THE
VISIONARY

THE
VISIONARY
DON PASSMAN

WARNER BOOKS

A Time Warner Company

"White Rabbit" © 1966, renewed 1994, Irving Music, Inc. (BMI). All Rights Reserved. International © Secured. Used by Permission.

Copyright © 1999 by Don Passman
All rights reserved.
Warner Books, Inc., 1271 Avenue of the Americas,
New York, NY 10020
Visit our Web site at http://warnerbooks.com

 A Time Warner Company

Printed in the United States of America
First Printing: June 1999
10 9 8 7 6 5 4 3 2 1

Library of Congress Cataloging-in-Publication Data
Passman, Donald S.
    The visionary / Don Passman.
        p.   cm.
    ISBN 0-446-52159-0
    I. Title
PS3566.A774V57   1999
813'.54—dc21   98-34907
                                              CIP

For my precious Shana and our boys, Danny, David, Josh, and Jordan. You are the light and foundation of my life.

and

For Bea Shaw, the source of my inspiration in all ways.

ACKNOWLEDGMENTS

I want to thank the following people, without whose contribution you wouldn't be reading this: My beautiful family—Shana, Danny, David, Josh, and Jordan—for your encouragement, your love, and your allowing me to disappear into the writer's cave. My three generations of editors: Bea Shaw, Shana, Danny, and David Passman. Mort Janklow and Eric Simonoff, for taking me on and using your considerable talents to sell the manuscript. Larry Kirshbaum, for your time, commitment, and friendship; for knowing when to be a tough coach, and for knowing when to be a cheerleader; and for teaching me the craft of writing. Your belief in me is something I'll always remember. Sandi Gelles-Cole, for keeping me together during the storms, and for showing me how to delve into the depths of characters. Sara Ann Freed, for your continued advice, your fine ear for dialog, and especially for teaching me the fine art of pruning. Dr. Richard Tuch, for your many hours of insight into the manuscript and the human psyche. Dr. Ed Ritvo, for your advice on all matters, large and small. Dr. Saul Faerstein, for sharing your experience in forensic psychiatry. Detective Fred Miller of the LAPD, for your advice on serial killers, and for your help in bringing Danny Talon to life. Dr. Mel Pollner and Dr. Jack Katz, for your insights into the field of sociology. Peter Gelb and Pat Jaffe, for your help with classical music. Kim Mitchell, for enabling me to get through the day and always making me look good. Kevin Marks, and the memory of Howard King, for your help with cross-examination techniques. Charlie Neeson, for being the quintessence of Evidence professors. And last but not least, John David Kalodner, for your detailed instructions on cleanliness.

THE VISIONARY

CHAPTER ONE

Lisa's head snapped forward with such force that it almost hit the coffee table. Within moments she was sweating profusely, and the room seemed to pulsate around her.

The evening had started routinely enough, save her exhaustion from the Latham meeting. The accounting firm where she worked, Engle & Loren, had been pitching the Latham Oil account for two years, and today they'd had a meeting with the company's decision makers. The six-hour "dog and pony show" had been in Latham's conference room, where the ceiling lights glared off a polished table directly into her eyes.

It was almost 9:00 P.M. when Lisa dragged herself into the bedroom of her West Los Angeles apartment. She dropped her clothes onto the floor, shook her blond hair free of the barrette, and splashed cold water on her face. She didn't have the energy to dry her face before moving to the living room, where she fell onto the tan couch and let the soft material envelop her.

Lisa had two reports due tomorrow, and she knew that if she didn't get to them quickly she'd risk zoning out for the night. So she stifled a yawn, folded one leg underneath her, and spread out the thick set of financials on her chrome-and-glass coffee table.

An hour or so later, it began. The episode started like the others: images flashing in her head like photos under a strobe light; visions striking her so rapidly that she sensed them more than saw them. She knew these incidents passed within a few minutes if she just relaxed, so she took a deep breath and laid her head back against the couch.

The first images were from her childhood. The petite Filipina nurse, from the hospital where Lisa had been taken after her injury. The AstroTurf thrown unevenly across a mound of freshly dug dirt. And a red-haired girl she couldn't quite place. All remnants of her psychic experiences twenty years earlier.

Suddenly she was seized by a new image: a tableau caught in a powerful camera flash, then shrouded in shadows after the burst of light. As she realized what she was seeing, her head involuntarily snapped forward, and she felt a jolt of electric current rip through her.

Lisa didn't recognize the young woman in her vision. A blond girl, apparently in her twenties. The woman was trapped in an empty room, screaming and running from an unseen terror. She couldn't find a place to hide, so she curled herself into a fetal position and covered her eyes, as if that could somehow shield her.

Lisa tried to look away, yet felt as if her head were being held, forcing her to watch. The spasms in her body became so intense that she fell roughly to the floor, scraping her face against the coarse carpet.

The images continued their assault. The nurse; the redhead;

the AstroTurf; the terrified young woman who seemed to be pleading for Lisa's help. Film clips projected on top of each other. Their soundtracks screaming for her attention. She began to pound the sides of her head with her fists, hoping it would jar the visions loose.

Several minutes later, the wave of images began to break apart. Feelings returned to the tips of her fingers, and as soon as she had enough control, she pushed herself to the window and flung it open. Then she took deep gasps of the cold night air, as if she had broken the surface of a dark pool just before drowning.

She had been foolish to think these episodes wouldn't intensify. Her attempts to deal with them on her own now seemed impotent, almost silly.

She had to do something more drastic.

And she had no idea what.

The figure watched from across the street, camouflaged in nighttime shadows. Adopting a mutt from the pound had been a brilliant stroke; everyone looks friendly and innocent with a puppy on a leash, and it's natural to stop and let them do their thing on the grass. So, night or day, you can look around all you want and be practically invisible. The last dog had been better; cuter, less conspicuous. This one had matted black hair and scratched constantly. Not that it mattered. The little bitch would get left on the streets later tonight, just like the others.

Across the street was the woman with shoulder-length hair. She was laughing and walking up to her apartment with that tall man. He looked like a wimp who couldn't protect her, yet everything had to be right. Which meant nobody else around. So if the wimp didn't take off in the next few minutes, it would have to be tomorrow night. Or the next. There was always time to do it right. And never time to do it over.

The dog strained against the leash, trying to run toward the couple across the street. As the dog's collar tightened, the mutt started coughing. The young woman glanced toward the sound, and the figure retreated into the shadows. After staring for a moment, the couple went back to their conversation.

Finally, the woman kissed the tall man on the cheek. As she turned to watch him amble away, her face was backlit by the porch light. She looked perfect. The best one yet. Sometimes the anticipation was almost as orgasmic as the event.

A light went on in the young woman's bedroom. The bedroom with a window she never locked.

A few moments later, the little dog scampered away, dragging the leash behind it.

CHAPTER TWO

At 7:00 A.M., Professor Michael Rennick locked his bicycle to the silver metal rack in front of UCLA's Public Policy Building, then started toward the Law School. At six foot five, with a full head of curly, black hair that he rarely took the trouble to comb, he was an imposing figure who moved with the power and fluidity of a long-distance runner.

Rennick walked briskly across the traffic circle, looking up at the tall eucalyptus trees that ringed the campus, creating the aura of a pastoral, intellectual island. The illusion worked well for him. Most of the time.

Holding the rickety handrail, he descended the steps to the Law School's three-story brick building and went to Room 1447. Rennick turned on the fluorescent lights, which seemed to wake up as they flickered to life. Then he sat down, put his feet on the podium table, and took out a stack of papers.

The early morning quiet, broken only by the buzzing of the

fluorescent lights, was his most productive time. He looked over the day's schedule that his secretary Bobbi had typed for him and saw that he had wall-to-wall meetings and classes. Rennick was a psychiatrist and a lawyer, on the faculties of both the UCLA Law School and Medical School, and in addition to a heavy teaching and lecture schedule, he saw a few psychiatric patients, was writing a *Law Review* article, handling a pro bono lawsuit for an environmental group, and acting as an expert witness in a case that would come to trial in three months. He was also committed to promote the paperback edition of his latest book, *Positive Healing*, with a media blitz in about six weeks.

He stuffed the day's schedule into his back pocket and studied his lecture notes for today's class. Rennick taught Evidence with an innovative slant: the psychology of persuasion. His approach was so novel that it had taken almost a year of politicking before the Law School dean allowed him to try it. In the four years he'd been teaching the class, his student ratings were consistently through the roof, and this year, despite scheduling the class at 8:00 A.M. to weed out the less dedicated, over two hundred students had applied for forty available spaces.

At 7:45, Rennick did a few squats to loosen up. The knees of his blue jeans stretched out along with his muscles. He wore jeans because they were comfortable, and also because it annoyed some of his colleagues on the faculty. In addition, the jeans had a practical value: Rennick was color-blind, and faded blue coordinated with almost anything else he happened to throw on. Or at least that's what he'd been told by people who weren't color-blind.

The sound of a door opening announced the arrival of the first students, and he straightened up, feeling a nice flush from the exercise. In marked contrast, the students filed in groggily, spreading out slowly over the four tiers of battleship-gray Formica desks. Their eyes seemed to be opening under protest, and the only sounds were murmured conversations, rustling papers, and a few slurps of coffee.

At exactly eight o'clock Rennick turned to face the class. He stood with his legs shoulder-width apart, and his tall, wiry frame radiated power and control.

"Today we're going to discuss cross-examination, which is the art of destroying a witness's testimony. Last time we talked about presenting direct testimony, where the witness tells a story you're trying to prove. On cross, your goal is to shake up that story.

"All trial lawyers will tell you there is nothing more believable than an eyewitness, and also nothing less reliable. What people testify becomes reality in the courtroom, and so the job of cross-examination is to probe and create doubts not just in the minds of the jury, but in the minds of the witnesses themselves."

Rennick leaned against the podium table and put his hands in his front jeans pockets.

"Before we get to the specifics, I'm going to rattle a lot of ideas you hold dear. In fact, I'm going to show you that everything you believe to be 'rock-solid reality' is only an illusion."

Rennick paused to let the thought sink in. He timed his pauses as carefully as he timed the cadence of his speech.

"I want you to open your minds up to the idea that everything you believe to be a certainty is only a mirage." He lowered his voice so they would have to strain to listen. "Reality is not an absolute. It's only something we all agree on. A shared delusion, so to speak. And one that changes from time to time.

"To the Greeks, the idea that the sun moved across the sky

was reality. To the Europeans before Columbus, the earth was flat. And who's to say that our beliefs today are any sounder?"

Rennick looked around. The eyes of each student met his.

"How many people here have been to Borneo?"

No one raised a hand.

"Me neither. So how do we know it exists?"

The class tittered.

A frumpled, redheaded student raised his hand. "Well, I've read about Borneo, and I've seen pictures of it."

"But we don't really *know* it exists, do we?"

Silence. "The reason we all think it's there is because we all think it's there. But how do we know it isn't?"

Rennick looked at Julie, the Ph.D. candidate in sociology who was auditing his class. Julie was also his "significant other," and when she smiled at him, he promptly lost his train of thought.

As he fumbled for a recovery, the back door flung open. A large man stormed down the aisle, breathing heavily like a bull on the charge. He had broad shoulders and a barrel chest, bulging out of a blue business suit that fought to contain them. His full attention was on Rennick as he clumped loudly down the aisle.

"Asshole!" he yelled. Before Rennick could react, the man's face was six inches in front of Rennick's. He spat on Rennick as he spoke, and poked his finger toward Rennick's chest.

"My wife says you've been calling her again," he bellowed, inching forward while Rennick inched back.

Julie bolted upright, suddenly quite interested in the proceedings.

"I'm telling you for the last time, if you ever see her again, you're a dead man."

Then, just as suddenly, he turned and huffed out of the class-room.

The students sat silently, in shock and disbelief. Rennick looked down, avoiding their stares. He shifted a few of his papers self-consciously, then turned his face to the class.

"Well," said Rennick. "What was he wearing?"

Stunned silence.

"What was he wearing? Ms. Lester?"

"Uh, a suit."

"What color?"

"Blue," said a disembodied voice in the back of the class.

"Good. Navy blue? Robin's-egg blue? Powder blue? Solid? Pinstripe? Be specific."

More silence, as it dawned on the class what was happening.

"Assume that you are witnesses who just saw this man commit a murder. The police have a suspect in custody, and they must discover whether they've caught the right person. You will have to testify in court, and he may get the death penalty. You can't play games with this. You must commit. What color blue?"

"Dark blue," came a tentative voice.

"Good. Dark blue. What color tie?"

"I, uh, didn't notice."

"Anyone want to help her?"

"Striped," came a voice in the back.

"What color stripes?"

"Red and blue maybe?"

"Red and yellow," said another with both assurance and doubt.

"Now we're getting somewhere," said Rennick. He glanced up at Julie, who winked at him. "Dark blue suit, striped tie with red and maybe yellow or maybe blue. How tall was he?"

"Big," said a voice from the back, and the students laughed, releasing the tension that had been building.

Rennick bored in. "You can't just tell the jury he was a 'big guy.' How big?"

"Over six feet."

"How far over?"

"Hard to tell; we were sitting."

"I'm six foot five inches. How many think he was over six foot two?"

About half the hands went up.

"How many think he was under?"

About a fourth of the hands, the last few straggling along tentatively. Rennick walked partway up one of the aisles, forcing the students to turn in his direction.

"What color was his hair?"

Two students answered simultaneously: "Black." "Brown." Upon hearing "black," the "brown" vote was changed to "dark brown."

"Did he touch me? How many think yes?"

About three-fourths of the hands went up.

"And how many no?"

About ten percent.

"Seems we're a little short of one hundred percent." He returned to the front of the class and put his hands on both sides of the podium. "Okay. You saw this incident five minutes ago, and look how fuzzy your recall is. How well do you think witnesses remember after hours, weeks, or months? In fact, it's often years before a trial. Also, look what peer pressure did. You may not want to admit it, but some of you voted along with the majority because you weren't sure."

He felt the rush he always got from connecting with his students.

"Reality is more elusive than you think. No matter how committed a witness is to her testimony, no human being ever remembers exactly what happened."

He leaned back against the table.

"When a witness is telling her story, the emphasis is on the witness. When you cross-examine, the emphasis is on you, the lawyer. The questions themselves are the stars, and they alone can create doubts. Think how you'd react to questions like 'Isn't it true that you were fifty feet away and can't be absolutely certain that he was over six-two?'

"Isn't it true that he was wearing a patterned tie like the one I'm now holding?" Rennick pulled a tie out of his jacket.

"Or was it a tie that looked like this?" He pulled out a similar second tie. "Or like this?" He pulled out a third tie and the class began to laugh.

Julie spoke from the back. "What about the ethics of chipping away at someone you think is telling the truth?"

Rennick liked it when Julie participated in the class. Or at least he liked it as long as he could field a response.

"Excellent question. In our system, everyone is entitled to an advocate. And there's a difference between what's true and what you can prove is 'true.' Remember, reality in the courtroom is what the judge or jury says it is, regardless of whether they're right or wrong. There's a great story of three baseball umps talking. The first one says, 'I call 'em as I see 'em.' The second one says, 'I call 'em as they are.' And the third one says, 'Because I call 'em, they are.'"

Rennick looked up at the door and shouted, "Jimmy, come back in."

As the doors opened, Rennick glanced at Julie, who was smiling warmly at him. She touched the tip of her index finger to her tongue, which was the signal to meet in his apartment after class.

Jimmy lumbered back into the classroom, now somewhat sheepish and self-conscious.

"Jimmy's a friend of mine from the drama department. For the record, he's six-three, two inches shorter than I am, and he didn't touch me; just a lot of poking in my direction. His hair is black. His suit is dark blue, as most of you said. His tie is red-and-yellow *patterned*, not striped. And by the way, he's not married."

"But you really are an asshole," said Jimmy.

The class broke into raucous laughter.

"That's it for today. See you on Friday."

The sound of shuffling books and papers immediately erupted. Julie and two other students joined Rennick and Jimmy at the front of the class. When the other students left, Rennick said, "Julie, meet Jimmy."

"Hi."

"Hey."

"Bye," said Julie, touching the back of Rennick's hand lightly as she left.

"Nice," said Jimmy.

"The class?"

"Nope."

"Didn't think so," said Rennick, his mind already heading toward his apartment.

CHAPTER THREE

Lisa fumbled for the snooze button on her alarm clock. She could still see the visions from last night's episode in her mind, although they were now only memories. She forced herself to sit up on the side of the bed, and she rubbed her eyes to shake off the last remnants. Her head cleared quickly, and she had a mental picture of chasing the images out with a broom, like chickens. The silliness of it made her smile.

She went to the window and let her face bask in the bright sunshine. A cool breeze blew the curtains into billows, rejuvenating her and affirming that she was back in reality.

She poured herself a full cup of coffee and turned on the local easy rock station. Even though she knew it was sanitized music for people in their thirties who liked to think they were still hip, she loved it. She swayed in rhythm to the music and watched the ficus outside her window dance in the breeze.

Lisa climbed into the shower and turned the spray directly

into her face. The water hit her with an invigorating splash and seemed to wash out the final traces of last night. She felt a surge of energy as her mood continued to brighten.

She hoped there would be feedback on yesterday's presentation to Latham Oil. If Engle & Loren got the Latham account, she might have a direct relationship with the client. And that might get her out of the managing partner's shadow, which she felt was keeping a rock on top of her career.

Lathering strawberry-scented shampoo into her hair, she began to sing.

Lisa drove to Century City, an office/retail development built on land that 20th Century Fox Studios was forced to sell after making the financially disastrous film *Cleopatra*. Her accounting firm, Engle & Loren, was located in a mid-rise building on Avenue of the Stars called Gateway East.

She strode out of the elevator on the ninth floor, with her customary perfect posture, still feeling the freshness of her shower. Lisa wore a chocolate brown business suit with just the collar of an eggshell silk blouse showing, and her blond hair was pulled back neatly in a french braid.

After locking her purse in her desk, she picked up the mail that was already opened, date-stamped, and sorted by the secretary she shared with four other staff members. The first piece was an issue of *Maritime Regulations*. This wasn't right. She didn't subscribe to that. Annoyed, she looked at the address and realized she had gotten someone else's mail.

She buzzed her secretary. An unfamiliar voice answered. Now she was really angry. This was the wrong day to be saddled with a raw temp. Lisa started to yell at the woman but checked herself and asked for the correct mail in a controlled voice. Then she slammed the phone down so hard that people around her looked up in surprise.

Whoa! Easy. It wasn't like her to be so upset over a small matter. She must still be jumpy from last night. Dammit. She thought she'd left her problems at home.

The intercom buzzed, startling her.

"Lisa, it's Phil," came a gravelly voice. "Can you come in?"

She got up quickly and walked to his office, where she found the other four members of the Latham pitch team.

Phil Trotter, the partner in charge, was a round, balding man in a perpetually wrinkled suit. Frown lines were etched into his face, and he kept a bottle of Pepto-Bismol in his desk drawer.

When everyone was settled, Phil got up and spoke in his usual staccato delivery. "We got the Latham account."

They all started cheering, high-fiving, and slapping each other on the back. Lisa broke into a broad smile. She was elated by the rush of victory, although she knew this account was going to take a lot of time and energy. She also knew that Phil's M.O. was to grab the glory while she and the staff did the work. Her mind raced to figure out how she could let the other partners know the value of her contributions.

When the roar calmed, Phil said, "Now we gotta deliver. So let's get to work. Lisa, stay a minute."

When the others left, Phil turned to her.

"Your section on financial controls at the regional level really impressed them. They mentioned it twice. Good work."

The compliment got to her, and she started to say something like "I didn't do anything so special." She quickly realized that was stupid and just said "Thank you."

Lisa walked back to her desk, high from the meeting. Clearly she would have a major role on the account, and she needed to get credit for what she did. Maybe if she carbon-copied the client on everything . . .

As Lisa neared her desk, she saw a woman duck underneath it. Who was that? What's she doing here? It was unlikely that the woman would attack her in public, yet you heard so many stories about violence in the workplace. Lisa became aware of the veins in her neck pulsing, and her hands began to shake.

It struck her that she'd seen this woman before. She was the blond girl in her vision last night.

Lisa turned away from her desk toward Earl Saunders, a six-foot-tall bookkeeper with huge biceps.

"Did you notice a woman hanging around my desk?"

Earl looked up blankly. "Huh?"

"I thought I saw someone crawl under my desk." The words rushed out of her. "I think she's still there. Would you go over there with me?"

"I guess." He dropped his pencil and stood up.

The two of them walked toward her desk. Lisa stayed a step behind Earl.

"Where?" asked Earl.

"Underneath. In the desk well."

Earl looked at her quizzically, then he leaned over and peered under the desk. By now they had gathered an audience.

"Nobody under there unless they're a leprechaun," Earl snorted.

Lisa moved next to him and looked underneath the desk. There was only a metal trash can with a brown plastic liner. Not enough room for an adult to even squeeze in. When she straightened up, her face was flushed red.

"I'm sorry. I'm a little jittery. Probably too much coffee or . . ."

"Whatever you're taking, share it with me after work," said Earl before he lumbered back to his desk.

The audience dispersed, as if responding to a silent cue. Lisa sat down at her desk and waited until she was sure that everyone's attention had moved on. Then she opened the drawer in which she kept the three books she had recently purchased. One of them, *Edges of Reality*, had really spoken to her, and she placed it behind an accounting journal to camouflage the cover. On the page marked with a Post-it, she read:

The border between "reality" and "perception" is not a bright line, as we usually assume. Mr. Black's reality is that the world is an unfair, hostile place, where people cheat you at every turn. Ms. White's is that it is full of kind souls who care about each other. Are they both right? Or both wrong? If there is only one reality, how can you explain the existence of both Mr. Black and Ms. White?

Many people who break with reality are merely attempting to cope with something unpleasant that has happened in their lives. It is a form of denial: they go to a place where the problem does not exist. When you solve the difficulty that caused them to withdraw, their need to "leave the world" disappears.

She closed the book and massaged her eyes. The words certainly rang true, although she had no idea what current "difficulty" might be causing her to "withdraw." Quite the opposite: Things seemed to be going pretty well.

She'd tried willing the episodes away with positive thinking. That hadn't worked. She'd also tried other techniques from the books she'd read, like relaxation routines and self-hypnosis. No better luck. Last night's episode, plus today's hallucination, were more serious. She had to accept that she wouldn't get better simply by reading books and exercising self-help.

Bruce Raymond, one of the partners, was on vacation for the week. She slipped inside his office and left the lights off, so as not to attract attention. After making sure no one was nearby, she cradled the receiver close to her mouth and then dialed the number.

CHAPTER FOUR

Rennick threw his notes into the saddlebag and climbed onto his bicycle. He sped down Circle Drive, onto Wyton, and then south on Hilgard toward his apartment, where Julie was waiting.

As he zipped in and out of the traffic, he remembered the first time Julie walked into his office. She was wearing a loose, peach-colored cotton dress, with no bra. Her face was a smooth-skin picture of openness and innocence, framed by soft, straight hair that she later told him was chestnut. Her eyes (she said they were hazel) hinted of an earthy sensuality underneath, and her tall frame and sense of confidence struck him with such force that he began to stammer.

Julie explained that she was a sociology graduate student at UCLA, and that she was writing a Ph.D. dissertation on the sociological dynamics of the courtroom. She had heard about Rennick's blending of law and psychiatry, thought it seemed relevant to her research, and asked if she could audit his class. Ordinarily Rennick didn't like to give up slots to auditing students, but he quickly decided to make an exception.

Their conversation led to a date the next night, and they began seeing each other a few times each week. They'd take in a foreign film at the Royal Theater on Santa Monica Boulevard. Or play Boggle, which they both played for blood. Or just walk along the beach in Santa Monica. Even though he admired her spirit, Rennick had refused to go with Julie on any of her daredevil activities. He found the idea of bungee jumping or skydiving slightly less appealing than having his teeth drilled.

Rennick wound his bicycle through the side streets south of Wilshire to his home. He lived on the north side of Wilkens, directly across from St. Paul the Apostle Catholic Church, in a funky, 1940s apartment that was rumored to have once been home to Judy Garland. His apartment had thick stucco walls, hardwood floors, and a multicolored stained-glass window in the front door that broke the sunlight into dozens of colors dancing in the entry hall. He hardly ever got around to cleaning the place, and he still hadn't had the courage to tell Julie how infrequently he changed the sheets.

Rennick had a habit of throwing his sports coats over the couch and taking another one the next day, so there could be two or three coats piled on top of each other at any given time. Today, as he pulled off his jacket, he was peeved to see that Julie had put away the last three he remembered tossing there. His annoyance came to an abrupt halt when he looked up and saw her standing in the doorway to the bedroom. She was wearing a brown tweed sports jacket she had stolen from the couch. And nothing else.

"Nice class today, Professor. Do you think I could get some private lessons? And maybe an oral exam?"

Rennick smiled and walked toward her. As he got closer, she slowly stretched her arms over her head, causing the jacket to fall open. His eyes went to the tiny Libra scales that she had tattooed on the left side of her pelvis, just below the bikini line.

"Don't be embarrassed by your gown," he said. "I *am* a doctor."

He took her in his arms and kissed her deeply. She began to unbutton his shirt, and he eased off her coat.

As she began to unbuckle his belt the phone rang loudly. Rennick kissed her and mumbled, "Leave it," without taking his lips off hers.

After two more rings, the machine picked up. Rennick's secretary, Bobbi, spoke over the speaker. She was sobbing so hard she could barely speak.

"Michael, I'm afraid there's some bad news."

The late afternoon sun was dying, making its last efforts to cast faded slats through the windows of Rennick's apartment. He sat silently on the couch, as he had for the last several hours, staring at cracks in the stucco wall. The lines seemed to form the grotesque silhouette of a face, and they blurred in and out of focus as he gazed at them intently. Sometimes the face seemed to be Andrea's; other times, it was the rough features of a man whom Rennick imagined to be her murderer.

Julie sat beside him in the darkening room, resting her head on his shoulder and holding his hand. Neither of them made an effort to turn on the lights, and neither spoke.

Rennick couldn't accept the fact that Andrea Baylor had become another victim of this killer that the police had been so impotent in finding. Andrea had been Rennick's first and only platonic female friend. Their relationship had blossomed out of a drama class he had taken to improve his teaching skills. They had read a scene from *Our Town* together, and their onstage chemistry drew loud applause.

While he never thought of Andrea as "pretty," she had intense green eyes, blond, shoulder-length hair, and a personality that far overshadowed her looks. Her soft voice and twinkling smile, which projected a sympathetic warmth, were so comforting that Rennick found himself sharing intimacies he hadn't told his closest male friends. Within hours after they met, he confided how difficult it had been for him to decide on a career. He described his convoluted road from Harvard Law, to Yale Med, and then to the specialty of mixing law, psychiatry, and forensics. She dubbed him a "Serial Obsessive," and he loved that turn of phrase. He was even more impressed with her ability to distill his psyche. Rennick also told her about his pattern of burning out not only on careers, but also on the women in his life. He even confided his fear that he might never form a lasting relationship.

On her side, Andrea told him how she had slept with the first boy who had shown any interest in her. The affair had led to her having a daughter when she was sixteen, whom she gave up for adoption. She told him how she stared at each little girl she passed on the street. And how she had the impossibly conflicted feelings of hating the father while looking for his face in the children.

After that night, they spoke every few days. He shared her happiness when she found a boyfriend, and he comforted her when the relationship fell apart a few weeks later. She lived through two of his unsuccessful relationships and, when he met Julie, she continually cautioned him to take it slowly, so he wouldn't burn himself out. Andrea also insisted that he talk to Julie about his fears of commitment. He still hadn't been able to do that, and he worried that without Andrea to prod him, he might never get there.

Without Andrea to prod him. Without Andrea at all. He would never see her again. Ever. It was a concept he couldn't handle. Professionally, he knew all about the grieving process. Yet that wasn't proving to be much help. His depression formed itself heavily around his shoulders, causing him to hunch forward.

He turned his mind back to the cracks on the wall, which again seemed to form the killer's profile. He imagined the man laughing smugly, arrogant that the police were so far behind. Rennick desperately needed to release his growing tension, yet he didn't know how. Andrea could have told him. He suspected she would have said to confide in Julie.

"I miss her," he finally said aloud. His throat was raw and it was odd to hear his voice after the long silence.

Julie squeezed his hand. "I do too. We have to be happy that we knew her for as long as we did."

"I am. That doesn't help much."

More silence.

"The last time I talked to her, I was late for a meeting. I cut her off short because I had to go. I should have talked to her longer."

"You couldn't have known it would be the last time."

More silence.

Rennick asked, "Did I tell you about the afternoon she called me out of a meeting with four lawyers who had hired me as an expert witness?"

"I don't think so."

"She had Bobbi break into this meeting and say that I had to come over right away. She wouldn't say why. Just that it was really important. So I made some lame excuse, left four very pissed-off lawyers, and rushed over to her place. I was expecting that she'd tell me she had some dread disease or something."

Rennick was smiling, remembering. "When I get to the door, she's holding these two dresses, one on a hanger in each hand. And she says, 'I've got a date tonight with this incredible guy I just met. Which dress should I wear?' "

"So I said, 'You got me over here to ask which dress you should wear?'

"And she says, 'Yeah. You're a guy. Which one do you like?' So I pick one, and she says, 'Are you sure the color goes with my eyes?' Then I remind her that I'm color-blind. We both started laughing so loudly that the neighbor complained we woke up her baby."

Julie giggled at the story. Rennick continued, his voice now animated. "So to get even, I call her a few days later and make her come over right away. When she gets there, I hold up a white V-neck T-shirt and a white crew-neck T-shirt, and I ask her which one I should wear."

Rennick and Julie began to laugh. It gave him a light-headed feeling, and his shoulders relaxed. After a few moments, the laughter faded into silence, and Rennick became aware of the facial muscles holding his smile. He strained to keep them in place until he finally had to let go.

It was now dark, and he could no longer make out the shapes in the room; could no longer see the silhouette formed by the cracks in the wall. The only sound was their breathing. He thought of Andrea, stuffed into some morgue refrigerator, and a dark claustrophobia squeezed his chest.

Rennick held Julie's hand tightly. Yet even with her so close, he felt alone.

CHAPTER FIVE

Detective Danny Talon of the LAPD cut the motor and leaned back against the headrest of his unmarked gray Dodge. He was parked on Corinth Avenue in West L.A., just below Santa Monica Boulevard, in front of the apartment in which Andrea Baylor had been murdered. Despite the cool December day, the morning sun was turning the car into a greenhouse.

As perspiration began to sprout on his forehead, Talon slouched down in the car seat and ran his large hands through his thinning, sandy brown hair. He still had the outlines of his high-school physique, albeit softened by the last twenty-some-odd years. Several twist-and-turn merit badges decorated his nose, and his left cheek had a jagged scar that ran down to his square jaw. His acorn-colored eyes, with dark crescents underneath, gave him the look of an animal that had been both predator and prey.

Talon popped a cassette into the tape player he'd illegally installed in the police car, and the melancholy strains of Dvořák's New World Symphony filled the interior. He moved his hands about an inch from his lap as he guest-conducted. Andrea Baylor was the third woman killed by this serial killer who'd been making the cops look like idiots for the last six months. All the victims were young women in their twenties, with shoulder-length blond hair, and apparently little else in common. The fucking reporters, whose idea of a big problem was having their computers freeze up, were milking headlines and TV ratings out of this, leaving the cops to bust their asses while the newspeople went on to cover some charity dinner at the Beverly Hills Hotel.

Talon's nickname on the force had once been Dr. Know, because he could pluck out the key thread of evidence that broke open a case. He hadn't heard that name much over the last year. Maybe it was because he had two high-profile homicides that had been lying on his desk for six months too long. Cases he would have quickly cleared last year. Or maybe it was because he fell facedown in a snow-white binge last year. Whatever.

The sweat felt like spider legs running down his back. He knew he had to go inside, yet he felt paralyzed. He continued looking up and down the street and reflected how the *Leave It to Beaver* neighborhoods of his childhood had been replaced with these cold monoliths of stucco. How the green yards were now concrete because it was cheaper than lawns and didn't have to be watered. And how the pounding of day-to-day life peeled the paint and cracked the walls, until there was nothing left between the people and the scum on the streets.

The car was now a sauna, and his clothes were drenched and shriveled. He thought about Lieutenant Wharton, his immediate supervisor, and the shots Wharton had been taking at him lately. Wharton had always hated Talon, and the sentiment was totally mutual. Wharton's anal-compulsive by-the-book approach, versus Talon's street tactics, had put the two men on a collision course since the day they'd met at the police academy. And Talon's slip with the nose candy had given Wharton the ammunition to lock and load.

Wharton had tried to keep Talon off this case, telling Captain Ramson that he was "unstable." Talon knew that Ramson had pressured Wharton to put him on anyway. So now Wharton was doubly pissed, and was inserting himself directly up Talon's ass. If Wharton had been smarter, he'd have insisted on Talon; this case had all the markings of an *Unsolved Mysteries* episode.

Fuck Wharton, he thought. I'm no Kilrenny. Kilrenny was the last guy Wharton forced out. Talon had visited him about a month ago, and found Kilrenny sitting at a wobbly card table outside a little jewelry store. The man had gained thirty pounds, and his gut almost covered his gun belt. He'd looked up at Talon with those droopy eyes and said, "It ain't so bad."

Talon rolled his head slowly in a circle, stretching his neck, and felt his body ache with echoes of high-school football injuries. He forced his mind back to the case. The physical evidence was nil, and the unrelated victims meant no predictable pattern.

The temperature in the car had gone beyond discomfort. Talon felt like the heat was purging him, washing the poisons out of his system. Yet he didn't move until the second movement of the symphony ended. Then he pushed Stop on the tape player and sat for a few more minutes before getting out of the car.

Once outside the car, the cold air hit Talon's perspiration and gave him the chills. He walked rapidly to a tan stucco apartment house with two scraggly palm trees in front. One of them was a putrid brown and looked like it was in the final throes of a slow death. A building sign said *Golden Palms* in wooden letters covered with small metal circles that shimmered in the sunlight.

The black wrought-iron rail wobbled under his grip as he went up the steps. In a nearby apartment a baby cried, and Talon thought about the mothers of the victims. He imagined how they had comforted these young women when they were infants. Changing and dressing them. Pushing them in strollers through the parks on sunny days, while they chatted with other mothers doing the same. Covering their little heads against the sun and rain. Watching them carefully in the supermarket. All that energy into raising a kid, just for her to end up slaughtered like some animal. He felt for the mothers, who would have news cameras shoved in their faces and neighbors staring at them like they were freaks. With holes in their lives that would never heal. All so that some creep out there could get his jollies.

Up ahead, he saw that apartment 12 was crisscrossed with yellow police tape. He fumbled with the key and the door groaned open. Then he stood at the entrance before going inside.

Talon didn't have a good feeling about this one. Rojas, who had been the detective on the case until yesterday, was a first-class detective. Yet he had found only one suspect, who was currently impersonating the Invisible Man. He also felt bad karma over Rojas's being laid up from a drive-by shooting yesterday. At a fucking picnic—right in front of his wife, for chrissakes—by some gang kids going through initiation. The kids got away clean, and Rojas was in a coma with tubes up his nose.

Talon finally stepped through the tape into the dark apartment. The curtains were drawn and the air was stale, an instant reminder that the scene was over twenty-four hours cold. He knew he didn't have to be very careful, since Rojas had already been over the scene with the criminalists. He also knew that he couldn't expect to find anything, for the same reason.

First he opened the drapes to let in the sunlight. The room seemed to grasp desperately at the light, like a person dying of thirst reaching for water. He stayed at the window for a while, letting the sunlight sear his face, then he sat down on the couch, laid out a stack of photos, and read through Rojas's case notes.

Three single women in their twenties. All of them living within a few miles of each other in the West L.A. area. All of them killed and mutilated in the same bizarre way. The victims had shoulder-length, blond hair and their faces resembled each other, but there was no evidence that any of them were connected. The first and third victims had roommates, which was unusual because serial predators usually go for women who live by themselves. Since he hit both these victims when the roommates weren't around, it meant he'd watched them carefully enough to know when they'd be alone. That also meant he was bolder and more aggressive than most. Which fit with the fact that the time between killings had shrunk from almost four months to about four weeks.

He flipped a page of the spiral notebook and continued reading Rojas's notes. Myra Powell, the first victim, had worked in a bar in Santa Monica. Her roommate told Rojas that she had a boyfriend named Bart, but no one knew the guy's last name, and no one had seen him since the murder. So far, Bart was the only suspect. Betty Sanchez, the second victim, had worked as a manicurist in West L.A., near the Westside Pavilion. She

moved to L.A. from Camarillo within the last year and didn't
have a lot of friends. Andrea Baylor didn't have much of a profile because her case was only a day old. Nice girl from St. Louis
who had moved to L.A. a few years back. Worked as a secretary
in an insurance firm, and described by her neighbors as "warm"
and "sweet."

A loud knock on the door startled Talon. He sprang up and
his hand went reflexively to his gun.

A young uniformed officer with deep-set eyes, buzzed black
hair, and a neatly trimmed mustache walked through the door.
He had the thin waist and enormous chest of a bodybuilder.

"Detective Talon?"

"Yeah. Michaels? Come here and tell me about this shit."

David Michaels had been on duty when the call came from
Baylor's roommate, and he and his partner had been the first on
the scene. When Michaels sat down on the couch next to Talon,
Talon realized his hand was still on his gun. He forced it onto
his lap.

"Tell me what you know," said Talon.

"Basically, nobody saw nothin'. Either a window entry or
somebody who knew the victim, 'cause there wasn't any sign of
force."

"Who found her?"

"Roommate. A guy named Bernard Downing. He says he's
just a friend. That's probably true, since it's a two-bedroom
apartment. He works as a nurse at Cedars-Sinai, and three witnesses say he was on duty the whole time."

"What happened?"

"Downing got home 'bout nine-thirty yesterday morning.
He works nights and gets off at eight, but he went grocery
shopping after work. When he got here, he found her door
closed. That's not normal, he says, 'cause she never closes it

when she's gone, and he knew she was always at work by seven thirty. So he knocks a few times, and when no one answers, he pounds. Says he thought maybe she was sick or somethin', so he opened it. Anyway, he sees her all carved up with an extension cord in her face. I guess he kept his lunch 'cause he's a nurse and used to that shit. Then he calls nine-one-one, and my partner and I come over. We call Rojas, who gets here in about a half hour. Tough thing about Rojas, huh?"

Talon pictured Rojas's body exploding in bursts of blood as the punks fired shots into him. He picked up the stack of photos he'd put on the coffee table, crumpling the edges in a tight grip.

"You okay, Detective?"

"Yeah." Talon showed Michaels a picture of an open window. "This the bedroom window?"

"Yes."

"It was open when you got here?"

"Yep."

"Any footprints on the carpet?"

"Nope. Larson, the criminalist, said it looked like the carpet had been brushed to cover 'em up."

Talon bristled. Any asshole who was this careful had to be seriously bad news. Someone on a fanatical mission from the planet Dementia.

He flipped to the next picture, which looked even less promising. It showed a nightstand with clothes carefully folded in a pile. Talon flashed on a loved one delivering her clothes to a mortician, to dress the corpse.

"This was beside the bed," said Michaels, smudging the photo of the clothing with his index finger as he pointed to it. "The killer cut off her clothes and folded 'em up like the fuckin' laundry."

"Any blood on the clothes?"

"No."

Talon figured there was no blood because the killer had cut the material carefully enough to avoid the skin. He felt him enjoying the victim's fear that her body was next.

Talon went into Baylor's bedroom, with Michaels trailing behind. On top of a desk were brick-and-raw-lumber bookshelves that sagged under a row of books. A small fern in a clay pot seemed to be withering from the loss of her company. The bottom desk drawer was open, and he saw a line of neatly printed plastic tabs on the hanging dividers. He flipped through them quickly and saw nothing unusual.

Talon went to her dresser and carefully picked through the drawers: a locket, panties, bras, costume jewelry. In the back of one drawer, he found two condoms that were so old the tinfoil had cracked. He closed the drawers and studied the room. Almost every flat surface had framed pictures of people or dogs. One burled wood–framed photo appeared to be her family. Probably her parents and a brother. They were waving goodbye. It was signed in the lower right, *Andrea: Don't become a weirdo in California! We love you, Mom, Dad and Chris*. Ah shit.

Talon felt Andrea's presence. Around and through him. Clinging to him for help. He closed his eyes and concentrated on what might have happened to her.

Suddenly he felt Michaels touch him on the shoulder. Talon reflexively grabbed Michaels's wrist and twisted it into a lock, forcing him onto the ground.

"Don't do that!" spat Talon.

Michaels didn't offer any resistance. "Detective, Detective," he said, his words muffled because his mouth was pushed into the carpet. Talon dropped his grip and sat back on the bed. It creaked under his weight.

"Sorry, kid," said Talon.

Michaels stood up, rubbing his wrist. "Nice move, Detective," he said shakily before taking a half-step back.

As Talon started to get up from the bed, he noticed a digital clock radio on the nightstand that was blinking the wrong time.

"Has there been a power outage here?"

Michaels shrugged. Talon thought maybe the power had overloaded when the killer did his electrical thing, although the body would probably provide enough resistance to prevent that. He went into the living room and checked the time on the electric clock. It wasn't digital and the time was close to the right time, which didn't rule out an outage of a minute or two. That would cause the bedroom clock to blink and not change the time significantly on a nondigital clock. He then spotted a digital clock on the oven. It wasn't blinking. No outage.

Talon went back to the bedroom. The crime-scene investigators wouldn't have unplugged and replugged the bedside clock, so the killer might have done it. Maybe trying to confuse the cops as to the time of the killing. He made a mental note to check the clocks at the other crime scenes, then set down the photos and put on a pair of latex gloves. He placed the clock in a plastic evidence bag to be checked for prints with the laser.

Back in the living room, Talon picked up another photo. It showed Andrea Baylor's nude body tied to the bed on her back, spread-eagle. Each wrist and ankle was bound with what appeared to be a piece of nylon stocking. She had silver duct tape over her mouth, and her throat had been slashed deeply. He could see the electrical cord snaking away from her to an outlet.

"No one heard any struggle?" asked Talon.

"No. The duct tape obviously took care of any screaming. Another friendly service of your local True Fucking Value."

Talon flipped to the next photo. It showed a closeup of the killer's trademark: two metal prongs connected to the electrical cord and stabbed into the victim's eyes. The result was that a victim's face was scorched and the coroner couldn't touch the body without getting shocked.

Talon stared at the dark, jagged pulps in the sockets, the remains of the seared eyeballs, and the radiating electrical burns. No matter how many he saw, murder photos were obscene. A few cops got off on them, and went into homicide so they had a reason to look. Others had no feelings, or so they claimed. Talon just got pissed off that humans could do things like this to each other.

The fact that the crime scene was so organized told him this was someone pretty smart, with an IQ in the 125-plus range; probably a college graduate. Maybe even a professional. The display of the body was a statement, although he didn't know what it meant. The fact that all the victims had similar looks suggested that the killer had been done wrong by one of the victims or, more likely, by someone who looked like them. Because there was no clear evidence of forced entry, he either charmed his way in, or came ninja-like through the open window. Either way, he was likely a psychopath, which meant he could lie to your face without any twinge of conscience. The kind of killer where the neighbors always said, "But he was so quiet and polite."

Talon made a note to check the coroner's report to see if she was raped. According to the first victim's report, she probably had been—the coroner hedged between rape and rough consensual sex. The second clearly hadn't. There was subdermal hemorrhaging in the first two victims' throats and wrists, indicating that they'd been manhandled. He expected to find the same here, unless she'd been forced onto the bed with a weapon. Or unless the killer was a charmer who'd talked her into the kinkiness of being tied up.

The prongs were a real mind-fuck. They had to mean something seriously sick, and Talon wanted an expert opinion. He knew who to call.

"Did Rojas ask what side of the bed she slept on?" asked Talon.

"Not when I was around."

Talon made a note to ask the roommate. The covers were pulled back on the left, so if she usually slept on the right, it could mean someone had shared her bed. That would be someone Talon wanted to meet.

He went back to the bedroom and opened the drapes. Talon squinted along the window's aluminum track and didn't see any fibers or blood, or any evidence of the window having been forced open. He hoped the criminalists had had better luck finding something, though he doubted it. He then went into a corner, turned to face the room, and moved his head slowly from left to right. After lowering himself into a squat, he swiveled his head again. Talon had stumbled onto this technique early in his career, when he leaned down to tie his shoe just before leaving a crime scene. Looking at the scene from a new angle, his eye caught a bullet casing that he'd missed during a two-hour search.

Talon stayed in his squat, and the personality of the killer radiated through him, icing his innards. He understood that the only emotion this asshole felt was the orgasmic release of the game. The high from killing and successfully eluding the cops. He sensed that this fucker might even turn into a "taunter" who played cat-and-mouse games just to be sure the chase kept going. Talon hoped so. Taunters were cocky, and cocky people made mistakes.

Talon forced himself to disconnect from his prey. Sometimes, climbing into a killer's persona, he felt the exhilaration of these sickos when they tortured a victim. The release of rage and sexual energy. And sometimes he secretly worried whether those impulses were powerful enough to overwhelm him. Like trying to hold some tiger on a thin leash.

His knees creaked as he got out of his squat and started toward the door. He had to make a call about those electrical prongs.

CHAPTER SIX

As the sun set, the faces of the crowd were lit eerily by the flickering candles that each mourner held in their hands. The light accentuated their cheekbones, giving the faces a drawn, cavernous look, and each exhale was visible in the cold evening air.

The people stood in silence, transfixed by a young, long-haired woman who sang a cappella in a soprano voice that seemed to weep with each phrase.

"A time to be born, a time to die . . ."

Rennick shivered in the chill and awkwardly tried to balance the rose and candle in his hands. The smell of burning cloth still lingered, a remnant of his having cradled the flame so close to his jacket that it had begun to smolder. Even though he knew intellectually that Andrea Baylor was lying in her casket a few hundred feet away, he still couldn't accept it.

Julie stood beside him, and he put his arm around her. They

were outside the Good Shepherd Chapel, in the foothills above the San Fernando Valley. Beneath them, shadows trailing the sunset cloaked the valley. As tiny lights blinked on, Rennick thought of the families snug in their houses. Mothers calling their children, exhausted from play, to come inside now. And he thought of Andrea, being called home the same way.

The woman continued singing. "A time to cast away stones, a time to gather stones together . . ."

Rennick's tall frame towered above the crowd. He guessed there were more than a hundred people gathered around the steps of the chapel. He only recognized Andrea's parents, whom he had once met briefly. Two tiny people, each with parts of Andrea's face, holding each other and sobbing.

As if sensing his feeling of isolation, Julie took hold of the hand he had draped on her shoulder. He looked into the warmth of her face, then hugged her so tightly that he could feel her heartbeat against his chest.

"A time to every purpose under heaven . . ."

The song concluded and a silence hung in the air, punctuated only by an occasional sob. After a few moments, the young woman began to sing again.

"A-ma-zing Grace, how sweet the sound . . ."

His lips moved almost imperceptibly with the words. Julie also sang softly, and he could feel her voice resonating through him.

When the song ended, the crowd began to move toward the chapel. Holding Julie's hand tightly, he stooped through the low doorway and saw that the chapel was a small replica of a Gothic cathedral, lit only by candelabra. The dark, heavy beams in the vaulted ceiling resembled the rib cage of a decaying skeleton, and shadows cast by the flickering candles darted into nooks and crannies, as if trying to escape the room. Rennick avoided looking ahead, as he had already glimpsed the icy gray, metal casket, and he could hear the others break into sobs as they lay their flowers on it.

When he edged closer, he was not happy to see that the casket was open to show Andrea from the waist up. He didn't want this to become his last memory of her, and he stopped in place, holding his ground until a gentle push propelled him forward. As soon as he arrived at the casket, his eyes involuntarily went to her face, which looked like cold ivory in the shadowy light. Considering what he understood had happened to her, they'd done a presentable makeup job. He searched the face, hoping for a sign that she recognized him and knew he was there.

Looking at the closed eyelids, he tried to picture her bright green eyes, which were now misting in his memory. The face before him was no longer hers. It was only a mask, a crude portrait. He fought to remember what she looked like in life. To remember their long phone calls and intimate talks. The disappointments she had in her own relationships at the same time she encouraged his intimacy with Julie.

His knees felt weak, and he had the absurd thought of leaning on the casket for support. Now he could no longer envision her eyes. He could no longer see her face. All he could remember was the sound of her voice, with its singsong cadence, and even that seemed to be fading. He could hear her words echoing softly, as if she were walking away from him down a long hallway.

Rennick stood up straight and gently laid his red rose on her chest, adding to the uneven pile of flowers left by the others. The roses looked to him as if they too were in mourning, unable to hold themselves up in their grief. He found himself gasping, hardly able to breathe in the tomblike atmosphere of the chapel. His jaw began to quiver, and he bit his lip, trying to hold in his feelings. Julie supported his large frame as best she could, and he felt as though he were leaning too heavily on her.

His tears spilled out softly, warm against his cold cheek, and he was both embarrassed and relieved to finally cry. He turned away for solitude, only to see Andrea's parents. All of them spontaneously hugged each other and moved as one in rhythm to their weeping.

CHAPTER SEVEN

Lisa sat in her kitchen, warmed by the morning sunlight that spilled across her shoulder. She took a sip of coffee and closed her eyes. The sun was bright enough that she could see it through her lids. In her mind's eye, she imagined the white light breaking up into colors, like passing through a prism. She wondered if that meant there were rainbows ahead. Or if everything was about to break into pieces.

As if in response to her query, the episode began. Her mind first wandered casually to the images, almost like a daydream. Then, within moments, she was fully engulfed.

Lisa found herself riding a horse at fast gallop. In the dark countryside, with twilight enveloping her. She couldn't tell where she was, or even see if any low branches were hanging across the dirt road. The horse moved beneath her rhythmically as she whipped him with a crop. The wind stung against her face, and even though she was panicked about where it would take her, she continued whipping the horse. In the last shards of light, she could see that she was raising welts and lines of blood on the horse's flanks.

The horse galloped faster and faster, his rib cage heaving beneath her. She grabbed his neck and found herself slipping forward, feeling the large neck muscles pulse with each gallop. Then came the sound of a stumble and the horse's front legs collapsed. He fell forward at an angle, and her body's momentum threw her over his head. She knew she'd be crushed if the horse fell on her, and she began to scream as she flew into the air.

Suddenly, as if she had ripped through a dark canvas into a different reality, she was back in her kitchen. She found herself gripping the seat of her chair so tightly that her fingers were numb. Her forehead was soaked and her breathing labored.

Lisa never rode horses. In fact, she was afraid of them, although she had no idea why. The only time she'd even been around them was when she was a little girl and her family lived on a farm in Arkansas.

Why would she have such a vision now?

Rennick walked slowly through the swirls of early morning fog that hovered above the UCLA campus, still encumbered by the guilt of resuming a normal life when Andrea and her family could not.

After slowly climbing the Janss Steps, he stood for a moment at the fountain, listening to the trickle of water. It was already 7:40, much later than he usually arrived on campus, though he still had twenty minutes before his Evidence class. The thought of teaching law seemed hollow and absurd. The legal system could only react to situations after the damage had been done, and that could never really make things right. He slapped his hand through the water, splashing it onto the sidewalk.

Rennick ambled past Royce Hall, a reddish brown, brick structure of porticos and arches, and it looked to him as if the arches were weary, about to collapse under the strain of holding up the building. On the grassy area in front of Royce, a group of Asian students played a touch football game. The ball bounced in front of him and he walked by without stopping to throw it back.

He still hadn't made love to Julie. As much as he wanted to connect to her soul, his body wouldn't cooperate. And the fact that she was so understanding only made him feel worse. He remembered lying beside her, almost afraid to touch her, as if his depression were somehow contagious. Maybe it was an unconscious desire to force her away, so she would be free to find someone who would treat her better. Or maybe it was a convenient way for him to avoid facing his own issues. He and Julie were at that point when his inability to commit usually sabotaged his relationships.

A passing student bumped Rennick back to the present. He wandered down the crisscrossing paths of Dickson Plaza, past three-hundred-year-old Moreton Bay fig trees, toward the Law School. Even the smell of baking cinnamon buns from Lu Valle Commons couldn't lift his spirits.

By the time he arrived at his classroom, it was 7:55. He pep-talked himself with the notion that he owed the students his best, then straightened his posture and walked to the podium.

After shooting a quick look at Julie, he started the lecture.

When the class ended, Rennick headed to his office on the second floor. He passed the *Law Review* offices and glanced in at the frantic activity of students trying to get out the current issue.

Bobbi, Rennick's secretary, was a bleached blonde in her early fifties. He suspected that her heavy makeup and low-cut dresses were "inappropriate" for law school decorum, yet Rennick never cared. She always doted on him and made sure he showed up where he was supposed to.

As he walked in, she handed him a thick stack of phone messages.

"You look like you're feeling better," said Bobbi.

"I guess. It'll take some time."

Rennick thumbed through the phone messages. Three calls from the lawyers who had hired him as an expert. A call from the *Law Review* editor, reminding him his rewrite was overdue.

"Detective Talon's here," said Bobbi. "He's waiting inside."

"Was I expecting him?" asked Rennick, still looking through his messages.

"No. He said it was important and asked if he could wait. I figured you wouldn't mind."

"Mmmmm." Rennick had met Talon a few years ago, when they both worked on the murder of a wealthy businessman named Elton Sudbury. Rennick hadn't seen him since.

Rennick quickly flipped through the rest of the phone messages and saw two calls from a Lisa Cleary. "Who's Lisa Cleary?"

"A lady who wants to hire you as a therapist."

"Who referred her?"

"Your book, *Edges of Reality*."

"Tell her I'm fully booked and give her the usual referrals."

"Got it."

Talon stood up as Rennick went into his office. The office was "decorated" in the same style as his house, but without

Julie's moderating touch. There were books open everywhere, and the closed ones were stacked in piles that leaned precariously. His desk was so completely covered with papers, pens, coffee cups, and other paraphernalia that the cleaning crews gave up trying to dust after the first three weeks of every semester. The only nod toward decor was a photograph of the 1982 Supreme Court justices, which had been left by the office's previous occupant.

After a few minutes of small talk, Talon got to the point. "So, Professor. You wanna do it again?"

"I'm flattered, Danny, but I don't have time for forensics right now. I've got work piled up to my eyeballs." That was only partly accurate. He no longer enjoyed forensics as much as teaching and writing.

"This is an interesting one."

"I'm sure it's fascinating. I just don't have the time."

Talon shifted in his chair and began straightening out a paper clip. "Lemme put it another way. I really need you."

"There's a lot of good forensic psychiatrists out there. I could recommend—"

"The others are academic assholes who talk about 'major trends in psychiatry' but can't tie their fucking shoes. I need you, Professor."

Rennick leaned back in his chair. "Well, that's one of the most unique compliments I've ever had."

"At least let me tell you about the case."

Rennick hesitated, then said, "All right. Go ahead."

"It's this serial killer who's popping off young women and frying their eyeballs with an electric cord."

Rennick blanched. "Oh no. I can't get involved in that one. The last victim was a friend of mine. It'd be way too painful."

"Shit, Professor. I'm sorry. I had no idea."

They sat in an awkward silence.

"Think I could bum some informal, big-picture advice?" asked Talon.

Rennick didn't answer right away. "I don't know. You mean about the general issues?"

"Yeah. Whatever."

Rennick looked at his watch. "I don't know. . . ."

"I'll make it quick. I'm doing okay with the routine stuff, but I'm hitting a brick wall with those prongs in the eyes. You heard about those?"

"Just what I saw in the papers."

"The killer puts nails on an electrical cord and spikes 'em into the victims' eyes. It's done after death. You got any idea what it could mean?"

Rennick thought for a moment. "Putting them in after death means torture isn't part of the motivation."

"Thank goodness for little things. What could the electrical thing tell us about the killer?"

"I couldn't say without knowing more about the case," Rennick answered tentatively.

Talon pulled his chair closer. "This asshole plans his kills like Norman Fucking Schwarzkopf. All the crime scenes are 'evidence free,' and there's no witnesses. His final product looks like the meat display in a goddamn supermarket."

"If the nails were postmortem, how were the victims killed?" He wasn't sure he wanted to hear this. Maybe if he skimmed the surface, he could at least point Talon in the right direction. Maybe that would help find Andrea's killer.

"Their throats were cut," Talon responded, pushing a stack of photos in front of Rennick. "This is the first victim, Myra Powell."

Rennick slowly lowered his eyes to the top picture. Powell's throat had been savagely slashed open, as if she had been attacked by an animal. The prongs and electrical cord made her resemble a robot that had been plugged into the wall. That could be it, thought Rennick. Turning her into a mechanical object controlled by the electrical power. Yet he felt that was too simplistic. The care and attention that the killer put into setting up this display signaled something much deeper.

"They were tied up with their own stockings," Talon continued, walking around and looking over Rennick's shoulder. "Duct tape over the mouth."

"Was anything missing from the victims' homes?" Rennick knew that in crimes this bizarre, killers often took something to remind themselves of the experience. A lot of these guys masturbated over the "souvenirs."

"Nothing that's been reported. Rojas's notes say he checked the area around each crime scene for shoes, purses, and shit like that. Didn't find anything."

"Sexual assault?" An image of Andrea being brutalized flared in his mind. He really should tell Talon to leave.

"Myra Powell, the first victim, was either raped or had rough sex shortly before death. The other two victims weren't sexually assaulted."

Rennick's eyes opened in surprise. "Really? Are you sure the same man killed the other two? When there's a sexual assault, you almost always see the pattern repeated."

"Can't ever rule out a copycat, but I'm ninety-nine percent sure we're looking at the handiwork of one wacko. The M.O. was identical."

"Was the sex before or after death?" asked Rennick.

"Coroner says before."

"That means a more aggressive killer. On the other hand, raping only the first victim says that rape isn't the dominant aspect of the crime. He's a sexual aggressor, probably driven by a sense of inadequacy, but this is a 'put the women in their place' power play."

"No pun intended?"

"Pun?"

"*Power* play?"

"Talon, you're an asshole."

"It's one of my best qualities."

Rennick spoke while staring out the window at a young woman walking a bicycle on the sidewalk. "Stopping the rapes could also mean the second and third victims did something to keep him from getting an erection."

"How's that?"

"Someone who ties up women like this wants to make them passive. Since you say Myra Powell's trauma could have been caused by rough sex, maybe she knew the killer and cooperated. If the other victims were strangers and resisted him, the rejection could have made him so angry that he was impotent."

"Interesting."

"It could also be that he found the killing so satisfying that sex was no longer necessary. Whatever it means, the stopping is highly significant."

"So what about the electrical angle?"

Rennick flipped to the next photo. He literally heard a scream in his head as he realized it was a picture of Andrea Baylor's corpse. Rennick slapped it upside down on his desk and moved to the opposite side of the room—but not soon enough to lose the image from his mind.

His mouth filled with a bitter taste, as if he had ashes on his tongue, and the smell of melting candle wax from Andrea's funeral burned his nostrils. "I can't help you on this one, Danny. It's too hard for me."

"I understand," said Talon softly. "I'm gonna leave the copies of files I made for you. If you don't want to read them, toss 'em out. You got an open invite if you change your mind."

"Not this time."

Rennick stuffed Talon's copies into a bottom drawer that he never opened, then forced himself to concentrate on next week's lectures.

An hour later, Bobbi buzzed him on the intercom. "It's that Lisa Cleary again. She refused to take the referrals and insists on talking to you. She says she's had some psychic experiences as a child that are related to her current problems."

"Psychic?" Rennick wasn't sure he believed in psychics, but he found himself intrigued by the idea of psychic experiences weaving into mental disorders. That was a new topic. He was impressed that this lady had been clever enough to hook him, and he figured that was worth a five-minute phone call.

"Okay. I'll take it." Rennick closed his door and put his feet on the desk.

"Dr. Rennick. Thank you for taking my call." He heard a slight tremble in her voice.

"Sure. I'm afraid I'm a bit rushed, though. How can I help you?"

"Your book really speaks to me. I feel certain you're the one to get me through these difficulties."

"Thank you for the kind words, but I have to tell you that I take very few patients. If you want to tell me a little about yourself, I'll be happy to give you a referral." That was his standard line, and it allowed him to politely turn down people he wasn't interested in seeing.

"This is kind of embarrassing."

"I don't make any judgments."

There was a silence on the line before Lisa continued. "I've been having these episodes where my mind is . . . how would I say it . . . 'captured' by some images. I can't control when they come. They just show up and take over my consciousness."

"What kind of images?"

"When I was young, I had a head injury and afterwards I had some psychic experiences. They stopped when I was fifteen. A lot of what I see is related to those old visions."

"What do you see?"

"There was this hospital where I was recovering after the injury. I see myself lying there, talking to a Filipina nurse. I also see this little redheaded girl I can't quite place. I think I knew her when I was a child. And there're some new images. This young woman I've never seen before, running around all sweaty and panicked. Like she's trying to get away from something. And there's a scene where I'm falling off a horse."

"You think these are psychic images?"

"Not all of them. Some are just memories. The others . . . I'm not really sure what they are."

"When did the episodes start?"

"About six months ago."

"I assume they're getting worse or you wouldn't be calling."

"Yes."

"Is anything particularly stressful going on in your life right now?"

"Not really." She hesitated, as if to say more, then stopped.

"Are these episodes different from the ones you had as a child?"

"Yes, although it's hard to explain how. The new ones are . . . well . . . threatening." Her composure had been slowly deteriorating as she spoke.

Rennick reflected on what Lisa had said. She sounded bright

and articulate, which he liked in a patient. She was also scared, which was usually a good motivation to recover. He understood why she had called him, since his book *Edges of Reality* dealt with experiences similar to hers. Usually these episodes were repressed memories that surfaced in response to a current trigger. He had an excellent success rate with these syndromes, simply by rooting out the underlying trauma. The psychic aspect of her visions was an intriguing twist. And he could use a new challenge right now, if only to get his mind out of the funk.

"I'd be willing to meet with you for a consultation. I don't promise any more than that, and I'll give you a referral if I can't get involved."

Her voice brightened. "Could I come in today?"

CHAPTER EIGHT

Talon parked his car and walked toward the Hollywood Division Police Station on Wilcox. The building was constructed of tawny-colored bricks, stained by the streaks of dirt that had dribbled down over the years. Several of the bricks were missing, leaving random holes that made the building look like an old, craggy fighter with a few teeth missing.

He stomped up the gray stone steps, then he elbowed his way through the morning's catch of human debris. The main area resembled the set of a 1950s police show, with tan walls, a few offices with wavy-glass partitions, and gunmetal-gray desks jammed together without any thought of efficiency. Phones rang and people shouted as they moved in and out, like the nerve center of some mission where no one was in control.

Over the years, Talon had been offered transfers downtown to Majors, where they handled the biggest homicide cases. He had always turned them down, mostly because he'd been in

Hollywood so long that it felt like home. As things worked out, with his success rate, he still got a lot of high-profile cases. Not to mention the hairy-assed ones.

Talon was still pissed that Rennick refused to help him with this case. It was like losing an arm before going into the Ultimate Fighting Championships. Rennick was the only shrink he'd met who had any common sense. The only other forensic psychiatrist he knew came directly from Nerd Central and talked like he was reading out of a textbook.

Talon chewed up a spitball and hit a four-footer into the wastebasket. Then he pulled the papers from his in-box and saw the report from VICAP—the FBI's database of violent crimes—that Rojas had ordered a while back. The damn thing was dated over a week ago, and Talon realized it had been misdirected through the Van Nuys Division before landing on his desk.

He flipped through the VICAP report and found a few cases of electrocution: people being pushed onto subway rails, a guy shoved into a power-plant generator, and the like. Totally fucking useless. He checked the search words and saw that Rojas had only looked for "electrocution." Talon filled out his own request, adding electrical cords and clocks to the search. He also added "stockings" and "throat."

Talon rubbed his beard stubble. The only lead was the missing boyfriend of the first victim, and all he knew about him was the first name, Bart. On the other hand, that was more than he knew about any other human being connected to this case.

Time to look for Bart.

Rennick saw patients in a small, stark office located in the Public Policy Building. He shared the room with a visiting professor, so Rennick only had access in the afternoons. At least there was nothing on the walls to distract the patients.

Lisa Cleary arrived precisely at 4:00 P.M., which was the only time Rennick could squeeze her in. He had told her he had thirty minutes, and he'd instructed Bobbi to call him at exactly 4:30 so he wouldn't miss the faculty meeting at 4:45.

Rennick observed Lisa carefully as she walked in. She was stunningly attractive, with features that were almost perfectly proportioned. Her sapphire blue eyes were so electric that he could see their brilliance even through his color blindness. She carried herself with authority and looked him directly in the eye with an intensity he had observed only in his top students.

Rennick saw that she was blinking much faster than normal and sensed a nervousness that she was doing a good job of hiding. While much of it was the awkwardness of visiting a therapist for the first time, he saw something deeper. A tight knot of emotion that she kept under iron control.

Lisa sat in the desk chair and shifted her position clumsily. She pulled down her skirt so that it covered most of her thighs.

They spoke superficially for a few minutes, then Lisa told him about the young woman she'd thought was hiding under her desk, and her vision of falling off a horse.

"You said these incidents started about six months ago?" asked Rennick.

"Yes. At first they were just images from my childhood. Like casual memories, almost daydreams. They gradually got more intense, and now I can't control them. Whenever they happen, I space out and lose track of where I am. What if it happens while I'm in a business meeting? Or while I'm driving or crossing the street?"

"These episodes started when you were a child?"

"Yes. When I was about fourteen years old I had some psychic experiences. They stopped about a year later, and I haven't had any since."

"I'm not sure I believe in psychics." That was mostly true, although he wanted to see her reaction to a direct challenge.

Her eyes seemed to flare slightly, then she composed herself. "I'm used to people being skeptical or thinking I'm crazy." She looked directly at him with a slight smile. "Although you're not supposed to say I'm crazy, are you?"

"Touché. Tell me about your psychic episodes."

"When I was fourteen, I fell off my bicycle and got a brain concussion. I remember waking up in this ancient hospital. It smelled like alcohol and had these white glass, acorn-shaped light fixtures hanging from the ceiling on long cords. I was lying there without a remote control, trapped into watching some Sunday morning religious program, when this short Filipina nurse came in shaking a thermometer. She put it in my mouth and took my wrist to measure my pulse.

"As soon as she touched me, I saw this flood of images. It felt like electricity jumping a circuit and blasting on at full power. I saw this scene in my mind, almost like I was standing there. The nurse was at home, kicking off her shoes and unzipping her uniform. This big man came into the room, looking upset. I could smell liquor on his breath. They started talking, but I couldn't hear the words. I could just see him getting madder and madder. Finally, he took off his belt and hit the nurse across the face. She started bleeding and tried to back away. He caught her and kept beating her."

"What did you do?"

"I started to cry, and the nurse hugged me. Her added touch intensified the visions. I knew that she had lost a baby from the beatings. And I saw into her future. She was in a hospital bed, with her jaw wired shut. Her face was black and blue. I tried to hold her so tightly that nothing could hurt her, and the harder I hugged, the more vivid the scenes became. Finally I said to her, 'Why do you let him beat you?'

"She jumped back and said, 'What?'

"I said, 'Your husband beats you, doesn't he? He's a big man, with black hair. He uses his belt. It's brown leather with a silver buckle.'

"She pulled my arms off her and started backing away.

"'Why do you say that?' she asked.

"I told her that I saw it in my mind, and I asked if it was true. She wouldn't answer me. She just backed out the door, shaking her head."

"Did you ever find out if it was true?"

"I was sure it was true when she started to cry."

"But you didn't really know?"

"Well . . . I guess not. Although I've had other visions that I knew were true."

"Such as?"

"A premonition where a parking space was going to be. Knowing what someone was going to say before they said it. Other things, too."

Rennick thought to himself that everybody has experiences like that. He wondered if she had played up the psychic angle just to get in the door.

"Were any of these other visions more significant?"

"Yes."

"Like what?"

She looked away from him, out the window. The sunlight struck her face and had to be directly in her eyes. She didn't squint. "Those are long stories. You said we only had a half hour. I promise they were accurate, and I'll convince you of that if we continue."

Rennick could see that these were emotional hot spots. Whatever the visions were, she seemed to genuinely believe in them. Even though his curiosity was piqued, they were short on time and there were other areas he wanted to explore.

"Tell me about your family life."

"I was an army brat. We moved all over the place. Virginia, Texas, Alabama, Arkansas, New Mexico, California, and Colorado. I never spent more than two or three years in one school. Just long enough to finally make friends before moving on and becoming the new kid in town again. And, of course, when I got out of high school and wouldn't have had to move anymore, Dad retired and settled down."

"Dad? Are your folks divorced?"

She fluttered a bit at the question. "No, they didn't divorce. My mom died when I was fifteen."

"I'm sorry."

"I'd always had a love-hate relationship with my mother, and going through puberty with a military dad was no day at the beach."

"You said your visions started when you were fourteen and then stopped a year later. Was that right after your mother died?"

She looked surprised at the statement. "Yes. Right after. I hadn't thought of it that way. You think that's related?"

"Good chance. There are few things more traumatic than losing a parent, especially in adolescence. Often—"

The phone rang.

"It's four thirty," said Bobbi. "Do you know where your ass is?"

"It's on its way to the faculty meeting."

"Right answer."

When he hung up, Lisa leaned toward him. "What do you think? Can you help me?"

"I need to think about it and check my schedule. I don't know if I have time to take on a new patient."

"I know you're the one to get me through this," she pleaded. "Please. I'll pay whatever you want."

"It isn't about money. It's about time. I won't get involved in something unless I can commit to do it right."

"When will you let me know?"

"In the next day or so."

Walking to the faculty meeting, Rennick replayed Lisa's session in his mind. Her case was intriguing, and he felt certain he could help her if he got involved. She appeared to be a classic case of suppressing a trauma and having it show up in some inappropriate manner; in her case, the visions. However, her trauma seemed much darker and more disturbing than most of the patients' he'd treated. He guessed the visions were related to Lisa's mother, since they stopped after her death. But why did they start up again?

The psychic angle was also fascinating. If she really was psychic, assuming that such a thing existed, he wondered what happened when these people had psychological problems. The interweaving of suppressed emotions and psychic experiences had to be unlike any disorders he'd ever studied.

He went into the Law School Building and started up the stairs. Even though his schedule was close to overload, treating her might be just the diversion he needed right now.

*　　*　　*

The killer sat alone, sipping a 1982 Pinot Noir and writing in the secret journal:

Saturday.

The urges are coming back. They feel like vibrations that start slowly, then increase in intensity until they're almost overwhelming. Like my own private earthquakes, which is an interesting thought. Maybe these urges are related to earthquakes on some primitive level. After all, isn't everything connected to a single source of energy?

The woman from the supermarket looked promising. Strutting around with her tits stuck out, like they were on a shelf. Almost begging for it. Unfortunately, she's been too street-smart. She even made eye contact with me, for God's sake. Why should I waste time with someone like that when there are so many who are naive and vulnerable? Fuck her.

This Pinot Noir has nice legs. And a fragrant smell of grapes fermenting in the shade. I should pick up a few more bottles.

The woman who lives on Sawtelle continues to be the first choice. She's almost as good-looking as the street-wise slut. I've watched her driving carpool, shopping at the market, getting her nails done. She's a little timid, but that's more than offset by her striking looks. That freshly scrubbed, All-American wife and mother face. She probably bakes cookies in the shape of Christmas trees. And she's got one of those smiles that says, "Let me help you." An offer I'll definitely be accepting.

The others are still on the list, but my research isn't far enough along. The one on Sawtelle will be next, although she's out of town for a while. No matter. Exercising restraint is good discipline. And a little waiting makes the climax more satisfying.

Climax. Wonderful word. Just writing it causes another wave to roll over me. Like a warm ocean surf.

The impulses are coming more and more often. Maybe it's because the performances are getting easier with practice. Or maybe it's because they're addictive.

It doesn't really matter.

CHAPTER NINE

As she approached Talon's desk, Mary Waters pushed her clear-plastic glasses up the bridge of her nose with an index finger. She was a tiny woman with jet black hair, wearing a white lab coat stained with brownish smears. Her thick glasses, already inching their way back down her nose, made her eyes look three times their actual size.

"The evidence collected at the Baylor scene is spotless. No prints, fibers, or other oddities. Just like everything else in these murders."

"Yeah. We're chasing Mr. Clean."

"We tried the laser on the clock radio. Sorry. No prints other than the victim's."

"I'm not surprised."

"You know about the shirt we found at Myra Powell's, the first victim?"

"I saw the notes in the file."

"Oversized shirt, extra large. Red and green plaid. Either she was into the gangsta look, or it belonged to a big guy. There were a few drops of blood on the collar that weren't hers or her roommate's. From the location, my best guess is a shaving cut. It's possible she nicked him during an attack, but the coroner didn't find anything under her fingernails. I think the guy cut himself shaving and it leaked after he got dressed."

"It's probably Bart, the invisible boyfriend."

Waters handed Talon a card with a fingerprint on it. "We got a magnifico print off one of the drinking glasses in Powell's kitchen. Not hers, not the roommate's. And no match in any records. That means the owner has no criminal record and hasn't been in a job that requires being printed. Unfortunately it's not a thumb print, so we can't use the Department of Motor Vehicles."

"This killer's been ultra careful," said Talon, steepling his huge fingers and springing them against themselves. "It doesn't add up that he'd leave a bloody shirt or a print on a dirty glass."

"He might've forgotten. It's obvious this is a sicko, and they do all kinds of inconsistent things. Remember the Leder case? The creep scrubbed the victim's bathroom with a toothbrush to get rid of blood and prints. Then he left a Polaroid in the living room that showed him standing next to the body in the tub."

"I suppose. It's even possible the boyfriend left the print on purpose. If he was real smart, he might use it as an excuse. Like, 'If I was the killer, would I be stupid enough to leave my prints there?'"

"Could be. Anyway, here's the video you wanted." She handed him the video taken at the Powell scene.

Talon had been trying to find out if the clocks had been

changed at the scenes of the first two murders. Unfortunately, the crime-scene photos didn't show any clocks. When he found out there was a video taken by Powell's investigators, he'd had Mary track it down.

Talon took the videocassette to a small conference room and fast-forwarded to images of the bedroom. Unlike the still photos, there was a quick shot of a clock beside the bed. He backed up, freeze-framed, and studied the clock's hands. The time code on the camera said it was 10:42 P.M. The clock beside the bed said 5:15.

He was right. The killer was turning back the clocks.

Julie knocked on the open door to Professor Thornton's office.

"Come in, come in," he said, waving her toward him. Thornton was a graying man with large ears that stuck out to the sides. His left shoulder always drooped a few inches below his right, so that it looked like he was perpetually carrying a satchel of books on his hip.

Julie walked into the office, which was an olive-drab cubicle piled high with blue-covered student exam books.

"Ms. Martin, I am very impressed with the rough draft of your dissertation."

She stopped her sit halfway through, then stood upright. "Well . . . thank you."

"Why did you decide to study sociology?" Thornton asked.

"It started with a sophomore course. I had an extraordinary professor at Dartmouth."

"Who's that?"

"Sandra Mell."

"Sandy? She's excellent."

"I remember the day I got hooked. Professor Mell took a piece of plaster out of the wall and asked if anyone understood what she was holding. We all sort of chuckled, until she went on to explain that you'd need a lot more knowledge than any of us had to truly understand it. You'd have to know how the forces of geology took thousands of years to produce the minerals. Why the university decided to build our classroom in the first place, and how that ties into society's decisions about funding education. How the people who constructed the building decided on this particular plaster material, and how they were trained to make that decision. How the janitors who left this speck had made a decision about what was clean and what was trash."

"Go on," said Thornton, shaking a few flakes of fish food into an algae-encrusted bowl on his credenza.

"She summed up by likening sociology to the Zen concept of seeing the universe in a grain of sand. She explained that sociologists see even the most trivial aspects of our daily lives as connected to the complexity of history and society. And that sociology looks at the whole chess games of our lives, while most of us are focused on the individual pieces."

Thornton was nodding enthusiastically. His head seemed to bob in rhythm with the fish that were flinging themselves at the flakes of food. "Yes, yes. Precisely. What else fascinates you?"

"How society perpetuates its values and mores. The way that our tribal instincts govern how we act no matter how advanced we become. Gender roles. Religion. Racial relations. Educational systems. These are usually instilled in us before we have the ability to make judgments about them."

"Why did you choose the court system for your dissertation?"

Julie sat down in the rickety chair. "Because it's a microcosm of society's way of saying who gets hurt and who is privileged.

The sociological process is intensified in criminal courts because the stakes are high and the process plays out quickly."

Thornton continued nodding approval. "You are just as articulate in speech as your papers indicated. And as I had hoped. That finalizes my decision."

"Your decision?"

"I called you in because I want you to join me at a lecture next week. Dr. Edmund Childs is coming here to give a lecture."

"Yes, I know." Julie was very aware of Dr. Childs, a famous Nobel laureate in DNA research. Childs had deserted science in favor of the humanities, and he was now a professor of sociology at NYU.

"I'd like you to meet him afterwards."

Julie reflexively stood up. "I could meet him?"

"He is looking for someone to train and I'm recommending you for the position. Your meeting would be the first step in that process."

"I . . . I . . . that's . . . wonderful. Thank you!"

CHAPTER TEN

Talon arrived at the Police Impound on Alvarado Street. Acres of cars sat waiting, like dogs whose owners had gone into a store. Cappy, the supervisor, was a skeletally thin man who looked like a starving POW. He greeted Talon with a tobacco-stained smile of crooked teeth underneath his trademark navy blue beret.

"Allo, Monsieur Capitain. How it goes?" he said cheerfully, exhaling a puff of his hand-rolled cigarette.

"Good, Cappy. Where's the car?"

"Section eight, space twenty-two, mon ami. Would you like an escort in the Cappymobile?" He pointed to a pea-green golf cart that appeared to have been repeatedly bludgeoned with a sledgehammer. Three black wires were strapped along the side with electrical tape.

"Nah. I'll walk. What time is Powell getting here?"

"Eleven bells."

Talon looked at his watch. He had fifteen minutes before Mr. Powell, Myra's father, picked up her car. Neither Talon nor Rojas had known that Myra Powell's car had been towed from a street-cleaning zone in front of her house and had been sitting in impound for almost three weeks. Talon had been notified when her father told Cappy that he was a parent of the serial killer victim.

"If he's here before I get back, keep him entertained," said Talon.

"I shall sing and dance my way into his heart," said Cappy as smoke slithered from his mouth.

Talon walked almost a half-mile to section 8, and saw the red Dodge Viper in space 22. It was covered with dust and grit, which swirled in his face as he opened the trunk. Nothing inside but a few newspapers, the spare, and a mildew smell. Same with the back seat and front. Talon popped open the glove compartment and saw a roll of breath mints, a cellular phone, and a handful of papers. He pulled out the papers and thumbed through them. On top was a laundry receipt, and Talon found himself thinking how she wouldn't need any more clothing. Below that was a warranty for a stereo, a few utility bills, and credit card receipts.

One of the receipts wasn't Myra Powell's. It showed a credit card in the name of Bartholomew Heath. Bartholomew. Bart. Maybe the boyfriend had just materialized.

Talon was itching to find Bart Heath. He jogged back to the front of the impound lot and saw a man standing with Cappy.

"Mr. Powell? I'm Detective Talon."

Powell was a bald man in his late fifties with callused hands that shook almost imperceptibly. Talon wasn't sure if the shaking was caused by a disease or by the recent trauma of losing his daughter.

"I'm very sorry about your loss," said Talon in a soothing voice.

The man nodded. His jaw quivered in an effort to hold in his emotions.

"After you called, I double-checked our reports," Talon continued. "We didn't find any ruby earrings in her apartment."

"They were her grandmother's. I know she had them here, because she sent us a picture of herself wearing them."

Talon remembered his conversation with Rennick about killers taking souvenirs from victims.

Bart was someone he seriously wanted to meet.

Within thirty minutes after leaving the impound, Talon rapped on Bart Heath's door. No one answered, and he went to the manager's apartment.

The manager, Eric Grimes, was a thin man in a burnt-orange polyester shirt. He held a coffee cup with a cartoon of a passed-out dog and cat, captioned WHO FARTED?

"Do you know Bart Heath?" asked Talon.

"Sure do. He's one of the tenants here."

"How long have you known him?"

"About a year or two."

"Do you know him well?"

"We ain't asshole buddies or nothin' like that. I say hello and he always says hello back."

"Do you know any of his friends?"

Grimes lowered his voice to a whisper. "I sure woulda liked to knowed some of the pussy he brought in. That boy attracted women like flies around shit. Some of 'em was real lookers, too.

And noisy bitches. Man, you could hear 'em wailin' in the bedroom at all hours. That Bart could fuck like a horse."

"Did you meet any of these women?"

"In my fuckin' dreams I did." Grimes pantomimed jerking off.

"Did he have any male friends?"

"Nah. When he weren't humpin', he spent a lotta time alone. Readin' books with titles you couldn't get your tongue around if you was a Ph.B."

"Do you know where he is now?"

"He's always disappearin' for a week or two. I know he's outta town now 'cause I'm holdin' his mail. That way nobody sees it pile up and gets no ideas."

"Did he say when he'd be back?"

"No. He usually don't."

"You know where he is?"

"On the road in his truck, I 'spect." Grimes broke into the chorus of Willie Nelson's "On the Road Again."

"Any idea how to reach him?"

"He ain't got no cellular or nothin' that I know about. Maybe he's got a CB radio or somethin'. 'Breaker, Breaker, there's a Smokey. . . .'"

"You know where he works?"

"It's probably writ down on his tenant app. You wanna grab a gander at it?"

"Please."

Talon took a step inside as the manager went into his bedroom. Mrs. Grimes, a small, white-haired woman with bony hands who resembled Norman Bates's mother in *Psycho*, sat knitting on the couch. Talon nodded at her and she scowled back.

After a moment, Grimes returned with Heath's form. "It

says here he works at somethin' called Hayashi Truckin'. Sounds like one of them Ore-ee-ental places, huh? Probably truck around sushi and chop sooey or somethin'." Grimes guffawed at his joke.

Talon wrote down the address, phone, and the name of Heath's immediate supervisor.

"Could I see Mr. Heath's mail?" Talon knew that looking at someone's mail was a federal offense, but he decided he wasn't going to mention it if Grimes didn't. He figured he was safe.

Grimes went back to his bedroom and returned with a small stack of envelopes. Talon thumbed through them quickly. He didn't care about anything except the dates. Talon saw that the earliest postmark was November seventh. The day after the murder of Andrea Baylor.

Talon drove up to the Hayashi International Trucking Company. Hayashi's "worldwide headquarters" were a small, corrugated-metal Quonset hut set on a cracked concrete parking lot in the City of Commerce, an industrial area just south of Los Angeles. The air smelled of diesel fuel as he walked past a chain-link fence with a rusted Beware of Dogs sign.

Mr. Hayashi was a wiry Japanese American with white hair who appeared to be in his sixties. When Talon entered, he was on the phone with his feet on his desk, enveloped in curls of blue cigar smoke.

Hayashi held the cigar between his fingers and waved it broadly in the air as he yelled into the phone. "Tell that bastard that if I don't have a check by tomorrow he can fucking well walk his fabric to Illinois." Then he slammed down the phone and stood up to face Talon.

"May I help you," he said in a soft voice, radically contrasting with the telephone display.

Talon showed him his badge. "I'm looking for Bart Heath. Does he work here?"

Hayashi took another puff, which shortened his cigar down to a saliva-soaked stub. Then he looked skeptically at Talon. "I run a clean business."

"I'm sure you do. Does Heath work here?"

"I only ship legal goods."

"That's real nice. I'll see if I can get you a medal from the City of Commerce. Now, does Heath work here or not?"

Hayashi's skeptical expression didn't change. "No one works here except me. I'm a clearinghouse for independent truckers. I match them with jobs and handle the paperwork, and I let them park their rigs here. I've known Bart for a couple of years. Did he do something wrong?"

"You know where he is?"

"No. I probably have his home address somewhere."

"I already got it. Is he on a job?"

"Not that I know of. He better not have taken a job through another clearinghouse. I'll string the bastard up by his johnson. Did he do something wrong?"

Rennick sat in his office, working through his backlog of phone calls. The first two were offers to act as an expert witness, which he turned down because he didn't have the time.

Bobbi came in with a revised draft of his *Law Review* article, which was still very rough, and still very overdue. He wondered if he could push it back to the next issue, although he figured that would leave the editors with a big hole in the current edition. He'd drop by the *Law Review* offices in the morning and see if he could sweet-talk them.

Late in the afternoon, when he was about halfway through the calls, Bobbi came in to say that Talon was there.

"Did he have an appointment?" asked Rennick.

"No."

"How did he know I would be in?"

Bobbi looked sheepishly over her half-glasses. "He's such a nice man."

Rennick shook his head in resignation. "Send him in."

"I know," said Talon before he even sat down. "You won't change your mind."

"That would make you the psychic of the week. Danny, don't pressure me like this."

"I just need some advice."

"Please. You know I can't get involved."

"Just hear me out. I got a high-profile case where my nuts are getting dry-roasted. My lieutenant has tried to kick my ass to Argentina for years, and if I fuck up this case, he's gonna get the chance. The only other forensic shrink I know has a voice that sounds like Mickey Mouse on acid, and he acts like he's got a broomstick up his ass. It's real simple. I need you. Can't you just, like, informally help me? Anybody who fries people's eyeballs like a fuckin' shish kebab has to be interesting psychologically. Aren't you even a little bit curious?"

"Under any other circumstances I'd be more than curious, but . . ."

"Look. I know it's painful because of your friend, but I'd keep your involvement to a minimum. And you'd be doing something for Andrea Baylor if you help lasso this dipshit. Just think what it'd mean to her family. And think how good it'd feel to help point a gun at the killer's head."

Talon stood up and waved his hands in the air. "Shit, Professor, I got anal bureaucrats slowing me down at the same time they're kicking my butt for results. You and me can wrap this up real quick if we work together. I've got a good lead on a suspect, and I just found something that nobody knows about."

Talon paused.

Rennick took the bait. "What?"

Talon leaned forward and lowered his voice. "The killer sets back the clocks at the crime scenes. I'm sure the time has something to do with it. Although I don't know what. The killings were all at night, between seven and eleven. I'll bet you can figure out what the clocks mean. Help me, Professor. I really need you. I'll owe you big time."

Reflexively, Rennick's mind began to spin out theories. The victims were symbolic of someone who had wronged the killer. Burning the eyeballs probably meant the killer never wanted them to see something again. Yet why electricity? Simply mutilating the eyes would do it. Maybe the killer worked as an electrician. Or was shocked as a child. Maybe it was connected to resetting the electric clocks, if they were electric. Resetting clocks might be as mundane as trying to confuse the cops about the time of death. But it could be something much more complex. Like a symbolic regression in time, as if to relive something from the past. Or to undo the painful experience that drove the killings.

Layered on top of this, Rennick felt a compassion for Talon. The guy was smart and dedicated, and he didn't deserve to go down on a case like this. And Talon was starting to get through to Rennick with his speech about avenging Andrea.

"Tell you what," said Rennick. "I'll talk to a friend of mine about whether I could be effective in a case where I'm personally involved. If he thinks it would compromise my ability to do a professional job, I won't do it. If he says I'm okay, then consider me conned."

"What's his name? I'll slip him a twenty."

CHAPTER ELEVEN

Rennick walked through the corridors of UCLA Medical School for the first time in over a year. The Med School and UCLA Hospital were tentacles of the same octopus, and the students were used to patients on gurneys, with IVs bobbling alongside them, being wheeled in and out of their corridors by white-suited orderlies.

He turned the corner into Corridor A, which housed the NPI—Neuro-Psychiatric Institute. Rennick followed the long cinder-block hallway to Office A-438, where the sign on the door read DR. MORRIS JOSEPH.

"Hi, Sally," Rennick said to the secretary.

"Hello, Michael." The plump, silver-haired lady, whose perfume was an overpowering magnolia, had been with Dr. Joseph for twenty-two years and knew most of the students by name. "Go on in. Dr. J's expecting you."

When Rennick walked into Joseph's office, it felt like returning to the womb. In some ways it literally was, because part of the training to be a shrink was to be shrunk yourself, and Joseph had been Rennick's psychiatrist.

Joseph's office was no more than ten feet by ten feet, and the only natural light came through an aluminum casement window with a lovely view of the parking structure. Floor-to-ceiling bookshelves, crammed to overflowing, covered one entire wall. Next to the shelves was a well-worn, taupe couch. It reminded Rennick of the couch he'd used at Yale Medical School when he was going through therapy with Joseph, and how he had had to lie at an angle to get his tall frame onto it. Across from the couch was a small, standard-issue metal desk, piled with papers and a cherry-wood stand holding several pipes on which the stems had been chewed like puppy toys.

Hanging on the only blank wall was the Clock. The Clock was a three-foot-long, handmade wall clock that Joseph's family had taken when they escaped from Germany during World War II, and Rennick knew that it symbolized their continuing life in the wake of the Nazis. He ran his fingers over the Clock's intricately carved mahogany cabinet while savoring the deep, melodious tick. During his therapy, Rennick had likened that tick to the way a mother's heartbeat must sound to her unborn child.

Joseph greeted Rennick with a warm hug. He was a short, round, grandfatherly man, with bushy eyebrows and gray-white hair that was rarely in place. His eyes were almond shaped, and they radiated warmth and caring. It was easy to see why many of Joseph's students referred to him as a country doctor, an image that Joseph rather liked.

"Michael, it is a delight to see you. You look marvelous."

"And you never change, Doc." Rennick was still so awed by Joseph that he could never call him by his first name.

They exchanged small talk for a few minutes, then Joseph broached the subject about which Rennick had called.

"You are quite correct to be concerned about compromising your integrity. Just as surgeons never operate on their own families, it would be difficult to profile a killer and maintain objectivity while you grieve for the victim."

"So I shouldn't do it?"

"I do not yet have sufficient facts to reach a conclusion. Please elaborate on your involvement with this young lady."

Rennick explained his friendship with Andrea, and his history with Talon. He also related the facts he had about the case.

Joseph listened, chewing on a pipe stem for most of the speech. When Rennick finished, Joseph furrowed his thick eyebrows and looked directly into Rennick's eyes. "What does your stomach tell you, my boy?"

"It tells me I'm confused."

"Indeed. You would not be here if that were not so. Yet your abdomen must be inclined in one direction or the other."

"I think I want to do it."

"Then you should do so. This is not the case of a spouse or child. While you obviously felt great affection for this fine young lady, I believe your analytical abilities are potent enough to avoid any significant impairment of your judgment."

"Are you sure?"

"One may never be sure in matters such as these. That is merely my opinion."

"Thanks, Doc. I think getting involved in something challenging would help me cope with her murder, by getting my mind off the depression and onto something productive. I'm also thinking about taking on this intriguing patient for the same reason."

"You are obviously teasing me with such a statement, and I

shall therefore oblige you wholeheartedly. Tell me about your patient."

Rennick explained about Lisa and her psychic experiences.

"Fascinating. I've also had a bit of experience with psychic phenomena."

"So you think it really exists?"

"Personally, I have no doubts that it exists. Have you not picked up the phone and known who was calling before they spoke? Or looked at someone in the next car, only to have them turn around?"

"I guess everybody has. I'm not sure that's more than coincidence."

"Let me tell you of an experience I once had in this arena. I was aiding the police in Providence, Rhode Island, and the case had them totally baffled."

Joseph told him of a nine-year-old girl who had disappeared, and how the family engaged a psychic named Werner Bamberger, a man with a goatee and a thick Austrian accent.

"Herr Bamberger handled some of the child's belongings, then began running around Providence, with much of the local constabulary following him like little ducks trailing after their mother. After several false starts, he finally led them to a remote cornfield and told them to start digging at a specific spot. About four feet down, buried deeply enough to avoid the farmer's plow, they found the poor child's body."

Rennick leaned forward in his seat.

"Next, Bamberger began raving about having visions of mountains. Mountains this, mountains that. Made no sense whatsoever. Within a few days, he summoned us to the apartment of a man named Berg. It turns out that *Berg* means 'mountain' in German, Bamberger's native tongue. When the police entered, they found the little girl's clothes, and Mr. Berg confessed.

"This experience made believers out of the Rhode Island police department, and I must confess I was rather impressed myself."

"So you believe in all this, Doc?"

"My story is not scientific, my boy. It's merely anecdotal. If you are asking my personal opinion, I will tell you that I am certain psychic phenomena exist in some form. If you are asking me as a scientist, I cannot tell you that they do."

"Do you know what's being done scientifically?"

"I have periodically read a few articles."

Joseph explained that psychic phenomena are referred to scientifically as "psi," and he described several recent experiments in the area. He related how a number of these used something called Ganzfeld, which is German for "whole field."

"In a Ganzfeld experiment," Joseph continued, "one person is the 'sender,' who studies a photograph and attempts to transmit the image to a 'receiver' in a distant room. The theory is that psychic signals are obscured by the din of normal sensory input, and therefore Ganzfeld attempts to cull out the noise."

Rennick turned sideways on the couch, dangling his long legs over one of the arms. "Like in a flotation tank?"

"Not terribly dissimilar. The receiver reclines in a double-walled room and listens to a mild white noise to block ambient sounds. To screen out visual input, they turn on a low-level red light and place small plastic hemispheres on each eye. Apparently they craft these hemispheres quite scientifically, by slicing Ping-Pong balls in half. Afterwards, the receiver is given four photographs and attempts to select the correct image."

Joseph explained that Ganzfeld experiments had a success

rate of about thirty-four percent, which was nine percent above the results of chance. Rennick thought that nine percent, while not overwhelming, held promise.

"For someone who doesn't know much about it, Doc, I'm impressed with your knowledge."

"It is my misfortune to have one of those minds that collects nonessential details and retains them beyond all necessity. And therefore I will tell you of perhaps the most interesting study, which was only completed in the last few months. A young doctor in Switzerland, quite by accident, was experimenting with electroencephalograms on a group of schizophrenic out-patients and a normal control group. Unbeknownst to him, two of the normal subjects were the Doretzyn sisters, rather well-known psychics from the Soviet Union who now reside in Lausanne. He happened to be using an electrode through the nasal passage to the back of the throat, and he found that both these ladies had a brain-wave pattern almost identical to people having a temporal lobe seizure. The doctor is now seeking funding to determine if, for the first time, there is scientific data to indicate an altered state of consciousness in the psychic persona."

"This is fascinating stuff, Doc," said Rennick.

"It is indeed, no matter how unscientific it might ultimately prove to be. Keep an open mind, my boy, and keep me informed of the progress with both your psychic patient and your forensics."

In the early evening, Rennick dragged himself into his apartment, exhausted. He took off his jacket and dropped it on the pile of coats that was once again growing on the arm of his couch. Julie was lying on the couch with her shoes off, reading *The Construction of Justice in a Democratic Society*.

She looked up at him and said, "Did you wear those clothes all day?"

"Yeah. Why?"

"I hope you didn't see anyone you needed to impress."

"What are you talking about?"

"Michael, you're wearing a yellow shirt and a burgundy coat."

"So?"

"So they're clashing like pit bulls in a dogfight."

He kissed her on the forehead. "They look good to me. That's one of the joys of being color-blind."

"Trust me. You're the only one who thinks they look good."

Rennick winked. "You take your chances when you get involved with the handicapped. An old girlfriend once numbered my clothes and made a list of what numbers went together. I lost the list about a week later."

He came around and sat on the couch.

"Do you see in black and white?" she asked.

"No. I see colors. It's just that certain shades of certain colors look alike. Dark reds and browns. Blues and purples. Oranges and greens."

"What do the colors look like to you?"

"I can't tell you. How would you tell a person who was blind from birth what the color red looks like?"

"Oh. That's weird." He began massaging her bare feet, and she moved them in counterpoint to his touch. "How was your visit to the Med School?"

"A trip down nostalgia lane."

"What did Dr. Joseph say?"

"He thought it wouldn't be a problem for me to work on Andrea's case if I wanted to. I think I'm going to do it. I also told him about that potential patient, and he gave me some information on psychic research."

Rennick summarized the information on experiments in psi that Joseph had described. He relayed how Joseph had distinguished telepathy, which is reading the thoughts of another; clairvoyance, which is the knowledge of events and objects; and precognition, which is the knowledge of the future.

"Joseph also told me about something called consensual psi. An outfit named Mobius had contact with a number of psychics, and they asked each of them individually to predict something. Then they acted on the majority opinion, and apparently found buried artifacts and things like that."

"So are you still cynical?"

"More like skeptical. Aren't you?"

"I don't have any problem believing in psychics," she said, closing the book and laying it on the floor.

"No doubts at all?"

"Not really. Haven't you found yourself knowing what someone's going to say before they say it?"

"I guess everybody's had those experiences. That doesn't make it scientific."

"I suppose not. But I still believe in it. Hey, guess who I'm going to meet."

"Who?"

She sat up cross-legged on the couch. "Edmund Childs."

"The Nobel laureate? That's impressive. How?"

"He's lecturing here next week and Dr. Thornton's invited me to meet him after the talk. He said Childs is looking for an associate, and I might have a shot."

"That's great. Isn't he at NYU?"

"Yeah. Going to New York would be a bummer. Anyway, I'm a long way from having to worry about it." Julie stretched her arms over her head and yawned. "I'm going back to my place. Although I could be persuaded to hang around if you're up for some snuggling."

"Oh, uh, well, I . . ."

"Don't feel pressured." An awkward pause. "Do you want to talk about it?"

"I'm just, you know, still sort of, uh, depressed, and a little preoccupied, and it's not . . . you, it's . . . you know . . . just me. I'm sorry. It won't be long."

"You might want to think about pushing yourself. It's been almost a week."

Silence.

"It's okay," Julie continued. "We have to get up early tomorrow anyway, don't we?"

Rennick had forgotten about tomorrow. Skydiving. He'd never even flown in a small plane, much less jumped out of one. When he made the promise in October, it had seemed like December was eons away. Now he thought he should be let off the hook because he'd agreed to do it during the "promise them anything" phase of their courtship.

"You know, I'm feeling a little off, and I have to prepare some new material for my class, and—"

"Not a chance, Michael. We set this date a long time ago."

"You know how much I want to . . ."

"I know *exactly* how much you want to. So don't try to con me. Pick me up tomorrow morning at six thirty." She got up and worked her feet into her shoes while standing.

"Maybe we should—"

"Did you get your car fixed?" she asked.

He didn't answer. "You didn't? Michael, we could get stuck."

Or maybe it won't start and we can't go, he thought.

"You're impossible." She kissed him, and he brushed her cheek lightly with his hand.

After she left, Rennick turned on his computer. It whirred and beeped through its usual routine. Then he connected to the Internet, found the Alta Vista search engine, and typed in the words *Skydiving* and *Safety*.

CHAPTER TWELVE

Unfortunately his car started just fine, so Rennick and Julie arrived in Hemet, a tiny desert community about sixty miles inland from Los Angeles, early in the morning. Even though the heat waves were still getting up to speed, the air shimmered visibly over the stark sand. The only signs of life were a few gray lizards darting between rocks before the sun got too hot for them to move.

The local vegetation consisted mostly of Joshua trees and cacti. To Rennick, the cacti looked like figures of people taunting him: "We've seen people like you jump out of planes and land on us without their chute even thinking about opening. Have a nice day." He imagined buzzards perched on the cactus arms, joining the chorus of jeers.

The airport turned out to be a strip of cracked asphalt next to a tower that looked like it had been built for a World War II movie. There were a few single-engine planes clustered around a ramshackle wooden building that had ACE'S FLYING SCHOOL stenciled in faded white letters on the side.

When the car stopped, Julie jumped out and sprinted toward a man who was waving at her. Rennick was suddenly absorbed in everything that didn't relate to jumping out of an airplane. He took his time carefully turning off the engine, pulling his keys neatly together, placing them in his pocket. Opening the car door, closing it, locking it. Looking around the airport and taking in the scenery.

When Julie reached the man, he picked her up. She kissed him, and he spun her around, with her legs bent at the knees and sticking out by centrifugal force. Rennick quickened his pace toward the two of them.

When Rennick arrived, the man put Julie down. He looked to be in his early twenties, tan, with jet black hair under a backwards baseball cap.

"Michael, this is Josh Stephens."

"Hi," said Josh. He grabbed Rennick's hand by the fingers and squeezed. Hard. Rennick felt like his eyeballs were going to roll out.

"Hi," Rennick answered, grimacing.

"Josh is working here so he can get enough hours to be an airline pilot."

"Only fifty-three more to go," he said, finally releasing the vise. "I teach flying just so I can get in the hours. It doesn't pay much, so I have to depend on tips." He winked at Rennick, who massaged his injured fingers.

"He's going to be our pilot today. He's taken me up four times already," Julie continued.

"Ever skydive before?" Josh asked Rennick.

Oh, sure. I was a paratrooper in Vietnam. "No."

"Ever been in a small plane?"

"I thought about learning to fly in college, but I found out you can't get a pilot's license if you're color-blind. I can't tell the red and green lights on the wingtips apart."

Josh didn't seem to be listening to Rennick's answer. "C'mon over here," he said.

"Over here" turned out to be a three-foot-high platform. Josh explained how even a bad landing shouldn't be any rougher than jumping off the platform, and demonstrated the right way to fall and roll when you hit. Rennick kept hearing the word *shouldn't* over and over in his head.

Julie jumped off the platform first, executing the roll perfectly. Rennick climbed up on it, and Josh explained the technique again. Then he gave him a push, throwing him off balance. Rennick landed hard and managed to roll, banging his shoulder in the process. No way was he going to show any sign of pain as he got up and dusted himself off.

"Three more times," said Josh.

After the rolls, Josh gave him a lecture on how to jump out and get into the free-fall position. He explained how to open the chute and guide your way down by pulling on the cords. Josh kept demonstrating on Julie, putting his hands all over her in the process.

By the time Josh was finished, Rennick was a pool of perspiration. The desert heat had gone from "Bake" to "Blast Furnace," though he seemed to be the only one who noticed.

After the ground school, they headed for the plane. It matched the ambience of the airport: a battered, single-engine Cessna, modified so that there were no seats except the pilot's. Instead of a door, there was an opening to jump through.

"How old is this plane?" asked Rennick.

"Not as old as you." Josh laughed.

And you live on people's tips? thought Rennick.

Josh walked around the plane, checking the elevator, ailerons, propeller, and fuel. Rennick ran his hand over the metal. It felt flimsy. He thought he could dent it with his finger and it wouldn't pop back. The fuselage was rusted in places. Some of the fiberglass was cracked. Did Josh see that? The tires looked worn. Were the treads okay? Did planes ever get blowouts?

Josh finished the preflight inspection as they put on their chutes. Julie got in first and held out her hand to Rennick. He took it and looked into her eyes. Rennick felt an electric current between them, and a pleasant stinging in his loins. He wanted to pull her out of the plane and take her back home. He motioned with his head toward the car and she giggled. Then she pulled him into the plane.

He quickly discovered that his large size didn't fit well into the small cavity. Standing up was out of the question, and he crabbed around until he could sit by lowering his butt onto the metal with a thump. When the engine started, it sounded like giant drums pounding right next to him. No. It sounded like he was inside a giant drum that was being pounded.

The plane jerked to a start and headed down the runway. Josh looked back and gave them a thumbs-up, to which Rennick responded with an "okay" sign. He thought about how the okay sign, a circle of your thumb and forefinger, meant "asshole" in Japan.

When they got above four thousand feet, it got cold. His sweaty hands began to freeze, and his teeth began to chatter. He hugged himself in an effort to keep warm. Julie and Josh seemed perfectly comfortable.

The plane dropped about fifteen feet in turbulence, and Rennick's head hit the roof. Josh waved to them without looking back, as if to say "No big deal." Rennick wanted to break his arm off and beat him to death with it, but he didn't know how to land an airplane.

Finally, they reached their peak altitude of twelve-thousand feet, where it was even colder. Julie motioned Rennick toward the door. He made a vague effort at unfolding himself, but ended up tipping over on his side against the vibrating floor. He looked up at her, and she was gesturing for him to hurry up. Josh looked back at him, smirked, and looked forward again.

Using his arms, he pushed himself up and inched toward the doorway. He stepped into the opening, holding tight with his hands, his legs planted firmly. The cacti below were undoubtedly laughing, while the buzzards checked their watches. Almost time for brunch.

Julie got close enough to scream in his ear. It sounded like a whisper in a hurricane.

"Just yell 'One-two-three-Go!' and jump on 'Go!'"

That sounded like something Josh had said on the ground. But it didn't sound like a good idea. His body wasn't cooperating. Are you kidding? it asked.

Then he heard Julie yelling in his ear. "One-two-three!" A foot against his rear end propelled him out the door before he realized what had happened.

The air hit him like a gigantic fan, and the noise of the whooshing was almost as loud as the plane engine. In the first split second, he had completely forgotten everything Josh had said on the ground. In the next, his body went into the position he was told to take: his stomach leading toward the ground, back arched, legs and arms out. It gave him a sense of control, and he moved his arms and legs to guide himself.

He felt like one of those beach balls he'd seen suspended on a stream of air in department stores. There was no sensation of

falling. It was more like being in a strong wind. He was leaning into it and relaxing, letting the wind hold him up. His face
felt like it was being pulled backwards toward his ears, even
harder than Aunt Minnie used to grab his cheeks. A jolt of
adrenaline hit him, and he began screaming like he did on a
roller coaster. Why not? No one could hear.

Julie appeared next to him, floating in the same position and
giving him a thumbs-up. Nice of you to drop by, was his first
thought, and he wished he could have said it to her. He returned the thumbs-up.

Now he was feeling even more in control. He could tilt himself up or down, move about. He was getting the hang of it.

Julie was gesturing to him in a way he couldn't understand.
He wrinkled his brow and shook his head to indicate he didn't
get it. She kept moving her hands, and she was starting to look
concerned. Uh-oh. What was wrong? He looked around and
saw nothing.

She maneuvered herself closer to him, and he thought he was
going to get a midair kiss. That would be cool. Instead, she
grabbed his cord and opened his chute. As it streaked above
him, he realized he'd forgotten all about it. "So one little thing
slipped my mind," he could tell the ambulance driver.

When the chute caught, the whooshing of the wind stopped
abruptly and it was dead silent. Julie was streaming below
him, since she was falling faster, and her chute was only now
opening. He watched it catch and billow into a brilliant hot
pink rectangle, like a blossom opening in time-lapse photo-
graphy.

He could see the target area on the ground, marked with a
chalk circle. He tried pulling the nylon cords until he got the
feel of how to maneuver himself toward it. The cords felt
smooth as they played through his hands, and he studied them

closely. Cords. Electrical cords. Why does someone use an electrical cord? The prongs were inserted after death, so it wasn't to inflict pain on the victim. What else? He remembered his fear of the skydive and reflected that some people are afraid of electrocution. Could the victim be dealing with that fear? Was it someone who had almost been electrocuted as a child? Or could it be that electricity is power? Asserting power over the victim. Someone wronged by a young woman. He felt that the cords were the key to unlocking the killer's psyche. The thoughts needed to simmer in his subconscious for a while before he could find a theory.

He looked down at Julie's hot pink parachute. Color. Something clicked in his mind. Despite the fact that he hadn't wanted Talon to leave copies of the files, he'd found himself reading them. And he'd learned that the electrical cords used by the killer were all gray. An unusual color for a cord and, according to the files, made only by two manufacturers. Unfortunately not unusual enough to mean there weren't over 75,000 of them sold each year. Rennick felt that the color was important. The killer had to go out of his way to get that color. Why gray? Gray is ambiguous. Maybe it wasn't color. Maybe it was lack of it. There was some meaning there for the killer.

His thoughts were punctured by the fact that he was rapidly approaching the ground. Julie, below him, was already landing, and didn't even have to roll. She ran forward and pulled her chute out of his way.

Rennick glided down smoothly and hit with a sharp thud. He remembered to roll, and it was rougher than jumping off the platform. It knocked his breath out for a second and he saw little white points of light. Then he stood up, wheezing, and looked for Julie. It was hot again.

Julie came bouncing up, with a wide grin. She jumped up into his arms, and he picked her up, giving her a massive kiss.

"You did it! How do you feel?" she said.

"It was a real rush."

"I knew you'd like it. Want to do it again?"

"*No*," he said before she finished the word "again."

CHAPTER THIRTEEN

Talon drummed his fingers on his desk, listening to the elevator music on the phone line. He'd been on hold for almost ten minutes.

Finally the music clicked off and a line rang.

"Jefferson."

"Mr. Jefferson, I'm Detective Talon. Did you get my letter and the court order to turn over information on Bartholomew Heath's MasterCard account?"

"Yes. I placed a flag on the account and we can fax you daily reports of the activity. Is this the correct number?" He read off the Hollywood Division's fax number.

"Yep. Did anything go through the account today?" Talon asked.

"No. We have a three-hundred-dollar hold for a hotel in Yucaipa from yesterday."

Talon's adrenaline level pumped up a notch. He knew that a

"hold" meant Heath hadn't checked out of the hotel: hotels estimate the bill and hold that amount when people check in. It's not released until the guest leaves.

"You have the name and address of the hotel?" asked Talon.

"I can get it. That's another department. The main computer only shows 'hotel' or 'restaurant' or 'retail' or —"

"This is real important, Mr. Jefferson. Can I wait?"

"It could take a while. May I call you back?"

"I'll wait for your call."

Talon hung up and paced around his desk. After five minutes or so, he sat down and started reading the files for the fourth time. Sometimes rereading them gave him a different perspective, like rearranging his cards during a poker game.

All of the victims had blond, shoulder-length hair, light complexions, high cheekbones, and heights of about five foot six. The first was Myra Powell, age twenty-six. Grew up in West Covina and moved to West L.A. three years ago. Roomed with Carol Wilson, who she met from a bulletin board at the supermarket. Worked in a bar called the Secret Dungeon. Boyfriend of about two months was Bart Heath, who was hopefully still in that Yucaipa hotel.

Second victim was Betty Sanchez, age twenty-eight. Grew up in Camarillo with eight brothers and sisters. Dropped out of high school and became a manicurist. Moved to Los Angeles within the last year, chasing an Afro-American boyfriend who races motorcycles. He dumped her about a month ago and was now living in New York, with lots of witnesses to his whereabouts at the times of the killings. No new boyfriends that anyone knew about. Sanchez was behind on her rent, credit card, light and phone bills. Other than a few collection agents, no enemies.

Andrea Baylor, age twenty-four. Grew up in St. Louis. In Los

Angeles about three years. Worked as a secretary in an insurance company. Very few friends, other than Rennick.

Talon didn't see any pattern among the women beyond their looks, and as far as he could tell their lives didn't cross. It wasn't unusual for looks to be the only connection between serial victims, but it was depressing because it meant there was no way to predict future moves.

He sat back and rubbed his eyes. Then he shook out four aspirin and swallowed them dry.

The phone rang and he dove for it.

"Yeah."

"Danny? It's Michael Rennick. If you still want me on the case, I'm in."

"Fuckin'-A!"

Lisa sat in Rennick's psychiatric office and tugged at the hem of her skirt. She was looking at him with a fragile expression, like a small child leaving her parents on the first day of school.

Rennick read over her patient form and noticed that she had just turned thirty-two. He was surprised to see that she was only four years younger than he was. He had thought she was still in her twenties.

"Happy birthday," he said.

"Oh, thanks."

"Did you have a big celebration?"

"No. I don't have anyone I care to celebrate with."

She continued to fidget and seemed so uncomfortable that Rennick suggested something he rarely used. "For therapy to be effective, it's important that you relax and clear your mind of all distractions. Since the biggest distraction is my presence, I'd like you to lie down on the couch, facing away from me."

She began toying with her thin blond braid. "Now?"

"Yes."

Lisa looked around, as if to get her bearings. Then she awkwardly sat on the couch with her knees tightly together. Finally, she lay down on her back, with her hands clutched across her stomach.

"All right. Take a few deep breaths and let them out through your mouth," said Rennick.

By the third breath, he could see her body beginning to relax. Her breathing slowed, and he began talking in rhythm to her respiration. The technique was one he had learned by mimicking Joseph's therapy, and it bordered between traditional relaxation methods and hypnosis. Once his phrasing was in sync with her respiration, he could slow his speech pattern and her breathing would also slow down. That created a subliminal rapport.

"Have you had any of these episodes since I last saw you?" Rennick asked. He avoided using her name because that might call the patient out of the state he was trying to get her in.

"Two. One new vision, and a repeat of an older one."

"What was the new one?"

Lisa described how she had seen her father as a young man, the way she remembered him when she was a little girl. He was dressed in a perfectly pressed, tan army uniform, standing at attention beside a door. She described how she walked toward the door and grabbed a brass handle that felt cold, almost wet. When she started to turn it, her father snatched her wrist and twisted her away from the door. Then he barked, "Off limits!" and went back to standing at attention. She tried the door two more times, with the same result, and then began pounding on his chest with her fists.

Rennick watched her body stiffen as she related the vision. "Then what happened?" he asked.

"The harder I hit him, the harder he threw me on the floor. I got up one last time and ran towards him, head first. Just before I would have hit him, he disappeared and I snapped out of the vision. I found myself shaking and reaching for a cigarette, even though I haven't smoked for ten years. It took me a long time to calm down, and I still can't get that scene out of my mind. What do you think it means?"

"Episodes like yours are usually a break with the present because something painful from the past has been triggered. The visions symbolically represent the old hurt. That's consistent with the fact that your father is young in the vision. The door probably represents a barrier you've erected to hide the old trauma. We'll get a better sense of what it is when we get further into therapy."

"I've had some unhappy childhood incidents, like everybody else I guess. But I can't think of anything that unusual."

"I'd be surprised if you could. That's what I'm here for."

"You'd think if it was that traumatic, I'd know what it was."

"It might not be anything dramatic to the world, just to you. Or it might be so painful that you have no conscious memory of it. Whatever it is, these things unfold over time, so be patient." Rennick controlled his voice, soothing her with his tone. He wanted to move her off this incident. "You said you had a repeat of another episode?"

"Yes. I had another vision of riding a horse. I was bareback, trying to hold on, and something really weird happened. I felt like my hands were slipping inside the horse's neck. Like I could feel all the mushiness of his innards. It was disgusting."

"Did you ride horses when you were young?"

"No. I didn't even particularly like them. We had horses on our farm in Arkansas, but I stayed away from them most of the time. I was afraid they'd kick me."

Rennick decided to probe other areas of her life, looking for hot spots. "Let's talk about your psychic experiences as a child. How did you feel about having them?"

Lisa described how she loved the episodes at first. She talked about the earliest incidents being small things, like helping her father find a parking space at the shopping mall. She told Rennick how her father had kissed her as a reward, which was special because he rarely broke his military demeanor.

"How did your mother feel about your psychic experiences?"

Lisa's expression abruptly soured. "She didn't like them at all. Our family was secretive about everything, and especially something that might be embarrassing. While she never outright called me a freak, I know that's what she thought. Like I was some Salem witch. When I tried to talk to her about my visions, she'd ignore me and go into her garden."

Rennick wrote down that the mother was definitely a hot spot. "What were some of your other episodes?"

Lisa described how she once held her friend Allison's backpack and had an accurate vision of Allison's mother, whom Lisa had never seen. She also saw Allison dating a boy who had invited her out only an hour earlier.

"Allison was the Western Union of the eighth grade," Lisa continued. "She told everyone what happened, so the kids all started asking me to 'tell their fortunes.' I was suddenly very popular."

"How did you 'tell their fortunes'?"

"First, I'd sit in a comfortable chair, and lean back into it. I didn't want anyone around except the person I was talking to. Then I'd take some object of theirs and rub it between my thumb and fingers while I closed my eyes. The feeling was really bizarre. I felt heat building up where I was rubbing, like two sticks starting to make a fire." Lisa began rubbing her fingers together as she spoke.

"The warmth would travel up my arm and I'd start sweating, like really sweating. Then I'd begin to see an image, very clearly, like I did with the nurse. I felt like I was standing in the scene."

"In the scene?"

"Yes. I once read something in my college psychology class that sounded very similar. The textbook described a brain surgeon who stimulated parts of the brain with an electrode, which caused people to have an intense vision. I remember reading about a woman who thought she was racing in a fast boat, with the water spraying her body, and the wind stinging her face. She said it seemed real even though she knew it wasn't."

Rennick knew about these experiments. They were conducted by two Canadian doctors, Penfield and Jasper, who were "mapping" parts of the brain. Her description of the results was right on the money.

"What kinds of visions did you have?" Rennick asked.

"I never knew what I was going to see. A lot of my friends had questions, but I wasn't very good at getting things on demand. They had to settle for whatever flowed through me at the time. Sometimes the events took place in the past, like childhood accidents. Or sometimes I saw the present, like Allison's mother. And the most spooky was the future, although the future was the least reliable."

"What kinds of things did you see about the future?"

"Usually nothing important. Once I saw that a girl was going to get grounded for sneaking out her window at night. Another time I knew this boy was going to make the football team. But sometimes . . . sometimes it wasn't so trivial."

Lisa's voice had changed jarringly as she spoke the last few words. Rennick looked up and saw that she had crossed her arms across her chest and was hugging herself. She stopped talking.

"You said you saw things that weren't so trivial," Rennick prompted.

Silence. He saw tears welling up in her eyes. Now it was time to intervene, because she was in a dark place and he needed to get her back. He called out in a strong tone, "Lisa!"

At the sound of her name, she sprang off the couch and rushed past Rennick. He moved reflexively to get out of her way, dropping his notepad.

Lisa opened her purse and dabbed her eyes with a Kleenex. As Rennick stood up clumsily, she turned to face him.

"I don't think therapy is a good idea for me after all. Thank you for trying." She stuck out her hand to shake.

"You shouldn't leave in this state. Stay and finish the session."

"I'm fine. Thank you."

Before he could shake her hand, she was gone.

Late in the afternoon, Talon finally got the call from the credit card company. Bart Heath, the first victim's boyfriend, had left the Yucaipa hotel early in the morning.

Talon stared at his desk, reflecting how he had missed the only suspect by a matter of hours. He gripped the arms of his chair so tightly that his fingers blanched. When he finally let go, his hands were so stiff that he could barely fish out the materials he had just received from the Department of Motor Vehicles.

According to his driver's license, Heath was six feet tall and weighed two hundred pounds. The picture showed a sandy-haired man with a wide, square face and light green eyes. Heath seemed to be sneering at him.

Talon leaned back. The tenuous connection to the killer that he'd felt at the Baylor scene had shriveled away. Why? He ran his huge hands through his hair and clasped them behind his neck. Why couldn't he get back on the killer's wavelength?

When it hit him, it was with enough force to propel him out of his chair. He wasn't getting his usual gut instincts because he hadn't been immersed in the case from the beginning. He needed to go back to square one.

Talon rushed out of the station and drove about fifteen miles over the speed limit toward West L.A. He parked in front of a Spanish duplex, with a red-tiled roof, on Federal Avenue. The building's walls were a dirty tan color, with blotches of a lighter shade that had been sloshed over graffiti. In front was a three-foot-high fence made of stucco posts with dark brown, rough-wood beams sticking between them. Several of the beams had fallen out of the posts and leaned against them like cripples.

The doorbell was a faded brass thumb-turn that looked like the key to wind an alarm clock, and he could barely hear its ring. A small, dirty-blond, owlish woman opened the door a crack, keeping the chain in place.

"Yes?"

"Did Myra Powell live here?"

The woman's eyes teared almost immediately. "Who are you?"

Talon flipped open his badge.

"The police have already been here. I talked to a Mexican guy for over two hours."

"Actually he was from El Salvador. And I know you already spoke to him. I'm new on the case, and I'd like to go over a couple of things again. Can I come in?"

"Do I have to do this?"

"Yes." That was a lie.

The door closed, the chain slid, and then she opened it. The woman had short, straw-colored hair that was matted close to her head, and her right eye had a nervous twitch. Talon noticed that she was wearing a white angora sweater, much too hot for the day's temperature. He knew that people who'd been victimized sometimes wore extra-heavy clothes. The thick layers made them feel more secure.

The room was filled with cardboard boxes, their flaps open as if they had put their hands in the air to surrender. All of the shelves were bare, and there was a cluster of drinking glasses on the floor next to a stack of old newspapers in which she had been wrapping them.

"You were Myra's roommate?"

"Yes. I'm Carol Wilson." She stood with her shoulders and head hunched forward, as if she were trying to make herself smaller.

"Danny Talon." He kept looking around and didn't offer his hand. On the dining room table, he saw a collection of New Age paraphernalia. Crystals, tarot cards, incense, and a collection of books. How could people waste money on this shit?

"These yours?" he asked.

"I guess they are now. They were Myra's. Her folks didn't want them. I don't know if I'll have room. I'm moving in with my lover, Nick. I haven't slept here since . . ." She turned away from him.

"So Carol—can I call you Carol? Were you and Myra close?"

"Not really. She was kinda nice, I guess."

"Was she into this New Age sh—stuff?"

"I suppose. She was learning how to tell fortunes with tarot cards."

Talon reflected on the irony of Myra's trying to predict her future as fate ended the process. He pulled the driver's license picture out of his pocket. "Is this her boyfriend, Bart?"

Carol's eyes flared in recognition, followed quickly by fear. "Yes," she gasped. "Is he locked up?"

"No. We only want to talk to him at this point. What can you tell me about him?"

"Can you, like, make sure he doesn't come around here?"

"At the moment, I'm afraid we don't know his whereabouts. Do you know where he is?"

"No."

"You know anybody who might?"

"No."

"What do you know about him?"

"Not much. He wasn't very friendly. When he came over, he told me to get in my room and close the door so they could watch television in the living room."

"Which room was Myra's?"

Carol's hand shook as she pointed to a closed door.

"Can I look in?" he asked.

"I haven't opened the door since . . . If you go in, please close it behind you."

Talon walked into the room and shut the door behind him. The bedroom smelled of dust and stale air. The mattress had been removed, and the only furniture was a bedside table that leaned away from the bare bed frame. He went over to the clock beside the bed and saw that it was unplugged. He put on latex gloves and put the clock in a plastic evidence bag, although he assumed there wouldn't be any prints. Then he went back into the living room and saw that Carol was sitting at the dining room table, with her back to Myra's door. He closed it loudly to let her know he was returning. She didn't turn around.

Talon lowered himself onto a chair next to Carol and began playing with a crystal. He could see about thirty of his faces in it.

"When you last saw Bart, did he have any facial hair?"

"I think he was starting to grow a mustache or a beard. It made him look like a homeless person."

"Did he ever spend the night here?"

"Sometimes."

"Did they, uh, disturb you on those nights?"

Her face reddened. "What do you mean?"

"Did they make a lot of noise?"

"Must you do this to me?"

"I'm sorry. It's important. Did they ever disturb you?"

"Yes."

"What kind of noises?"

"Detective . . ."

"What kind of noises? Were they fighting?"

"Well, I always assumed the groans were . . . were . . . lovemaking. But now that you mention it, I suppose it's hard to tell."

"So he could have been hurting her?"

"Maybe. It could get pretty loud."

Talon starting thumbing through the tarot cards and flipped over the Five of Cups. "When was the last time he was here?"

"The night before . . . she was . . ."

"Did he have any distinguishing marks? Tattoos? Scars? Injuries?" He turned over the Queen of Pentacles.

"Not that I noticed."

There was a loud knock at the door. Carol looked at Talon in panic, then at the door. The chain hung loose. Talon stood up as the door slowly opened. A stunning, six-foot-tall redheaded woman with long eyelashes walked in.

"Hi, Nick," said Carol.

The redhead gave Carol a hug and a kiss on the lips. Then she shot a look at Talon before speaking to Carol. "I thought we were going to finish packing tonight."

"This man is a policeman. I didn't know he was coming." Carol looked over at Talon. "We won't be long, will we?"

"No."

Nick disappeared into the bedroom.

"Uh . . . do you have any idea where Myra met Bart?" asked Talon.

"No."

"What did he do for a living?"

"He said he was a driver. A trucker, I think. I thought that was unusual because he said he had a master's degree in philosophy. The Zen of the open road, I remember thinking. He said trucking kept him close to real people."

Nick walked past Talon into the kitchen without acknowledging him. She had changed into a pair of tight blue jeans and was tying her blouse in a knot above her bare stomach. Talon adjusted his tie.

Talon and Carol spoke a few more minutes, until her answers became a series of "I don't know"s. When he stood up to leave, his eye caught one of the New Age books. It had a slick, electric-yellow cover that looked almost as if someone had colored it with a highlighter. On the front was a picture of a pyramid, like on a dollar bill, but with a star at the top instead of an eye. The title was *Vibrations of the Pyramids*. This New Age shit was really from another planet, thought Talon as his attention moved to Nick. She was facing away from him, bending over to feed her cat.

"Here, kitty, kitty," she said softly.

*   *   *

Lisa sat at her desk. Her eyes were on a page of financials, but her mind was still back in Rennick's office. She'd never behaved like that before. What could she possibly have been thinking, to chase down this famous psychiatrist and then walk out on him? Was she a complete idiot? He must certainly think so.

As if to confirm her hypothesis, she found herself slipping into a vision of the horse. While she rode, her entire body began sinking into the horse, as though she were descending into a quicksand mixed with the horse's blood and organs. A sickening, sticky muck was covering her body, and a rancid smell filled her nostrils, nauseating her.

She sank farther into the horse's body as he galloped faster. The horse had enormous ears, so she grabbed them to keep from sinking farther. Then she looked ahead at the dirt road on which they were running. The young woman from her earlier vision was floating above the ground. Next to her were two other women; now a fourth was joining them. All of them similar in looks: shoulder-length blond hair, trim builds. All suspended in the air.

As the horse brought her closer, she realized the women weren't merely floating. They were hanging from a huge tree, suspended on cords tied around their necks. Their bodies twitched spastically inside a clear material, like kitchen wrap.

Lisa bit her lip to keep from crying out, and she hoped the discomfort would keep her from slipping fully into the vision. She clenched harder, sending a sharp pain into her jaw.

Finally, the image began to dissolve. She went to the ladies' room and splashed cold water on her face. When she looked in the mirror at her reflection, her face appeared gaunt and strained. Dark circles had materialized through the makeup under her eyes, while wrinkles of crow's-feet scarred the corners.

She thought of her father, forbidding her to cry when she was a child. Drawing in a shuddered breath, she straightened her posture and tightened her stomach muscles. She gained more and more control as the moments passed.

When the last traces of the episode faded, she patted a wet towel on her eyes. Her father had been right. All the strength she needed was inside her. She could handle these episodes. There was no need for this psychiatric nonsense.

She continued to stare at her reflected image, and her face told her she was lying. She hadn't walked out on Rennick because of some inner strength. He had started to touch something deep inside her. She wasn't even sure what it was. Only that it was something no one else had touched.

CHAPTER FOURTEEN

Bobby Mullins, fresh from his bath, smelled like Ivory soap and baby shampoo. He got into bed wearing his big-boy pajamas, and his mother tucked him into the crisp sheets. He stared at the little clown with balloons on his night-light until he fell asleep.

Later that night, he was dreaming about somebody knocking. Maybe it was more like somebody pounding on the wall. In a half-sleep, he looked over at his night-light. The clown holding balloons was smiling at him. The thumping was in the next room.

He climbed out of bed, still foggy, and bumped into his door going out. The noises were coming from his mother's room. He toddled over toward it and saw that the door was closed with some light shining underneath. Mom never closed her door. The knob was cold to his touch, and his hand slipped as he tried to turn it. When he tried again the knob squeaked, and the light went out in Mom's room. He used two hands on the handle and finally made it move.

The noises in her room stopped as he pushed the door open. "Mom?"

He heard a crackling that sounded like fire. Now he was wide awake and starting to shake. The room was dark and he couldn't see very well.

Something moved! Oh. Just a curtain blowing in the window. No wonder the room was cold. Wait a minute. Mom never left the window open. Something was wrong. The shadows in the room made the furniture seem like monsters crouching in the corners. All eyes on Bobby. He thought about turning on the light but something told him he shouldn't. The monsters seemed to be coming closer. The wind "hooed" as it vibrated the window glass.

"Mom?" His voice shaking.

He saw someone stand up and look at him quickly. Plastic Man, Bobby thought to himself. Bobby screamed out loud, and Plastic Man jumped out the window. Very fast. He started to cry and felt himself peeing. He hoped he hadn't ruined his Mickey and Goofy pajamas.

Mom was on her bed, not moving. It was dark. She didn't sleep all spread out like that. Without covers. Without clothes. Something was really wrong. He felt his pee running warmly down his leg. He was sobbing and shivering. Should he turn on the light?

"Mom! Mom!" He pulled at her arm and she didn't answer. His whole body began to shake and he thought he should run. He didn't know where to go. He started turning around in place, looking for a grown-up to help, getting a little dizzy. He could taste his tears, all salty and runny.

Mom still didn't answer. He ran to the living room and

turned on the light. It stung his eyes. Then he dialed 911, just like on TV. It was hard because his hands were cold and shaking.

"Mommy's not well," he cried.

A man's voice replied. "We'll help her, little girl. What happened?"

"I'm a boy."

"Sorry, son. What happened?"

"I don't know. She won't move. Help her! Please."

"Is your daddy there?"

"He lives in Houston."

"Stay calm, sweetheart. We're sending someone right now."

Bobby left the phone off the hook and ran back into Mom's room. He didn't want to turn the lights on.

"Someone's coming, Mom," he said, taking hold of her hand. She was getting cold.

CHAPTER FIFTEEN

Rennick was sitting on his living room couch. He was so bored that he picked up Julie's copy of *Bias in American Criminal Justice*. It was possibly one of the dullest books he had ever read.

The phone rang.

"Michael? Danny Talon."

Rennick knew it was serious when Talon didn't use the nickname "Professor."

"Number four just came in," Talon continued. "I'm going to the scene. There's a little boy there who mighta seen something. Can you join me?"

Rennick knew the little boy would be in shock. Memories of Andrea Baylor flooded him. The thought of the child made him think of Andrea's parents. He remembered the image of those tiny people at the funeral, holding each other and crying. Their baby gone forever.

"Michael?"

"Sorry. How old is the boy?"

"I dunno. Four or five."

"Okay. I'll meet you there. I want to stop at a drugstore first."

Talon parked his car on Sawtelle near Santa Monica Boulevard and sat in the dark, listening to Chopin's "Military Polonaise." He hated homicides that were reported late in the evening, because the media monitored police frequencies and climbed all over the scene to make the eleven o'clock news. His routine was to park a block away so he could walk in unobtrusively, hopefully avoiding the bubble-headed reporters and assholes with cameras on their shoulders.

After a few minutes, he looked at his watch: 11:23 P.M. He yawned reflexively, since he would normally have been in bed for an hour and a half. Seven more minutes and they couldn't show him live on television.

After several polonaises, Talon got out of his car and walked past the newspeople, who were packing up their equipment. An Asian woman from one of the local stations recognized him.

"Detective Talon. Any leads on this electrical killer?"

He looked around conspiratorially. "We off the record?"

All the newspeople went quiet.

"Sure. The camera's packed up."

He cupped his hands around his mouth and whispered, "No comment."

The crowd grumbled and went back to packing. One man whispered loudly, "And you wonder why the media and police have such a cordial relationship."

Talon ignored him and walked up the sidewalk to a wood-shake apartment building with overgrown bushes covering most of the entrance. He passed a sign, lit by two badly aimed floodlights, that said GASTON MANOR.

The building was U-shaped, built around a central courtyard, and most of the neighbors had stepped out to watch the circus. Talon remembered an interview he once saw with the founder of a tabloid newspaper. The guy said he started the paper after he saw people crowd around the carnage of a traffic accident.

The door to Tanya Mullin's apartment was guarded by a uniformed officer. Talon recognized a photographer named Edison and a criminalist named Larson who were waiting outside for him. The uniform introduced himself as Lester Spears and logged in Talon. Talon surveyed the living room carpet from the doorway, and decided it wouldn't disturb any evidence to step inside. Spears and the others followed him.

The scene in the bedroom looked like the photos of the other crimes, with a gray electrical cord trailing off the bed. The woman, with shoulder-length blond hair, had been tied, nude and spread-eagle, to her bed frame with sliced-up panty hose. Beside the bed, her clothes were folded neatly in a pile. She had silver duct tape across her mouth, her throat had been cut savagely, and she lay in a massive pool of blood. There was a look of terror in her still open eyes.

Her eyes. They weren't speared with the prongs, yet he had seen an electrical cord. He walked closer and saw that they had been driven into her ears. The other end of the plug lay limply on the floor. Presumably the kid had arrived before the killer could plug in the cord.

Talon went to the bedside clock. It showed the correct time. Maybe that was also because the killer was interrupted. Or maybe the pattern was changing, since the prongs were now in the ears. He wondered when Rennick would get there.

Talon started toward the window and saw a large, faint footprint on the carpet. Much larger than the victim's. Because of the kid, the carpet hadn't been brushed. He said "Yes!" under his breath and dropped a white plastic evidence marker, which resembled an upside-down V, next to it.

Talon continued to survey the room and found nothing else. Then he went into his squat routine in the corners. On the third squat, his eye caught something lodged in the metal mattress frame. He almost missed it because it was close to the same color. He went over and carefully removed it with the oversize tweezers from his evidence kit. It was the broken blade of a hacksaw. Instinctively, he knew the killer was moving into something more bizarre. His gut was churning, and he found himself tuning in to the killer's frequency. There were going to be more serious mutilations. The other murders were merely a warm-up. Talon could feel the killer breathing, his rib cage expanding and contracting like a wolf working up for an attack. If the little boy hadn't come in . . .

"Where's the kid?" Talon asked Spears.

"In his bedroom with a social worker. His name's Bobby. His father's flying in from Texas to get him."

Talon went into the boy's bedroom and saw him huddled on the bed. Bobby was small and slight, with tightly curled auburn hair and very white skin. He was clutching his knees to his chest in a fetal position, sucking his thumb. An Afro-American woman with gray hair and a warm smile sat beside him, gently massaging his back. The boy was shaking.

"Bobby?" said Talon.

No response.

"Bobby?"

Nothing. Talon sat on the bed beside him.

"Bobby, I'm Detective Talon. I know it's rough, kid, but I gotta talk to you."

Bobby shivered. The social worker looked at Talon and shook her head no.

"This is police work, son. It's important."

Bobby looked up at Talon. His hand started toward him slowly. Talon moved closer, and Bobby touched the handle of Talon's gun.

"No!" yelled Talon, jumping up. "That could kill you!"

Bobby started to cry and pulled the covers up over his head. The social worker looked at Talon with a Now-look-what-you-did expression. Talon clenched his fists.

"Let me try," came a soft voice from the doorway. Talon turned and saw Rennick holding a white plastic bag. He motioned his head for Talon to leave.

Rennick sat on the side of the bed and spoke in a low, calm voice.

"Hi, Bobby. I'm Dr. Rennick."

Bobby didn't come out from under the covers, and the lump kept rocking back and forth in place. Rennick looked around the room and saw a toy space station.

"Did you ever hear the story about a little boy named Bobby who lived on a space station?"

The lump stopped moving.

"It was near an asteroid that lights our sky in winter, and sometimes on a clear night you can see it near the moon. There were these very bad warriors from the planet Zeus who wanted to capture the station, and the only one who could save it was Bobby. . . ."

Rennick continued spinning the story, and Bobby slowly

pulled back the covers. He didn't look at Rennick and was trying not to appear interested.

"The warriors from Zeus had eyes in the backs of their heads, and weapons called Zeus-swords that could cut through steel. The people living on the station were ready to surrender when Bobby started talking to them. . . ."

Bobby was sitting up now, finally looking at him.

". . . The Zeus king had the captain of the space station on the ground, and as they fought, they rolled towards the edge of the cliff." He paused. "Do you want to hear the ending?"

Bobby looked quizzically at Rennick for a long moment. His eyes were red yet dry of tears, and his head was cocked against his shoulder as if he were cradling a telephone. "Yes."

The social worker began to rub Bobby's back. She didn't look convinced that Rennick should be doing this.

"Bobby hit the Zeus king on the head with a rock, and when the king stood up, Bobby pushed him off the cliff. And everyone cheered, and they picked Bobby up and put him on their shoulders and carried him all over the space station."

Bobby sat there in silence.

"Did you like the story?" asked Rennick.

"I guess."

"Do you like to play games?"

"Sometimes."

Rennick reached into the plastic bag and took out a copy of *People* magazine.

"The captain of the space station radioed me earlier and said that you saw somebody tonight. If I show you some pictures, do you think you could tell me if any of them look like him?"

Rennick began flipping through the magazine, watching Bobby in his peripheral vision. He was afraid that looking directly at him might upset their fragile rapport.

Rennick pointed to a picture of Tom Cruise. "Did he have hair like this?"

Bobby shook his head.

"Did he have ears like this?" He pointed to a cartoon drawing of Bugs Bunny.

The corners of Bobby's mouth tried unsuccessfully to smile.

"Did he look like this?" asked Rennick, pointing to a picture of Denzel Washington.

"No. White skin."

Rennick flipped a few more pages.

"Wait," said Bobby, as Rennick turned the page to a home video ad. Bobby stared at it for a moment and then put his tiny finger on a picture of Robert Redford, in *Butch Cassidy and the Sundance Kid*.

"Blond hair?" asked Rennick.

"Yes."

"And a mustache like this?"

Bobby nodded. "He was Plastic Man."

"Plastic Man? Is that a cartoon character?"

"No. He was Plastic Man."

"I don't understand, Bobby."

"Plastic Man. I'm afraid to sleep tonight."

Rennick put the magazine aside. "Then you need my secret protector."

"What's that?"

Rennick took out his handkerchief and began to roll it up. Bobby watched curiously. Rennick then tied the middle and one end, pulling up two little corners, so that it looked like a mouse.

"This is Fred, your new pal and protector. Fred, do you want to see Bobby?"

Rennick flicked his finger under the mouse, sending it into

Bobby's lap. Bobby took the mouse and put it against his cheek.

"When I was your age, my uncle made Fred for me and I slept with him almost every night. He protected me and nobody ever came near." Rennick put his lips next to Bobby's ear and whispered, "Sometimes I still sleep with Fred." Bobby looked up at him. "Fred told me he's going to take care of you tonight and for as long as you want to keep him."

Bobby petted Fred, then put him against his cheek again.

Rennick started to get up, when Bobby clung to him. Rennick hugged him back.

"Dr. Rick?"

"Yes?"

"When's my mommy coming home?"

CHAPTER SIXTEEN

Lisa put her foot on top of the four-foot fence and pulled her forehead down to her ankle, holding the stretch for a count of thirty. It was her last stretching exercise before she started her run. She liked exercising early in the morning, when the only other people on the trail were serious runners who left her alone.

Her breath was visible in the crisp morning air as she jogged along the dirt trail surrounding Rancho Park, the second largest park in Los Angeles. The exercise warmed and loosened her body, and the smell of freshly cut grass filled her nostrils. Within a few minutes, her mind was floating pleasantly above her body.

Over the last several days, there hadn't been any more episodes. Those horrible images—the four women, dangling from a tree; her sinking into the body of a horse—were only faded memories. While she feared that another vision might be lurking beneath the surface, at least for now she was back in control of her life.

She ran alongside Rancho Park Golf Course, then past several baseball diamonds and a soccer field. The fields were being watered by a fifty-foot rotating spray that pulsed rhythmically as it turned, and she reflected how the water rejuvenated the soil.

On the second lap, Lisa picked up her pace and began to break a sweat, further lubricating her movement. She wiped her face with the towel she kept around her neck, and a pinkish-brown-and-white-spotted dog came toward her. The dog ran with Lisa a few days each week, and she had taken to calling him Measles because of his spots. He fell in beside her and looked up with his one green and one blue eye.

About a hundred yards from the end of the fourth lap, she slowed down and Measles peeled off, looking for someone who was still running. Lisa then dropped to a fast walk, and felt a sharp runner's cramp in her right side. She stopped and pushed on the cramp with her fingertips.

She was standing on the basketball courts, next to the sandy play area. As she walked during her cooldown, she noticed a little girl, about three years old, rocking on a red metal horse that was mounted on a giant spring. The girl's mother was barking something at her and looking at her watch. The little girl ignored her, rocking harder.

"Jenny, Mommy is late for her yoga class. You have to get off now."

Jenny kept rocking and the spring squeaked loudly.

"Jenny! I said *now*! I said *off*!"

Jenny rocked harder. The mother grabbed Jenny's arm and tried to pull her. The little girl kept looking at the horse, gripping it with her other hand and her legs. The mother pulled again, and in the process dropped her purse, which spilled into the sand.

"You are in big trouble, young lady," said the mother. Then she smacked Jenny's arm so hard that the little girl started to cry and slipped partway off the horse.

Lisa flashed on her vision of sliding inside the horse. Horses. There was something important about horses. Why couldn't she remember?

The little girl's cries brought her back to the present. Lisa walked up to the mother and started picking up articles that had fallen out of her purse. The mother possessively pulled the purse away.

"I know it's none of my business," said Lisa, "but the little girl is scared. Perhaps—"

"You're right. It's none of your business." The mother grabbed the articles out of Lisa's hand and stepped between Lisa and the items on the ground. "Would you excuse us, please?"

"I just—"

"I said, would you excuse us, please?"

Lisa looked at Jenny, who was rocking hard and hugging the horse's neck. The metal horse.

That was when it hit her. The memory of the horse from her childhood. She had suppressed it so deeply that now she wasn't even sure it had happened. The memories continued to flood Lisa's consciousness, and she bit her tongue to hold them in. She clenched so hard that the salty taste of blood filled her mouth.

Rennick sat beside Talon's desk. The air-conditioning was out, and in a building with windows that didn't open, that meant working in a sweat box. Talon had rolled up his sleeves and loosened his tie. Perspiration dribbled off his face and saturated the top of his collar. Rennick folded back his sleeves and picked up a notebook to fan himself.

"Here's the latest," Talon began. "The credit card company said that Heath, the first victim's boyfriend, used his credit card at a motel in Yucaipa two days ago. Unfortunately, he was gone by the time we found out. Now I have the account set up so I can get on his ass the next time he checks in somewhere. He hasn't been back to his apartment, so he's gotta stay somewhere. Hopefully we'll bag him in the next couple of days."

"I'd like to go over a strategy before you interview him."

"Done. What do you make of the electricity going into the ears this time?"

"I think we're dealing with someone striking back at an authority figure. Teacher. Principal. Parent. First he keeps them from seeing him do anything wrong. Now he stops them from hearing. I think he'll be polite and obedient on the outside. Eager to please. Someone who probably works in a place where he has to perform exactly as instructed. Not too far under the surface, there'll be a lot of dark thoughts that we can hopefully ferret out in an interrogation."

Talon pulled out a handkerchief, which was already soaked, and wiped it over his face. It only seemed to smear the sweat around. "There was something else. I found a hacksaw blade in the mattress springs."

"I don't like that."

"Me neither. I think we're going to see some more surgery next time. This performance was interrupted, so he didn't get to the climax. We did get one break, though. The killer didn't have time to brush the carpet, so we know that our man wears a size-twelve tennis shoe, and that we're looking for a big motherfucker."

"Is the boyfriend that size?" asked Rennick.

"I don't know about the size of his tootsies, but he's six feet. And he fits the general description we got, thanks to you. You were impressive handling the little boy, Professor. Very impressive."

"What a horrible thing to have happen to a child." Rennick fanned himself with the notebook. "Bobby said he saw 'Plastic Man.' Any idea what that means?"

"None whatsoever."

CHAPTER SEVENTEEN

Talon hung up the phone, ecstatic, and started to dial another call. Before he finished, Wharton grabbed his arm and motioned him into his office.

"Close the door," the lieutenant barked.

Talon watched Wharton smooth back his black, shiny hair that always looked wet, like he had just stepped out of the shower. He was a thin man with a hook nose, and his clothes were always perfectly creased.

"Where are you on the serial killer?" asked Wharton.

"We got a break. There's enough circumstantial evidence around the first victim's boyfriend to bring him in for questioning. I just hung up with a credit card company who said the guy checked into a motel in Eureka, California, last night. I was about to call the locals and invite him in when someone grabbed my arm."

Wharton leaned back in his chair. "Good. The mayor just

called and said he needs to announce something. You got enough to arrest this guy?"

"Not even close. There's no physical evidence to tie him to any of the crimes. I don't even know if he was in town for some of them."

"We need somebody to offer up. Even if he fizzles, we have to look like there's progress."

"We'll look stupid if we pick up the wrong guy and go public with it."

"We don't have the luxury of time. His Honor, the mayor, has his balls on the barbecue. The boyfriend will buy us some time if we haul him in. And if he turns out to be the wrong guy, you'll have to be sure you get the right one before anyone finds that out. So arrest him."

"Arrest him? I can't do that before I have anything."

Wharton smoothed back his hair. "Then get something."

Rennick wasn't surprised when Lisa called back. Some patients show their resistance by being late and canceling appointments. Her walking out of a session was unusual, yet clearly part of the same syndrome. The fact that she had taken the initiative to return meant she was committed to the process. At least for now.

She lay down on the couch in his office and relaxed more easily this time, which Rennick also took as a positive sign.

Rennick decided to start far away from the topic that shut her down in the last session, then ease toward it. "Tell me more about your parents. Let's start with your mother."

"I remembered something important that I think is related to my freaking out last time."

So much for easing in, thought Rennick. "What was that?"

"I told you that I've had these visions of riding a horse. A few days ago, I was in the park watching this little girl on a rocking horse. And it clicked together. I remembered something horrible from my childhood about horses."

Rennick wondered if she was using this topic to avoid dealing with her parents. He decided to find out.

"I'd like to hear about the horses after I've learned a little more about your family background. Can we start with your mother?"

Lisa tensed her lips in frustration. "I'd really like to talk about the horse."

"And we will. Tell me about your mother."

A beat of silence. "There's not much to tell."

"What do you mean?"

"Mom spent more time with her gardening than with me or my brother. She grew prize irises, and she was always outside talking to the flowers or going to some gardening meeting with a bunch of old ladies. We were latchkey kids before the word was invented. Then she died."

"When she was around, how did she treat you?"

Lisa described how her mother mostly ignored her, and how the other members of her family only spoke to each other when necessary. She also described how her mother had major mood swings and could be nasty and abusive.

"Did she hit you?" asked Rennick.

"No. Just a lot of yelling."

"What about your brother?"

Lisa coughed into her hand. "I haven't seen him since he joined the army when he was seventeen and I was fifteen. My dad had to sign for him because he wasn't eighteen. I wouldn't know him if he walked in the door."

"Were you close as kids?"

"No."

"How did your father treat you?"

She seemed to be staring into the distance. "We didn't have much to say to each other."

"Did he hit you?"

"No."

"Did he otherwise abuse you?"

"What do you mean?"

"I mean in any way."

"You mean sexual?"

"Sexual. Verbal. Any kind."

"Not really. He gave me the silent treatment when he was angry."

"Does any particular event stand out in your mind?"

She paused for a few moments. "Well, there was an incident with my first boyfriend."

"What was that?"

She began to play with the hem of her shirt as she described how her father caught her kissing her boyfriend, Larry, when she was sixteen. Her father chased him out of the house, yelling at him to stay away from his daughter.

"What did your father say to you afterwards?"

"Nothing. Absolutely nothing. He stormed into his bedroom and slammed the door. I was afraid to go near him."

Rennick noticed a slight waver in the tone of her voice. He sensed that there was an issue she was fighting to keep hidden.

"Did you ever talk to your father about it?"

"No. I was too embarrassed. And he wouldn't talk to me at all for two weeks."

"What have your relationships with other men been like?"

"I didn't date at all for a couple of years after that. I buried myself in schoolwork. In fact, I've never really dated much."

"Never?"

"Not really."

"Even now?"

"I'm too busy with work."

"When was your last serious relationship?"

Lisa stiffened her muscles. "I never really felt like I needed one."

For a woman so attractive, thought Rennick, this was very unusual. The childhood trauma might be more serious than he had anticipated.

"Are you homosexual?"

"No."

"Have you had any sexual relations over the last few years?"

"Do we have to talk about this?"

"We don't have to do anything that makes you uncomfortable."

"Then let's move on."

Rennick noted the hot spot and wrote himself a reminder to approach it in a later session. "When did you last see your father?"

"When I was in college. I had an apartment in Denver that was only a few miles away from him, and I used to call him or drop by every few weeks. The conversations were stilted and he was always in a hurry to leave or get off the phone. One day I decided to try an experiment. I didn't call him and waited to see how long it would take him to phone me. The answer turned out to be forever. After three months I finally called and found out that his number was disconnected. The man had moved and not even told me. I didn't see any reason to call him after that."

"All right. Now let's talk about the horses. Tell me what you remember."

Silence. Tears pooled in her eyes.

Rennick gave her a few minutes, like letting out the line on a kite. He watched carefully, as he didn't want her drifting too far away.

"Lisa?"

No response. She began to hug herself tightly. After a few moments, she said, "Do you remember my telling you I've had visions of a redheaded girl I couldn't quite place?"

"Yes."

"Her name was . . . Sarah Wayne." Lisa began rocking back and forth, with her arms crossed over her chest. She didn't speak for several minutes, and Rennick chose to let the silence hang.

"I don't know if I can talk about it."

"Yes, you can. Follow me, Lisa. I'll help you."

She shuddered as she released a long sigh. Then, with her voice garbled through the tears, she began to talk.

Officers Wilson and Sweet of the Eureka police department sat outside the Driftwood Motel in an unmarked car, sipping luke-warm coffee from paper cups. Wilson counted the sticks of driftwood used to make the Driftwood sign.

The men had gotten tired of showing up and finding Bart Heath gone. So this afternoon they sat where they could see both the one-story motel and the parking lot. Their attention alternated between Room 6 and a Peterbilt cab-over with *Hell-raiser* written in sparkling script on the door.

About 3:30 P.M., a large man with light blond hair who was wearing aviator sunglasses came out of room 6 and walked toward the Peterbilt. Without looking at each other, Wilson and Sweet got out and started toward him.

"Excuse me," said Sweet, as the man opened the door of the truck. "Are you Bartholomew Heath?"

"Who are you?" said the man, climbing into the cab.

"Eureka Police," Sweet answered, holding out his badge. "Are you Bartholomew Heath?"

The man reached underneath the seat of the truck. Sweet reflexively yelled, "Freeze!"

Heath moved across the seat and opened the passenger door. He was halfway out of the truck when Wilson, who had been waiting on the other side, grabbed his arm.

"My partner said freeze, asshole."

Heath swung at Wilson, glancing him across the face. Wilson managed to hold his grip on Heath's arm just enough to keep him from bolting. Heath struggled, then wrenched free as Sweet arrived and snapped open his metal baton to its full length. He hit Heath against the back of the knees, which immediately took him down. Then he put Heath's arm into a hammerlock while he handcuffed him.

"It seems we have a whole pharmacy in here, Mr. Heath," called Wilson from the cab of the truck. "Several shades of white powdery substances and matching hypodermics. I suppose you wear this pair of ruby earrings when you go out dancing?"

"Do you have a search warrant?" said Heath, who was being jerked upright by Sweet.

"We don't need one, thanks to your reaching under the seat. Incident to an arrest, we're entitled to search the immediate area. You're not too smart, Mr. Heath. All we wanted was to ask you a few questions. Now you've got resisting arrest, assaulting an officer, and possession of some substances that I don't think are gonna turn out to be baby powder."

Sweet pushed Heath toward the unmarked car. A group of four or five people gathered to watch. "Mr. Heath, you are under arrest. You have the right to remain silent. Anything you say . . ."

Lisa lay stiffly on the couch, speaking through her tears. "Sarah Wayne was a girl down the street when we lived in Williamsburg, Virginia. She had red hair that she wore in a ponytail, and freckles all over her body. She was very athletic, with lots of energy, and spent most of her afternoons riding horses."

Lisa described how Sarah invited her over and asked for a reading. Lisa had taken Sarah's horseshoe key chain and begun to rub it in her hand.

"I closed my eyes, and almost right away I knew something was wrong. I saw this dark, cloudy field, and I felt a cold gust of wind. I must have looked strange, because Sarah asked if I was okay. I still regret that I didn't just say no. It would have been over." Lisa curled up on her side and began to cry.

"Relax and roll onto your back," Rennick said evenly. "Take a couple of deep breaths." Rennick handed her a tissue, which she took without looking up.

"I saw a saddled horse without a rider. Its bridle was pulled over its head and dangling to the grass. The horse was in a meadow, poking its nose at something on the ground. When it shook its head with a loud whinny, I jumped physically.

"Then there was another scene. It appeared the way . . . what would you call the opposite of dissolving? Sort of like a photo being developed."

"What was it?"

"I saw . . ."

Lisa started shaking. She turned on her side and curled into a fetal position. It seemed as though the memories were pummeling her body with a myriad of silent blows. He waited without talking. It took several minutes for her to recover.

"I saw Sarah falling through the air. She was screaming and thrashing her body in all directions. The horse was falling beside her. They hit the ground with this loud, sickening crunch, and then there was dead quiet. Sarah's neck was bent at this impossible angle, and there was blood all over her. She didn't move. The horse lay on its side, speared with some branch or something, and he had thrown up blood from his mouth. He was trying to roll over and kept whinnying in pain."

Lisa described how she couldn't tell Sarah what she'd seen and instead ran out of her house. She'd gone home and found her mother.

"I explained what had happened and asked her what I should do. Mom was very decisive. She said I should tell Sarah's parents, and without waiting for my reaction, she called Mrs. Wayne and handed me the phone. Then she sat there gesturing for me to start talking.

"I told Mrs. Wayne about my psychic experiences, and that I wasn't always right. Then I explained what I had seen and she asked me if this was some kind of a sick joke. She told me I was mentally ill and slammed down the phone."

Rennick flipped a page of his notebook. "What happened after that?"

Lisa described how she saw Sarah the next day in school. Sarah said that her parents had forbidden her to ride horses because of Lisa's call. Sarah slapped Lisa's face and ran off crying.

"A few days later, my girlfriend Linda asked me if I'd heard about Sarah. She told me that Sarah had sneaked out early one morning to go horseback riding. The horse had tripped and thrown her off. Sarah fell against a sharp rock and broke her neck. She was paralyzed. Now I know this sounds horrible, but I remember feeling relieved. That she wasn't dead."

"Did you ever see Sarah again?"

"A few times at school. She was in a wheelchair with one of those motors on the back. We both pretended not to see each other. She looked so sad and helpless. Teachers had to carry her into the bathroom because it was up a flight of stairs." Lisa's eyes began to tear. "I still feel responsible."

Rennick spoke calmly. "Sarah's accident wasn't your fault. You only told her what you saw, and you couldn't be responsible for how she used the information. You at least gave her a chance to avoid the tragedy. And in any event, it was a long time ago and you can't un-ring bells. You have to let it go."

"I hear the words. But it still hurts. How long will it take to get better?"

"This injury has had almost twenty years to fester. You've now begun the healing process, which is like cleaning and bandaging an infected area. It will take some time."

"How long?"

"I'm afraid nobody knows that."

A silence. "Doctor?"

"Yes?"

"I should tell you about another vision I had recently."

"We only have a few minutes left."

"It could be important."

"All right."

"I was riding on a horse, and again I was sinking into his body. It was even more sickening than before. I held onto the horse's ears to keep from falling completely into him. They were these huge ears, almost like a donkey's. And it felt like there was something hard inside them. Then I saw four young women ahead on the road. Each with shoulder-length, blond hair. They were hanging by their necks, like they'd been lynched. Their bodies dangled from cords that were tied to a large tree branch. They were all bloody and they were wrapped in some kind of cellophane. I still get sick thinking about it. Do you think this is related to Sarah? What do you think it means?"

Rennick's heart thudded in his chest. Four young women. Tied with cords. Bodies in cellophane. Plastic. Plastic Man. That wasn't public. A horse with large ears and something in them. Nails in the last victim's ears. Also not public.

Holy shit.

CHAPTER EIGHTEEN

Julie had no sense of time as she listened to Dr. Edmund Childs, NYU's Nobel laureate in DNA research who had left the biological sciences in favor of the humanities. His defection had caused tidal waves in academia, mostly because of his radical views of the social sciences, and his lectures were always over-subscribed. This afternoon, over two hundred students crowded into a room built for 150, and almost a hundred others spilled into the hall.

Childs was a short man, balding to a gray fringe, who wore a dark suit with a wide lapel that had been out of style for at least a decade. A commanding voice resonated from his tiny frame, and the room was otherwise silent.

"I left the study of DNA because the manipulation of genetic material was leading us to a Hitleresque system of discrimination. Science marches inexorably toward such goals, without any thought of the racism and elitism that may follow in its wake.

That is why I have joined you of the humanities, to take a stand against such a cataclysm.

"Sociologists have historically been relegated to chronicling what has been, with only a few maverick souls offering theorems for the solutions. Today you must shatter those shackles, and declare yourselves players on the field of a troubled world." Childs's voice had risen to an authoritative timbre, and his face reddened as he delivered the final words. "Without the sociologist's perception of humankind's primal mentality—those primitive instincts that so often override our intellect—we are doomed to repeat the failures of history."

There was a beat of silence, after which the audience, as one, rose to their feet and began to cheer and applaud. Childs loosened his tie like a football player pulling off his helmet after a winning touchdown.

Julie was the last to stop her applause. She then made her way to the front, high with the anticipation of meeting a legend whose works she had studied since her sophomore year. Dr. Thornton, her Ph.D. faculty adviser, took her arm and led her through the crowd to Childs.

"Ed, this is Julie Martin," said Thornton.

Childs turned the full power of his attention on Julie. The intensity almost caused her to look away. "So you're the one," said Childs. "Stay for a moment after the others leave."

It was over thirty minutes before Childs made his excuses and dismissed the remaining fans. He picked up his papers and motioned for Julie and Thornton to walk with him.

"I apologize for talking on the run, but I have a flight to Boston in an hour and a half. I assume Bill told you that I'm in need of an assistant professor. In addition to a teaching position, it would involve working on my study of biological warfare policies in developing nations. You may have heard of the project?"

"Yes, of course." Who hadn't? thought Julie.

"Tell me about yourself."

Julie explained her background, her studies, her passions. Childs proved to be a decent listener, which Julie took as a good sign—most of the people she'd met in exalted positions only wanted to talk about themselves.

Childs opened the door of his rented white Taurus and turned to her.

"Are you familiar with my 1978 paper comparing the functionalist and conflict approaches to sociology?"

"Yes. It was required reading in two of my classes."

A smile played at the edges of Childs's mouth. "And what is your opinion of my hypothesis?"

"It, uh, well, it was a breakthrough when it was published."

"Yes, yes. What do you think of it by today's standards?"

"I believe that the general thinking today . . ."

"I didn't ask you about general thinking. I want to know your opinion. Hurry up, now. I've a plane to catch."

Julie hesitated, then decided on honesty. "I'm afraid I find it a bit dated. You brilliantly analyzed the divergence of the theories but didn't contemplate the interactionist construct."

Childs's eyes bored into her. Out of the corner of her eye, she saw Thornton shaking his head.

A long silence sat on Julie's shoulders until Childs finally spoke. "I find it a bit dated myself. Not too many people would have told me that to my face. Here's my card. Send me some of your writing samples."

He then closed the door and drove away. Julie and Thornton spontaneously gave each other a high five.

Lisa looked up from the couch at Rennick.

"Doctor? Are you all right?"

Rennick was still processing her vision of the four young women, the plastic material, and the objects in the horse's ears.

When he finally spoke, he could only rasp. "Lisa, these images . . ."

"Yes?"

"Have you heard about the young women who were recently killed in the West L.A. area?"

"Of course. I bought a dead bolt for my front door."

"Were you aware I'm working on this case?"

"No."

"These visions . . . I think they may be connected."

Lisa sat up and turned to face him, keeping her knees tightly together. Her face was washed with fear, and she hugged herself defensively. "How could that be?"

"I don't know. Have you ever had any psychic images of a crime?"

"No. Never."

"Would you consider talking to the police about some of the things you've seen?"

"I couldn't do something like that. It would feel like some kind of side show. Do you think I should?"

"I didn't say you should. I only asked if it was something you'd consider."

"You think I should do it, don't you?"

"No, no. I didn't say that. You shouldn't do anything that makes you uncomfortable, especially when it's something this personal."

"I need to think about it."

"Please. Let me be clear: I'm not suggesting you do this. I'm not even sure it's a good idea. This whole thing took me by surprise, and I spoke before I thought it through."

"I'd have to think about it."

*   *   *

After Lisa left, Rennick sat at his desk, swinging his keys hyp-
notically like a pendulum. He studied them pensively, allowing
his vision to blur in and out.

Despite his continued protests, Lisa seemed convinced that he
wanted her to talk to the police. He finally said flat out that it
wasn't a good idea, and she still insisted on thinking it over. It
was a classic sign of the dependency stage of therapy, where the
patient does everything to please the therapist's perceived
whims. He hadn't meant to do that.

His theory of her disorder was quickly turning into fool's
gold. Whatever was going on with Lisa was far more complex
than the usual denial of current problems. Her flights from reality were growing increasingly dark, and now they were mixing
with psychic visions of the crimes.

The intercom buzzed, jarring him into dropping the keys on
the desk. It sounded like a tray of glass crashing on the floor.

"Detective Talon's here," said Bobbi.

Rennick wanted to tell him about Lisa, yet what he learned in
therapy was confidential. He hadn't thought to ask her if he
could say something, and therefore he couldn't. While psychiatrists were used to keeping juicy secrets, sometimes it was excruciating.

"We finally got a break," said Talon as he whirled into the
room. "Heath, the first victim's boyfriend, turned up in Eureka
and is now the guest of the city's hospitality. I'm going up to pay
my respects tomorrow. Since you offered to join me on a trip
through his sexual fantasies, you're cordially invited. The plane's
at ten and I'm trying to get the City of L.A. to spring for your
ticket."

"I can't leave tomorrow. I've got meetings with people who
are coming in from Arizona. Can you wait a day?"

"No. Wharton's up my ass to deliver this guy."

"I'll at least go over some interrogation strategies with you."

"Thanks. There's more. Yesterday I got a report back from VICAP, the FBI database. It had about ten possibles, some of whom were dead, and others back in prison. But there were two real likelies. One is living in Passaic, New Jersey, and was there when two of the murders went down. So that takes care of him. The other is a guy named Marvin Lofton, who's an MDSO. He did a girl about six years ago in San Francisco, with a similar M.O. No electrocution, which is why the first VICAP report didn't turn him up. But he raped a young woman, tied her to the bed with electrical cord, and cut her throat."

"That sounds promising."

"Lofton went to the loony bin for it, then had a miraculous recovery. The asshole dropped outta sight about two years ago. His last known address was in San Francisco and we can't find him even though he's supposed to register as a sex offender. Shocking as it may seem, some people disregard their civic duties. I think he's using a phony name because there's no DMV records on him and his social security number hasn't been used for over two years. There's no property in his name, and no utilities. Here's a copy of the file I got from San Francisco PD."

Talon handed a thick packet of papers to Rennick. It was stamped MDSO—mentally disordered sex offender.

"Did you check his prints?"

"Yeah. They don't match the one we found in Powell's apartment. That turned out to be Heath's print, which means diddly since he was her boyfriend and around there legitimately."

Rennick flipped through the packet and saw Lofton's mug shot. He had soft, boyish features, almost pretty. Black hair, clear skin, and a straight nose. The only blemish was wide gaps between his teeth, which peeked through a smile that seemed to say "I know something you don't."

"Lofton has a long history of mental illness," Talon continued. "Rich boy gone bad. His folks were apparently loaded. Made money in adult diapers or some shit like that. He's been in and out of funny farms since he was in his early twenties. One shrink said he had major hang-ups about women, and a lotta anger. Du-uh. He tried to molest a court-appointed female shrink, which ain't exactly a brilliant move if you want a recommendation of leniency. Though I guess it's smart enough if you're pleading insanity. A regular poster boy for 'Sickos R Us.'"

"Sounds like a great guy."

"The San Francisco Parole Board decided he'd straightened out and let him go. And he's apparently been a good little boy for the last four years, since he hasn't been arrested for anything."

San Francisco Parole Board. Rennick felt that meant something. What was it? He couldn't reel it in.

"Do you know the color of the electrical cord that Lofton used?" asked Rennick.

"No. Maybe it's in the file. Why?"

"I think the gray color means something. Unfortunately, I have no idea what."

"Color of brains? Gray matter?"

"Maybe. Or something ambiguous. Gray isn't black or white. Maybe a bisexual. If the first victim was raped and he stopped afterwards, that could be connected. We're also dealing with a chameleon. Meaning he blends in with whoever's around him. Putting nails in the ears means he's evolving, but the cord color stays gray. It means something."

"Beats me."

The two of them sat in thought. Rennick was feeding on Talon's high energy. His gut was kicking in and he closed his eyes. He could almost picture the killer. Good looking, engaging smile. Smart enough to be this careful. Carried himself with authority. Hiding a ferocious anger inside, shut away like the fires of a boiler behind a heavy door. Overheating until the boiler exploded.

Lisa's hand ached from taking copious notes during the three-hour meeting with the president and the chief financial officer of Latham Oil. Rex Manford, the president, was a strikingly handsome man with chiseled features, close-cropped brown hair, and black eyes. Constance Fry, the CFO, was in her late forties, with a strawberry birthmark on her neck. She wore a wrinkled dress that draped loosely over her massive girth, and she kept a pencil behind her ear. Fry had been drilling the four Engle & Loren accountants for most of the meeting.

"So to sum up the bullshit you've been giving us for the entire morning," said Fry, "you really don't have any idea how to avoid the depreciation recapture, do you?"

The others from Engle & Loren sat stone-faced, looking at Phil Trotter, the partner in charge. Lisa shook the cramps out of her hand.

Phil sounded drained when he finally spoke. "It's unrealistic to think we can solve a major problem like recapture in just a few hours. . . ."

"You've had weeks to work on this," shot back Fry. "We made it clear when we interviewed you people that this was our number-one priority."

The president studied the argument intently, like an emperor watching gladiators. Lisa thought of him giving a thumbs-up or thumbs-down when one of the combatants surrendered. She began to rub the back of her neck, which was perspiring.

Phil looked at Lisa, his eyes pleading for help. She looked

down and saw the reflection of his anguished face in the polished mahogany conference table. Lisa was afraid to speak up, especially in such a new relationship. She also worried that, because she was fatigued from the three-hour meeting, she was at risk of triggering another vision. She pretended to study her notes.

Phil said, "The laws are drawn specifically to prohibit what we're trying to do. To find a way—"

"We know what the laws say," snapped Fry, with more than a trace of sarcasm. "We want some creativity. Our former accountants were a bunch of old ladies, and that's why they're history. We thought you people were going to be more practical." She shook her head, as if to say the situation was hopeless.

The president's eyes shifted back to Phil. Lisa thought he looked done for. The idea of talking terrified her. Still . . .

"I have a thought," she said quietly.

"Huh?" said Fry.

"I have a thought," she said more loudly.

All the eyes turned to her. Phil looked like a drowning man who thought he saw a life raft.

"I haven't finished the research, but I have some ideas that look promising."

"So what are they?" asked Fry.

"Well, if we assign the depreciated assets to a limited liability company owned by Latham, there's no taxation on the transfer. We can later shift the LLC's ownership into an offshore entity in a country like the Netherlands Antilles, where there's no local tax. That company can contract with the Netherlands, which has a U.S. tax treaty. If we operate there for at least three years, it should establish a foreign domicile. Then we could sell the assets to a non–U.S. company, and there would be a reasonable chance to keep the gains offshore. There's no guarantees, of course, but if it works it would eliminate the depreciation recapture."

Dead silence. Lisa was certain that she had just made herself look like a moron and couldn't look at any of them. She was on a high wire, and the crowd was holding its breath because they saw that the wire was frayed and about to snap. She realized she was holding her breath as well.

"Brilliant!" said Fry. "*That's* the kind of thinking we need. What's your name?"

The president smiled, and Lisa imagined a thumbs-up to her gladiatorial skills. Phil's eyebrows were raised almost an inch over his eyes.

The meeting broke up and she walked back to her desk, still glowing from the victory. She hummed softly under her breath. As she started through her stock of phone messages, she saw one that confirmed her next appointment with Dr. Rennick. She ran her thumb over his name, studying the handwriting.

This man was amazing. His digging into the recesses of her mind was both frightening and exciting. And, more important, it was working. The episodes had lightened up over the last few days, and she was feeling in control. She had just made it through a stressful meeting without any difficulties at all.

Dr. Rennick's words about helping the police kept ringing in her mind. The thought of intentionally having a psychic vision in front of strangers was terrifying; she didn't even like to talk about these experiences. And what if nothing came to her? She'd humiliate herself and Dr. Rennick. On the other hand, maybe she owed it to the victims. Despite his denials, she felt certain that Rennick wanted her to do it. If he was working on this case, maybe it would help him. He was helping her, so she should help him.

CHAPTER NINETEEN

The windshield wipers squealed back and forth on the drive from the Eureka airport to the police headquarters. Talon had tuned out the conversational missiles being lobbed by the young officer driving him, and his full concentration was on Heath. He always felt a little on edge when he finally got to interview someone he'd been chasing, and he funneled the energy into reviewing his questions. He was disappointed that Rennick hadn't come along, although he hadn't given him much notice. At least they'd worked up a strategy.

Eureka, California, is a seaside community that evidently went to great pains to keep its historic look. He watched the heavy rain pour down on ramshackle houses that looked like they had been beaten into submission long ago. He was sure the postcards called them "picturesque."

The police headquarters were located near a wharf that smelled like fish. A group of seagulls sat on the pier's cracked, wooden posts, with their wings folded against the assault of the rain. In stark contrast, the police building was a modern concrete structure, with a porcupine of radio antennae on the roof. Chief Tufts, a paunchy, balding man with a gold-framed front tooth, greeted him at the car with an umbrella. Talon got out into the sharp cold, and the wind blew the rain sideways onto him, thumbing its nose at the umbrella.

As they walked down a long corridor toward the visitors' room, Talon shook off his soaked jacket.

"We found a pair of ruby earrings in the truck," said Tufts. "Did they belong to one of the victims?"

"The first victim, Heath's girlfriend, was missing ruby earrings," said Talon. "I'm willing to bet they're hers, although that only proves he's a thief, not a killer." Talon thought about the fact that Heath hadn't fenced them. That was consistent with the theory that he'd taken them as souvenirs.

"Whatever he is, he was carrying a two-year supply of drugs for a family of six, so he won't be bothering the outside world for a while."

Tufts waved to a guard behind a thick glass pane and the door in front of them opened with a loud buzz. They walked down another hall and into the visitors' room. It was brightly lit and furnished only with a table and chairs. A bailiff brought out Heath and an Afro-American woman dressed in a dark blue business suit. Her hair was cut close to her head, and she wore large, silver hoop earrings. She stuck her hand out to Talon.

"I'm Shauna Zitan of the Eureka Public Defender's Office."

Zitan and Heath sat down. Heath was a rugged-looking man who appeared to be in his late twenties. He was about six feet tall, with light brown hair and a clean-shaven square jaw. Talon remembered Powell's roommate saying that Heath had started a beard and wondered if he'd shaved to change his looks. Heath was slumped in the chair with his legs stuck straight out, as if he wanted to trip somebody. Talon noted that his feet were big enough to match the size-twelve print they'd found at the Mullins scene.

The bailiff walked over to the door and folded his arms across his chest. Talon remained standing.

"Mr. Heath, did you know Myra Powell?"

"Is this related to the drug charges?" asked Zitan.

"No, ma'am."

"What is this about?"

"Ms. Powell was murdered."

Talon watched Heath. The only reaction he could see was that Heath squinted.

"Is Mr. Heath a suspect in the murder?" asked Zitan.

"I'll let you know when we finish. Did you know her, Mr. Heath?"

"I was unaware of any murder investigation," said Zitan. "I need some time to confer with my client."

"I'll wait outside," said Talon.

Fifteen minutes later, Zitan opened the door and motioned for Talon to return. When he came back in, Heath was sitting up straight in his chair and intently watching Talon's moves.

"So, did you know Myra Powell?"

"Yeah, I knew her," said Heath.

"Did you know that she's dead?"

"Yeah. Everyone in L.A. knew she was killed by some nut."

"You don't sound very broken up."

"I dated Myra some. It's not like we were married."

"We found a plaid shirt with your blood type on it in Myra's apartment. We also found your fingerprints on a glass in her kitchen. Can you tell me where you were on June fourteenth, the night Myra was killed?"

"I was at home."

"Were you with anyone?"

"No."

"Do you know a Betty Sanchez?"

"I don't think so."

"Where were you on October sixth, when Betty Sanchez was killed?"

"I have no idea."

"Do you keep a log or a diary. Or a calendar?"

"Nope."

"How come a college-educated guy like you is driving a truck?"

Heath looked at Talon's clothing. "I couldn't take running around in a suit with some tie choking my neck. I like seeing the world as it really is."

"Does shooting up heroin get you close to the real world?"

Zitan was on her feet. "That's way out of line, Detective."

Talon started pacing. In his peripheral vision, he saw that Heath was watching him closely and getting fidgety.

"Where were you on the night of November sixth? That was the night Andrea Baylor was killed, and it was also the night before you left L.A. for an extended trip."

"Don't know."

"Did you know a Tanya Mullins?"

"No."

"And I don't suppose you know where you were on December third, when she was killed?"

"Nope."

"Did you take a pair of ruby earrings from Myra Powell?"

He cleared his throat. "She gave those to me. I was gonna get them fixed. She said the clasps were loose and she was afraid she'd lose them. I have a friend who's a jeweler in Portland. He said he'd do it real cheap."

Talon thought he'd heard four-year-olds explain missing cookies better than that.

"How did you meet Myra Powell?"

"Picked her up at a bar in Santa Monica. She worked there."

"Were you and Myra dating steadily?"

"I don't date anybody steadily. She lasted longer than most. We went out a coupla months."

Talon thought it was time to ratchet things up. "Did she like her sex rough?"

Zitan was opening her mouth to object as Heath answered, "Yeah. She liked it rammed in real hard."

"The way I hear it, she dumped you." That was a lie. Rennick had suggested it as a way to stir up Heath. "You musta felt real stupid when she crapped all over you, huh?"

Zitan shot into action. "That's irrelevant and offensive, Detective. I'm instructing him not to answer."

"I think his state of mind is real relevant. Last time I looked, revenge was still on the top ten motives list."

"You've got no motive as to any other victim."

"Oh yeah? Well, maybe he decided he liked killing women." Talon turned back to Heath. "I know I'd feel like I'd been deballed if someone dumped me. Maybe it doesn't bother you 'cause you're used to it."

"She didn't dump me. I dumped her." Heath grabbed the sides of the table tightly, and the muscles in his arms bulged. Talon figured a few more pricks and the balloon was going to burst. Apparently so did the bailiff, as he took a step closer.

Talon kept stabbing. "I also hear you have trouble getting it up. You probably have a lotta trouble satisfying women, don't you, Heath? Can't stay with one woman 'cause they find out you're a phony when you get 'em in bed, huh?"

"This is the most outrageous—" started Zitan, too late. Heath leapt to his feet, shoved the table over, and grabbed for Talon's throat with both hands.

"C'mon asshole!" shouted Heath, who now had Talon's windpipe under his thumbs. His eyes were bulging with blood. "Right here. Right now."

Talon couldn't breathe. Heath had taken him off guard, and was stronger than he'd figured. His head was feeling light, and the pain in his throat was excruciating. Heath was now yelling like a soldier on the charge.

Talon forced himself to concentrate. He summoned his concentration into kicking Heath in the groin. The kick was a little off target, but close enough to make Heath bend forward and let go. Talon spun sideways and side-kicked Heath so hard that he slammed into the wall, then collapsed to the floor, stunned. Talon knew that Heath was now helpless and yet he couldn't stop himself from barreling toward him. He imagined grabbing his hair and slamming his face into the cinder blocks.

The bailiff leapt between them. Talon kept moving toward Heath until the bailiff thrust the end of his nightstick into Talon's solar plexus. That sent him backwards, coughing. He looked up to see the bailiff shaking his head no, like a referee sending a boxer to the corner.

Heath lay limply against the wall, whimpering, the loser in a dogfight. Talon forced himself to look away. He rubbed his throat, which was still pulsing from the attack, and realized his whole body was shaking. He felt foolish for having been caught off guard—something that hadn't happened in years. And the violent rage he'd felt at Heath. That button hadn't been pushed in a long time.

CHAPTER TWENTY

Rennick met Talon at the Blue Bird Coffee Shop. The diner was located across the street from the Hollywood Division Police Station, and its decor was authentic 1950s. There were candy-apple-red booths, for which hundreds of Naugas had given their Hydes, and pink Formica tables with boomerang-shaped squiggles. Loud conversations and clanging dishes provided the background music. The patrons were cops, locals, and a few bail bondsmen, either looking for business or taking a break from the rigors of springing slimeballs from captivity.

Rennick ordered decaf from a lacquer-haired waitress, whose name was Darlene according to a crooked pin on her apron. Talon had the fully leaded caffeine.

"So how did you enjoy your date with Mr. Heath?" asked Rennick.

"Well, he didn't confess in tears like they do on TV. And he developed CRS for his whereabouts during the murders."

"What's CRS?"

"'Can't Remember Shit.'"

"How'd our interrogation strategy work?"

"I guess I don't have your finesse. He tried to strangle me."

"Strangle you?"

"No big deal. I've been strangled by better punks than him. Truth is, I mighta gone a little over the edge myself, 'cause I kept seeing dead women the whole time we were talkin'."

"Getting strangled is one of those telltale signs that you've gone too far."

"So I learned."

"You think Heath's the guy?" asked Rennick.

"I got some serious doubts. Heath's a crude bully, and our killer is an artist."

"I agree about the artistry, but you said Heath has a master's degree in philosophy. He could be a different person under the surface."

"Wharton agrees with you. Or, more accurately, he doesn't give a shit whether Heath is guilty or not. He's pressuring me to give him up to the press. I'm holding off the dogs as long as I can. There's nothing concrete to connect him to the crimes."

Darlene put their coffees on the table, clinking the cups against the saucers. She picked up the quarters left by the last patron with her red-and-gold-flecked Krazy Glue nails.

Talon took a large gulp of coffee and then threw an antacid tablet into his mouth. "What did you think of Lofton's file?" The white bits of tablet were visible on his tongue when he spoke.

"He's certainly got the brainpower, and the sexual hang-ups fit. On the other hand, his crime scene was trashed, not neat like this killer. That means a very different personality."

"Was that a yes or a no?"

"It was a possible. Usually the disorganized types stay that way, although some of them change as they get older. I could give you a more educated guess if you let me interview him."

"You'll be the first to know when I bring him in for a little game of To Tell the Truth. He's still being Mr. Elusive."

Talon fiddled with his spoon, running his huge thumb over the concave surface. "I got the lab report on the Mullins crime scene. The carpet footprint wasn't clear enough to tell us what kind of shoe he wore. Just that he's a big fucker. And he didn't leave any prints, fibers, or precious bodily fluids. They even tried taking prints off Mullins's body, which they can sometimes do if the victim's skin is tight. It turns out the sonofabitch was wearing gloves."

Talon took another sip, then set his cup down roughly. He began drumming his fingers on the table.

"I studied how the victims were cut," said Rennick. "The slicing was neat and methodical. Starting with the jugular and moving across. Each cut went deeper."

"Yeah? You think it might be a doctor?"

"No. From the look of the wounds, the coroner thought the weapon was a kitchen knife, which a pro wouldn't use. And there wasn't anything anatomical about the cuts. So my guess is that he's a careful amateur."

"Did you look at the Lofton file? Were the cuts on his victim similar?"

"Yes, but much more haphazard. Although it's been a while since that killing, so he might have improved his craft."

Darlene refilled their cups and smiled broadly, which moved great amounts of makeup on her cheeks.

Rennick shifted slightly in his seat. "I have something off-the-wall that we should discuss."

"A little comic relief would be welcome right now."

Rennick looked out the plate-glass window as he spoke. "I'm treating a patient who's had some psychic experiences. During one of our sessions, she told me about a vision that seems to be related to this case."

"You're joking."

"I'm . . . no. It's not a joke."

Rennick described Lisa's vision of the hanging women, the plastic, and the hard objects in the horse's ears. "She offered to handle the evidence and see if she could find anything helpful."

"I worked with a psychic once before."

"You did? What happened?"

"She wasted my time for almost two weeks and came up with exactly jack shit. I don't want to turn my back on anything that might help, but I ain't got a lot of time to kill these days."

"I'm not pushing this. She's a little fragile psychologically, and I have mixed feelings about her getting involved. I only brought it up because she kept insisting."

Talon took a sip of coffee, then sat for several moments in silence. "She really saw women in plastic?"

Rennick arrived five minutes before the four o'clock appointment and waited on the steps of the Hollywood Police Station. He looked at his watch and wondered if Lisa would change her mind. Then he took off his coat and draped it over his shoulder. Even though it was December, the hot Santa Ana winds blowing across the desert made the day a scorcher, and he was starting to perspire.

Lisa arrived exactly on time, smelling of a jasmine perfume. She was wearing a navy blue skirt, and her blond hair was pulled tightly into a french braid, although a few rebel strands had worked their way out and reached into the air for freedom.

They walked up the steps and went inside. As they got closer to the waiting room, Lisa began to fidget with her purse, and Rennick noticed that she was beginning to shiver. He stopped her and said, "If you don't want to do this, it's okay."

"I'm fine."

She turned away from him and walked to the reception counter. Behind it was a large woman with short black hair, several chins above a tight collar, and laserlike eyes.

"Dr. Rennick and Lisa Cleary to see Detective Talon," said Rennick to the desk clerk.

"Please sit," she answered officiously. "I'll tell him you're here."

Talon appeared a few minutes later, wearing a rumpled brown suit and a loosened tie. Rennick introduced him to Lisa, and his enormous hand swallowed hers when they shook. The desk clerk buzzed them into the chaotic central area, which was crammed with desks and noise.

They went across the room, then through an unmarked door, and the noise disappeared abruptly. The only sound was the squeaking of shoes on linoleum as they walked down a long corridor lit with flickering fluorescent lights.

Lisa's gait had become wobbly, and she was perspiring more and more. She was also shuddering visibly.

"Are you okay?" asked Rennick.

"I feel like I've got an icicle sliding down my windpipe," she said with a forced smile. "But I want to do this."

Rennick felt like he should stop her. She seemed to sense his thoughts and moved ahead of him.

At the end of the hall, Talon opened a door to an interrogation room and gestured for her go inside. Rennick thought the term *room* was somewhat pretentious, as the windowless, bare-walled cubicle was hardly large enough for three folding chairs and a metal table. Four blue-gray cartons sat on top of the table.

Talon opened the containers and stepped back. He and Rennick looked at Lisa, who was staring at the boxes. Her expression reminded Rennick of a diver standing on top of the high board for the first time, realizing that the water looked a lot farther away than when she was on the ground.

"Was there a dog in here recently?" asked Lisa.

"A dog?" responded Talon.

"A large yellow dog. I'm just . . . sensing one."

"I doubt it. We don't allow animals in here."

After several minutes of silence, Lisa walked over to one of the cartons and took out a blue dress, a bra and underwear, and cut-up nylon stockings. She examined them closely, then put back everything except the stockings. She moved to the other boxes and gathered hosiery from each.

Rennick and Talon watched her hold the stockings against the light, creating a smoke-gray gauze. She ran them across her fingertips, in long, rhythmic strokes, then put them under her nose and inhaled deeply. Finally, she dropped all but one pair, which she rubbed against her cheek.

Lisa was perspiring heavily. It looked to Rennick like the sweat was running into her eyes, as she was squinting from the sting. She seemed oblivious to everything except the stockings as she began rubbing her thumb and forefingers together, with the nylons in between them.

After several minutes, she began speaking in a monotone that seemed to come from deep inside her. It was lower in pitch than her normal voice, and seemed to resonate in her chest.

"She's sleeping quietly on a chair. Moonlight falling across the room. She's covered with an Indian blanket. She shivers because the window is open and it's cold outside. On the table is a picture in a silver frame. An older couple with a cat.

"Someone's coming through the window slowly. Breathing in slow, measured breaths. Spilling over the sill into the room, without a sound."

Lisa suddenly jerked, spasmodically.

"Her arms and legs are tied to the bed with her stockings. She's got silver tape over her mouth, and she's trying to scream."

Lisa began flailing her arms, as if she were falling. "I'm . . . I'm not there anymore. I'm on top of a huge clock tower. The hour is chiming, vibrating through me. The bells are getting louder and louder."

Lisa shrieked and grabbed her ears in pain.

"The chimes are striking faster and faster. I'm looking over the edge. I can see the clock's hands spinning fast around the face.

"There are two young women up here with me. They're holding hands. One is the victim I just saw sleeping. The other looks just like her. Her stockings are here too. On the floor somewhere. The two women are laughing and whispering in each other's ears. I can't hear what they're saying. I feel like I'm going to fall off the edge. Help me!"

Rennick grabbed her. All the muscles in her body were tense, and her clothing was soaked, as if she had been in a rainstorm. He began to shake her. Harder and harder. Slowly, her muscles relaxed and she straightened up. Her eyes were still closed.

"I'm back in the victim's room. The killer is wearing a plastic raincoat and moving slowly, methodically. Standing in the shadows; I can't see well. Still breathing calmly, rhythmically. Taking out a knife. Holding it in a gloved hand. Her clothes are being cut off and folded. She's writhing, lifting herself off the bed as far as the stockings will stretch."

Lisa's tears flowed into her perspiration. "Standing over her. Cutting her throat. Blood spreading from the cut. More gashes. There's an electrical cord. Nails. Her eyes—oh God!

"Stop!" she screamed.

She opened her eyes and looked around, clearly disoriented. Then she looked down at the stockings in her hands. Her face twisted in terror, and she threw the stockings as if they had suddenly caught fire. Her knees collapsed and Rennick caught her. She clutched him around the waist and pressed her head against his chest. He stood there awkwardly, feeling his clothing moisten from her perspiration.

"It's a compulsion," said Lisa. "It's going to happen again and again." She released Rennick and walked into a corner. Facing away from him, she adjusted her skirt and tried to push in the loose strands of hair.

Still facing the corner, she said, "Would one of you please pick up the stockings? I'm sorry I threw them. I don't want to touch them again."

Silently, Talon picked up the hosiery and dropped it into the carton. "Ms. Cleary," he said, "I'd like to talk to Dr. Rennick alone for a minute."

"Certainly."

"Why don't you relax in here. We'll go outside."

Lisa collapsed into one of the chairs and began fanning herself with a yellow pad.

"What the fuck was that?" said Talon shakily, as soon as the door closed.

Rennick didn't answer for a moment. "I have no idea. If I

didn't know her better, I'd say we were dealing with a delusional psychotic."

The two men stared at each other. "That thing about the plastic raincoat," Rennick continued. "It suddenly clicked: that's what Bobby Mullins meant when he said it was Plastic Man."

Talon looked at him, his eyes blinking rapidly. "And she talked about clocks moving. Shit, Professor. Nobody knew that."

"She also said that two of the victims knew each other. Is that possible?"

"Rojas checked that out and came up empty. I did a little snooping and also got zip. But it's possible. I'll check again."

They stood for a long while without talking. Talon kept shaking his head, and Rennick began to move his in sympathy.

Rennick worried about what he'd done to his patient.

Talon sat at his desk. He hadn't answered the phone since Rennick and the blonde had left.

Plastic raincoat? Clocks? She even said something about a large dog. Talon had found out that a blind witness brought a seeing-eye dog into the same interview room this morning. There's no way Lisa could have known that.

How the fuck did she do it? He'd seen magicians do tricks that were just as mind boggling. Because he didn't know the secret didn't mean it was supernatural. And he'd seen "Helpful Harry"'s show up in investigations. Most of them turned out to have an angle. They wanted to be in the papers. Or they wanted to sell their story to the papers. Or they had a grudge against some guy they wanted to finger.

Wouldn't it be nice if she was exactly what she'd said she was—a pipeline to information he couldn't get any other way?

Maybe she was on the up-and-up. Maybe she could lead him to something important. It was certainly worth another look to see if any victims knew each other.

Or was there a nastier explanation? Had she been at the crime scene? Women serial killers were virtually unknown, and the few around were usually caregivers who poisoned victims out of their misery. But maybe Lisa was a friend of one of the victims. Or even an accomplice.

Who was this girl?

He aimed to find out.

CHAPTER TWENTY-ONE

Julie walked back and forth in Rennick's apartment, feeling like a tiger pacing in a small cage. She had left a lecture early so they could meet, and now he was almost an hour late.

The sound of keys in the door announced Rennick's arrival.

"I'm sorry," he said, throwing his coat onto the pile on the couch.

"You knew I had to leave something early to rush over here. It's really rude for you to be this late."

"I know, I know. I'm sorry. I lost track of time with Talon. This psychic stuff is fascinating. I won't do it again. I promise." He made a Scout sign with his right hand.

"You're always exactly on time. So when you're not, it makes me nuts."

"If I was late more often, then it would be okay?"

Arguing with lawyers, she thought. What a pain in the ass.

"You have a message on your machine," she said.

Rennick walked over and listened to the recording. "Professor? Danny Talon. I found Lofton's sister today. She seemed happy not to know where the asshole is. Told me he used to torture birds and cats when he was a kid, and I thought you'd want to put that in your profile hopper. I hope you enjoyed our little trip to the Twilight Zone today. I know it was good for me. See ya." The machine clicked off.

"The Twilight Zone?" asked Julie.

"Yeah." Rennick described what happened when Lisa handled the evidence at the police station.

"That's spooky."

"I know. And it was really hard on her."

"But it doesn't excuse your being late."

"Okay. Okay. What's for dinner?" he asked.

"Cold food from the Dancing Greek. It was hot when you were supposed to be here."

Greek food, thought Rennick. Greek. His subconscious had been looking for something, and Greek was connected to it. What?

Julie took the tinfoil off a plate of souvlaki. "I met Edmund Childs after his lecture last night."

"Cool. What was he like?"

"I've never heard anyone think in such big concepts. He made me feel like a pea-brain."

Rennick laid out the place mats and silverware. "What about the job?"

"I think he liked me. He wants some writing samples."

"That's wonderful!" said Rennick. That's horrible, he thought. "You'd have to go to New York?"

"I'm a long ways from getting a job offer. But yeah, it would be in New York. Which is a bummer. I hate places with concrete and glass and people all piled on top of each other. Not to mention what it does to our relationship."

Rennick felt the silence hanging over him. "If you really hate New York, you shouldn't go."

She stared at him and blinked several times. "Well, it's a long shot. I'll deal with it if it becomes real." She turned away.

Lisa lay in bed with the window open. She shifted into a comfortable position on her side, then snuggled her face into the down pillow. A gentle breeze carried in the aroma of moist night air, along with the faint singing of a mockingbird.

Having the visions today had been frightening. Yet she had done it, and now she savored the high of conquering a fear. She replayed the events in her mind, enjoying how they were far less terrifying in retrospect. She couldn't have done it without Dr. Rennick, who had made her feel safe. Like getting on a two-wheeler, knowing he would be holding the back of the bike.

Lisa remembered how her father had done that when she was a child. She still had the vivid image of the first time she rode a bicycle by herself. How she looked back and was shocked to see her father a half-block away. How she fell over when she realized she was balancing herself alone.

She felt her facial muscles tense when she remembered her father. She'd been thinking more about him in the last few weeks than she had in years. The man didn't deserve any of her time or attention. He'd given up all rights to that when he let go of much more than just her bicycle.

She turned over on the other side and ordered herself to think about something else. Anything. Work. Latham Oil. Her—

An image of the Powell girl's mutilated body began creeping into her consciousness. It wasn't nearly as vivid as the one today, yet it was vivid enough. Lisa fumbled for the light and sat up quickly. She pressed her fingertips against her temples, willing the images to leave.

To her surprise and pleasure, they disappeared into the distance, like a movie closing to a pinpoint. She continued sitting for a few more minutes, just to make sure the images didn't return.

When she finally turned off the light and lay back down, she pulled the cool sheets up over her shoulder and took a deep breath of the evening breeze. It hadn't been so difficult to get herself out of that downward spiral. Maybe today had made her stronger. As long as she could chase the images away that easily, they shouldn't be a bother in her life.

The mockingbirds seemed to sing a little louder as her lips relaxed to a tranquil smile. She closed her eyes and drifted into a deep sleep.

CHAPTER TWENTY-TWO

Talon pored over the files, trying to find a connection between the victims. Lisa's prediction had prompted him to try once more, yet he'd found nothing.

With dead ends in all directions, he decided to go to the apartment of Betty Sanchez, the second victim, which was the only scene he hadn't checked out. Even if this psychic stuff was voodoo, it couldn't hurt to get the vibes of another victim.

Sanchez had lived in a two-story apartment building on Ohio Street in West L.A. It was painted some putrid shade of green, and dried weeds covered most of the sidewalk. Talon found the building directory inside an alcove that was lit by a broken bulb, and he pressed a button next to the handwritten *B. Sanchez*.

A man's voice answered and buzzed him in. Talon walked toward the back of the building, past a dog that threw itself against a screen door trying to get at him. He knocked on the door of apartment 4, and a short, light-complected man with a pencil mustache answered. When Talon stepped inside and closed the hollow door, the unit's walls vibrated like a flimsy movie set.

"I'm Arturo, Betty's brother."

"Detective Talon. I appreciate your coming down to Los Angeles."

"I had to come eventually. We've avoided packing up her things, but the landlord wants everything out next week or we have to pay for another month."

"Do you know much about Betty's friends?"

"Sorry, no. Betty moved here about a year ago, and I stayed in Camarillo. She came up to see us but I never got down here. I worked six days a week. There's eleven of us in the family and our parents need my help."

While Talon was listening, his eyes surveyed the apartment. With all her life being packed away, it seemed like Sanchez's personality was evaporating, leaving only the bare walls to get ready for somebody else's idea of home. And taking off a little more of the sheen every time it happened.

"I think she had some financial problems," Arturo continued. "They shut off her phone over a month ago, and the power company is scheduled to close her down next week."

Talon had tuned out the last few words. His attention was now locked on a book that had caught his eye. A book with an electric yellow cover, which looked like it was colored with a highlighter. A book with a pyramid on the cover.

Leaving Arturo standing there, Talon went over and took the book off the shelf. *Vibrations of the Pyramids*, by Asan-Aziz Al Ghiza. He remembered that Myra Powell, the first victim, had had the same book. Was that a coincidence? An odd tingle rippled from his neck to his tailbone.

Talon flipped through the pages of the book. It looked like New Age bullshit: connecting with the rhythms of the universe and all that. Then he saw a handwritten name inside the front cover.

Myra Powell.

Lisa yelled loudly as she pushed out another rep of her bench press. After having slept for almost nine hours last night, she had awoken with several new ideas for Latham Oil's depreciation recapture, and was now lifting more weight than she could ever remember.

She squeezed out one more rep, then clanked the bar into the rack and lay spent on the bench. Her chest pulsed from the exercise as she looked around the gym while recovering for the next set. Benny's Body Shop on Third Street was the gym where she had worked out for the past year. It was a no-frills former warehouse, and most of the patrons were professional dancers and bodybuilders. The gym's gray industrial carpet was scarred from the heavy weights that had dropped on it, and the air was saturated with perspiration. The only music was an old radio that could barely be heard over the banging of weights and the whir of a floor fan.

Lisa went over to the pec-deck machine and began squeezing the pads together in front of her. She concentrated on using her chest muscles, not her arms, as she watched her form in the mirror. Just like the bench press, she was able to use heavier weights today, and she could feel the blood flushing her chest muscles with the warm glow that bodybuilders call a "pump." With each rep, the pump spread out, and was now buzzing through her entire body. It gave her a floating feeling, almost as though she were hovering in space.

On the third set, the gym seemed to be getting colder. It

was subtle at first, then quickly grew uncomfortable. She looked around the room to see if anyone else was reacting. Just then a young woman walked through the door, on the arm of a blond man. Or was his hair gray? She couldn't tell in the light. Lisa couldn't see his face, but his mannerisms looked familiar. Did she know him?

The woman turned toward Lisa and stared at her. First curiously, then intently. As if she were going to say something.

Lisa knew this woman. She had just seen her. Could this be the woman whose stockings she'd handled? That was impossible. She was dead. Lisa started toward the woman and found she couldn't move. She felt as if she were paralyzed.

Now the woman was strapped to the pec-deck machine next to Lisa's, struggling to get free. The man suddenly whipped her across the neck, and she screamed as a line of blood erupted in the whip's track. The whip went up again, then slashed across her chest. Her clothes ripped in its wake, exposing her breasts. Blood splattered on Lisa as colors erupted from inside the woman's body, like a spectrum of searchlights flooding into the room.

Lisa told herself forcefully that this wasn't really happening. She looked in the mirror, hoping to anchor herself in reality. The reflection showed that she was still in Benny's, sitting on the pec-deck machine. While she tried to control her breathing, she saw the outlines of a skeleton appear inside her body, as if she were becoming transparent. She could see her veins, arteries, and muscles, and she saw her blood pumping in bursts from her beating heart.

Then she was no longer in the gym.

First she saw a street, with a grass parkway in the middle and older brick buildings stretching for several blocks. Teenagers were sitting on the parkway benches, smoking, laughing, sharing brown paper bags crumpled around bottles. Two young Latinos kicked a soccer ball back and forth, while another boy deftly bounced a ball off his thighs and ankles.

Then she saw a wholly incongruous image: a dragon. It was complete in every detail: fire exhaling from its mouth; hemlock green skin that stretched and dangled when its head moved slowly back and forth; mustard yellow eyes looking at her suspiciously when she came into its view.

Next she was in an alley. There were scattered trash cans with cats darting among them. In front of her was a figure, whose face was in darkness, using a metal pole to pry open the door of a large, brick barbecue pit. Placing a tan plastic bag inside the door, then starting to close. . . .

"Are you all right, miss?"

Lisa became aware that someone was talking to her. The scene in her head popped like a soap bubble, and she was disoriented, almost dizzy.

"Are you all right?" repeated the voice.

She blinked to clear the fog. The woman strapped to the pec-deck was gone.

A hand touched her shoulder and she jumped. "Can you hear me?"

She turned her head toward a man with long black hair, who was muscled and bulging out of a T-shirt that read POWER PUNCHING. Her heart was still beating rapidly.

"I'm sorry," she said. "I just spaced out for a minute."

"Are you okay?"

"I'm fine. Why? Am I staying on the machine too long?"

"No. Your finger's bleeding."

Lisa looked down and saw it was true. The blood had already pooled into a growing circle on her leotard, and it was dripping into a puddle on the carpet. As soon as she saw it, her finger began to sting, and the sight of blood brought back an image of the woman being slashed on the machine. Her stomach soured.

"I'll get you a bandage. You should wash it off."

Lisa awkwardly put the finger in her mouth, tasting the salty flavor of the blood. More of it flowed than she had anticipated. She hurried to the watercooler and spit the blood into the drain, coughing a few dry heaves in the process. Then she ran the cold water over her finger to numb it.

A vision like this would have sent her into panic just a week ago. Maybe this therapy was really helping. She felt the rush of staying calm in the face of danger, as if she had somehow taken control of a wild horse that bucked beneath her. Definitely progress.

Lisa put a Band-Aid on her finger. Maybe there was something useful in what she'd seen. Could the killer be this gray- or blond-haired man? Did the alley really exist? Had the killer hidden something there?

She thought about calling Dr. Rennick and asking if the police wanted the information. Yet she hated to disturb him, and she felt funny talking to him outside of therapy. It had been really awkward at the police station. Seeing her doctor in another setting like that.

She had a session with him tomorrow. She'd tell him then.

CHAPTER TWENTY-THREE

Small brass bells tinkled as Talon opened the door of the Higher Karma Bookstore on Westwood Boulevard, between Wilshire and Santa Monica. This morning, Talon had been hopeful that the Pyramid books might open a crack in the case. Six New Age bookstores later he hadn't found shit, and he was getting nauseous from the smell of incense.

Higher Karma was a tiny place, with no more than twelve or thirteen half-empty bookshelves, and one wall that still had the dirty outlines of a Frozen Yogurt sign. Indian sitar music played softly, and the room smelled of curry as the clerk put down a Styrofoam box of aromatic food. He was maybe thirty-five years old, with chalky skin and almost white hair, wearing a loose-fitting batik shirt.

"May I help you?" he asked, his voice singsongy as if he were from India.

Talon flipped open his badge. "You sell a book called *Vibrations of the Pyramids?*"

The man recoiled from the badge, and the singsong disappeared. "Oh. Yeah. Sure do. Here." He hurried around to the shelves and handed Talon a copy.

"I don't wanna buy one. I just need some information."

The clerk looked puzzled. He continued holding out the book for a moment, then recovered his composure and replaced it carefully on the shelf, as if he were hanging an invaluable oil painting.

"How may I help you?" The singsong was back.

"You sell a lot of these books?"

"Oh yes. It is one of our best-selling titles."

"How many?"

"Eight or ten a year."

"You know anything about the people who bought them?"

"Sorry. We don't keep those kinds of records."

"You know any places where people who read this sh— uh . . . book might get together and talk about it?"

"Yes. There's a center on Motor Avenue where the committed gather. I will write out the information for you."

The clerk floated back to the counter, flipped through a Rolodex, then wrote in fancy calligraphy on a Post-it. Talon stuck it in his pocket and turned to leave.

"May I make an observation?" asked the clerk.

"Huh?"

"I consider myself a student of humankind. Please don't think I'm being intrusive, but I feel a need to help anyone who seems to be in distress. In the same way I would aid someone lying on the sidewalk."

"Yeah. So? What's your point?"

"I read your aura as somewhat troubled. There are a number

of techniques I could suggest to adjust it, and they would lead you to a kinder, happier place."

Talon seriously considered telling him where to put his aura.

Talon parked next to the Center For Ethereal Learning on Motor Avenue, near the Santa Monica Freeway overpass and between an autobody repair shop and a bar that advertised satellite TV.

He pushed aside some beaded curtains that slapped back into his face, and he had to stop himself from ripping them off the door frame.

Past a few dozen metal folding chairs was an office at the back. A grossly heavy man sat behind a desk with his feet propped up. Because of his weight, his eyes looked tiny compared to the rest of his face. He was wearing a shirt on which dozens of colored fish swam around, and he was reading *The Wall Street Journal*.

"Mr. Plimpton?"

Plimpton folded the paper neatly, then stood up with great effort.

"Yes, I'm Gerald Plimpton," he answered in a voice that wheezed from the exertion of standing.

"Detective Talon. We spoke on the phone."

"Ah, yes. Please sit down." Plimpton was already lowering himself into the double-wide seat.

"You give classes here on *Vibrations of the Pyramids?*"

"Not really classes. More like discussion groups that I facilitate. I ask the participants to read a chapter before each meeting, and then—"

"Do you have a record of the students that come through?"

"Yes, although I'm afraid they're not too well organized."

"Do you remember any of these women?" Talon pushed across photos of the four victims.

"I know these two," said Plimpton, pointing to Powell and Sanchez. "Myra and Betty. I introduced them to each other."

Talon pulled his seat closer to the desk. "Tell me about them."

"Myra had been coming to the Pyramid class for a while before Betty showed up. Betty originally enrolled in my Mysticism class, and I asked if she was related to Myra because they looked so much alike. When she said no, I told her to come meet her twin. They hit it off right away and spent a lot of time together."

"Did they ever come in with men?"

"Myra had a large boyfriend that came a few times. Not big like me. I mean a tall, muscular guy. He yawned and looked at his watch for the whole class. Distracted me so much that—"

"What did he look like?"

"Blondish."

"You know his name?"

"Bart, I think."

"Did Betty know him?"

"Oh, yes. They came in as a threesome."

Gee, thought Talon. Ol' Bart done plumb forgot to mention that in his interview. "Did anyone else come in with them?"

Plimpton attempted to lean forward, and got as close to the desk as his stomach would allow. "One night Myra told me she was meeting another man after class, and that I shouldn't tell Bart about him."

"Did you see the other man?"

"Just briefly. He came in and picked her up when the class was over."

"What did he look like?"

"He was older. Maybe in his forties. I'm not so good with ages. Graying, I think."

Lofton would be around forty, thought Talon. Also, gray could look blond in a dark room. Especially to a five-year-old Bobby Mullins. On the other hand, the older guy could be some innocent asshole that Powell had started dating. If Heath had found out about her cheating, he could have popped her in a jealous mood. Maybe the other murders got started when Heath found out he liked killing.

His instincts still said it probably wasn't Heath, and even if he was wrong, the guy wouldn't be killing anyone from the Eureka jail. Talon's instincts also said that Lofton could be the guy. It bothered him that Rennick had reservations about Lofton, since their guts usually matched. But there wasn't anyone else on the list.

He needed to find Lofton. Pronto.

CHAPTER TWENTY-FOUR

Lisa lay on the couch in Rennick's office, describing the incident in the gym. Rennick noticed that, although she appeared relaxed, her hands were clasped tightly in front of her as if she were guarding her pubic area.

"You never saw the face of this blond- or gray-haired man?" he asked.

"No."

"Did he look familiar in any other way?"

"Yes. But I can't place it."

"Think about it. It could be important."

"I have been. I can't quite grasp it. If there's even anything there."

"Besides this vision in the gym, have you had any other episodes?"

"Nothing serious."

"What about not so serious?"

"Not . . . not really."

"Nothing at all?"

"Well . . . do dreams count?"

"They might shed some light on what's happening."

"I had a dream about a horse again. I was buried in the ground up to my neck and I couldn't move. This dark figure was riding a horse toward me, like he was going to trample my head."

Odd, thought Rennick. He had assumed the horse images were related to Sarah Wayne, her redheaded friend who fell off the horse. Rennick thought they would dissipate now that she remembered the incident. This dream seemed unrelated to Sarah. Much darker, and potentially much more troubling.

"Were you actually being buried in the dream, or were you already in the ground when it started?" he asked.

"I think I was already . . . no, wait. I remember. How did you know?"

"I didn't. That's why I asked."

"I was forced to dig the hole myself. It was this sort of mud that kept sliding in, so it was hard to make any progress. I was down at the bottom, using a piece of wood as a shovel. Everything was all mushy and yucky."

That fit with the mushy feeling of sinking into the horse she had described earlier. "You said you were forced. Who was forcing you?"

"I couldn't see him."

"Him. A man?"

"Yes. He made me take off all my clothes."

"Was he watching you undress?"

"I guess. I couldn't see him in the shadows."

"Were you sexually aroused?"

Her body tensed and her grip tightened over her pubic area. "No. It was disgusting."

Rennick's instincts told him he was heading in the right direction, yet he didn't know where it might lead.

"Lisa, we have to get into some areas that are going to be uncomfortable. It's important. Will you go along with me?"

No answer.

"Lisa?"

She nodded.

"Have you ever had sexual intercourse with a man?"

"I don't want to talk about this. Do I have to?"

"You certainly don't have to. But if you want to get better, we need to get into these experiences."

Silence.

"Have you ever had sexual intercourse with a man?"

". . . Yes."

"What was your first experience?"

"College. A friend of my roommate's."

"Was it a serious relationship?"

"No. We dated a few months."

"Did you enjoy the sex?"

"No. It was horrible. It hurt and I got very bloody."

"Did you sleep with him again?"

"No. I never saw him again."

"Your choice or his?"

"I never returned his calls."

"Have you slept with any other men?"

No answer.

"Lisa?"

"Why do we have to talk about this?"

"I think it's related to what's going on."

"How?"

"I need more information before I can tell you."

"Isn't our time almost up?"

"We have plenty of time. Lisa, have you slept with any other men?"

Tears spilled onto her cheeks as she shook her head no.

Rennick wasn't surprised. "Why not?"

"I'm just not, you know, interested in sex. It was such a horrible experience."

"Do you masturbate?"

"How could you even suggest something like that?"

"I didn't accuse you. I only asked."

"No."

"Do you ever get sexually aroused?"

"I don't want to talk about this anymore."

Rennick didn't feel he could push any harder right now. He was beginning to form a theory, although it would take more probing to see if he was right.

Lisa broke his train of thought. "Do you think the visions I had in the gym could help find this killer?"

"I don't know."

"I'd be willing to help look for the alley. We could see if there's something inside that brick thing."

"Your handling the evidence last time was hard on you. I don't think you should go through something like that again. But with your permission, I'll pass along the information you gave me."

She sat up and looked directly at Rennick. Her makeup had run, yet the energy had returned to her eyes. "You can tell them everything I said. But I could do much more if I went along. It'll be hard to find that alley without me. There must be hundreds that look just like it. I could, you know, ride around with the police."

"I don't think that would be good for your recovery. Now that some time has passed, you've probably forgotten how rough it was for you to handle the stockings."

"I remember perfectly. I think it made me stronger. And I'd feel irresponsible if I didn't help when I could."

Rennick looked at her for a long while before he spoke. "Let me think about it."

Rennick arrived at Le Petit Bistro in Westwood Village, a restaurant that took great pains to look like a sidewalk café of the owner Rene's native Paris. The walls were plaster, with red brickwork peeking through cracks, and accordions accompanied by mandolins played through the speakers. The waiters, each with a French accent of varying accuracy, glided among the customers.

Rennick sat at an outdoor table in the sunshine, idly fingering his water glass while he waited for Dr. Joseph. It was another hot December day, courtesy of the Santa Ana winds. He watched an overweight lady rush by with a tiny dachshund that was moving its legs at light speed trying to keep up.

Dr. Joseph arrived and clapped Rennick on the shoulder as he sat down. Rennick made small talk and played with the rock candy stuck to a wooden swizzle stick that came with the cappuccino. Then he rearranged his silverware and began building a little house out of the sugar cubes.

Joseph placed a corner of the red cloth napkin into his collar and smoothed it against his chest with several long strokes. He carefully lifted the cappuccino and swallowed a small sip, causing his Adam's apple to bob up and down.

"So, Michael. It is an utter delight to have your company not once, but twice, within a short time. To what do I owe this honor?"

"It's about my psychic patient. The one we discussed."

"Ah, yes. How fareth Cassandra, the prophetess?"

"It's pretty eerie. She touched the victims' stockings and gave a reasonably accurate description of the crimes. She was wrong about seeing an Indian blanket and some other details, but she had the major elements right. She also said that two of the victims knew each other, which the police didn't know at the time."

Joseph swallowed another sip of cappuccino, then dabbed his lips with a free corner of the napkin. "Eerie indeed. There is something rather discomforting about the entire psychic business. It challenges many truths which we assume are bedrock."

"Doc, she had another of these visions and saw the killer hide something. For all I know, it could be an important clue. Or a total hallucination. Whatever it is, she wants to go to the police and help, and I'm worried that could set back her recovery. When she handled the stockings, she almost collapsed. Letting her do something like that again seems risky. Maybe irresponsible."

"All of that sounds perfectly rational. What is the other side of the polemic?"

Rennick unconsciously began playing with his spoon as he spoke. "There's a chance that facing her fears might help her overcome them. And she might help find the killer. This is a case where a lot of young women are in jeopardy, and the cops aren't doing very well."

"So we have a somewhat balanced equation. What do you think should be done?"

"I don't trust my motives, Doc. I'm worried that my curiosity to see if she could do it, along with the need to bring in this killer, is coloring my judgment."

"Judgments are always colored, my boy. Indeed, it is that very color which separates great decisions from mediocre ones. What do you believe to be the proper course?"

"For her sake, it's very risky. For the sake of the community, she should help."

"And on balance?"

"I'm pretty confused."

"Ah! That is the first item of clarity yet to be uttered." Joseph chuckled. "Have you included her desires to be of assistance in your evaluation?"

"I suppose so. Although in a sense that's irrelevant. You don't let a kid play in the street because he wants to."

"Yet this is not a small child. From your description, she is a rather bright, articulate lady."

"So you think she should do it?"

"I did not say that. I am merely probing the situation. I do not believe there is a right or wrong answer. This one will have to come from within you, Michael. Know that you have excellent judgment, and that you will make the correct decision."

By late afternoon, Talon had interviewed most of the neighbors around Tanya Mullins's apartment. His feet were beginning to throb, and his collar was tightening up.

Next was Mrs. Bernice Winslow, whose apartment building was almost directly across the street from Mullins's. When she opened her door, the smell of baking bread immediately lit Talon's taste buds. Mrs. Winslow was a silver-haired woman who looked to be in her seventies, and she stood a few inches shy of five feet. She was wearing a white terry-cloth bathrobe, and Talon guessed that was as dressed as she ever got.

He declined a glass of water, thinking he wouldn't refuse some of the bread if she offered. The plastic covering on her couch crackled as they sat down, and Talon explained that he was investigating the Mullins homicide.

"Have you noticed anything unusual over the last few weeks?" he asked.

"Did you say weeks?"

"Yes, ma'am. Sometimes the perpetrators observe the scene beforehand."

"Oh. I didn't think something that old could be important. I suppose I should have called."

"Called about what?"

"That man who came here several nights in a row."

Talon slid closer to her, causing the plastic to squeal.

"A man?"

"Yes. He was walking a dog. I don't really like to snoop, but I couldn't help noticing. I'd never seen him before."

Talon opened his notebook and began writing. "Did you get a look at him?"

"His dog was a cute little black thing that scratched a lot."

"What about the man?"

"He stayed close to the wall of my building, so I couldn't see him very well. If you go over to my window, you'll see it's hard to look straight down."

"What did you see?"

"I think he had a mustache."

"Was he old? Young?"

"I'm sorry. I couldn't tell."

"Blond, brunette?"

"He was wearing a baseball cap."

"What color?"

"It was dark outside. I'm not sure."

"Any insignias on the cap?"

"I just couldn't see that well. I don't see so well to begin with."

That would damage her credibility as a witness, Talon thought. Not that she'd seen enough to mean diddly in court. "Do you remember anything else?"

"One night he was carrying a plastic grocery bag."

"How often did he come?"

"Every night for a while. He stopped coming right after the—oh, dear. I should have called, shouldn't I?"

"That's all right, ma'am. Is there anything else you remember?"

She furrowed her brow in concentration. "No. I'm sorry. Would you like a slice of homemade bread?"

Detective Paul Jordan rubbed his pockmarked cheeks as he walked along Venice Boulevard toward the yellow sign with black letters that said MAR VISTA BOWL. Because the alley's parking lot had been full, he had walked almost an entire block to the old building. The street was dark, since the shops were closed at this time of night, and the building seemed to lean away from him.

Jordan adjusted his tie and wondered if checking out this boring Cleary broad was punishment for something he accidently did to Talon. Or, since everyone knew that Wharton was jolting Talon's balls with a cattle prod, maybe it was just Talon's way of torturing somebody else so he could feel better. Whatever it was, investigating her background was about as interesting as watching paint dry. Thank God he was down to the last few pieces before he put in his report.

He opened the door to the bowling alley and was assaulted with the noise of clanking pins and beer bottles, punctuated with occasional cheers and laughter. The lanes were full, and computer-generated scoreboards buzzed on TV screens above each one. A blond waitress with candy-apple-red nails wove through the crowd, gyroscopically balancing a tray of drinks above her head.

Jordan saw the collection of crimson-and-yellow bowling shirts on alley 24, with the words *Olympic Metals* sewn in fancy script. He worked his way toward them.

"Any of you guys Ron Cleary?"

"That's me," said a thin, tightly built man. Cleary appeared to be in his early fifties, and was slumping on the bench with his feet propped against the scorekeeper's chair. He looked like a former fighter, wiry and dangerous. Jordan had learned years ago that even an old lion can kill you if you piss him off.

"I'm Jordan. We talked earlier."

Cleary made no effort to get up. "Yeah. So whaddya want?"

"Do you want to talk privately?"

"No one can hear over the racket. Whaddaya want?"

"I want to ask some questions about your daughter, Lisa."

"I ain't seen her in years."

Odd, thought Jordan. He expected the usual drill about why the cops were snooping around.

"How many years?"

"Hell, I dunno. Fifteen maybe. Maybe more."

"You talk to her during that time?"

"Nope."

"You're up, Ron," said one of Cleary's teammates. Without looking at Jordan, Cleary picked up a highly polished gunmetal-gray ball. His form was smooth, and he laid down the ball without out a sound. It glided down the lane, then hooked sharply into the one/three pocket, scattering all ten pins with the satisfying crash of a strike. His teammates clapped him on the back. Jordan looked up and saw that Cleary's score was 206 in the eighth frame. Since Jordan averaged about 120 per game, he was impressed.

Cleary sat down without looking at him. "Anything else?"

"You know anyone who's been in touch with her?"

"Nope."

"She ever had any trouble with the law?"

"Not that I know of."

"You know where she works?"

"Nope."

Jordan probed a little longer, got absolutely zero, and headed toward the door. On instinct, he looked back and saw Cleary staring at him. Cleary made no attempt to hide his stare or break it off. Jordan turned and kept walking, feeling Cleary's eyes on him the entire way.

CHAPTER TWENTY-FIVE

Lisa sat in the back seat, while Talon and Rennick were in front. They were looking for the street she had seen in her episode at the gym: a wide street, with a grass parkway in the middle, lined with older brick buildings. According to Talon's research with the traffic cops, there were fourteen streets in Los Angeles that matched that description. After almost three hours in Talon's gray Dodge, they had seen nine of them.

Lisa shifted her position, leaning into the corner where the seat met the door. She hunched her shoulders forward. "I'm sorry. It felt so real."

"It's okay," said Rennick. "We understand this isn't an exact science."

"I'm running outta time, Professor," said Talon. "There's two more I can hit on the way back." He made a U-turn at the corner, causing the tires to squeal.

Lisa traced her finger along the window glass as they headed west on Sixth. The street was lined with markets, florists and other small businesses, most with bilingual English/Korean signs. She watched a Korean woman sweep the sidewalk in front of an immaculate electronics shop, and she wished that she was back in the world of accounting where everything was neat and orderly.

Talon turned the car off Sixth onto Lafayette Park Place, and Lisa suddenly felt an intense surge. She moved her head toward the window so rapidly that she hit the glass.

"This is it!" she said. It was just as she had pictured: a green parkway, benches with teenagers crowded on them, and rows of brick apartments over stores.

"Up ahead on the right. There. That one." She reached in front of Talon and pointed out a red brick building with dull yellow paint that had peeled in large spots.

Before the car fully stopped, she leapt out and ran toward the building. The vibrations increased as she got closer. Lisa closed her eyes and moved her palms slowly across the rough surface of the bricks. The wall felt as if it were purring with the murmur of a ship's engine.

Sounds of laughter and clanging dishes brought her back to the street. Ignoring Talon and Rennick, she ran toward the sounds. They came from a crowded Chinese restaurant whose patrons were laughing and talking loudly. Lisa placed her forehead against the glass and watched.

On a wall near the window, she saw a calendar that seized her attention. The calendar had a picture of a dragon, just like the one in her vision. As she stared at the image, the dragon came to life, winking at her as it exhaled flames with an audible blast of breath. She jolted back against Talon.

Lisa turned to face him. "I saw an alley. It must be behind the building."

She jogged ahead of them into a passageway between the buildings. As she rounded the corner, she saw an alley almost identical to the one in her vision. The fire escapes were black metal bars that looked like charred skeletons of a bygone era. Clothes hung across several of the escapes' rails, and barbed razor wire blocked access to the apartments. In the background were the sounds of televisions and mothers shouting in Spanish. She hadn't foreseen the foul odor of garbage mixed with urine.

Half in shadow, at the far end of the alley, Lisa saw a large incinerator that looked like an oversized brick barbecue. She immediately recognized it as the structure from her vision. Her knees began to give, and she grabbed Rennick for support. His strong hands steadied her.

"Is that the grate?" asked Rennick.

"Yes . . ."

A sudden sandstorm blocked her vision. Lisa found herself leaning into a wind so strong that it held her up. It howled loudly in her ears and pitted sand against her cheeks. She covered her face to continue breathing, and her sinuses felt raw and thick with a gritty mucus.

After a few moments, the storm lightened. The brick structure was now inside a translucent pyramid, whose tip was glowing an iridescent yellow.

"Yes," said Lisa. "There. Inside the pyramid."

"Pyramid?" said Talon. "Pyramid?!"

She started toward the incinerator, slowly, so that Rennick wouldn't release his grip. The energy around her intensified when she stepped inside the pyramid, almost as if her body were vibrating. It grew stronger as she neared the iron door on the structure's belly.

As soon as she touched the grate, Lisa felt a surging connection to her vision. She saw colors swirling from the door in a whirlpool, just as the colors had spurted from the body of the young woman in the gym. Amethyst, ruby, topaz. Forming a vortex that drew her in. Now she could see through the iron door. Inside was a tan plastic bag that glowed like a dying ember.

Lisa tried to open the grate, which felt like it was welded shut. Her fingers were rubbed raw within a few seconds of pulling at the rough surface.

"Lemme try," said Talon, who applied his huge hands to it. Lisa reluctantly moved back, but only a step. Talon grunted, yet the door still wouldn't give. Lisa's eyes caught a rusted pipe on the ground, and she remembered the killer using a lever in her vision. She handed the pipe to Talon, who worked it behind the door. He leaned his weight on it, and the door groaned open.

Lisa elbowed past the two men and thrust her head inside. Ashes stirred by prying the door wafted into her nostrils and covered her face. Talon and Rennick tried to look in, yet she held her ground.

It was dark and her eyes took a moment to adjust to the light. She saw what appeared to be a cat, but then it turned, and she saw that its tail was naked skin. It was a huge rat that bared its teeth and hissed at her. She screamed, banging her head on the small opening as she retreated and fell hard onto the pavement. Rennick helped her into a sitting position. Her head throbbed from hitting the door, and she was covered in perspiration and ashes. She couldn't summon the energy to stand up.

Lisa watched Talon take out a tan plastic grocery bag that showed no deterioration, and therefore couldn't have been there long. Using a ballpoint pen, he removed an inside-out pair of latex gloves and a balled-up clear plastic raincoat. Both were stained with blood.

When Lisa saw the objects, she gagged, and her mouth filled with a sour bile. Her eyes teared, and she spit out the bitter liquid.

"Take some deep breaths," said Rennick. "Slower."

"Can I touch the gloves?" she asked. Her voice was frail, and the aftertaste of bile was still in her mouth.

"No," answered Talon. "They could be evidence. One of the witnesses saw a man with a plastic grocery bag." He sounded like the wind had been knocked out of him.

Lisa leaned back against the bricks, whose rough edges gripped her hair like tiny barbs. She began to bang her head against the wall, at first softly, then harder. She wanted to knock these images out of her brain. Again and again. Harder. Harder.

Rennick's hand came between her head and the wall, gently cushioning the blows. A feeling of utter helplessness seized her, and she lowered her chin against her chest in resignation. Then she began to sob aloud for the first time in her adult life.

CHAPTER TWENTY-SIX

Talon and Rennick walked to Talon's desk at the Hollywood police station.

"Jesus, Mary, and Joseph, Professor. Talk to me."

Rennick kept replaying the scene in his mind. He remembered how Lisa had run around touching the walls. If she had been a street person, they'd have locked her up. And the most bizarre part: He felt like he was getting in tune with her.

"I wish I knew what to say," Rennick finally answered.

"Did you tell her about the pyramids?"

"No."

Talon played with a rubber band. "What do you think she'd find if we took her to the crime scenes?"

"I don't think she could handle such an intense experience. You saw how she fell apart. Whatever she's getting, there's a price tag."

Talon began folding a paper accordion. "It's obviously not

worth her sanity. And as good as she is, there's still something about her that doesn't sit right."

"What do you mean?"

"Nothing I can put a finger on. In fact, the boys doing background on her say she's just what she seems to be. At least so far. I just can't shake the feeling that something's off." He played the paper accordion in and out.

"Lisa's pretty troubled right now. Maybe you're reacting to that."

"Yeah. Maybe. Probably. Anyway, I hope what she found will point us somewhere. You got any ideas how I can write up the way we found this shit?"

"How about the truth?"

Talon snorted. "Maybe I'll say I made an antenna out of paper clips and got the location from a spaceship broadcast. That's a little more believable."

Thursday.

This afternoon I sat across from her in an organic food cafe. She was at the next table, no more than three feet away from me. So lost in her book that the lettuce leaf speared on her fork dangled halfway between the plate and her mouth for almost four minutes. I pretended to drop my napkin just so I could lean past her chair and catch a whiff of that shampooed blond hair. I could have licked the back of her neck and she wouldn't have noticed.

Most people jump at their first instincts. Like animals. They're the ones who fail. Picking the candidate is easy, you see. Spending the time to confirm your choice is what separates the hacks from the artists.

This one is superb. I've been watching her for two weeks now. She lives alone. She leaves her windows unlocked. It's almost too easy. I suppose that's one of the bonuses you get from playing a *longer game. Over time, you get some tough ones, and you get some that lay there like a $20 bill on the street.*

I watched her for the full forty-seven minutes she was in the restaurant. I studied how her mouth moved in little circles when she chewed. Sometimes she ran her tongue over her lips. Each little move clawed at my insides. Stirring up feelings that only come from this.

Talon drummed his fingernails against his teeth as he sat on hold. Then he began stapling the same piece of paper over and over.

The woman's voice said, "The mayor is now on the line." Talon stood up reflexively.

"Detective Talon?" came the strong, calculatedly friendly voice.

"Yessir."

"Sam Jarvis. How are you and Ellen?"

"Uh, Elaine and I are divorced, sir."

"Oh. Sorry. My information must be a little stale." Perfect laugh. Laughter ends. Serious voice. "Danny, how are we doing on this case? I'm catching hell in the press because Chris Armstrong, who will almost certainly run against me next year, is painting us to look like buffoons. We're getting calls from young women who are scared to death. And the Westside merchants are complaining that business is off because single women won't go out at night."

Talon drummed his nails against his teeth, then stopped when he worried that the mayor could hear it through the phone.

"Well, sir," answered Talon, "we really don't have much to go on. This guy's been so neat and careful that he hasn't left us much. I—"

The voice grew more authoritative. "I need to report some-thing to the press. What have you got?"

"I just found some evidence, but it hasn't been analyzed. And I have a couple of suspects. But we shouldn't make this public. I—"

"Perfect. That's just what I'll say. 'We've got several leads that we can't make public.' But that only buys us a week or so. I'll need something concrete by then. Am I clear, Detective?"

Talon hung up the phone and continued stapling the piece of paper until he ran out of open spots. Then he tossed it into the trash and started through one of the piles on his desk.

A few minutes later, he saw Wharton approaching his desk. Perfect.

"I heard the mayor called you," said Wharton.

"Yep," answered Talon without looking up.

"So how are you doing on this case?"

"It's coming."

Wharton sat down on the edge of Talon's desk, pushing over some papers with his butt. "Is there anything I can do to help?"

Talon looked him directly in the eye. "Why do you bother playing charades? You don't want to help me. You hope I fall on my ass."

Wharton began to clean his fingernails with a pocketknife. "If you're worried, I could pull you off the case. 'Course, I don't think that'd look so good on your record. But if that's what you want . . ."

"What I want is for you to get your butt-cheek off my desk and let me do my job."

Wharton finished cleaning his nails, shedding little droplets of gunk onto the floor. Then he got up, smiled at Talon, and walked away.

*   *   *

After the experiences in the alley, Lisa got in bed early. By six the next morning, when she couldn't sleep anymore, she went to work and opened up the office. An hour later she was on her second cup of caffeinated coffee, which was something she never drank. It gave her an odd combination of wired and exhausted, and made her hands so jittery that her pencil shook.

In the late morning, Phil Trotter called her into his office. She was surprised to find Constance Fry, the chief financial officer of Latham Oil. Fry and Phil were sitting at a small table covered with work papers.

"Come in, come in," said Fry. "I thought you were going to be in this meeting in the first place." Fry glared at Phil, who didn't look at Lisa.

"We've checked your idea through our tax attorneys in Washington and the Netherlands," Fry continued. "They both say it's excellent. In fact, the Dutch lawyer wants to use it for another client."

Lisa tried to warm her hands by rubbing them behind her back. "I . . . I'm glad it worked out."

"Worked out?" Fry laughed. "I want you to look at a few of our other trouble spots. We'll start with our plans to go into the drilling accessory business. I'm sure your tax planning will be better than the assholes we have at the home office."

Phil didn't look nearly as happy as Lisa was beginning to feel.

"Now," continued Fry, "sit down and look over these projections with me."

Lisa sat next to Fry at the small conference table, and Fry pushed several pages in front of her. Phil stood behind them.

Fry went through the financials line by line, and Lisa concentrated hard. Several ideas occurred to her, yet she kept them to herself until she could do some research. If they merged with a company that had a huge loss-carry forward, that could shelter a lot of phantom income. Another idea would be to base their operations in a foreign country. The Kenyan government was aggressively going after new businesses and offering twenty-year tax exemptions.

When they came to an item marked "Cutting Tools," the words seized Lisa's attention. Cutting tools. Sharp instruments. Knives. She felt herself being pulled into a vision. Oh no. Not now.

She saw the knife. A young woman, face in darkness, tied to a bed. Lisa felt as though she were being pulled upward, and prayed she wouldn't start speaking in the monotone voice. . . .

A hand shook her shoulder.

"Ms. Cleary?"

She was jolted back into Phil's office.

"Are you all right?" asked Fry.

"I'm sorry. I've just gotten over some low-grade bug, and it's made me a little spacey. It isn't contagious."

Fry continued as though nothing had happened. Phil did not look pleased.

CHAPTER TWENTY-SEVEN

Julie ran into her apartment, hoping to catch the phone before it stopped ringing. Her jock friend Bill was supposed to call about snowboarding this weekend, and she'd missed him three times.

Panting, she grabbed the phone. "Don't hang up on me, you hunk."

"Certainly not," came the authoritative voice.

"Who is this?"

"Dr. Edmund Childs. Is this Julie Martin?"

Oh shit. She sat on the bed and tried to steady her breathing. "I'm sorry, Dr. Childs. I was expecting someone else."

"So I gathered. I've read your papers, young lady. They are quite impressive."

"Thank you."

"I have reviewed over sixty résumés and writing samples, and I am prepared to offer you the professorship here at NYU.

You will work harder than you ever imagined possible, and you will learn more than you suspected there is to know. I shall require a four-year commitment if I am to make that kind of investment in you. I do not want you to make this decision hastily, but I will need an answer within two weeks."

"I'm . . . that's . . . wonderful!"

Talon was sitting in the guest chair beside Rennick's desk, with a stack of papers on his lap. He handed the top few to Rennick and started talking.

"Our Ms. Cleary went to Colorado State and earned herself an A-minus average. Here's her DMV records. Only one ticket for unsafe passing two years ago. No arrest records or rap sheets. For the past ten years she's lived in three apartments around the West L.A. area. Her mother died about seventeen years ago. She hasn't seen her father or brother for a long time, even though both of them are local. Father's an ex-army guy on a pension who likes to bowl. He worked in Special Forces, then was forced into the radio corps because of a broken leg. Brother's an 'automotive consultant' who arranges the shelves at Pep Boys."

Talon leaned back and stretched his arms over his head. "For the last seven years, Lisa's been pushing paper around an accounting firm called Engle and Loren. Her credit is a Visa and a Mastercard, both paid timely. So to sum it up in one word: Boring."

Talon handed Rennick the next packet, a juvenile court file from Santa Rosa, California. It concerned Lance Cleary, Lisa's brother.

"This case file says it was sealed," said Rennick. "That means it isn't a public record. How did you get this?"

"I got ways. Don't ask."

As Rennick read through it, Talon narrated. "Seems Big Brother Lance had a lot of trouble with the law. They got him in Alabama for petty theft and vandalism of a grammar school when he was thirteen. Then he moved across the country—Virginia, Arkansas, New Mexico—graduating along the way to auto theft, desecrating a cemetery, assault, and robbery. Because he was a juvenile, they assigned a social worker."

Rennick noticed a handwritten note from a social worker who had spent several sessions with Lance. He read it out loud.

"'Ronald Cleary, subject's father, stated that he did not believe in social work, and was rude and belligerent throughout the interview.'"

Rennick flipped through the papers and came to the last page. It said that the court had agreed to drop the charges if Lance joined the army. The notation said that he did, and so the case was dismissed and the file sealed.

"So what does this do to your instinct that something's not right about her?" asked Rennick, laying down the file.

"I guess I'm okay with her. I got nothing to say otherwise."

"Well, it doesn't matter anyway. I'm going to insist that she stop working on this case. That thing in the alley was way too rough on her, and I feel guilty for having let her do it. My gut said it was a bad idea, and I let my curiosity outvote it."

"So I guess we'll have to struggle by with planet Earth methods from here on."

"Did you get a lab report on what she found?"

"Yeah. Blood type AB. Same as Tanya Mullins. Not common, but not that rare. DNA will say for sure if it's Mullins, but it's close enough for me. Unfortunately, no prints or blood of the killer."

"Speaking of the killer, I've worked up a profile."

"I hope it's more interesting than Lisa's."

"It is. Since all the victims were in their twenties, with shoulder-length blond hair, we're dealing with someone done wrong by a woman with those looks. Probably an authority figure who caught the killer in some kind of cookie jar. His obsession with those looks means these aren't chance encounters. He stalks the women and learns their habits. Which means he lives in the same area as the victims."

"Go on."

"The other key feature is 'meticulous.' That indicates someone intelligent, probably a college graduate. The fact that the bodies were displayed, instead of hidden, means we're dealing with a man who's proud of his work. It also means the killings will happen more frequently, since he'll want to show us how skilled he's getting."

"Great."

"All this points to someone with a lot of self-confidence. He's likely a loner, though he's capable of being sociable when he wants to. You know how common it is for neighbors and friends of serial killers to say they can't believe such a nice, polite guy could do something like that."

Talon stood up and looked out the window. He twirled the venetian blind cord in his fingers. "So far you're depressing the shit out of me. No pattern, a smart and aggressive killer, and a more frequent body count. Thanks, Professor."

"Any time. Since the victims were white, he's most likely a Caucasian. Statistically, he's in his twenties to forties, although I suspect he's in his thirties or early forties. If he was much younger than thirty, he wouldn't have the maturity to be this careful. If he was much older, he might not have the strength to overpower the women. The coroner's reports say none of the victims were drugged, and the autopsies all showed evidence of their being manhandled around the throat, wrists, and ankles.

With three of them, there was also damage to the solar plexus, probably from a punch. All this means a strong killer."

"Makes sense."

"The sexual assault on Myra Powell, the first victim, points to a killer who's not likely over thirty. Sex offenders usually stop after thirty unless they're child molesters. However, we're still not sure she was raped, and the fact that the other victims weren't sexually assaulted makes this part dicey."

Talon continued staring out the window as Rennick continued. "Now, the clocks. That's potentially the most interesting. I'm still not sure yet what it means, but it's important that the killings all happened between seven and eleven at night. Killers have circadian rhythms, so—"

"Circadian? That's a twenty-dollar word."

"*Circa* means 'around'; *dia* means 'day.' It refers to the earth's twenty-four-hour cycle and the way your body chemistry changes from morning to night. The reason you get jet lag—"

"All right, all right. I get it."

"Sorry. My professorial instincts kicked in. What I meant was that our killer may act differently at night. So when you find Lofton, we should interview him in the evening. If he's our guy, nighttime will make it easier to set off whatever drives him."

"As soon as I find his ass, it's yours. So far, everybody who knew this guy seems happy that he's missing. I did get a new lead this morning. He apparently worked in a San Francisco grocery. . . ."

San Francisco. Rennick had known there was something important about the San Francisco Parole Board the first time he heard it. What was it? Then he remembered the food from the Dancing Greek Restaurant that Julie had ordered the other night. There was something important about that, too.

The bulb flashed and he had it. Of course. Pete Demetris. His fellow resident at Yale Med School. He knew that Pete consulted for the San Francisco Parole Board.

Rennick interrupted Talon. "Danny, I got an idea." He pulled out the Yale alumni directory and dialed Pete's phone number in Marin County. While it was ringing, he cupped his hand over the mouthpiece and said, "You're not here, okay?"

Talon nodded.

Rennick got Demetris, and they exchanged small talk for several minutes.

"Pete, I need a favor."

"Sure."

"I'm helping the LAPD track a serial killer, and one of the suspects is a guy who went through the San Francisco Parole Board. The bureaucrats are seeing who can out-delay each other, and I wondered if you could cut through the red tape and let me know if the parole board has anything that could help."

"Are we on or off the record with this?"

"Totally off."

"Gotcha. That'll make it a lot quicker. Give me the info and I'll see what I can do."

Julie came running up to Rennick in front of the Law School and jumped into his arms.

"What?" He laughed.

"I got the offer!"

"From Childs?"

She nodded and kissed him on the lips.

As he spun her around, his excitement plunged into a deep crevice. She might be going to New York.

"Are you going to take it?"

"I don't know. I can't think straight because I'm still high from the call. C'mon. Buy me an iced tea."

They sat in Lu Valle Commons, nursing drinks in waxed paper cups.

"I didn't think I'd ever consider living on the East Coast again," said Julie. "Do you know what having Childs on my résumé could do?"

"It would be phenomenal. I'm really happy for you." He tried to sound like he meant it.

"So you think I should do it?"

"I can't make that decision for you."

"I know. I want your opinion."

"It's a tough one."

"That's a great insight."

"I can't say I'd be real excited about your moving away. On the other hand, I don't want to be selfish."

She placed her hand on top of his and stared directly into his eyes. "I sort of like the idea that you might be selfish."

Rennick knew what he was supposed to say. He heard Andrea Baylor's voice urging him to tell Julie he loved her. Instead, he looked out the door of the cafeteria. "It's not fair to you and your career for me to put that on you."

Her smile disappeared and she took back her hand. There was a long silence, and he felt like he'd just wounded a kitten. Ah shit. This was the part of relationships he could never get right.

Rennick took a sip of the iced tea, still looking out the door. The waxed cup seemed slippery in his hand.

When he stole a look at Julie, she was looking away and biting her lower lip. He reached for her hand, and she got up and left.

CHAPTER TWENTY-EIGHT

Talon sat in his living room, watching the Lakers lose to the Orlando Magic. He had the sound turned off and was listening to Mozart's D Minor Piano Concerto. It was a CD featuring the St. Paul Chamber Orchestra, with Chick Corea conducting. While it wasn't the best known recording of the work, it had a lot more passion than some of the famous ones. Talon unconsciously began to sway with the music, and it looked to him like the basketball players were also moving in rhythm.

He took a sip of his warm Dr Pepper, which was starting to go flat. Like the players, he felt like he was dancing to music he couldn't hear. All the hard evidence in this case was useless. Nothing to prove Heath was anything more than the first victim's boyfriend. At least the asshole was in jail. Talon needed to find Lofton, and hopefully Rennick's lead would short-circuit the morons up north. Yet without hard evidence to connect Lofton to the crime, even finding him would be a dead end.

The feeling that he was missing something taunted him. In the past, just being at the scene got his juices going, and theories came to him so fast that he could hardly scribble them down. Now they were coming like some mail-order record that didn't show up until after he'd forgotten ordering it.

He nudged up the music volume and rubbed his eyes. His body ached, and he felt a distantly familiar tingle. Unfortunately, it wasn't a brilliant insight. It was an urge for some cocaine to sharpen up his senses. Talon went into the kitchen and poured the Dr Pepper down the sink. He knew it was dangerous to even fantasize about drugs, and he willed his thoughts back to the pivotal day he'd decided to get away from them.

It had happened over fifteen years ago at a storefront on Sunset Boulevard, whose pasty white marquee announced $$ 4 UR BLOOD/PLASMA in huge red letters. Talon was a regular, since you could give plasma more often than blood, and he used the extra bucks for a little Colombian marching powder.

He was sitting next to a balding woman with long wisps of straw-colored hair and a man in his twenties who coughed so deeply that it vibrated the frayed couch. After he gave blood, Talon was in a hurry so he skipped the orange juice and cookies. That left him weak, and shortly after he staggered out, he was jumped by three men. He remembered the sickening sound of his face cracking, and the helpless feeling of lying on the pavement while they took his money and his dignity. Two bystanders laughed at him; just another street scum whose life didn't even register on their radar screen.

With a broken nose and no money for cocaine, Talon resolved to turn his life. He managed to walk to his girlfriend Elaine's house, who cleaned him up, got him into a Twelve

Step program, and filled out the LAPD application for him. Within two years, they were married and he was on the force.

Like a lot of ex-addicts, he needed something to obsess about. For Talon, it was a seventy-to-eighty-hour workweek. That made him an excellent cop, but cost him his marriage after a few years. A few months back, just after his fortieth birthday, the department shrink told him to cut his hours. She said that being a workaholic was his way to avoid dealing with his feelings. "Fuck that" was how Talon summed up those feelings, though he did drop to sixty-hour weeks for a while. Shortly afterwards, the hours crept back up.

The cocaine kept singing his name. He'd heard people in program say the urges never went away for good. He could handle them. He just needed some of that obsession for work. Wherever the fuck it was tonight.

Talon fell back into the lumpy chair and watched the Lakers go down in flames.

Rennick and Julie rode their bicycles along the Venice Beach path. The setting sun spread a triangular path across the water as it turned the sky shades of rose and amber behind wisps of pink cotton clouds. Or at least those were the colors that Julie told him were there.

The sun edged closer to the horizon, and the salty sea breeze chilled Rennick through his windbreaker. The beach was deserted except for a few Frisbee players and kite flyers. Rennick loved to watch the kites, since some of the best flyers in the world hung out on Venice Beach. They were experts with small, maneuverable "fighting kites" that they handled with the graceful finesse of fly fishermen. Mixed in were the casual flyers, who let the wind move their kites at will, preferring to harmonize with nature rather than try to control it.

The ride to Redondo Beach and back had been the quietest couple of hours Rennick could remember spending with Julie. In fact, so were the last few days. Ever since she was offered that New York job and he had failed to make a full commitment to their relationship, she'd been cool and unavailable. He didn't want to lose her, yet it was awfully soon for her to expect a long-term pledge. Not that he'd ever been able to give anyone a long-term pledge.

He looked over at Julie, who kept her eyes ahead and didn't seem to notice him. She looked striking with the sun behind her, silhouetting her figure against the horizon He kept staring hoping she'd turn. Finally, he gave up and shivered in the growing cold.

A couple of miles later, they left the bike path and wound up to San Vicente Boulevard. It was a wide street, with a grass parkway that was turning crisp and pale in the winter weather. Over the last several days, Andrea Baylor had been haunting his conscience, urging him to tell Julie his feelings. As they crossed Fourteenth Street in Santa Monica, Andrea won.

Rennick pulled his bike alongside hers and said, "I feel like we've been distant for the last few days."

She turned her head and stared at him like he'd just made an incredibly stupid remark. Then she looked back at the road without answering.

"Julie. I'm trying to talk. Give me some help."

"What do you want me to say?"

He didn't have any idea. "I guess I'm pretty confused about your job offer, too. I can't stand the idea of your going away. And I know you're looking for a commitment from me to stay, and I'm scared to make it."

He couldn't believe he'd gotten the words out. He could feel Andrea beaming. He also felt vulnerable and naked.

Julie slowed her pace, and he dropped back to stay beside her. Her face softened. "I loved the first half of that. And at least you're being honest with the second."

"I've just been so . . . stressed lately. I don't know if I can make a long-term decision while I'm under this much pressure."

"That's a pretty weak excuse, Michael. You love pressure. You create pressure if there isn't any."

"No I don't."

She laughed. He didn't.

"As bright as you are," Julie continued, "you don't see what's going on in front of you. You're teaching. You're seeing patients. You're writing books and articles. You're becoming obsessed with this criminal case."

"I'm managing to handle everything."

"At what price? Your personal life? Your relationships?"

"I have it under control."

"The fact that you think so is the problem. You really don't get it."

"I'm trying to be honest with you."

"You're not being honest with yourself."

"That's not true."

"Michael, this conversation is going nowhere." With that, Julie stood up off her seat and began pedaling faster, shifting into the higher gears. She pulled a hundred yards ahead within seconds.

Without thinking, he stood up and pumped the pedals hard. As he shifted into a higher gear, his competitive instincts kicked in, and his only focus was to catch her. He pedaled harder, but the gap between them wasn't narrowing. The gears on his bike screamed for the grease he'd never gotten around to putting on them.

As the race continued into Brentwood, they zoomed up San Vicente Boulevard, passing joggers, bikers, and even some of the cars. He saw Julie waiting for a red light where Barrington Avenue crosses San Vicente, and he knew this was his chance. With aching legs and sweat stinging his eyes, he began to weave recklessly between cars. Rennick was within ten yards of her when the light changed and she sprinted off.

Even though she was lighter and faster than he was, he knew that, about three blocks ahead, Wilshire Boulevard took a downhill dip near the veterans' hospital. While light riders do better on the uphill, heavy riders have an advantage on the downhill.

As he turned onto Wilshire and began to gain speed, he looked down at the chain to see what gear he was in. He was already in the highest gear, so he stood up on the pedals and pushed hard. When he looked back up at the road, he saw that while he had his eyes on the gears, a car with its hazard lights flashing had pulled over and stopped in the No Stopping zone. The driver's door was opening directly in front of him.

Rennick's reflexes were good, but he didn't have a chance. He was going too fast to brake without flying over the handlebars, so he swerved to the far right, hoping to miss the car and run onto the shoulder.

The bike skidded onto its side and he slid for an interminable distance. His cheek was inches from the pavement, and he could feel the heat of the road surface rushing by. The sliding motion twisted his knee with a loud snap just before he slammed into the car's rear bumper. Rennick shook his head in disbelief that this was happening to him.

His mind shut out the pain until he came to a halt. Then his senses returned with a vengeance, and his leg throbbed with such intensity that he yelled out loud. The people from the car rushed toward him.

"I'm calling an ambulance," came a man's voice. Rennick lay there feebly, realizing he was going to be crippled for a while. The pain and humiliation were now turning into anger. He kept replaying the last few seconds. If he hadn't tried to race Julie. If he had looked up sooner. If he had talked about his feelings while they were sitting on a couch.

Behind him, he heard a bicycle coming to a halt and a kick-stand squeaking down. Footsteps approached and then, like an angel materializing, Julie was standing over him. When she took off her helmet, her chestnut hair fell from under it, loosely framing her face. She got down next to him, looking very concerned.

"I'll get my car and come back for you," she said. She took his hand and stroked it gently. Her touch was soft and soothing against the pain.

"Meet me at UCLA Emergency," he said. "These folks called an ambulance."

As if on cue, he heard a siren in the distance.

Later that evening, Rennick hobbled back into his apartment on a single crutch. He had never used a crutch before, and he hated the clumsiness. His knee alternated between sharp and dull pains, as if playing some symphony of torture.

He awkwardly lowered himself onto the bed. As instructed in the emergency room, Julie rolled up a sleeping bag and put it under his knee. Then she rustled in the freezer for frozen peas, which the doctor had suggested because the bag could be molded to fit his kneecap.

He was lucky. It was only a sprain, although it was a helluva sprain. While painful and ugly, he knew that sprains weren't long term. Still, he was going to be sore for a few weeks, and the first couple of days were going to be the worst. He thought about helplessness being the most depressing of human emotions, and that cheery thought sent him into an even deeper funk as Julie arrived with the Jolly Green Giant. At least he didn't have to talk about their relationship for a while.

Rennick sank back into the bed and closed his eyes. If he lay very still there was a minimum of pain. The warm tingle of dead weight flowed over him, and within a few minutes he had fallen into a heavy sleep.

CHAPTER TWENTY-NINE

On the evening of the accident, the doctors had told Rennick to stay in bed for a minimum of three days. The next morning, he limped into his office with great difficulty. He used only a cane, because he found the crutch cumbersome, which had seemed like an excellent decision when he left home. Now that his knee was throbbing like a tympany drum, he was having second thoughts.

Bobbi stood up as he walked in.

"The injured soldier returns from battle," she said with a salute.

"And a grand battle it was."

"You never did tell me why you were racing down Wilshire Boulevard."

"It's not important."

"C'mon. Give."

He mumbled the answer. "I was trying to set the land speed record, and I couldn't catch Julie."

"Oh. I see why you didn't tell me." She pointed to his cane. "You joining the Hell's Angels?"

Rennick held up the polished ebony cane that Julie had brought him. The handle was a fake-ivory skull with eyes of iridescent rhinestones.

"Actually, I like to think it's a symbol of the Grateful Dead. The truth is that Julie thought it looked like a shrunken head and was therefore appropriate for a psychiatrist."

"I knew that girl had class," said Bobbi. "Do you need anything? Ice? Pillow for your knee? I already called to get you a handicapped parking pass."

"Could you fill the ice bag in my briefcase? I ate last night's ice pack."

"Excuse me?"

"Never mind. What's on deck today?"

"The dean's office called twice. You missed the last ethics committee meeting, and he expects you there today sharply at noon. He said the word *sharply* three times."

"Sharply. Got it."

"Mail's on your desk. Your eleven-o'clock's already down in the faculty lounge."

Rennick had forgotten that he temporarily had to see patients in the faculty lounge. "How long before they're through painting the office?"

"University Maintenance says two days. That means about six weeks."

"Six weeks? A quickie."

"By the way," Bobbi continued, "I had a bitch of a time getting the key to the faculty lounge. It seems they don't like to open it until noon unless you're related to the chancellor."

"Or having an affair with him."

"That'd probably work. Though it's not for everyone. At least since he turned eighty-two and got the shakes."

"Gee, Bobbi, I ask you to do one little thing for me . . ."

He fell into his chair, to rest a couple of minutes before making the trek down the hall. The phone buzzed.

"It's Pete Demetris," Bobbi yelled through the door.

Rennick quickly grabbed the phone.

"I got some information on this guy Lofton," said Pete. "You didn't hear it from me, okay?"

"Understood."

"Lofton is a serious sicko. And a mean one at that. There was a real debate whether he should have been paroled. He squeaked by on a three-to-two vote. What swung it is that he agreed to get MPA injections."

Rennick knew that MPA stood for medroxyprogesterone acetate, a drug that reduced testosterone levels—almost like a chemical castration. That radically reduced sex drive, although some men still committed sexual offenses while taking it. A few offenders volunteered for it, or for similar drugs like DP or CPA, because they thought it made parole boards more lenient. The ploy had obviously worked for Lofton.

Rennick also knew that these chemicals could make people look normal on the outside while things were rough underneath. The drug could also explain why Lofton went from a disorganized killer to an organized one—if it reduced his animal impulses, he might be able to keep them under intellectual control.

"Pete, you're a pal. I owe you one."

Rennick hung up and turned over the conversation in his mind. He remembered that only the first girl had been raped, and he wondered if this could be why. Maybe Lofton was off the drug for a while, got scared after the rape, and went back on. His injection records might show the dates, and if they matched, the information could be valuable. That is, if anyone could find either him or his records.

Wait. His medical records. Of course. Rennick quickly called Talon.

"I got this off the record, so we have to protect my friend."

"Got it."

"I found out that Lofton is taking MPA. Check the State Pharmaceutical Board. If he's taking it, we can trace him through the records."

"He's probably using a different name."

"If you find the last date he took it under his real name, you could look up the people who started taking it right after. There won't be that many. Since it keeps you from getting an erection, MPA's not exactly popular with the druggie set."

After an hour of snaking through bureaucratic switchboards, Talon learned that Jerome Tibbit had the information on MPA prescriptions issued in California. He finally got Tibbit on the phone.

"We'll require a court order," came a nasal voice on the other end of the phone.

"Already issued. It'll be on your desk by tomorrow. How long will this take?"

"From the time we actually have the court order in hand . . . certified, of course . . . we could probably rush it through in about . . . six weeks."

"Six weeks! I could have four more dead bodies by then!"

"There's no need to raise your voice, sir, or I will terminate this conversation."

Talon steeled himself. He'd learned years ago that throttling these rubber-stamp assholes only slowed down the process. "Sorry if I yelled, Mr. Tibbit. It's just that we've got a serial killer loose down here, and this could help us identify him."

"I suppose I could expedite this to maybe four weeks or so."

"Please, Mr. Tibbit. Isn't there a computer or something where you just push a button?"

Tibbit snickered about an octave higher than his speaking voice. "Sir, there are sixteen regions in this state, and each one is organized around a center that has its own discrete system. Thus the material must be sorted manually. You also indicated that you wanted multiple years, and records over two years old are stored on tape backup in Stockton. They must be retrieved, shipped to Sacramento, collated, coordinated with the current data . . ."

Talon wrapped the phone cord tightly around his hand. His fingers began to blanch from the pressure as he concentrated on controlling his voice. "Thank you for your time."

He hung up the phone and dialed back the State Pharmaceutical Board.

"Who is Jerome Tibbit's supervisor?"

Rennick hung a hand-written Do Not Disturb sign on the knob of the faculty lounge before going inside. The room had two khaki-colored leather couches, and a dinette with four navy plaid chairs. The rest of the decor consisted of a microwave, a refrigerator from which mystery smells emanated, and a couple of ceramic lamps thrown in for a homey touch.

Lisa was sitting on one of the dinette chairs. She stood up as he walked in.

"What happened to your leg?" she asked.

"I had a bike accident."

"Are you okay?"

"I'm sore as hell, but I'll be fine."

The refrigerator's hum was the only sound in the room.

He told her to lie down on the couch, take a few breaths, and relax. Rennick elevated his leg with another chair, then discreetly took out the ice pack and put it on his knee.

They spent several minutes reviewing the last session.

"How have you felt since the incident in the alley?" he asked.

"Much better. I've come up with some innovative ideas at work, and my boss loves them. I'm sleeping better, and I'm lifting heavier weights at the gym. Strange as it sounds, I think these intense experiences are making me stronger."

"That's a good sign. On the other hand, they've been pretty rough on you."

"Only for a little while. Then things get a lot better."

Rennick had an idea. "Have you ever considered consciously calling up these visions?"

"You mean on purpose?"

"Yes."

"No."

"This is only a suggestion, and if it doesn't feel right, don't do it." He explained about the Ganzfeld experiment that Joseph had described, where people tried to receive psychic information by blocking sensory input with white noise and Ping-Pong ball halves over their eyes. "If you learn how to make these visions appear on command, maybe you could grow to make them disappear the same way. Also, you could do it at home in a controlled environment, without an external stimulus like the evidence that could trigger such an intense experience."

"Ping-Pong balls?"

He chuckled. "I know. It sounds silly. But it might help."

"I'll think about it."

"Okay. Did you have any more visions of horses?"

"Why do you keep bringing that up?"

"Because you've had so many episodes involving horses. They're connected to something important. And the fact that you're getting defensive is an indication of that. Did you have any more?"

"Well . . . yes."

"What?"

"I had this dream about a horse lying on me. It was on its side and I was underneath. He was so heavy that he was crushing me and I couldn't breathe. Like the other dreams, I was, like, melting into the horse. I was getting covered with his mushy, gooey innards. It was really sickening."

"Lisa, do you remember anything from your childhood like this?"

"No. I don't like horses."

"You said you lived on a farm that had horses. Did a horse ever hurt you?"

"Not that I remember. Doctor, I want to tell you about something that happened when I was fifteen. I've never told anyone about it."

"What about the horses?"

"This is more important."

"You're trying to change the subject."

"I know. This is really important."

He looked up and saw that she had folded her arms across her chest and tensed her body. Rennick knew he had to unpeel the layers around the horse incident slowly, so he decided to back off for now.

"Okay," he said. "Tell me about it."

The refrigerator hummed patiently in the silence that followed, gurgling periodically.

"I . . . I . . . we were living in Santa Rosa, California. It started with a dream, which woke me up in the middle of the night. I found myself sitting up in bed, panting to catch my breath. I was sweating so much that the sheets were soaked. I couldn't sleep for the rest of the night, because I couldn't get the image out of my head."

She stopped talking. The refrigerator coughed, as if the motor were about to die.

"What did you see?"

She didn't answer for a few moments. "I saw a funeral. A gray metal casket being put into the ground. The lowering device creaked as one of the funeral directors turned a crank. There was a mound of dirt to the side, with pieces of AstroTurf over it. I saw a minister reading from a Bible that he held in one hand. People were crying. No one paid any attention to me. When I tried to ask what was going on, I had no voice. Like I was a mute."

Now tears were streaking across her cheek, and Rennick was pleased that she was able to let out her emotions. "Go on," he said gently.

"At first I thought it might be Sarah, the redheaded girl with the horse. Maybe she was going to die from her injuries. But it was an adult coffin. After the thing with Sarah, I felt like I had to warn somebody that they were in danger. Only I didn't know who."

"Was it a recurring dream?"

Lisa described how the dream started out weekly, then came almost every night. She closed her eyes, and her voice went into the "trance monotone" she had used when touching the evidence.

"I came home from school one day and my father's car was there. That was strange, because he never got home before six-thirty. I went into the living room and saw him sitting on the couch with my brother. I knew that something horrible had happened."

Lisa's body was relaxed and her voice was controlled, virtually emotionless.

"What happened next?"

"They looked up at me. My brother had been crying and his eyes were red. My father, who never showed any feelings, had tears on his face.

"Dad was in the military, and he was a fanatic about keeping in shape. He had a tightly muscled build, like a swimmer, and you always felt his strength. That day he was ashen. He stood up shakily and had to use the arm of the couch for support."

"How did you feel about seeing him like that?"

"It was sad. Even though I hated the way he intimidated me, it was scary to feel like my pillar of strength was gone."

"What did he say to you?"

"I remember how he choked on the words. 'Lisa, I have some very bad news. This morning, Mom had a hemorrhage and was taken to the emergency hospital.'"

"The words stung me. And I knew there was more: 'By the time the ambulance got her to the hospital, it was too late. She's passed away.' His jaw quivered as he tried to keep from crying. He once told me how he delivered news to widows about their husbands, and I knew he was trying to put on that face. It wasn't working, but I let him think he was fooling me."

"What did you do?"

Lisa described how she ran into her parents' room and saw the bloody bed and plastic packets that the medics had left be-

hind. She then ran to the bathroom and threw up before returning to her room.

"I had a rocking chair that I got for my fifth birthday. It had
my name painted on a little banner that was carried by pink
dancing bears. I sat on the arms of it, hoping it wouldn't break.
I rocked for hours, creaking on the tiny little chair, holding
Kitty. Kitty was a little gray stuffed cat with one eye missing.
I used to sleep with her when I was three or four. She was
lumpy and matted from years of hugging, and she smelled like
my childhood. She also made a wonderful tear sponge."

Rennick noted that, even though Lisa was describing the
most cataclysmic episode of her life, her voice had stayed in the
monotone and her body was relaxed.

"What happened next?"

"Late in the afternoon, when it was getting dark, I realized
Dad wasn't coming into my room, even though I'd left the
door open. I tiptoed out into the hall to see where he was. No
one had turned on any lights, so I was moving through the
shadows. I checked the kitchen and the den, and finally I
peeked into the living room.

"My brother Lance was gone, and Dad was sitting on the
couch alone. I stood there and watched him. He was sitting
still and staring into space. With his shoulders rounded forward. I walked up to him and tried to talk. He wouldn't answer me. He just kept staring, almost without blinking. After
a few minutes, I tiptoed back to bed and cried myself to sleep."

Lisa told Rennick about the funeral, which was on a bright
and sunny day in an old cemetery whose granite headstones
looked like a neighborhood of haunted houses. The service was
in a small chapel with peeling paint. Only a handful of people
showed up, and even the tiny room looked empty.

"Lance didn't come to the funeral at all. We didn't know where he was that whole day."

"Did you ever ask Lance where he went?"

"Yes. He told me it was none of my business."

"Did your father ask him?"

"I don't know. They didn't fight about it. It seemed like Dad had no fight in him."

"What happened next?"

"When we got to the graveside, it was almost identical to my dreams. There was a mound of dirt covered with AstroTurf, and the coffin was just like the one I had seen. The strangest part was this surreal feeling that I had already done this. It was comforting in an eerie sort of way."

Rennick had felt the emotion return to Lisa's voice during the last few moments. He looked up and saw that she was again tense, and had crossed her arms across her chest.

"I stood next to my dad during the service," she said gruffly. "He didn't look at me once. Not once. I tried to hold his hand. It was cold and limp and he wouldn't take mine. I finally quit trying, because it was such a horrible rejection."

Rennick controlled his voice, hoping to guide her anger down gently. "In a perfect world, none of us would ever do anything to hurt anybody else. Your father was in pain. I'm not defending him, because his neglect caused you horrible anguish. But now that you're an adult, you could have another way to look at it."

Lisa was quiet for a few moments, and Rennick left her alone with her thoughts. Then he continued. "Have you talked to him about this since you grew up?"

"No." The reply was immediate and hostile.

"I think you might get something out of doing it. Even if you don't reconcile, you'll learn a lot about yourself from how you react to meeting him. Look at the strong emotions we've stirred up just by considering it."

Lisa shot back angrily, "He doesn't deserve any of my time or attention. And besides, I haven't had any contact with him for over fifteen years. I don't even know where he lives. Or if he's alive."

"You wouldn't be doing this for him. You'd be doing it for you."

Lisa turned her face to the back of the couch and curled up. She finally spoke so softly that Rennick could barely hear.

"No."

CHAPTER THIRTY

Talon felt like someone was standing on his eyeballs with spiked heels. He picked up the phone and jabbed in the numbers so hard that it moved the base across his desk.

"State Pharmaceutical Board."

"Lemme have Henry Norton." His tongue barely cooperated in forming the words.

"Just a moment."

While Talon was on hold, his ear was blasted with a talk radio show. ". . . vagrants sleeping on the park benches. Filthy, dirty, animals. We should ship 'em off to Berkeley or one of them other People's Republic cities. . . ."

"Norton."

"Mr. Norton? Detective Talon of the LAPD."

"Hello, Detective. Aren't you the one who wanted the MPA records?"

"Yessir. We got a real nervous situation down here, and this material might make a big difference. I was wondering if there's any way you could speed it up."

"Hold on a moment."

The talk station came back on. ". . . street cleaner's brushes scratched the paint right off of the side of my new car. Okay, so I wasn't supposed to park there, but for the love of Pete . . ."

"Tibbit," came a higher-pitched voice.

Shit, thought Talon. This was the asshole who told him it would take four or five weeks. He felt his neck muscles tighten and the spiked heels on his eyeballs went into a tap dance.

"Mr. Tibbit, this is Detective Talon. Mr. Norton transferred me over. Do you have that material on MPA yet?"

The refrigerator temperature of Tibbit's voice moved toward Freezer. "Oh yes. I remember you. You yelled at me."

"I'm sorry about that. I really need this information. . . ."

"I think I may have received the raw data, but you must wait your turn in line. It will be another week or two before I can assemble it. We're quite busy."

"I'll take the raw data. Just fax it down."

Tibbit laughed through his nose. "That's dozens of pages, with very confidential information mixed in. I couldn't even consider letting it out."

Talon slammed down the phone and stared at it.

A few minutes later, he had an idea. He called his pal Squeaky in the Sacramento police department.

"You got a friend in Vice?" asked Talon.

"Sure," answered Squeaky.

"I need a favor, and I'll be up this afternoon. If this works, I'll owe you big time."

Talon came out of the Sacramento airport terminal and shaded his eyes against the bright sun. Squeaky got out of a blue

Crown Victoria and waved at Talon. A stunning blonde got out of the passenger side of Squeaky's car, which nearly caused a cabdriver to hit an old lady in the crosswalk.

The blonde looked like she was almost five foot ten and was wearing a tight dress that barely restrained her topside. As Talon approached, he saw she had a few facial scars under the heavy makeup, and that her dress was wrinkled and stained around the seams. Even so, the overall effect would work just fine.

"Danny, meet Lola."

"Hi," she purred.

"Pleasure."

Talon explained the plan as they drove to the records building. She laughed out loud.

"What do I owe you for this?" Talon asked Lola.

"Nothin'," answered Squeaky. "Lola got a free pass for doing you this little service."

Squeaky stayed in the car, while Talon and Lola went inside the Pharmaceutical Records Building. At the front desk was a young man with stringy hair and a tiny nose.

"Does a Jerome Tibbit work here?" asked Talon.

The man looked up and his eyes widened as he stared at Lola, who was touching the tip of her tongue to the side of her mouth.

"Yes," he answered without looking at Talon.

Talon leaned in and whispered, "It's his birthday in a few days. This lady is, well, his present. And she's a surprise."

"You sure this is for . . . Mr. Tibbit?!" Talon thought the man was on the verge of dribbling saliva out of the corner of his mouth.

Talon fished a laundry receipt out of his pocket and pretended to read it. "It says Jerome Tibbit. He work here?"

"Yeah."

"Can you find an excuse to get everybody into a room, then call in Mr. Tibbit? I promise he'll never forget this birthday." Talon winked, although the young man still wasn't looking at him.

"I guess." He began making calls.

About fifteen minutes later, most of the staff had gathered in a conference room, and the receptionist called Tibbit.

"Mr. Tibbit, Dr. Weeks is here from the Surgeon General's Office. Yes, *the* Dr. Weeks. Mr. Lawrence and Mr. Melville are with him in the conference room, and they asked you to come in right away."

"Where's Mr. Tibbit coming from?" asked Talon.

The young man led him to a door and pointed toward Tibbit, who was standing up at his desk and straightening his narrow tie. He was a thin, gawky man who had pimples despite being in his midthirties.

Talon made a mental note of the desk location, then turned to the receptionist. "Do you think you could take Lola to the conference room and tell everyone to yell 'Surprise' when Tibbit gets there?"

Lola sidled up next to the young man and took hold of his arm.

"Uh, sure." Talon thought he could see the man's heart beating in his neck.

"I'll need someone to unzip me," she said to the young man as they walked away.

As soon as they disappeared, Talon headed for Tibbit's desk. From the looks of this geek, he couldn't depend on his being gone very long.

The desk was neat and clean, and unfortunately locked by the fucking anal compulsive. He probably locked the damn thing when he went to piss. Talon found a letter opener on another desk and wedged it into the locked drawer. It broke off. He then tried a pair of scissors and began to work it loose.

From the other room, he heard a muffled chorus of "Surprise!"

The metal drawer was starting to bend, and he finally pried it open with brute force. Inside were dozens of hanging folders, all neatly labeled and color-coded. None said "MPA."

In the distance, he heard a distinct ". . . not my birthday!" Oh shit. This was the kind of guy who raised his hand at the end of class and said "You forgot to assign us any homework."

He heard the sound of footsteps coming down a hall. Talon quickly grabbed as many papers as he could stuff into his coat, then pushed the drawer shut and started away from the desk. A door in front of him flung open, and a very red Tibbit charged through. Tibbit made eye contact with Talon, then looked at his desk. His mouth opened and he turned redder.

Talon didn't give Tibbit time to react. He ran outside and got into Squeaky's car, yelling at him to step on it. Lola was already in the car, having left as soon as Tibbit caught on.

When they were safely on the road, Talon took out two twenties and handed them to Lola.

"You don't have to do that, Detective. I didn't do very much."

"You were great."

She shot a quick look at Squeaky, then took the bills. "I could give you a little something extra if your friend wants to look the other way."

"That's okay, Lola. Just take the night off."

On the plane, Talon found the MPA documents in the material he'd taken. It was a blurry fax of a fax, and totaled sixteen pages of single-spaced typing. The records listed the names randomly, with their addresses, phone, prescription history, and dates.

Talon quickly located the records of Marvin Lofton, with the out-of-date San Francisco address. As expected, Lofton dropped off the list right around the time he disappeared. So Talon looked for names of people who started right after that date.

By the time he landed, he had gotten through about a third of the shit. His eyes were watering from the slick fax paper and the glare of overhead reading lights. So far he'd marked three possibles, putting a star next to the ones who lived in L.A.

At a stoplight on the way home, he found another record for Lofton. Why was there a duplicate? He looked closer. It wasn't Lofton. It was a Marvin Logan.

Talon instinctively knew it was him. He flipped back to the Lofton records and saw that Logan started taking MPA right after Lofton stopped. He lived in Brentwood, a fancy part of L.A. It fit with the "rich boy gone bad."

Talon drove directly to Logan's condo, which was located in a six-story, plush building on McClellan. Over the intercom, Logan nervously reacted to the arrival of a cop. Talon took an elevator with gold-flecked mirrors up to Logan's sixth-floor unit.

When Logan opened the door, Talon saw a slim, perfectly groomed man wearing an expensive burgundy velour jump-suit. Logan had graying hair, a neatly trimmed mustache, and clear braces that had almost closed the gaps between his teeth. Still, Talon recognized him immediately.

"Mr. Logan?"

"Yes?"

"Were you formerly known as Marvin Lofton?"

Logan's pasty skin drained of its minimal color. "Why are you asking me that?"

"I have a few questions about your recent activities."

"I've done nothing wrong. I've worked very hard to lead a model life."

"Then you were known as Marvin Lofton?"

"I want a lawyer before we talk any more."

After her shower, Lisa propped one foot on the tub and applied Oil of Essence to her leg in long, deep strokes.

Ever since Rennick had mentioned the idea, she'd been debating whether to bring on these visions intentionally. Going through therapy and not listening to the doctor seemed like a stupid thing to do. Not to mention that he might stop seeing her if she ignored him. This Dr. Rennick was such a charismatic man, and she knew that her finding him attractive was one of the reasons he could help her. But lie down with Ping-Pong balls over her eyes?

She put her other leg on the tub and massaged in the oil. Lisa realized she was afraid to put herself into a psychic state intentionally. Who knows what might fly out if she opened that cage? This didn't seem like a good idea at all. Rennick was really pushing her to the edge in a lot of ways. All this talk about her father. She supposed psychiatrists always went into family history, yet that didn't mean that contacting her father was a good idea. He wasn't worth any of her time and attention.

She began oiling her shoulders and arms. She had gone to Rennick for help with her visions, not her family. It'd be enough if she did the Ping-Pong ball thing. Maybe she would do that.

Maybe.

*　　*　　*

Marvin Logan stood at the men's room sink in the law offices of Sandy Baris. After placing his tie over his shoulder and rolling up the monogrammed sleeves of his custom shirt, he rubbed his palms with Purell liquid hand cleanser from the small bottle he always carried and washed each hand past the wrist. Finally, he used a paper towel to turn off the faucet, then to open the men's room door. Logan knew that only forty-one percent of men wash their hands after using the lavatory, and so the door handle was disgustingly germ-laden.

He approached the receptionist seated behind the curved blond-wood-and-chrome counter.

"Is Duke ready yet?" he asked.

"Mr. Duke will be with you shortly."

Logan grunted. He'd already been kept waiting eleven minutes. He tried to distract himself with the decor: a painting of abstract slashes that was taller than he was, a thick glass coffee table, and a rug that looked like a lot of cotton balls stuck together. He figured Baris spent at least a hundred thousand decorating his offices. No big surprise, at the three hundred dollars per hour Duke had quoted him. He'd wanted Baris to handle his situation personally but gotten some song and dance about Baris's being in a lengthy trial. The woman who answered the phone had said this guy Duke was first class. He'd better be, at these prices.

The receptionist brought him a Coke. Logan took a napkin and wiped off the top of the can. Sure enough, it was filthy. About a quarter of the time they were. He poured the Coke into a glass, which at least looked clean, and thought about how his cleanliness was so far from the adventures of his youth.

Logan had grown up in a wealthy San Francisco family, with everything in his life being measured and planned. All that ritual seemed to come easy to his sister, yet he could never get the hang of it. He'd had to wear a uniform to the Thurston School, and it itched and choked his neck. Often he ditched school to hang out with some of the locals at a burger joint in North Beach. When his truancy caught up with him, he was expelled from Thurston—like he really cared—which produced stern lectures from his father and prayers from his sister. When he was fifteen, and after two more schools had booted him, his parents shipped him off to a boarding school in Arizona. Rousted out of bed early for calisthenics, and a birch paddle for discipline. Yet he finally met guys he could relate to. Guys with desires like his. Guys who could understand his Special Games.

The Special Games started when he was twelve. One of the older boys in the neighborhood told him about Edna, a sixteen-year-old girl who lived a few blocks away. She liked to shower at night with the curtains open, and the best way to look in was to hide behind a large air-conditioning condenser just outside her window.

So night after night, Marvin sat alone, watching Edna soap herself up in the shower. He remembered her dark nipples growing erect when she first got into the water; the exquisite view of her moist pubic hair when she turned at just the right angle. Sometimes she even rubbed herself there a lot longer than it could possibly take to get clean. Marvin couldn't have cared less about the whirr and clanging of the air conditioner not more than six inches from his ear. Nor did he care about the grime and toxic smells it had to be throwing directly into his face. Quite the contrary, he had grown to feel a kinship with the machine. Each doing their dirty work alone and unseen; a partnership in which the noises of the air conditioner masked his own.

He looked at his watch again. Three thirteen. Whoever this

Duke was, he was a rude sonofabitch. Logan sat back on the couch and remembered how he had continued his Special Games in college. At San Francisco State, he started taking pictures through a sorority bathroom window. He kept them hidden in a locked trunk at the foot of his bed and took them out when he needed to handle himself. Which was six or seven times a day by the second semester of his freshman year.

None of the sorority girls could compare to Edna, although he found some close seconds. One girl he nicknamed Blondie always kissed another girl when they thought no one was looking. One night they locked the bathroom door and started undressing each other. Logan was too excited to even take pictures. Just as they were fondling each other's breasts, he felt a strong arm on his shoulder pull him upright. He almost came on that fucking security guard.

Logan looked at his watch and took another sip of the Coke. And of course there was that "incident" four years ago, where things got out of hand. He hadn't intended to cut that woman's throat. He figured he'd just tie her up and look at her while he did things to himself. She looked so delicious tied up on the bed. Her legs spread wide, for viewing at any angle he chose. So maybe he decided to stick it inside her once or twice. Adults do those things. He just wanted to have his fun and move on. It would have all been so perfect if she'd just shut up.

But the bitch kept threatening him. And screaming. Shrill, loud shrieks. He finally taped her mouth, then worried that someone might have already heard her. And they might come into the bedroom. He couldn't let that happen. The next part got rather surreal. It was like someone else took over his body and picked up the knife. He couldn't let her tell.

He'd been such an amateur, thought Lofton. They'd found him almost immediately, and he had no choice but to fool them into thinking he was crazy, so they wouldn't fry him. It worked perfectly. They just locked him up and labeled him a sex addict, plus some other horrible words. A convenient compartment in which to put little Marvin. He was shuffled from one mental institution to another, until they put him on MPA. The drug stopped the urges, but it left him limp and without passion. At least until a day or so before he got his weekly shots.

"Mr. Duke can see you now," said the receptionist. Logan looked at his watch. Three sixteen. Next time he'd call first, to see if this guy's running late.

Duke had a small office, jammed with papers and haphazardly stacked files. Logan was surprised to see a kid who looked like he was in his twenties, with thick brown hair and oval glasses. Three hundred dollars an hour for this? At least the guy was sharply dressed in a gray suit and cognac tie.

"How long have you been doing this?" asked Logan.

"I'm older than I look," said Duke. "I'm thirty-three and I've been here almost nine years." Duke sniffled and blew his nose. From his eyes, he looked like he had a cold. Logan was annoyed that they had shaken hands. He took out a foil packet of Vinox—an antibacterial towelette used by emergency medical personnel—and wiped his hands.

"This could be a serious matter," said Logan.

"I'm very experienced, Mr. Logan. I just did an appeal that got someone off death row. Tell me what happened."

Logan hesitated. "Well, the police came to see me and I have no idea why."

"I do. I called a contact of mine in the Hollywood Division. Detective Daniel Talon came to see you, and they think you might be involved in these serial killings of young women."

"What! That's ridiculous."

"I'm glad to hear that. Why do you think they came to you?"

Logan looked over at a framed photo of Duke on a ski slope. "I had some problems in the past. From what I read about these killings, there could be some similarities."

"So they're going to be snooping around. Should we have any concerns over what they might find?"

Logan stood up and slapped Duke's desk, sending a few papers scurrrying for cover. "That's insulting!"

Duke stayed seated and wiped his nose with a Kleenex. "Cut the melodrama, Mr. Logan. It was a question, not an accusation. And I'm only asking because you can't afford to have me surprised. Now sit down and talk to me."

CHAPTER THIRTY-ONE

Rennick and Julie turned off Interstate 10 onto Alabama Avenue, then onto Highway 38, a two-lane road that would take them up to Big Bear. Big Bear is a tiny community nestled in the pines of the San Bernardino Mountains. It consists mostly of cabins built around a small man-made lake, which is frozen in the winter and dotted with boats in the summer.

For the last five years, Rennick had rented the same cottage for the same December weekend. He had brought a different woman there each year, and they had all succumbed to its charm. Julie was obviously more than just another conquest, and he was looking forward to sharing it with her for the first time; perhaps taking her to the cabin would represent a closure of his womanizing days. He also hoped this weekend would be the first time he made love to her since Andrea died, and he worried whether he could hold up his end of the bargain.

As they went higher into the mountains, his ears popped

and patches of snow appeared on the ground. A chill wriggled its way into the car. Julie turned the heater on High and gently massaged the back of his neck. He felt the stress of his workload fade, winding out of sight like the road behind them.

"I thought this weekend should be like going to Fantasyland," said Julie. "So let's not talk about anything stressful."

"You have no idea how happy I am to hear that."

"And to that end . . ."

"Yes?"

". . . I've got a little surprise for you," she said playfully.

"Oh yeah? What?"

"It's a new outfit."

"Tell."

"I slipped over to a place on Highland called Slinky Lingerie." She began rubbing his neck in a sensual, circular motion. "I bought a sheer nighty. Very short. The front is held together by some tie strings that I thought you'd like undoing."

Rennick felt himself getting excited.

"What was Slinky Lingerie like?"

"To be honest, most of the customers were these frumpy, older women. Some of the straightest-looking ladies you've ever seen: gray hair, sensible shoes. Amazing."

"What else did they have there?"

"I'm sorry to say I passed on the edible panties and nippleless bras. But get this. There were these little U-shaped metal things in a fishbowl by the cash register. I asked what they were, and guess what the girl said?"

"What?"

"Tit clips."

*　　*　　*

The cabin was a rough-redwood A-frame built into a small clearing in the pine trees and set back so that it was invisible from the road. They pulled into the driveway just as daylight was fading. The powdery snow gently reflected the last glimmers of sun, and a fawn's tiny tracks were the only blemish in the soft white blanket.

Rennick got out and took a deep breath of the chilly, pine-scented air. They were still wearing the light clothes of the seventy-five degree day they'd left behind in Los Angles, so he quickly limped to the house while Julie carried the bags. The cabin was furnished rustically and had a massive stone fireplace in the living room, next to a picture window overlooking a meadow. Beside the fireplace was a built-in bookcase, stocked with paperbacks and board games.

He made two cups of hot chocolate, started a fire, and sat on the couch to watch the blaze grow. It was now dark outside, and he hadn't turned on any lights in the living room. The fire crackled and hissed as its flames stretched to the top of the fireplace, casting long shadows across the amber glow of the room. He decided to unwind there for a few minutes before looking for Julie, so he propped his feet up on the coffee table and rested his recovering knee. The smell of burning wood mixed with the warm aroma of hot chocolate.

Rennick wasn't sure how long she had been there before he turned to look. In fact, he wasn't even sure why he turned, as she had materialized beside him silently. Maybe it was her perfume, an erotic, flowery fragrance. Or maybe it was just his sense of her presence nearby.

Julie was standing at the end of the couch in the new lingerie, a sheer black two-piece that hid little of her body. His imagination had underestimated its sexiness. The top was tied together loosely in the middle, and his mind was already untying the strands. He slowly moved his eyes downward, languishing on each part of her body. She ran her hands sensually down her sides, never taking her eyes off him.

Julie reached over and touched his hand, which he had casually draped across the back of the couch. He looked at her longingly, feeling both helpless and powerful, then gave her a slight pull. She came around and sat beside him on the couch.

"I . . . I . . . I'm a little nervous," said Rennick. "I'm not sure I'll be able . . ."

"Just relax," she whispered. "We'll only go as far as you're comfortable."

They spent a long while on the couch, kissing tenderly. Then she straddled his lap, facing him, and began to unbutton his shirt. His fear of failure gripped him, then mercifully subsided.

She nuzzled her face against his chest as he laid back his head. After she eased off his shirt, he untied her nighty top. In his excitement, even that simple an act was difficult. When he finished, the sides fell away.

She gently guided off the rest of his clothes, and he lay back on the couch. Then she slid on top of him and they coupled gently. He almost began to cry, desperately thankful for the intimate connection from which he'd been so isolated. Here in the woods, with people far away, they blended with the primal sense of nature and made love in an increasing crescendo of sounds and feelings, finally collapsing into a tender and powerful embrace.

Afterwards, they lay spent on the couch, exhausted and perspiring, speaking only in caresses. The fire was dying down, and a fresh snow had begun to fall, filling the bay window with tiny white confetti.

Rennick found himself thinking about Julie's moving in

with him. The idea had crept into his thoughts without the usual panic. Maybe it was time. Someday he wanted to live with someone. Why not now?

Yet something tugged at him, holding him back. Perhaps it was just his fear of making that kind of commitment. He didn't want to ruin the moment, so he forced himself not to think about it. Now all he wanted was to savor their intimacy.

Julie began to snore softly, which brought him back from his twilight sleep. It also stirred his practical side, as he realized they would be stiff and cold from sleeping naked on the couch. He wanted to move to the bed, yet he didn't quite have the energy. So he set his mental snooze button for five minutes and hugged her firmly, which caused her to stir and smile.

Rennick basked in the warm contentment, feeling as if he were floating in space. Ah, what would it matter if he was a little cold or stiff?

CHAPTER THIRTY-TWO

Lisa sat in her apartment, looking at the brown paper grocery bag that held her supplies for tonight's experiment. She'd been ignoring them all evening. Maybe she should postpone it again, like she had last night. And the night before.

The idea of deliberately calling up the visions frightened her. Yet she was getting them anyway, and she had to retake control of her life. She trusted that Dr. Rennick wouldn't tell her to do anything harmful.

It was nine o'clock. If she was going to do it, she had to get on with it. Lisa stood there, staring at the materials for a full ten minutes. Then she grabbed the bag in a quick swipe and took it into the bedroom.

She laid out the supplies on her bed and inspected them like a hiker looking over provisions before a journey. It had taken her three Ping-Pong balls before she'd cut one in half without squashing it. Next to them was a small red light she'd bought

in a camera store, several sticks of incense, an Enya CD, and a
pocket radio with earphones. She had gone to Sharper Image to
buy a machine that made the static-sounding white noise Rennick had described, and had found out that it cost one hundred
and fifty dollars. A nice salesman whispered that she could get
the same thing by tuning a radio in between stations, and so
she'd hauled out her twenty-dollar portable.

Lisa let her eyes wander from object to object before finally
starting. She screwed the red darkroom bulb into a lamp beside
her bed. Then she lit the incense called Rasta Dreams that
she'd bought from a Jamaican in a colorful shirt on Venice
Beach. A thin curl of smoke filled the room with a sweet
aroma. She decided to go with white noise instead of the Enya
CD, as she really liked Enya and thought it might be distract-
ing. So she put on headphones and tuned the radio to a soft static that sounded like rain.

She listened to the static for a long while, debating if she
should continue. Finally, she turned out all the lights except
the red one, and the room immediately looked like a bordello.
When she lay down and put the Ping-Pong balls on her eyes,
she felt that the plastic eyes and red light must make her look
like a Kermit the Frog hooker.

While deep breathing and counting backwards, she relaxed
into the bed. The white noise blocked out the sounds of the
city, as well as her extraneous thoughts, and she found herself
unconsciously rubbing her thumbs and forefingers together. As
her relaxation grew deeper, it felt like the resonance of magnetic vibrations buzzing through her.

Abruptly, as if a dark curtain had been snatched aside, Lisa
found herself flying above a street. The feeling of being in the
air with no support made her stomach drop, and she felt like
she was on the dip of a roller coaster. The sensation also made

her gasp in panic, and she flailed her arms for support. Then she realized she wasn't falling. She was gliding effortlessly through the air.

About thirty feet below her was the Chinese Theater on Hollywood Boulevard. Its famous neon sign was blinking even though it was daytime, and hundreds of tourists crowded together, jabbering in multiple languages. They were flashing photos of each other and putting their feet in the concrete celebrity footprints. Next she saw an iron gazebo with chrome legs in the shape of women, which she recognized as standing on the corner of Hollywood and La Brea. Then, as she continued east above Hollywood Boulevard, there was a synagogue on her left with a stained-glass Star of David on the front.

Lisa floated above several acres of greenery and then came to a gentle landing among a number of garden patches. She was standing in a small area enclosed by a Cyclone fence, which had a few scraggly patches of cultivated earth and little wooden spears through seed packages.

She saw a freshly dug patch of dirt. A wooden-handled knife, smeared with blood, was suspended in the air above it. A shaft of light thrust upward from the ground toward her. It began as a pinpoint, then enlarged into an intense brightness. Expanding until all she saw was a white blaze. Blinding her to the point of pain, like a searchlight directly in her eyes. . . .

Lisa sat up in bed with a jolt, causing the Ping-Pong ball halves to fly off her eyes. Her sudden transportation back to her bedroom was frightening and jarring, making her feel like she'd been thrown out of a moving car. She was sweating profusely, and she could feel blood rushing in her ears.

A euphoria welled from her stomach into her chest, erupting into laughter. For the first time in her life, she had taken control of her visions. And just as Rennick had predicted, it felt liberating.

Lisa combed her fingers through her perspiration-soaked hair. On top of everything else, she sensed that she'd seen something important to the investigation.

The Sunday drive home from Big Bear was uneventful, at least after Rennick finally got the car started. Julie teased him again for not having gotten it fixed, and he said he'd charge the battery. She gently pointed out that it wouldn't have started at all if the battery were dead. That sounded logical. He'd never been all that mechanical.

Rennick parked the car in front of Julie's apartment. He was still savoring the last embers of the weekend's glow.

"Come spend the night with me," he said.

She stroked his arm as she spoke. "It's very tempting, but thanks to your athletic skills, I haven't slept all that well for the last two days. And I have an early class tomorrow, so I'll take a rain check."

He drove home without putting on the radio, then limped and dragged his suitcase to the door. In the two days he'd been gone, Rennick's apartment had developed the stuffy, stale smell of an abandoned dwelling. He left his bag just inside the front door and threw his keys on the coffee table. Then he put a kettle of water on the stove.

He was pleased to see there was only one message on his answering machine. He pushed the button and listened to it rewind.

"Dr. Rennick, this is your answering service. A Ms. Lisa Cleary called your office and left the following message."

Lisa's voice was breathy and high with energy. "I did what you said. I tried the Ginzberg thing, or whatever it's called, with the white noise and Ping-Pong balls. You were so right. It felt amazing to take control. And I think I've seen something that could help the police."

The teakettle began to whistle from the kitchen, and he put his ear next to the machine.

"Please call me as soon as you can. I'll be up late tonight. We should act on this Monday morning." She left her phone number, which Rennick wrote on a piece of junk mail. The machine beeped again and shut down.

He took the kettle off the stove and it whimpered into silence. Then he poured a cup of hot water and dunked a bag of chamomile tea before calling Lisa.

"Oh, Doctor. I meditated like you told me and it was amazing. The images were so clear. And I felt totally in control. More importantly, I think I may have seen where the murder weapon is hidden." Lisa described her vision. "Should we get Detective Talon and look?"

"Lisa, you shouldn't be handling evidence. That's been very hard on you."

"No, no. It's helping me. After I get over the physical stress, I feel incredibly energized."

"I don't think it's a good idea."

"This was the first time I've ever called up a vision and felt in control. What you suggested was amazing. Please. Let me repay you by helping with the murder case."

"I'll sleep on it."

CHAPTER THIRTY-THREE

Rennick sat down at Talon's desk. He explained Lisa's vision of Hollywood, then said, "So she thinks maybe she found the murder weapon."

Talon massaged his eyes with his index fingers. "After her last performance, I'm in. Though I can't shake the feeling something about her ain't kosher."

"You still feel that way?"

"I dunno. Probably just my built-in paranoia. Helpful Harrys—and Helpful Harriets—who show up out of the blue usually have an angle. Like maybe to watch what we're doing." Talon opened his eyes, which were now red.

"You said you checked her out and didn't find anything unusual. If she was involved in these crimes, would she go out of her way to lead us to evidence?"

"Probably not. Although every once in a while a smart one drops some clues because they ain't having fun unless the cops are close behind. I'm sure she's legit. And frankly, at this stage, I'll take help from a fuckin' fortune cookie."

"So we visit the tourist attractions of Hollywood?" asked Rennick.

"Bring your camera and Bermuda shorts."

Lisa stood with Rennick outside the Hollywood Police Station. She watched him pace back and forth, which was awkward with his limp.

"I have serious reservations about your doing this," he said, stopping to point a finger in her face. "I'll only be involved if you agree to stop immediately when I say so. That means no argument. Agreed?"

"Yes, yes."

"If this is really the murder weapon, it could be more powerful than anything else you've done." His voice was rising in pitch.

"I know."

"You sure you still want to do this?"

"Yes."

Rennick shoved his hands into his pants pockets. "Have you called your father?"

Lisa turned her side to Rennick. "I don't have his number."

"Have you tried to find it?"

"I guess I could try harder."

"I think it's important for your recovery."

Talon walked up before Lisa had to respond. They got into his car, and Lisa distracted herself by looking out the window at the white geodesic dome of the Cinerama Theater on Sunset and Ivar. She began to fidget as they turned onto Hollywood Boulevard near the area of her vision.

When she described her images to Talon, Danny knew immediately where to go. He told her that Wattles Park was the grounds of a former mansion on Hollywood Boulevard, near the Chinese Theater. Part of the park was divided into small gardens, which the city rented out for people to grow flowers, vegetables, or anything else legal. It was also across from Temple Israel, a synagogue made famous when Elizabeth Taylor converted to Judaism there before marrying Eddie Fisher.

She blotted her moist palms on the car's upholstery as they pulled into the parking lot of Wattles Park. An older man with leathery tanned skin walked with a slight stoop toward the car. A large ring of keys jangled from his khaki cloth belt.

"You must be Clarence," said Talon, extending his hand to the caretaker.

"Yep." Clarence's hand vanished into Talon's. "You folks want to see my gardens, eh?"

They walked on a narrow dirt path, past a Japanese tearoom and a small lily pond with hundreds of multicolored koi. In the distance was a manicured hill with picnic benches in the shade of huge birch and eucalyptus trees.

Clarence opened a white wooden gate marked GARDENERS ONLY. Beyond it was a Cyclone fence, about four feet high, against which butted the end posts of other Cyclone fences, cutting the area into about forty squares. Some of the plots were well kept while others ran the gamut from sloppy housekeeping to full-scale neglect.

"The units are numbered, but they ain't exactly in order," said Clarence.

Lisa walked slowly along the fence to the right, letting her fingers ripple over the metal grating. At the first corner she turned left, down a narrow passageway between the plots, then returned and continued along the fence. Nothing called to her.

Suddenly she snapped upright, like a dog who had just

caught a scent. Lisa felt a pull to the left and started off at a fast clip. She stopped at a locked gate with the number 8 on it. There were planted rows, each with little sprouts, and wooden stakes speared through packages of seeds. There were also weeds closing in from the perimeter, as if in slow attack. She rattled the gate, trying to wrench it open.

Clarence tried several keys until he found the right one. "This one belongs to Mrs. Sipes," he said, turning the key in the padlock. "She doesn't come here very often."

Lisa shoved the gate aside and rushed through. She closed her eyes and began rubbing her thumbs and forefingers together. Heat built up in her hands, as if a match had been ignited. She stopped, turned slowly in place like the needle of a compass, then followed the almost gravitational pull that beckoned her. She didn't open her eyes until she stumbled on a wooden stake.

Lisa found herself near the corner opposite the gate. She dropped to her knees, oblivious to the dirt she was getting on her dress, and crawled on all fours. Just ahead, she spotted a mound of freshly turned earth, camouflaged with dried weeds. She pounced on the mound and began digging with her bare hands, flinging away the ground like a dog looking for a bone. She was oblivious to the perspiration and dirt that covered her.

Suddenly she scraped something solid. The sound of her fingernails across plastic caused her stop and look. It was a beige plastic material. She scratched across it to remove the dirt. Faster. Harder. Like shredding open a package.

From a distance, a voice that sounded like Rennick's was shouting something. After a few grunts, it took on meaning. He was saying, "Stop!"

Lisa ignored him and dug faster. In the corner of her eye, she sensed his stepping closer. The dirt she was excavating sprayed his trousers.

"Lisa!" she heard Rennick yell sharply.

She stopped and sat up on her knees. Her heart beat rapidly, and her breathing was in gasps. Her eyes never left the beige plastic.

Rennick helped her stand up. "You said you'd stop when I told you to."

"I'm okay. See how much stronger I am now? My clothes are a mess, but I'm in control."

He looked skeptical.

Talon snapped on a pair of latex gloves and lowered himself to finish the dig. He worked slowly and carefully, touching only the earth and not the object, to reveal a beige-topped Tupperware container, about six by twelve inches. He lifted it out with the care of an archaeologist handling a five-thousand-year-old artifact.

Lisa rushed to his side as Talon pried off the lid. Inside, she saw a knife wrapped in a bloodstained, blue piece of cloth. Next to it was an ivory-colored sealed envelope.

CHAPTER THIRTY-FOUR

Rennick sat in his office, paging through the lecture notes for his five o'clock seminar, "Expert Testimony." His eyes read the words while his mind replayed the morning's dig in Wattles Park.

He rubbed his neck and the vertebrae cracked softly. Lisa had performed amazingly well. While she'd lost it when she started digging, she came around pretty quickly afterwards. Maybe she'd had a breakthrough and was close to recovering from these episodes. He was glad he'd suggested the Ganzfeld idea.

The intercom buzzed.

"Detective Talon on line one," said Bobbi.

Rennick really didn't have the time. Well, maybe just a minute.

"Mr. Lofton and his lawyer have blessed us with an audience," said Talon. "Tomorrow morning at eleven if you can make it."

"If you can reschedule for an evening, that'd be better. Our killer's a night creature."

"Right. I'll try to rebook him. I also got some preliminary info about this morning's festivities. The little Garden of Eden we visited is rented to a Mrs. Fanny Sipes. She's eighty-three years old and lives with fourteen cats. A total Froot-Loop, but probably harmless. I'm checking with her friends and relatives, though I don't think she's got anything to do with this. The killer just helped himself to her real estate."

"I can't say I'm surprised."

"I'm rushing a lab report on the Tupperware, knife, and envelope. I wanted to open the letter but they said no dice. They wanna check for saliva."

Bobbi came in and pointed at her watch. Rennick nodded and waved her away. "What about the cloth that was in the Tupperware?"

"I remembered seeing a blue dress in the evidence container for Myra Powell, the first victim. Sure enough, there was a piece of cloth cut out of an inside seam that nobody noticed. The lab'll tell us officially if the cloth's a match, but I'm telling you right now it is. The shape fits and they're the same color."

There was a beat of silence before Talon continued. "So does any of this stuff tell you more about the killer?"

Rennick stood up and started pacing. It wasn't an easy pace, as his knee still ached and the phone cord was like a leash, jolting him every time he reached the end of it. "Leaving a note with the knife, and placing them in a semipublic place, means the killer is starting to show off. That's a good sign. People in that mode can start to make mistakes."

"Heath coulda done it before he got locked up. There's no

way to tell how long the stuff was there. Did Lofton ever do shit like this?"

"There's nothing in his file about it. But people change. And whoever it is, I think he's getting more brazen."

"From your lips to God's ears."

That evening, Rennick and Talon walked into the interrogation room to meet Lofton and his lawyer. Lofton was already sitting at the table. He was a pale-skinned man who was perfectly groomed, and Rennick saw that he was trying to effect a calm he didn't feel. The man wore an expensive, navy blue pin-striped suit and a starched white shirt with an L on each cuff. In his breast pocket was a burgundy silk kerchief, which matched his paisley burgundy-and-navy tie. His thinning hair was graying, and he had it combed straight back. Rennick knew that Logan was only thirty-five, and yet he appeared to be in his late forties or early fifties. He also felt that the gray hair could have looked blond in the pale light when little Bobby Mullins, the son of the fourth victim, saw Plastic Man.

Next to Lofton was a young man who apparently bought his clothes from the same tailor. The man introduced himself as Leon Duke, Lofton's lawyer, and handed Rennick and Talon his card. It said he was with the offices of Sandy Baris, whose name Rennick recognized as one of the top criminal attorneys in L.A.

Rennick began formulating a strategy to go after this guy. He already had an idea, based on how Lofton was dressed.

"Mr. Lofton, why didn't you register as a sex offender?" asked Talon.

"He's not required to do so," answered Duke. "The court found him not guilty by reason of insanity, so he's never been convicted as a sex offender."

"That's a gray area, Mr. Duke."

"This is how we interpret the statute, Detective. If you disagree, we can let a court decide."

"And my name is Logan," Lofton added. "Please call me that."

"Well, Mr. Lof—Logan, have you heard about a series of young women who were murdered over the last few weeks?"

"By the guy with the electric cords? Who hasn't?"

"It seems they were cut up real similar to the way you once sliced a woman."

Logan visibly squirmed in his seat.

"Is Mr. Logan a suspect?" asked Duke.

"Not now."

Duke whispered to Logan and then said, "My client's statement is that he has paid his debt for that unfortunate incident in his past. Since then he's been a model citizen, and has controlled his difficulties with medication. He receives weekly four-hundred-milligram injections of MPA, and they're administered by a Dr. Paul Rudnick. I can supply his medical records if you wish."

"Yeah, and I also have the high blood pressure and leg cramps to prove it," said Logan. Rennick knew those were side effects of MPA.

Duke continued. "Mr. Logan has no involvement in these crimes."

"Is that right, Mr. Logan?" asked Talon.

"That's correct. If you tell me the dates, I'll tell you where I was."

Talon read off the dates and Duke wrote them down. "We'll get back to you," said Duke.

"Mr. Logan, I'm Dr. Rennick, a psychiatrist. I consult with the police, and I'd like to ask you a few questions."

Silence.

Rennick continued: "What kind of work do you do?"

"I sell computer software."

"Where do you live?"

"Brentwood."

"Apartment or house?"

"Condo."

"Brentwood condos are pretty expensive. Does selling software pay that well?"

Rennick could see Duke about to say something and then check himself.

"When my parents passed away," said Logan, "I inherited a sizable amount of money."

"Are you married?"

"No."

"Do you have a steady relationship with a woman?"

Duke barged in. "This is not *The Dating Game,* Doctor. If you don't have anything more relevant, I believe we're finished."

Rennick spoke forcefully. "In crimes committed by deviates, like this one, psychiatrists have a lot of latitude. Look up *People vs. Chandler,* a California Supreme Court decision. If you want to leave, go right ahead. The police will get a subpoena and make sure Mr. Logan's record shows that he refused to cooperate."

Rennick walked over and yanked open the door, gesturing for them to walk through it. Duke and Logan sat still. Talon covered a smile with his huge hand.

When it became obvious that they weren't budging, Rennick closed the door, sat down, and continued calmly, as if nothing had happened. "Do you have a steady relationship with a woman?"

"No."

"Do you grow vegetables?" Rennick liked to use this technique, where he dropped in random questions that only the killer would know were connected to the crime. Normally the killer had a visceral reaction. Unfortunately, Logan only looked puzzled.

"No," he said.

"Where did you grow up?" Another innocuous question, and Rennick didn't even listen to the answer.

"Do you have ivory-colored stationery?"

"No." It was apparent from his face that Logan thought Rennick was crazier than he was. Or was he hiding something? Rennick wasn't sure.

"What kind of car do you drive?"

Logan puffed up a bit. "A Lexus."

"Do you own a knife?"

Logan reddened, then looked down. The question had scored an emotional reaction, but Rennick knew it could just be Logan's feelings about the prior murder.

"I, uh, guess I got some in the kitchen. Maybe a pocketknife."

Now that he had Logan off balance, Rennick wanted to break things open. He had an idea that anyone dressed this fastidiously would overreact to disorder, so Rennick poured a small amount of water on the table, about six inches in front of Logan. Logan stared at the puddle. "Why did you do that?" Logan asked.

Rennick didn't answer.

"Do you have a tissue, or a towel?" asked Logan.

"Leave it," said Rennick.

"Why?" asked Duke.

"Because I say so. Mr. Logan, when was the last time you had sex?"

"This can't possibly be relevant," said Duke.

"Quite the contrary. The display of nude bodies means the murders were sexually motivated, and your client has a history of sexual assault. Therefore his sex life is very relevant."

Logan kept staring down at the puddle, then up at Rennick. He was beginning to twitch uncomfortably.

"When did you last have sex?"

Logan took out his burgundy handkerchief and began neatly mopping up the water. When he finished, he didn't want to put the wet handkerchief in his pocket, so he held it out awkwardly.

"I'm instructing him not to answer," said Duke

"No sweat," said Rennick. He poured out another puddle of water. "Unless you're taking the Fifth, we'll subpoena him."

"Don't do that! Stop it!" said Logan.

"These young women deserved what they got, didn't they, Mr. Logan?"

Logan mopped up the water with his handkerchief, and Rennick poured out more.

"Don't!" Logan exclaimed. He looked at Rennick and flames ignited behind his eyes. "You bastard!"

"They deserved it, didn't they!"

"This interview is over," said Duke. He stood up as Logan started to mop the last spill. Then both of them scurried out while Logan held his dripping handkerchief by one corner.

Rennick sat at Talon's desk after the interview. "What do you think, Danny?"

"You sure chimed his fucking clock."

"Hopefully that'll lead to his doing something stupid."

"A lot about him fits. The way he dresses, he's gotta be squeaky clean in whatever he does. The light skin and mustache are right. He also looked like a size twelve or so shoe, though it's hard to imagine him in anything besides Gucci leather. And of course we ain't got shit that would impress a jury. What's your take?"

"I think he's hiding something. It could just be his guilt about the old killing. Or that he's uptight about being here, like the way you feel guilty going through customs."

"He looks like a primo candidate to me," said Talon. "I'm gonna check out his ass six ways from Sunday."

Lisa had watched her brother Lance call girls on the phone when he was in junior high, and she had teased him mercilessly. If there was a girl he was too nervous to call, he'd punch in all but the last number. Then he'd stare at the phone, working up his courage to hit the last button.

Now Lisa was sitting there, with the phone receiver cradled against her shoulder, having dialed all but her aunt Jane's final digit. She fidgeted with a pencil, flipping it rapidly up and down, then chewing on the eraser. Finally, she took a deep breath and hit the last number.

"Hi, Aunt Jane. It's Lisa."

"Lisa, you pretty thing! How are you, darlin'?" Aunt Jane was one of the last true southern belles.

"I'm fine, thanks. Aunt Jane, do you have my father's phone number?"

"Yes, I believe I do somewhere. Is anything wrong, darlin'?" Aunt Jane was also one of the world-class gossips.

"No, not at all. I just want to talk to him."

"Oh." Aunt Jane sounded a little disappointed. "Did I tell you I've planted some lilies in my garden this year? The pictures on the packet look like they're going to be the most beautiful creamy white you ever saw. The man at the nursery said they would make me the envy of the neighborhood. Not that I care about that." Lisa found herself smiling. She hadn't talked to her aunt in almost five years, and the lady was going on as if they'd spoken yesterday.

"I finally had to fire my yard man, Roddy," her aunt continued. "He kept letting the weeds grow something awful, and once he pulled up the flowers. His sister Sarah cleaned on Fridays, so of course I had to fire her too. The girl I hired to replace her . . ."

"Aunt Jane?"

"Yes, dear?"

"Could you please look for my dad's phone number?"

"Oh. Certainly, honey. I'm sure it's here somewhere. Hold on. I'll go look."

Lisa heard the clunk of the phone being placed on the table. In the distance was the sound of her aunt pulling out drawers and ruffling papers, all the while humming softly. Then silence.

After about five minutes, Lisa was sure that Aunt Jane had forgotten about her. She couldn't hang up and call back, since the phone was off the hook. She tried yelling into the receiver. On the third yell, she heard an "Oh!" in the distance, and then footsteps to the phone.

"Here it is, darlin'," said Aunt Jane, with no acknowledgment of having left her dangling. "Ron is living in Sunland now."

"Sunland? He's in L.A.?"

"If that's where Sunland is."

"Yes. It's about twenty minutes north of here." Even though she never wanted to talk to the sonofabitch again, she couldn't believe he was living that close and hadn't tried to call.

"I'd never hear from him if I didn't call every few months," continued Aunt Jane. "He doesn't even tell me when he moves. I get the new numbers from the phone company. They're so thoughtful about that. It used to be an operator that told you. Now it's a robot voice of some kind . . ."

"Aunt Jane? His number?"

"Oh, yes. Here it is, darlin'." Aunt Jane fumbled through several papers and read her the number.

"Thank you."

"You're welcome, honey. When you get ahold of him, would you kindly remind him that he has a sister?"

"I will."

"And tell him to call me. Between you and me, I worry about Ronny. He hasn't been right in the head since your mother was murdered."

Lisa bolted upright, as if she had just been slapped across the face.

"Did you say murdered!?!"

CHAPTER THIRTY-FIVE

Rennick stepped out the door of his apartment, heading to his early morning Evidence class. As he unlocked his car door, he heard the telephone ring. He hobbled back inside just as the ringing stopped. Although he was running late, he hit star-six-nine, got the Hollywood Police Station, and asked for Talon.

"Professor, I got the lab results on the Wattles Park stuff." Rennick thought Talon's voice sounded tired and groggy.

"And?"

"The Tupperware, knife, and envelope were clean. No fingerprints, saliva, hairs, or fibers. The envelope is a cheap, common one, sold through Pic-n-Save. Same with the Tupperware. There's hundreds of thousands of 'em around."

"How about the cloth?"

"It's a definite match to the Powell dress. The lab says it was soaked in B-positive blood, which is the same as Powell's. Since the dress didn't have any blood on it, the piece was probably used to wipe the knife."

"What did the note say?"

"It said, 'You're too late.' Whaddaya make of that?"

Rennick sat down on the couch. "It could mean the killer wants to get caught. By saying 'You're too late,' he could be pleading with us to hurry up, so there won't be a next time."

"You really think someone this careful wants to get caught?"

"Not consciously. But at a deeper level, the reason they're being so careful is that they know they're doing something wrong. On the other hand, it's possible the note is just the opposite of a plea for help. It could be an arrogant 'You can't catch me.'"

Talon was silent for a moment. "My gut tells me he's gonna visit another young woman real soon. The time between the last two killings was ten days, and it's been eight since Mullins."

Rennick stood up and began pacing. "I got an idea. This guy had problems with a woman who looks like the victims. Can you check out the women around Lofton and Heath? Girlfriends. Mothers. Sisters. Maybe one of them has shoulder-length blond hair. Or had it when she was in her twenties."

"Lemme see what I can do."

Suddenly Rennick remembered his class. He realized that it started in seven minutes, and raced out the door as fast as his knee would allow.

In the late afternoon, Julie sat in the Law School library watching the sun cast long shadows across the room. The room was cavernous, with rows of dark oak tables widely spaced on either side of the center aisle. Open casebooks clustered around students scribbling on yellow pads and softly clicking notes into laptop computers.

Julie preferred the Law School library to UCLA's main library because it was quieter. For the last four hours, she'd been roughing out her Ph.D. dissertation. The topic order didn't flow, and she had a lot more gaps in the research than she would have liked. Her eyes watered, and she pushed the papers away as she let her mind take a break.

She knew she was avoiding a decision on the New York offer, and the ticking of the deadline clock was growing louder each day. Less than a week left. Michael's indecision had been a big help with her procrastination, although she hated to admit that.

Julie took out a yellow pad, drew a line down the center, and labeled one side "Pro" and the other side "Con." On the Pro side, she wrote "Opportunity of a lifetime," "Excellent challenge and education," "Career guarantee." On the Con side, she wrote "East Coast weather," "Big city," "No Michael."

Three pro and three con. Not as big a help as she'd hoped.

As she stared at the list, she found herself doodling a question mark next to "Michael."

CHAPTER THIRTY-SIX

Talon knew from the popping flashbulbs that the mayor had entered the foyer of City Hall. Just in time for the six o'clock news. His Honor walked up to an arsenal of microphones, each with multicolored call-letter signs. The roomful of reporters began shouting questions.

"I want to read a prepared statement first," he said in a honey-smooth voice.

The room calmed to an uneasy silence. Talon stuck his hands in his pants pockets, shifted his weight to one leg, and leaned against the back wall. He glanced over at Wharton and caught him looking. Wharton turned away.

"The police have made some great strides in this case," said the mayor. "We have a number of leads, and one breakthrough that we can't jeopardize by discussing it publicly. We expect to have a major announcement in the next few days."

That's it, thought Talon. The end of a perfect fucking day.

He pushed off the wall and started toward the door, wondering what these leads and breakthroughs might be.

Lisa headed north on Interstate 405, toward her father's house in Sunland. As the traffic crept slowly in fits, a cacophony of noises assaulted her: car horns, truck motors, and rap music from the next car. She repeatedly tapped her steering wheel.

The call to her father had been awkward to the tenth power. Of course he hadn't recognized her voice, which wasn't surprising since he hadn't heard it for over fifteen years. When he repeated her name, she thought he almost sounded happy to hear from her. That was enough to spark her into wondering if they could re-create the few times she'd been Daddy's little girl. The idea excited and frightened her.

The traffic came to a halt near the Anheuser-Busch Brewery. Seeing the beer-company sign reminded her of sitting on her father's lap while he watched football on television. She couldn't have been more than three. Dad always kept a bottle of beer in his hand, and she remembered its bittersweet odor filling her nostrils. When he got excited by a play, he sometimes spilled a little on her dress. She always loved that, because it meant the fragrance would be with her all day. Now the only thing she could smell was diesel fuel from the freeway.

The closer she got to her father's house, the more the neighborhoods deteriorated. Lisa hadn't anticipated that. While she had pushed herself to make a comfortable life, maybe her father had never recovered from the blows he'd been dealt. Maybe he'd suffered more than she knew.

She arrived in Sunland and saw that it was a semi-rural area with small houses on large lots. She turned onto Lisbon Drive and began looking for the address. Lisbon was a street of tiny, one-story houses with crooked foundations, broken chimneys, and dry, patchy lawns. In front of a house with shattered windows, a group of kids were laughing and playing with a truck tire.

Her father's address was painted crudely on a bent tin mailbox that didn't quite close. Lisa pulled her green Toyota into the gravel driveway, stopped the engine, and sat in the car. Her father's clapboard house hadn't been painted for years, and large patches of dirty blue paint had peeled off to reveal an avocado green below. His yard was mostly dirt, with patches of crabgrass and an unidentifiable attempt at a lawn. To one side were several rows of scraggly corn underneath rusted clothesline poles that stood like abandoned crucifixes.

She put her keys back into the ignition and debated whether to start the car and leave.

Talon was almost out of the Hollywood station when a receptionist flagged him down and gave him the phone.

"Danny," said Rennick, "Lisa just told me that her mother was murdered about twenty years ago. Her memory of it is pretty vague, and I think it might help her therapy if I had some details. Do you think you could get me the file?"

"Twenty years ago? That's a real pain in the ass, Professor. Do you really need it?"

"I don't *really* need it. I'm asking a favor."

"Shit. You know I can't refuse that. Where was she killed?"

"Santa Rosa."

"Santa Rosa! I ain't got any contacts up there."

"You macho cops are always helping each other. C'mon. Make a call. I'll owe you one."

"You'll owe me two. Gimme the goddamn information."

*   *   *

Lisa pulled the keys out of the ignition and got out of the car. When she stepped onto the front porch of her father's house, it sagged and creaked under her weight. A wooden screen door, with the screen pulled out of the edges in several places, covered the open front door. She could hear voices from a television inside. Lisa took a deep breath and worried how opening these old wounds was going to feel.

She pushed the bell. No sound. So she knocked on the frame of the screen door. No response except a lawn mower commercial from the television. Finally she opened and closed the screen door roughly, making a banging sound. A voice from inside said, "Come in."

The living room furniture was sparse, and in varying degrees of fray. The walls were covered with a peeling, powder blue wallpaper that had little pink flowers in the design. Yet the room was neat and clean, as if awaiting an inspection. On the wall to the left was a locked gun case, with pistols, rifles, and bayonets neatly positioned inside. Above the cabinet was a framed collection of her father's medals that she remembered him wearing on dress occasions.

Lisa stood in the door, behind her father. Ron Cleary made no attempt to turn around. He was sitting on the couch, watching a bowling tournament. The announcer whispered, the ball rolled, pins flew, and the crowd applauded. He motioned her to come around without taking his eyes off the set. She walked to the side of the couch and looked at him.

He turned to face her, and looked her up and down. She did the same. He was still wiry and muscular, though his face was creased and the skin sagged under his arms. His hair was salt-and-pepper, and he had a gray stubble of a beard. His blue eyes were slightly cloudy, faded with age.

"You look like your mother."

"Do I?"

She thought he almost made a move to get up. Maybe to come

up to her. Even hug her. For a moment she saw herself with him as a little girl at the park. She remembered riding in his arms, snuggling close to his chest. Her lips against his sandpaper cheek. She felt his arms holding her tightly. One of the few times when his military shell melted.

If he had started to move, he stopped himself. Or maybe the move was just her imagination.

"Dad, how are you?"

"I'm okay. You?" His eyes moved between her and the television.

"I'm fine. I'm an accountant."

He waited for the crackle of the pins before answering. "I never did get what accountants do. Pushing pencils around paper all day long. I understand building things. Making things."

"We keep track of the money when people build things and make things."

Silence.

"Are you working?" she asked.

"I'm in between jobs."

Silence

"Dad, I started having those visions again. Do you remember when I had them before?"

"Of course I do. You embarrassed the hell out of all of us. I thought they stopped."

"They did. They started again."

Roll of the ball. Pins crash. Applause.

"Dad, I'm seeing images of murders. It's scaring me. It makes me think of Mom's death. And how you and I were never the same after it—"

"Is that why you came? To talk about your mother?"

"No . . . I . . . well . . ."

He stood up and faced her. She saw that his clothes were wrinkled and faded. "I don't want to talk about your mother."

"Dad, was she . . . killed?"

He didn't look at the television despite the sound of the rolling ball.

"Yes."

"Why didn't you tell me?"

"I don't want to talk about it."

"I do, Dad. Please. I need to. I have a right to know what happened. When Mom died, it tore up my life too. I'm trying to heal."

"You sound like one of those TV shrinks. They're always saying 'Liberate your pain,' or some such bullshit. The thing with your mother is history. Ancient history. Put it behind you and move on with your life. That's how you deal with it."

"When you cut me off after she died, I felt like I lost both of you. We've never talked about it. Please." She hated herself for begging, yet she could hear Dr. Rennick's voice urging her on. Dr. Rennick had seemed so sure that she would learn something important from her father.

Ron sat back down and stared at the TV.

"Daddy! Look at me!" she almost shouted.

His head slowly turned to her. She could feel the tension within him. As they stared at each other, she suddenly saw the familiar image of a horse. Galloping toward her, with her father riding bareback. She watched him sink into the horse's body, just as she had done in her earlier visions.

Ron spoke brusquely, breaking her trance. "Marrying your mother was a mistake that I want to leave in the past. I never understood how you and your brother kept worshiping her when all she did was beat the hell out of you."

Suddenly Lisa flashed into a memory. For the first time in years, she remembered her mother hitting her. The way her mother's perspiration sprayed on Lisa with each blow. She could see her mother's face, possessed and focused on the task. She felt the sharp sting of each slap and saw the look of crimson welts.

Her father had turned his attention back to the television. At least she could wipe the tears without his seeing her.

"Good-bye, Father," she said, turning to leave.

"Lisa," he said.

She halted abruptly. She hadn't heard him say her name like that since she was a child.

"Yes, Daddy?"

He wasn't looking up.

"There are things about your mother's death you don't want to know."

"What things?"

He picked up the remote and turned up the television volume. The meeting was over.

Lisa stared at his profile, realizing she had been cut off all over again. Just as he had left her alone in her room after her mother's death. Just as he'd refused to take her hand at the funeral. She hated him. And she wanted his love.

She knew there would never again be contact between them. At least she'd tried everything she could. And at least finality was easier to handle than uncertainty.

She walked out the door.

Ron Cleary's eyes were on the television, but as soon as the screen door banged shut, he turned down the volume and listened for her car. He heard it start, followed by the crush of gravel as it pulled out of the driveway. When the sound of the motor disappeared down the street, he grabbed his pair of gloves from the drawer and ran out the back door.

In the garage was his heavy punching bag, hanging from the ceiling and anchored to the floor with a chain. Virtually exploding into the bag, he began throwing punches. Yelling in animal cries with each one. Cleary pushed himself to the max, putting his fist, shoulder, and hips into the blows. Faster. Harder. The sweat began to pour off him as he danced back and forth while pummeling the bag. Jab. Jab. Punch. Harder.

Faster. His shoulders were moving back and forth in a blur. Harder.

Within a few minutes, he was exhausted. He was breathing in labored gasps, and he felt as if somone were thrusting sharp pins into his ribs. Cleary fell into the threadbare easy chair that he kept in the garage, and it protested with a cloud of dust. He dropped his head onto his hands and commanded himself to regain control.

Within sixty seconds, his breathing and pulse were back to normal.

CHAPTER THIRTY-SEVEN

Rennick knocked on the door of Mrs. Thomas, his apartment manager. Inside he heard the clattering of dishes, followed by the padding of footsteps. She opened the door and finished wiping her hands on a faded blue apron.

"Oh, good evening, Dr. Rennick," she said in her chirpy voice. Mrs. Thomas was a squat little lady in her sixties, with a twinkly smile. Her apartment and front porch were filled with ivies, ferns, ficuses, and other assorted green plants, some of them five or six feet tall.

"Hello, Mrs. Thomas. Do you have a package for me?"

"Yes indeed. That nice policeman dropped it off this afternoon. It certainly looks bulky."

She waited for a crumb or two of information, like a dog begging for a treat.

"May I have it please?" Rennick said.

"Oh, yes," she replied, as if getting the package had completely slipped her mind, silly her. She picked it up off a table by the front door and handed it to him. "It sure is bulky," she said, pausing again. When he didn't take the bait, she finally said, "Have a lovely evening."

"Thanks. You too."

Rennick turned and walked to his apartment, which was only a few feet away. He could feel Mrs. Thomas's gaze following him, just in case he opened it on the spot or otherwise revealed some valuable data. He unlocked his door and waved to her before going inside. She waved back, totally unself-conscious about staring.

The evening was turning chilly, and a cold breeze wormed its way in with him. Julie was in the kitchen, humming as she stirred the sizzling onions that she was browning. The wonderful smell permeated the apartment.

He walked in and grabbed her from behind. She turned around and kissed him.

"What's in the package?"

"It's from Talon." He grabbed a knife and started cutting carrots.

"So what's in it?" she asked.

"It's about a patient."

"Is this TWENTY QUESTIONS?"

"Sorry. It's a file I need to review."

"Aw. I was hoping you'd take the night off."

The way she said it melted the last of his attempted nonchalance. He grabbed her again and kissed her fully on the lips, feeling as flushed as an adolescent on a date with his dream girl. She giggled and hugged him tightly.

Their activities came to an abrupt halt when sour fumes suddenly filled the room. It was the unmistakable odor of onions turning into charcoal. They both grabbed for the skillet and

Rennick won. He hobbled on his game knee to get it outside, and a trail of dark smoke followed behind like some demonic force.

Julie opened the windows and they held their noses long enough to put two frozen dinners in the microwave and head for safer ground on the living room couch.

"I promise I won't work long tonight," said Rennick. "I just want to take a quick look at this file."

"I understand," she responded, taking the package and flinging it across the room. He looked at her in disbelief, then looked at the file. It was crumpled from the throw, and sat limply in a corner like a defeated boxer.

"Julie, it might be important. I have to . . ."

"See if you think this is important." She started unbuttoning her blouse, which hung loosely as she worked her way down.

"That's not fair," he managed to say while staring at the exposed sides of her breasts.

Now she was unzipping her jeans, wiggling them off, and stepping out. He could see a dark triangle through her light pink bikini panties. She hooked her thumb in one corner of the panties and slowly pulled down the side.

He got up and whispered in her ear. "I just have one request."

She pulled her blouse slowly off her shoulders, holding it up so that it barely covered her breasts. "Yes?"

"The last time we made love on a couch I was sore for two days. Can we get into the bed?"

"Sure." She cupped her hand over his crotch. "Although I can't guarantee you won't be sore. You already seem to have some swelling."

Rennick lay in bed next to Julie. He waited until he could hear her snoring, then carefully lifted the covers and got up. He was totally silent, save one slip against the bedside table that didn't seem to wake her.

In the living room, he turned on a table lamp, retrieved the file from its corner, and sat back into the couch. Then he yawned deeply as he began to read the murder file on Lisa's mother.

Martha Cleary, Caucasian female, age thirty-six. Date of death, residence address, next of kin . . .

He felt heavy and tired. The material was less than exciting, and so far useless. He yawned again. One more page and he'd put it away and go to sleep.

That was when he saw it.

Rennick's stomach somersaulted, and a shot of adrenaline jolted him awake. He grabbed the phone and dialed.

A voice grumbled, "This better be important."

"I'm sorry to wake you, Danny. It's Michael Rennick."

"Oh. What's up, Professor?"

"Did you read this Cleary murder file?"

"No. You said it was for Lisa's therapy, so I didn't see any reason to."

"We have to meet first thing in the morning. Are you going to be in?"

"Yeah, why?"

Rennick explained what he'd found in the file.

"Holy shit," Talon responded.

"I'll meet you seven thirty at the station," said Rennick.

Rennick went into the kitchen, breathing through his mouth to filter out the remains of the onion stench. He grabbed Louisiana chicory coffee, the strongest he had, and filled the coffeemaker with water. He knew he was going to be up for a while.

CHAPTER THIRTY-EIGHT

Rennick awoke to find one eye stuck shut as he tentatively opened the other one. The sunlight coming through the window was glaring in his face, causing the working eye to squint in pain. His mouth was dry and foul-tasting, and his neck and body were twisted at an odd angle. As he gained his bearings, he realized he'd fallen asleep on the couch.

He found that his arm was asleep when he finally got up and started a fresh pot of coffee. Julie had left a note: *Bye.* That wasn't so good. No "Love" or even "Have a nice day." She was probably pissed about his getting up and working. Had he promised he wouldn't work? He couldn't quite remember.

Rennick saw the clock on the stove. Seven fifteen. Dammit. Talon was expecting him in fifteen minutes, and the station was twenty minutes away. He walked in fog toward the shower.

* * *

Lisa awoke in the morning with a scream and sprang into a sitting position. Her heart was thumping in her temples, and she was sweating so profusely that the sheets felt like bathwater.

The dream had been intensely vivid, even more so than her visions, and she was relieved to know it wasn't real. She had dreamed of her mother, who looked just as she had when Lisa was little. A bright-faced woman with a warm smile and sapphire-colored eyes, wearing blue jeans and a red-checked shirt. In the background was her father, dressed in his military uniform, guarding a door. Just as he had in Lisa's earlier dream, when Lisa tried to get through the door and he shoved her away.

Martha Cleary was flirting with Ron. Smiling, touching his face, whispering in his ear. He stood rigidly at attention, ignoring her. Lisa tapped her mother on the shoulder. Martha spun around, and her smile slashed into a snarl. "Lisa, what are you doing here?"

"Mommy. Where have you been? I've missed you."

"Stay away from us. You have no idea what's going on here. Go away."

"Mommy, please."

"You're having those visions again, aren't you? You know how dangerous they are. Look what they've done to your family."

"I can't help it, Mommy. They just come."

"Stop them. And stay away from us. You're going to get yourself in big trouble, young lady." Martha shoved Lisa backwards, much harder that her father had done in the previous dream. Lisa hit the floor roughly, unable to breathe. Martha stood over Lisa like a fighter waiting to see if an opponent had the nerve to get up. In the background, her father remained at attention.

Her mother stabbed a finger toward Lisa's face. "Stay away, you hear me?"

Before she could answer, Lisa was in the second part of the dream. Even now, sitting in the daylight, those images terrified her.

As if dialing 911, she called Rennick's office.

"I'm sorry. Dr. Rennick won't be in until later this morning."

Lisa then called his emergency answering service and left a voice-mail message.

"Dr. Rennick, it's Lisa Cleary. Please call me as soon as you get this. It's urgent. And I'm frightened."

The police station was bustling at eight when Rennick arrived for his seven-thirty appointment. He sat in the chair beside Talon's desk and, because his neck was stiff from sleeping on the couch, he turned his whole body to look at Talon.

"I went through the Martha Cleary file last night, so let me give you the highlights."

Talon began flipping the pages while Rennick spoke. "As I told you on the phone, Lisa's mother was killed almost exactly the same way as these victims. She was tied to the bed with her stockings, and her throat was cut. The killer was careful enough not to leave any prints or fibers. The major differences were no electrical cord, and more haphazard butchering. Still, it's pretty close for a coincidence."

Rennick began talking more rapidly. "The father was a suspect, and he didn't have an alibi. Just his word that he was 'out driving around by himself.' According to the file, he's a tough cookie: army Special Forces, trained in hand-to-hand combat. There were two calls by the wife for spousal abuse, both of

them withdrawn before pressing charges. But there was no evidence to link him to the killing, and he wasn't charged."

"So it looks like we ought to nose around about Daddy," said
Talon.

"Yes. Why don't you find out what he's been up to over the
last few years."

Talon continued thumbing through the file. "Professor, did
you notice where this murder occurred?"

"Santa Rosa. Where's that?"

"Northern California. Not far from San Francisco."

Rennick's eyebrows went up. "Lofton territory. He was living there at the time."

"Right. He'd have been about eighteen years old then."

"Can you find out what he was doing at the time of the murder?"

"It ain't so easy to check where somebody was a coupla
weeks ago, much less seventeen years. If I'm lucky, I might find
out he smoked in the boys' room. But I'll give it a shot."

"What about Heath?"

"He was in grammar school."

Rennick hesitated before the next question. "Do you think
you could get someone to watch Lisa's father?"

"Based on what? That he was never charged for a killing seventeen years ago?"

Rennick groped for the best way to say it. "I didn't know
any of this, and I wouldn't have done it if I had, but . . ." Rennick paused, as if grimacing from a sharp pain. "The fact is, I
sent Lisa out to see her father. It turned out to be unproductive
psychologically, which isn't your problem. But I'm worried I
might have put her in danger. That's why I was hoping you
could get someone to watch him."

"Professor, you know how short-handed we are. I'll check

him out thoroughly, but I can't tail him at this stage. The only thing that points at this guy is ancient, and they couldn't even nail him then."

Rennick paused. "Do you think she's in any danger?"

"No more than before she went out there. If the guy wanted to pop her, he'd have found her already."

"I guess. . . ."

"I actually have a different worry," Talon continued. "If he starts to look like a suspect, I'm worried Lisa might try to warn him. So I'd rather you don't tell her about our checking him out."

"What? Lisa hates the sonofabitch. She only called him because I insisted. And she didn't even know her mother was murdered until a few days ago."

"You're probably right. But play it my way."

CHAPTER THIRTY-NINE

Marvin Logan came into his condo with his arms full of grocery bags. He placed them on the counter and began his usual routine of washing the tops of the tin cans. With all the clerks and others who handled those cans, he didn't understand why everyone didn't take these simple precautions. The amount of gunk he took off would turn people's stomachs.

He dried the cans with paper towels, washed his hands with Purell, and then moved his laundry from the washer to the dryer. Even though he had a housekeeper five times per week, he insisted on doing his own laundry. Who knew whether Louisa might clean the bathroom and then handle his clothes? It was better not to take any chances.

Logan neatly hung up his slacks and sport shirt, then put on the navy suit with a subtle taupe herringbone pattern. He chose a rep tie that picked up the taupe, fluffed a white silk handkerchief into his breast pocket, and studied his reflected image.

He had finally organized his life as well as his wardrobe. All the pieces had all been clicking into place so nicely. And now the cops come nosing around, stirring things up. How could they expect him to go on like nothing had happened? Logan never did well when he was being watched. As a kid, he'd always been a great soccer player in his backyard, only to fall apart in games with other kids. He remembered what the older boys had said. "Lookit the dork! What a sissy."

So maybe he had some problems. Who didn't? Maybe his problems got a little out of hand now and then. Everyone makes mistakes. He'd worked so hard. He shouldn't have to perform for the cops like some circus dog.

He pulled out the pocket silk, folded it neatly, and placed it in the handkerchief drawer. He'd go without a silk today, since it reminded him of that mean-spirited psychiatrist.

Rennick walked into his office, and Bobbi looked up from her computer.

"Lisa Cleary got here about fifteen minutes ago. She wouldn't stop pacing back and forth, and it was making me so jittery that I thought about jumping out the window. I put her in the faculty lounge instead."

"Thanks. Starting the day with a suicide always puts a pall on my mornings."

"Remember that at bonus time."

"In all seriousness, give her a little slack. You'd be upset too if you kept seeing horrible visions."

"Oh, you've met my ex?"

Rennick chuckled. "I give. You win. Cover me while I'm gone."

He walked down the hall, past the gray metal lockers. One or two students said hello, and he waved by rote. He really didn't have time to see Lisa for an unscheduled appointment, yet Bobbi had said her call sounded desperate. He supposed it was the same as a surgeon whose patient had a burst appendix. But that didn't add any hours to the day. How had he gotten himself on a treadmill that was moving so much faster than his feet?

When Rennick opened the door to the faculty lounge, he tried to conceal how much her looks shocked him. Her hair was disheveled, and the skin under her eyes was a sickly blue-black. Her clothes were wrinkled, and her blouse was tucked in unevenly.

She stopped pacing and ran toward him. "Thank you for letting me come in on such short notice," she said rapidly. "I had this terrifying vision last night, and I'm sure it's significant." Her voice was shaking.

Rennick told her to lie down on the couch, and he started a relaxation routine of deep breathing. It took almost ten minutes to get her into a shakily composed state.

"Tell me what you saw."

Her body tensed again, and she began violently shaking her head. Rennick stood up and said forcefully, "Lisa!" She froze at hearing her name.

"I had a dream last night," she said. "It was even more vivid than the visions I've had while I'm awake. There were two distinct parts. In the first, my father was guarding a door. Just like the dream I had before, where he pushed me away. This time my mother was there too. She scolded me for having these visions again, and shoved me on the ground. Then she said to stay away. What do you think it means?"

"Your having these visions is stirring up lots of repressed

feelings about your parents. It sounds like your subconscious is protesting the intrusion."

"Why would my mother be guarding the door with my father?"

"When you deal with childhood fears, your parents lose the power and authority they had over you when you were little. This could represent their last attempts to keep you under control."

"How do I find out what's on the other side of the door?"

"It will come out in therapy. You're making excellent progress. I know it seems like things are falling apart, but it's necessary for you to get through this. We have to open the wounds before they can heal. You've seen how much stronger you get after dealing with your visions."

Lisa lay there without speaking.

"You said there were two parts to your dream," Rennick continued.

"Yes."

Silence. "So what was the second part?"

"I don't know if I can talk about it."

"Go slowly. Stop if you need to."

She lay a long while before speaking. "I . . . I saw this same killer who's been in my other visions. Standing over a girl tied to a bed with nylons. It wasn't one of the other victims. I've never seen this woman before. She had a mole on her left cheek. The knife looked like the one we found, but new. Shiny, razor sharp. This time I saw a lot more detail. I saw her skin being peeled back under the blade. This gaping wound in her neck split open and her head fell back. Blood spurted several feet into the air, like a fountain. This long, gray cord came out of her body. Spilling out like it was her intestines." She gagged as if she was going to throw up.

The reference to a gray cord raised the hair on the back of Rennick's neck. The color wasn't public. "What happened next?"

"I woke up this morning in a panic. The vision was so vivid that I'm sure this is real. If the murder hasn't already happened, it's going to very soon. The only other time I had such a vivid dream was when I foresaw my mother's funeral."

Lisa broke into tears again. Rennick let her cry.

"The most frustrating part is that the killer's face is always in the shadows. I try to get around in the scene, and there's this invisible barrier that keeps me from getting close. I feel like such a failure."

"These images are not objects that will bend to your will. You have to take them as they are and not chastise yourself for what they aren't." Rennick spoke calmly, yet he was beginning to worry. She seemed close to losing the separation between reality and hallucinations, which would be a serious downturn. It might mean medication and possibly hospitalization.

Lisa suddenly began speaking in the trance monotone she had used in the police station, an eerie, detached voice, like a medium at a séance. Rennick looked up and saw that she was lying still, with her body relaxed.

"There's an apartment. Wind chimes made of brown ceramic, in the shape of fish, tinkling in the window. A round, multicolored candle is burning with the smell of jasmine. The young woman has a mole on her cheek. She's sitting on a bed with a calico spread. Humming while sewing something. No. Not sewing. She's reading. Lost in the book. She lives alone, in an apartment. It's nighttime. She's left the window open, and the killer is slipping inside. Quietly, no sound. Plastic raincoat and latex gloves. Getting bolder. Not waiting for her to sleep . . ."

Lisa's monotone was dissolving. "New knife. Sharpened blade. Coming up behind her. Turn around! Turn—"

She was panicking, flailing her arms wildly.

"Lisa!" Rennick shouted.

She sat up, blinking rapidly. Her chest heaved with labored breaths.

"Wha—what?" she stammered.

Rennick spoke slowly. "Lisa, you're okay. You're here. In the faculty lounge. Don't worry. Everything's okay." He was bending his ballpoint pen to the point of snapping.

"I'm s-sorry," she stuttered.

"There's nothing to be sorry about. It's okay."

"Dr. Rennick, help me." She began to cry, cradling her head in her hands.

"I'll help you. But you must do what I tell you."

"Yes. Anything."

"First, look at me." He wanted eye contact, to keep her from slipping off again. She self-consciously glanced at him, then quickly looked away. He stared directly into her face.

"Look at me, please." She did. With her running makeup, she looked like a waif caught in a thunderstorm. "I'm going to give you some pills. . . ."

"No pills," she shot back.

"You need—"

"No pills. I won't even take an aspirin. No."

"Do you want my advice or not?"

"I won't take pills."

"Do you want to get better?"

". . . Yes . . ."

"Then you need to take something to get through this. Have your pharmacy call me and I'll give them a prescription for something called Haldol. You only have to use it until you get on top of these episodes. Hopefully that will only take a few days. Think of it like using a crutch until a broken leg heals."

"I'd have to think about it."

"Tell me you'll do it."

"I'll . . . I'll do it." She looked away as she said it.

CHAPTER FORTY

Lance Cleary dragged in from a long day on his feet at Pep Boys. He fell onto the living room couch, kicked off his shoes, and grabbed the TV remote. His wife, Cheryl, popped the top off a beer, and Lance took a long pull.

The phone jangled loudly.

"Lance Cleary?" asked the voice.

"Yeah. Who's this?"

"Your father."

Dead silence.

"Who is it?" whispered Cheryl.

He put his hand over the phone. "It's my father."

"Your father? Why the hell is he calling? Did somebody die?"

Lance motioned her to be quiet and spoke into the phone. "What is it?"

"We need to meet."

"Why?"

"I'll tell you when we meet."

Lance hesitated. Almost twenty years and he waltzes in? The old man had to want something. Lance didn't owe him shit.

"It's important," said Ron.

"Okay, I guess."

Talon sat down in Rennick's office. Rennick noticed that Talon's left eye was starting to droop, and that he had been wearing the same suit the last few times they'd met.

"You okay, Danny?" asked Rennick.

"I'm fine. I got some info on Ron Cleary."

"That was quick."

"With the similarity to Martha Cleary's case, I figured the guy should get a front-row seat."

"What'd you find?"

"Cleary lives on an army pension. Doesn't seem to do much except watch TV and fix old cars. He was in the Special Forces till he broke his leg in three places. They were gonna discharge him for disability, but he squawked so much that they benched him in the radio corps. His main pastime is bowling with a league that meets in Mar Vista. That's a long ways from Sunland, and within a couple of miles of the victims. When he isn't bowling, he hangs out at a bar called the Palomino in North Hollywood. Country-and-western place. He also goes to a bar called the Jester in Sunland near his house. That's a my-dick's-bigger-'n'-your-dick kinda place, and he got into three fights there over the last five years. Won 'em all pretty quick."

"What do you make of all that?"

"Well, he doesn't have any qualms about shoving people around. But we ain't got nearly enough to put a leash on him. I want to keep him on the radar screen, and if we get something that even hints in his direction, I'll bring his buttocks in for some up close and personal time."

"You don't have enough to question him now?"

"Whatta we got? That his wife got slashed seventeen years ago? He wasn't charged for that, and even if he had been, the trail's dead cold. There's no physical or even circumstantial evidence that ties him to our killings."

"What about his bowling near the victims?"

"It seems a little odd, but it doesn't make him a killer."

"No. I guess not."

"I got someone checking out Lance Cleary, Lisa's brother," said Talon. "He lives in Culver City, near the MGM studios. That's also near the victims."

Talon closed his eyes and rubbed the lids.

"Danny, you okay?" asked Rennick.

"I'm fine."

"I figure this thing has been rough on you."

Talon stood up. "I'm fine."

"Psychiatrists get a lot of money to listen to people's problems, and I'm all yours for free."

"I'm fine," Talon said on his way out the door.

CHAPTER FORTY-ONE

Julie and Rennick sat at Le Petit Bistro, the French restaurant in Westwood where Rennick had met with Dr. Joseph. As they picked through their salade niçoises, Julie brought up the topic.

"We haven't discussed my offer to go to New York."

Rennick took a few sips of water. "What's your thinking?"

"I'm pretty confused. On a professional level, there's no doubt I should take it. A decision to work with Childs is a no-brainer."

"Agreed."

"Personally . . ." She looked directly at Rennick. "I don't really want to live on the East Coast for four years."

He looked up at a poster of the Loire Valley. "I don't blame you. I hate New York."

The only sound for the next few moments was Rennick chewing lettuce.

"How do you feel about my going east?" she asked.

He poked at a chunk of tuna and answered while looking at the plate. "Well, you know I'm supportive of whatever you think is best."

"You don't think you should be part of the decision?"

"I don't think I can decide what's the stronger priority in your life. That's such a . . . you know . . . personal choice."

Julie put down her fork. "You really aren't making this easy."

Rennick felt as though the room were closing in around him. He knew exactly what she meant as he said "What do you mean?"

"You know I'm talking about you and me. We're not children, Michael. We've both had some wild years. . . ."

"You've had wild years?" he said with a laugh.

"This isn't the time for jokes."

Rennick had only been partly joking. He'd always thought of Julie as pretty straight. What kind of wild years? he asked himself.

"We've been dating exclusively for three months," Julie continued. "I'm in love with you, Michael. I need to know what kind of commitment you're willing to make to me."

He knew he should tell this beautiful, brilliant woman that he wanted her forever. Yet the thought of making such a commitment terrified him; as did the idea of losing her. This was definitely the point in relationships where he blew it, he thought. If he had any decency, he'd tell her to find someone without his hang-ups.

Rennick finally answered. "If things keep going the way they are, I don't see any reason why we wouldn't continue—"

Julie stood up. "That's not exactly a strong affirmation of our relationship."

"I didn't know I'd have to make one at this stage. I'd hoped we could just let things, you know, grow organically."

"We don't have that luxury right now."

"You're saying you're not going to New York if I make a commitment to you?"

Julie hesitated. "Well . . . I want to know where we stand before I make a decision."

"Listen to what you said. You want me to make a commitment so you can decide if you want one. That's not fair."

"This is coming out all wrong." The light reflected off her moist eyes. "I'm sorry this job offer is accelerating things. I can't help it. I love you and I'm confused."

He took her hand and whispered, "I guess I'm confused too."

Tuesday.

Tonight I watched from a street corner. The lights in the apartments came on one at a time, and I saw people in easy chairs watching television, cooking in the kitchen, and actually talking to each other.

The dog I bailed out of the pound sat still at the end of the leash. Someone must have trained this one, so it might be worth keeping. Then again, who gives a shit. The pound gasses these mongrels by the truckload, so there's a steady supply without having to feed or house them.

It took me three days to find the right vantage point. It's against a building across the street, back from the streetlight just enough to make me invisible. When I'm standing there, her apartment building is a fish tank.

She got home right on time, and it took exactly forty-two seconds from the time she opened the wrought-iron security door until the lights went on in her apartment. She always peels her clothes off first thing, then runs around nude before putting on that powder blue chenille robe. It's amazing how so many women run around with their tits and pussies sticking out like that. She even stood at the window with her robe open, like she was advertising the goddamn things. And they wonder why there's so much crime.

The first floor of her building has wrought-iron bars over the windows. The second floor is unsecured. It's stupid how people feel so secure on the second floor. This girl never even locks her bedroom window. Yesterday she hung out some wind chimes. I wonder if that's her idea of a burglar alarm. Like it would take more than two seconds to avoid them.

I crossed the street and moved up against the wall of her building. So close that I could smell lamb chops grilling in a first-floor apartment. Above me, I could hear her singing by the window. It'll be an easy jump from the carport to that window. I've calculated and recalculated it for days. I've mentally rehearsed it so many times that my muscles can feel the moves.

Planning is like the blueprint for a building; execution is the construction. Adrenaline is the mortar that holds the bricks together.

Even though it was only nine thirty at night, Lisa was already yawning. She dropped her robe on the floor and slipped under the sheets. The cool fabric moved pleasantly against her. As she reached for the light, she saw the pills that Dr. Rennick had prescribed. They were still on the bedside table, inside a white paper bag that was stapled shut. While she had no intention of taking them, she had picked them up in case he called the pharmacy to check. The idea of something alien in her system was disgusting. A good night's sleep would be the best medicine.

Rennick had taken her very far. Now she could make her

own judgments. Which did not include pills. She was on top of the visions, she told herself. After she left the therapy session this morning, she'd had her most productive workday in months. Just like the other episodes. She lost control during the visions, then was stronger afterward.

Lisa now felt a pleasant drowsiness. She stretched, yawned widely, and snuggled under her big, fluffy marshmallow comforter.

On the stereo, the Jefferson Airplane is singing "White Rabbit":

> *One pill makes you larger*
> *One pill makes you small*
> *And the ones that mother gives you*
> *Don't do anything at all*
> *Go ask Alice*
> *When she's ten feet tall*

Danny Talon is dancing with his big sister Karen to the music of his favorite album, *Surrealistic Pillow*. Karen and her friends love how he calls it "Furry Kisses Pillow," which makes perfect sense to nine-year-old Danny because his favorite song on it is about a white rabbit.

> *When you go chasing rabbits*
> *And you know you're going to fall*

Danny and Karen hold hands, facing each other and leaning back while moving together clockwise. Karen has her eyes closed. Her tie-dyed bandanna is holding the crown of her straight brown hair in place, while the ends swirl around her shoulders.

When men on the chessboard
Get up and tell you where to go

Incense fills the air, and the black light is making her room look like a funhouse. Her friends are lying on the floor and bed, passing around the funny-looking cigarette and moving in time to the music. One of them is wearing glasses with lenses that look like crystal doorknobs.

Now everyone is sitting on the floor in a circle. Their arms are around each other's shoulders, swaying in unison, while they sing along with John Lennon's "Give Peace a Chance." Danny is feeling a little funny. The music is smearing pretty colors in his head. Is Karen's bed starting to move? Karen says don't worry. It's cool. So it must be okay.

Later that night, when everyone's gone home, Danny is lying on Karen's bed. His head is by her feet, and her toenails are glowing purple in the black light. She's playing her nylon string guitar that's missing one string. "Greensleeves." Danny closes his eyes and feels the music move through him. Her sweet voice sings, "Alas, my love, you do-o me wrong. . . ."

"I don't want you to go away to college," Danny says when she finishes.

"Don't you want me to have a good time?"

"Yes. I want you to have it here."

She rubs his cheek with her toes. "I'll miss you, Danny."

"I want to go with you."

"You'll come to visit me. I'm just going to Sonoma."

"I don't mean visit. I mean I want to live with you."

Karen sits up and takes his hand. "I'd really love that. But the college won't let people come there until they're seventeen. And I'm depending on you to take care of Mom and Dad. When I'm gone, you're in charge of the house."

"What about Dad?"

"He's a grown-up. You're the kid in charge."

"Oh."

Danny pulls out a Bazooka bubble gum that has shaped itself to his pocket during the two days it's been there. He peels off the paper and splits it not too evenly. He gives the smaller piece to Karen and quickly puts the bigger one in his mouth. She starts to chew.

"Mmmm. Your bubble gum is the best."

"Really?"

"Honest."

Karen looks back and forth to see if anyone is around. Then she leans close to Danny. The small wooden beads around her neck rattle softly. She smells like vanilla.

"Danny, let's make a secret pact."

"Okay," he whispers. "What?"

"I want you to have these." She takes off her beads and puts them over his head. He sits up straight and looks down at them, running them between his thumb and fingers.

"Wow! These are cool!"

"What do you say?"

"Thank you. Thank you."

"I promise I'll call you every week while I'm away," Karen says, taking hold of his hand. "And you promise you'll look after Mom and Dad. A deal?"

"Deal."

"Say 'I promise.'"

"I promise."

Danny Talon awoke. It was dark out, as it always was on winter mornings.

He lay in bed, replaying the dream in his head. He reached out his hand in the air, pretending to give Karen's hand a last squeeze as her fingers slipped out of his grasp.

His alarm buzzed rudely. Five A.M. He stumbled toward the shower, groped for the knobs, and turned the water almost all the way to Cold. The spray hit him directly in the face.

He hadn't thought about Karen's pact in years. Even when she appeared in his prior dreams, it was just an image of her floating in front of him. Never talking. Why would he dream about it now?

He turned the water all the way to Cold and let out a quick yelp.

CHAPTER FORTY-TWO

Lance Cleary locked his helmet onto the motor scooter, then combed his hair in the rearview mirror. When he was satisfied with the look, he walked toward Al Penny's, a fifty-year-old diner on Washington Boulevard in Culver City. Lance had chosen Penny's because it was close to his house. He figured if the old man really wanted to see him, he could haul his ass in from Sunland. Lance was actually surprised that his father had agreed. This must be pretty important.

Penny's had a long counter, round swivel stools, and only three tables. A jukebox played fifties music on forty-fives, and the patrons were gray- and blue-hairs who looked like they were ready to keel over. Lance had intentionally come ten minutes late, so he knew his father had to be there somewhere.

Lance spotted him at a table in the back. Even though he hadn't seen his father since Lance left home to join the service, he recognized him right away. The guy looked pretty good, and Lance hoped he had the same genes. Genes were about the only thing they had in common.

His father didn't reach out to shake his hand, so Lance just sat down. To his surprise, Ron Cleary looked nervous as he kept clicking the glass salt and pepper shakers against each other. Lance never remembered seeing his father any way other than in control. The master of the house. The supreme commander. Now a jittery old man. In fact, Ron looked smaller than he remembered.

"Your posture is weak," said Ron. "You ought to stand up straighter."

"Yeah, yeah. So what's this all about?"

Ron took a sip of coffee and looked around the diner. "You remember a conversation we had right after your mother . . . died?"

Now it was Lance's turn to look around the room. "'Course I do. What about it?"

"The cops have been nosing around lately. And your sister showed up too."

"Lisa?"

"You got another sister? Of course, Lisa. Has anyone been to see you?"

"Uh, yeah."

"Who?"

"Some cop."

Ron tensed. "What'd he want?"

"He wanted to know about you."

"Shit." Ron picked up a quarter lying on the table and flipped it into the air with a *ping*. "What'd you say?"

"That I ain't seen you in years."

Ron slapped the quarter onto the table. "Listen. The things we talked about back then were private. I was real upset and I said some stupid things. I don't want you to ever talk to anybody about it. Understand?"

Lance sat in silence.

"Gimme your word that you won't talk to anyone. Not Lisa. Not the cops. Nobody."

"You don't got any right to tell me what to do."

"I'm your father."

"You maybe dropped some sperm a while back, and I guess that makes you my father, but you ain't exactly been a picture of what I think a father oughta be."

"You some expert now? You got kids?"

"What's it matter to you? You ain't given a shit about my life for years, and that's fine by me."

Ron leaned back. "Okay. You're right. I don't have any right to order you around. So I'm asking. Nicely. Will you do this for me, please?"

Lance could see that his father had a hard time getting those words out. He almost felt sorry for him, which was the last thing he'd expected.

"I guess."

Ron gave a short nod. "You need anything, Lance? Like some money or something?"

"I guess I never got enough dough."

Ron fished a twenty out of his pocket and pushed it across the table. Lance put his hands on it, then stopped. Taking the money felt too weird. He didn't need to owe this guy shit. "Forget it. I don't need nothin' right now."

Ron took back the money and the two of them sat silently for several moments. Finally, Ron got up and left with the check.

*   *   *

Michelle Harris's big toe played with a drop that hung on the bathtub spigot. Her head rested all the way back on a pink inflatable seashell, and her arms floated freely in the warm water. Its surface was covered with a thick foam of bubbles, whose lilac fragrance filled the room. The only light radiated from four thick candles that cascaded wax down their sides.

She was still glowing from the day's victory. The agency loved her sketches for Reebok's national campaign, and they wanted her to submit ideas for America Online. Her boss said this meant a promotion and a raise.

Michelle toyed with the bubbles on her fingers and wished that Roger were in town to share the news. And to share the bath. She closed her eyes and sank deeper into the tub. The water seeped into her shoulder-length blond hair as she imagined his touch all over.

A half hour later, the candles began to sputter and the water was cooling down. She reluctantly climbed out and grabbed the fluffy burgundy bath towel. Then she dried herself in long strokes, savoring the soft fleece against her skin.

Michelle walked nude into her bedroom and pulled on a sweatshirt that said LOVE ANIMALS, DON'T EAT THEM. After a quick debate, she decided not to wear anything else.

The apartment felt stuffy, so she opened her bedroom window. A cool breeze drifted in, and her wind chimes jingled in the draft. She poured herself an unfiltered apple juice, put on a CD of harp music, and snuggled into the overstuffed kelly green chair, whose fabric was worn soft and cuddly with age. The upholstery caressed her bare lower body.

After settling into just the right position, Michelle turned on the brass reading light and opened her new book by environmentalist Aubrey Chernin. She was hooked on the first page by his discussion of the scientific and medicinal possibilities of the rain forests. She shifted in the chair, putting one foot underneath her.

An hour or so later, she noticed that the room felt chilly. Had she opened the window too far? She didn't think so. Usually she just opened it a crack. She looked around but couldn't see the window from her chair, so she continued reading.

A few minutes later there was a gust of cold wind and she thought she heard something. She looked around and didn't see anything. Maybe she should check the window. Yet she was into a really fascinating section of her book. In a minute. Just another page or two.

Rennick hated faculty parties. Small talk with a bunch of people whose asses he was supposed to kiss, forced laughter, professors pontificating about some obscure theory of the Napoleonic Code's influence on modern society. And if that wasn't enough, the phone was ringing so loudly that it drowned out their conversations. Everyone was ignoring the ring. Why the hell didn't someone answer? Rennick seemed to be the only one who heard it, since the others just kept talking. Didn't anybody else care? Disgusted, he looked around for the phone and couldn't find it. The damn ringing grew louder and louder.

Gradually, Rennick realized he was asleep in bed, dreaming of a party. Not exactly an escape from the rigors of the day. Groggy and disoriented, he reached over to answer the phone and knocked his alarm clock off the table. It was followed immediately by the phone. At least the ringing stopped.

His head felt three times its normal size as he groped for the phone's handset in the dark, unwilling to open his eyes. Finally, he gave up and looked, since nothing felt like a phone. The clock on the floor read 2:13 A.M.

"Yes?" he managed to say hoarsely.

The voice on the other end came rapidly and loudly, like the staccato fire of a machine gun. "It's happening! I know it! It's happening right now. Or it just happened."

"What's happening?" said Rennick, cupping his hand around the phone in hopes he wouldn't wake Julie.

"The murder I told you about. The girl with the mole on her cheek. I know it. I feel it. I'm sure of it."

"Lisa, there's nothing we can do about it now."

"I'm scared. I keep seeing it over and over. The girl. The wind chimes. I saw the killer walking a small black dog with hair that looks like dreadlocks. I saw this girl being cut apart. And electrocuted with a gray cord. There were nails in her ears. Doctor, these visions are getting worse. I can feel the killer's pulse. It's like we're breathing in the same rhythm. How do I make them stop?"

"Hold on a minute." Rennick stumbled into the living room and picked up the extension. He pitched his voice lower and spoke slowly, in counterpoint to her panic.

"Are you at home?"

"Yes."

"Are the doors and windows locked?"

"Yes."

"Then you're safe. You just need to calm down. Do you want to go to the emergency room at UCLA?"

"No! They'll shoot me full of medication."

"I think it might be—"

"No. Please. I just need you to talk to me," she whimpered. The whimper was a good sign. It was a ratchet away from panic, and hopefully he could guide her down gently.

"I've been doing so much better," she continued. "This is the first time I've fallen apart in days. Please. I know you keep saying I have to open the wound before I can heal, but I feel like I just ripped off the scab."

"You're okay, Lisa. If the murder is real, it's too late to help, and we can deal with it tomorrow. If it's not, then you had a nightmare and it can't hurt you or anyone else. Either way, if you don't want to get medical treatment, there's nothing we can do tonight."

"I'm so scared."

"I can prescribe Xanax to help you sleep. There's an all-night pharmacy in West Hollywood that delivers."

"No. Please. No pills. Just talk to me for a few minutes."

Rennick sat back on the couch. "All right. Take some deep breaths and relax. Okay? Go on. I can hear you breathing over the phone."

Lisa took a few deep breaths, and he listened for the telltale sign that each one was a little longer and a little slower, which meant she was calming down.

"Good. Now I want you to get into bed and relax. Even if you can't sleep, resting is almost as good. Drink some warm milk if you like. I know it's a cliché, but it actually has chemicals in it that relax you."

The fact that she was quiet meant she was listening.

"It's all okay, Lisa. You're going to be fine. There's nothing we can do tonight. Get in bed, and we'll talk tomorrow. Call me back if you want a prescription for tranquilizers."

"Thank you," she said weakly before hanging up.

Rennick rested his head in his hands and massaged his scalp. This was not what he had in mind when he talked about opening Lisa's wounds. She had much deeper problems than he had guessed.

He didn't want to wake Julie, so he returned to the bedroom silently by stepping on his toes before his heels, a technique that his father once told him Native Americans used for hunting. Just as he was about to slip into bed, Julie turned on the lamp. He shielded his eyes from the searing light.

"Michael, goddamn it, I'm sick of your putting our relationship behind everything else in your life."

He blinked repeatedly, trying to adjust to the sudden light. "What do you mean?"

"What do I mean? Don't be idiotic. You work twenty-four/seven, you drag your ass home exhausted, and when we finally have time together, you don't talk."

"Do we have to discuss this now? It's so late."

"See? You're doing it again. You had no problem getting on the phone with someone else at this hour."

His head was now throbbing. "Okay, okay. I'm sorry I've been so distant. But you know what my load's been like. I'm in the middle of a swamp, and I've got a lot of slogging whether I go forward or backwards."

"I know you have a heavy workload. The point is, you're using your work as an excuse not to deal with us."

He tried to touch her shoulder, and she pushed his hand away. "It's just that, I, uh . . . don't want to make a major decision when I'm under this much stress. I don't trust my judgment right now."

She stared at him for several moments, then said, "I see. Well, let me make it easy for you. You don't have to be a part of this decision at all."

Julie threw back the covers and got out of bed.

"What are you doing? It's almost three a.m."

"I'm going to my apartment."

"Now?"

"Now." Julie pulled on a pair of jeans and a sweatshirt as she spoke.

"No. Don't. Please. You shouldn't be out by yourself at this hour."

She went into the bathroom and Rennick followed behind. She stuffed her makeup and toothbrush into the Pooh bag, which was a child's plastic case with a picture of Winnie the Pooh. He had bought the bag for her on their first weekend away, because she'd forgotten her travel kit.

"Why are you taking your toiletries?" he asked.

She struggled to zip the bulging Pooh bag and didn't answer. Winnie, with his hand in the honey jar, smiled at Rennick.

Julie walked past him to the front door. Rennick trailed behind like a puppy whose owner was about to leave him in a kennel.

"Please. Don't go. I'm sorry. I'll cut back on my work. I'll—" His words bounced off the door she closed behind her.

CHAPTER FORTY-THREE

Rennick did not have an easy night. After several hours of dozing in and out, he finally fell into a heavy sleep. It was therefore with great annoyance that he became conscious of the phone ringing. The clock next to it said 7:00 A.M.

His mouth felt like it was full of foul-tasting cotton as he managed to snort a greeting.

"Morning, Professor," came Talon's voice. "I just called to let you know that I checked out Logan's alibis."

"And?" Rennick rolled over, remembering with a pang that Julie was gone. Instinctively, he looked at the empty bathroom counter where her Pooh bag belonged. That sent him into a nosedive depression.

"Logan's a major league loner," Talon continued. "That fits your profile but makes it hard to verify his whereabouts. He says he was at the movies, or watching television or surfing the Internet. The computer company shows he was on-line, but my techies tell me it only proves he logged on, not that he sat at the terminal the whole night. In short, I got zip-a-dee-doo-dah."

Rennick's mind was still on Julie. How could he have let the rift between them get this wide? He remembered the sound of her laughter when he landed in his parachute. Her brilliant perspectives on the law. The vision of their nude bodies lying spent in the afternoon, lubricated with beads of perspiration.

"Professor?"

"Sorry. I'm a little preoccupied. Danny, was there another murder last night?"

"Several. But none by our favorite asshole, so far as I know. And they'd tell me right away if there was. Why?"

"Lisa called in the middle of the night. She thought another one was happening."

"If it did, it ain't been reported yet."

Rennick hung up and grabbed a handful of aspirin. The lack of sleep and the memory of Julie's leaving, intensified by the missing toiletries, jackhammered against his head. He took the pills with a gulp of water, then fell back onto the bed. Before he closed his eyes, he called Julie's number and left a message on her machine.

"I'm sorry. Please call me. I love you."

Marvin Logan hit the Enter key on his laptop, which loaded the program for the demonstration. He was dressed in his charcoal gray pinstripe suit. While he waited, he looked down the long, highly polished, walnut conference table of Thurgood Industries. About fourteen empty chairs surrounded it, like knights ready for the battle. He figured the furnishings in this room alone cost over fifty Gs.

All of the vice-presidents had already agreed, and if the president and the CEO bought in, he could close the six-hundred-thousand-dollar software sale. He had worked on this transaction for five months, spending a lot of time pretending that these morons were his friends. He had even sprung for a nine-hundred-and-fifty-dollar dinner, in the hopes that it would close the deal. And that was out of his own hide.

The double door opened, and in came the entourage. Logan stood up. Everyone waited for the CEO, Morton Graves, to go in first. Graves was an old bastard, probably in his late seventies, who walked stooped over. The others followed in silence, like a line of cars behind a slow truck.

When the group finally sat down at the table, the CEO growled, "Get right to it. You got ten minutes."

Logan began the slide presentation. He talked along, explaining how the accounts payable program alone would pay for the package in eighteen months, since they could downsize the department by seven employees. The old man seemed to be going for it.

The slide show ended and one of the assistants poured a drink of water for the CEO. A few drops splashed on the table. Logan couldn't take his eyes off the drops. Just like that bastard shrink at the police station, he thought. Trying to get me to say something stupid. Who the fuck did he think he was dealing with?

"What did you say?" asked the president.

"Excuse me?" said Logan.

"It sounded like you used the f-word."

"I . . . I'm sorry. I don't think so." Oh shit. Had he said that out loud?

An assistant whispered into the CEO's ear while looking up at Logan the whole time.

"We'll get back to you," grunted the CEO, standing up. All the others stood in unison, then followed him out in silence.

"I'm sorry. . . . I'm sorry. . . ." Logan repeated.

They left without looking back.

CHAPTER FORTY-FOUR

The phone rang at seven on Wednesday morning. Rennick rolled over and picked it up. He hoped it was Julie, who had apparently unplugged her phone.

"Mornin', Professor. Have you seen the newspaper?" Talon's voice sounded deflated, like someone who was about to go down for the count.

"No."

"Page one, Metro section. Another victim. Same shoulder-length blond hair. Nails in the ears and a crispy-fried corpse."

Lisa was right, thought Rennick. There had been a killing.

"It ain't pretty," Talon continued. "Remember I found that broken hacksaw blade at the Mullins scene? This time we got the throat slashed with a knife, then the head cut off with a hacksaw."

"When did it happen?"

"Judging from the last time anyone saw her and the last day she took in her newspaper, Monday night."

Lisa had been right about the timing as well.

"Did the victim have a mole on her cheek?" asked Rennick.

"Yeah. I thought you didn't see the paper."

"I didn't. Lisa saw the mole in a vision."

A beat of silence. "Did she say anything else?"

"She said the killer had a dog with dreadlocks."

"A dog? I interviewed a woman near the Mullins scene who saw a man with a dog hanging around. Shit."

There was a brief silence. "The time's getting shorter between killings," said Rennick. "This sonofabitch loves the game. He'll go on until he's captured or dead."

"That's cheery news, though not so surprising."

"You're checking Logan's whereabouts on Monday?"

"Yep. At least there's one down—Heath's still locked up in the Eureka jail. I think it's time to invite Ron Cleary to this party. Want to come along when I interview him?"

"Yes."

"And you're also invited to meet brother Lance when he gets back to town."

Talon's last words were interrupted by the beep of call waiting.

"Dr. Rennick? It's Lisa." Her voice was calm and composed.

"How are you feeling?" he asked.

"I'm fine now. I'm sorry about calling you late the other night. Have you seen the papers?"

Rennick was surprised at the question. He'd assumed from her composure that she didn't know about the killing.

"No. Talon's on the other line telling me about it."

"Unfortunately, it looks like I was right."

"Yes."

"Doctor, I want to go to her apartment. With something this fresh, I could get very strong images."

"That's not a good idea."

"Why not?"

"Because it has the potential of seriously upsetting you."

"I'm feeling strong now, and I want to confront this in its most violent form. Don't you see the pattern? It upsets me, and then I heal. And every time I heal, I'm stronger."

"Going to a murder scene would be much more traumatic than anything else you've done. I don't like it, and I don't think you should risk it."

"I understand your concerns. But you can hear that I'm in a different place now. I see the whole thing more analytically. If I couldn't handle it, we'd both know very quickly, and I'd leave."

Rennick was impressed by her logic and control. Maybe she was right. Maybe the healing after each incident was making her stronger. On the other hand, the danger of her going to an actual crime scene was immense.

"No. Absolutely not."

"Dr. Rennick, I have to do this. I feel . . . well . . . drawn there. I owe it to these young women."

"You asked my professional opinion. I think it's a mistake that could do you serious harm."

A few seconds of silence. "I see."

She hung up.

Lisa found the murder victim listed in the phone book, under "M. Harris." Michelle Harris, the paper said, in the Pico/Robertson area. Seeing yellow police tape across the steps confirmed that she was in the right place. The day was cold, with an overcast sky and heavy moisture in the air, causing Lisa to pull the sides of her coat tightly against her. A chilly gust of wind ruffled the yellow tape.

The Babylonia Apartments was a 1920s two-story, boxlike building, with peach stucco walls and concrete steps that climbed to a small landing. Sometime in the last ten years, the owner had made a pass at converting the structure to a security building by adding wrought iron to the doors and first-floor windows. It obviously hadn't worked for at least one resident.

Lisa locked her car and walked along the sidewalk, sensing that the killer had taken the same path. If the vibes reached this far out, she could only imagine what she'd feel inside the apartment. She quickened her steps.

Dr. Rennick had been right about a lot of things, and he'd helped her so much. But he was only human, capable of an error in judgment like everyone else. She had to make her own decisions if she were ever going to be independent, and she knew he was just plain wrong about this one. This was where she needed to be.

As Lisa neared the steps of the death scene, she felt weaker. Something wasn't right. The vibrations from the building didn't feel the same as the other places she'd been. They were . . . darker. She hesitated, then stopped.

A uniformed officer on the stoop came toward her.

"May I help you?" he asked.

She considered turning to leave. The building both beckoned and repelled her.

"I've been working with Detective Talon on these serial killings," she finally said. "He's given me permission to check the scene." The lie came easily.

"Your name?"

"Lisa Cleary."

"Is Detective Talon expecting you now?"

"He's here?"

"Yes."

"Oh. No, he's not expecting me."

The officer eyed her suspiciously and went into the building. On the way, he whispered to another officer, who watched her while she waited.

The first officer finally returned. "I'll take you to Detective Talon."

Lisa missed a step on the way to the second floor, nearly falling down the stairs. By the time she walked down the second-floor hallway, she was beginning to shake. Apartment 23 was at the end, and when they entered, Talon put down his notepad and greeted her.

"Does Dr. Rennick know you're here?"

"No. I'm not sure he wants me to come."

Talon furrowed his forehead. "Why not?"

"He thinks I'm fragile. You can see I'm not."

She looked around and saw a picture of a gray wolf on one wall, and a poster of an albino tiger on another. In one window was a ceramic wind chime that looked like an octopus, with a cup-shaped top and tube-shaped pieces dangling like tentacles. They tinkled softly as a cold breeze rustled them, and she shuddered as she remembered her vision of chimes in the shape of fish.

Lisa was beginning to feel more energy around her. Intense, threatening forces, like she'd felt on the front steps. Maybe Dr. Rennick was right. This was disturbing. The energy radiated through her, like a low vibration moaning in pain, punctured by wind chimes that seemed to scream in terror.

She ought to get out of here.

"I'm no shrink," said Talon, "but if Dr. Rennick doesn't think—"

"It happened over there, didn't it?"

Her hand, as if on its own, pointed. She began walking with her eyes half closed, then stopped at the bedroom door. The covers on the bed had been stripped, and there was a huge blood-soaked stain on the mattress. Next to the bed was a multicolored candle in the shape of a ball, similar to the one in her dream.

When she realized how close it was to her vision, Lisa bolted and ran hard into Talon. She recoiled from the collision, stunned and disoriented. Before she could run again, a voice began speaking through her. Harsher than before. More jarring. It caused her chest to ache and her throat to burn.

"This is the same killer. Watching her for days. Outside. Across the street. With a small dog. Very careful. 'No one will notice if there's a dog.' I'm getting a clearer picture, but I still can't see the face. This is someone strong and agile. Methodical, calculating. The chase is part of the game. Striking back at . . . at . . . I can't tell."

Shadows were starting to surround her. They were rudely shoving her, as if asking, Who are you? What do you think you're doing?

"The killer is coming through the window. Over there. The girl is in a chair." She pointed toward the living room. "The killer is coming from behind. Quickly choking her unconscious. No time to scream. Dragged to the bed and tied up with her stockings. Cutting off her clothes. Starting to cut her throat. Deep gashes. My God! It's a saw."

The dark energy surrounded her like a pack of wolves moving in on wounded prey, signaling each other with nods as they tightened the circle.

"It will happen again soon," she continued. "It's getting easier with practice." Her body started moving. "Escape through the window there."

She found her body climbing out the window. Talon grabbed her. She roughly shoved his hand away. "I can feel it. Down the alley. This way."

"Don't go out the window," said Talon, gripping her more tightly. "It's two stories up." He pulled her inside and led her downstairs by the elbow, as if escorting a blind person through a maze. When they reached the alley, she began jogging.

"Along here. Carrying the bloody raincoat in a bag. This way." Lisa felt bands of energy along the alley, like runway lights guiding her way. When she ran into the street, Talon grabbed her roughly. A car's tires screeched and its horn blared. She pulled urgently out of his grip and continued across the way. Down a block, through a yard. Faster. Panting. Following the energy.

She stopped at a galvanized trash can behind a blue stucco house. It pulled her magnetically. She reached for the lid and felt Talon's hand intercept.

"If you think something's in there, don't touch it."

The can seemed to pulse, as if it were a breathing organism. Her compulsion to grab hold and connect was almost over-whelming.

Talon led her back several steps, then put on latex gloves and opened the lid. He looked inside, then at Lisa. After a hesitation, he took out a bloodied sports bag and unzipped it. She ran forward and looked inside.

A knife, a plastic raincoat, and a sealed ivory-colored envelope. All covered in blood.

Lisa began to vomit.

*   *   *

Talon walked Lisa to her car across the street from Michelle Harris's apartment. It began to drizzle as she sat in the driver's seat with the door open. He stood beside her on the pavement. Lisa hadn't stopped shaking for almost a half hour after finding the bloody bag. With her hair half undone and her blouse stained with vomit, she reminded Talon of a socialite he'd once found overdosed in an alley. Now, with Talon's jacket around her shoulders and a few sips of hot tea that one of the officers had fetched, she finally seemed to be calming down.

"I really think you should go to a hospital," he suggested.

"No. I'm all right. I just need some time to collect myself."

"Then let me call Dr. Rennick."

"Please don't do that."

"You're not in any shape to drive. I'll have someone take you home."

"I'll be fine in a few minutes. You don't have to stay."

Talon reached into her purse and found the keys. He took her hand, and she followed him docilely as he led her to the passenger side of her car. Then he climbed in and started the engine.

They drove to her apartment in silence. He walked her to the door and called a cab for himself on her phone.

"I'd get some sleep if I were you," said Talon.

She smiled weakly and held out her hand to shake. He hesitated for a second and then took it. As soon as they touched, her eyes closed and her face lost all expression. She gripped his hand with more strength than she looked like she had left. He tried to pull away, yet she held tightly.

"Detective, there's a pretty teenage girl. She has long brown hair, and she's very close to you. Her name starts with a K or C. Carol maybe? Or Cat? She loves you very much."

Talon felt like he'd been hit in the chest with a defibrillator.

He literally jolted back, almost losing his balance and falling against the rail. His tongue swelled in his suddenly dry mouth.

How? No one knew that his nickname for Karen was Kat, the initials on her little pillow. Karen Anne Talon. No one except his parents, who'd been dead for years.

Lisa continued. "She's . . . she's dancing with you. A dark room. Friends around. Laughing. She's blowing smoke in your face. Why would she do that?"

A flood of memory returned to his consciousness. Blowing smoke in his face. My God. Karen had gotten him stoned when he was only a small child, by blowing marijuana smoke into his face. Talon had totally forgotten.

He turned away from Lisa and began to cry.

CHAPTER FORTY-FIVE

Talon never drank. He wasn't critical of people who did, or against it morally. He just didn't like the taste or the way it made him feel. In fact, he hadn't drunk alcohol even in his wildest drug days. He knew his Twelve-Stepper buddies would strangle him for even thinking about blitzing out on booze. He didn't give a shit tonight. He could handle it.

Since he never kept any liquor around, he stopped to buy a bottle of Jack Daniel's. It rested next to him on the passenger seat during the drive home, like a dog on an outing.

Talon sat down at his dining room table without bothering to change his clothes, even though he usually couldn't wait to get out of the monkey suit and into an old set of sweats. He poured the whiskey into a glass and held it up against the light. The cheap overhead fixture lit the amber liquid as he swirled the glass around. After studying it awhile, he set the booze on the table without drinking. He wasn't looking forward to the taste.

Talon put on the third movement of Beethoven's Opus 130 and cranked up the volume. Then he picked up the glass and took a sip. Even though he only let the liquor sit in his mouth for a second, it stung like hell and tasted like a mixture of lighter fluid and mouthwash. He knew the first sip was the worst. After that, his taste buds were seared off.

Lisa's reminding him of Karen had disturbed him so much that he hadn't gone back to work. On top of a case that was crushing him, she had to bring up Karen. Talon had spent the afternoon walking aimlessly around Griffith Park's hiking trails in his suit and tie, oblivious to the rain and the mud it made. Until Lisa said it, he hadn't remembered what Karen had done. That she'd exhaled marijuana into his tiny face so he'd get stoned along with her. Why would someone do that to a little kid?

Talon took another sip, and the smell of alcohol clawed his sinuses. Karen's face drifted into his mind. She was floating in front of him, radiating youth and innocence. Her long brown hair, crowned with a tie-dyed headband, drifted about her in slow motion, almost as if she were weightless.

The sixties had arrived late in Valencia, California, and Karen had made up for lost time. Talon used to listen outside her room when she hung out with her friends. They played Jimi Hendrix, the Doors, and Led Zeppelin. When they caught him spying one day, to his delight and surprise, they invited him in, even though he was only eight and they were in their late teens. Karen always danced with him, and he felt the boys were jealous. Or at least he hoped so.

Karen's withdrawal began so slowly that no one noticed. At first she'd sit at dinner and not say anything. Then she'd refuse to come to the phone when someone called. Finally, she sat alone in her room and stared at the wall. Her friends stopped coming around. Danny tried to talk to her. She wouldn't answer. He knew she was mad at him. He must have upset her. But she wouldn't tell him what he'd done. She wouldn't say anything. He cried at night, trying to figure out why. He wrote notes to her in pencil, still in printing even though he could almost do it in handwriting. She never answered him. Mom said Karen had taken some "bad medicine" and would be okay. But Mom didn't look like she meant it.

Karen finally stopped eating with the family. In fact, she hardly ate at all. He overheard Mom and Dad saying they might have to put her somewhere. He didn't want her to go. It had to be his fault. What had he done?

Every night he begged her to come down to dinner. Every night she sat there without answering. The family ate with her place set and her chair empty. Mom and Dad talked less and less to him and to each other. And Karen just sat in her bedroom, without the lights on. Even at night.

Then one night Danny went to get her and she wasn't in her room. He tried the bathroom and found the door was locked. He rattled the knob, but there was no answer. He called Dad. Mom started crying. Dad threw his shoulder against the door over and over, almost like he was trying to hurt himself. The door finally popped open and Dad sent Danny to his room.

Talon remembered lying on his bed with a pillow over his face. He could still hear the screams. And the sirens and commotion that followed. His parents came in and said Karen wasn't coming back. They were dried out of tears. There wasn't anything to say.

Talon shook his head and took another sip of whiskey. This time he held his breath while he swallowed. Then he closed his

DON PASSMAN

eyes and listened to the music glide into a crescendo. His favorite part. The cavatina movement. He moved his entire body in rhythm and hummed along. This was the piece he played when he wanted cocaine so badly that his body screamed. In the days when he first got clean, he'd walk around the room, banging the walls in time to the music. Anything to let out the bursting tension. And most of the time he made it through, forming a bond with this opus in the process. Like buddies helping each other under enemy fire.

He sure could use a buddy right now.

CHAPTER FORTY-SIX

After Talon dropped her off, Lisa had felt so hot that she sat in a cool bath for almost an hour. She then developed chills, so she put on a sweatshirt and a sweater and shivered in bed underneath two blankets. She checked her temperature and found it was a hundred and three. Finally, she fell asleep in a pool of perspiration at four in the afternoon.

The next morning, she awoke feeling more energetic than she had in months. The fever had passed, and she was rested and alert. She washed several days' worth of accumulated dishes, vacuumed her apartment, and did two loads of laundry. Finally, she did some aerobics to her seventies disco album and finished off with a brisk shower.

Lisa continued riding the crest of her high at work. She made a serious dent in her backlog of paperwork, and marveled how these horrible episodes kept making her stronger. Even though the visions were growing more intense, her vigor afterwards was extraordinary. Like building a muscle, she thought. The strain of lifting tears it down, then it's stronger when it mends.

Because the Latham Oil people were coming in this afternoon, she stopped working on the backlog and took out a clean sheet of paper. They wanted to expand into drilling accessories, but it was uneconomical because of the Value Added Tax assessed on their French manufacturing plant. VAT was one of the hardest to avoid, and she'd been trying to come up with a scheme for over a week.

As she stared at the blank page, her thoughts meandered to finding the bloody sports bag yesterday. Now it seemed a distant memory, with no emotional charge. She really was getting better. The bag had been in a garbage can. A can. A can is a container. Containers are used in shipping.

Of course! If the components were made in France with non-VAT-country materials, then shipped to a non-VAT country for assembly, they couldn't avoid the tax, but they could reduce it radically. She'd have to study several countries' treaties with France to be sure, yet it seemed promising.

Lisa walked with a bounce toward the international tax library.

The morning sun lit Talon's face harshly as he drove north on the 405 Freeway. Rennick noticed that his hair was disheveled and that his eyelids appeared heavy. When he spoke, his voice was hoarse.

Talon explained his experience with Lisa at the Harris murder scene.

"How could you let her do that?" barked Rennick.

"She just showed up and started before I could do anything about it."

"That was irresponsible. I told her to stay away."

"Well, you didn't tell me that. So go yell at her. Shit, Professor. Chill out."

Rennick slapped the dashboard hard enough to make his finger sting. "You're right. It wasn't your fault. I'm just upset about a lot of things."

"So put that energy into figuring out what this new evidence means."

"It means our killer is turning stone-cold aggressive. Leaving clues virtually in the open like that. Typing a note in advance for us. This guy is really giving us the finger. I only hope his cockiness will lead to a blunder."

"Seems like we've been waiting a long time for that."

Talon turned off the freeway toward Ron Cleary's house in Sunland. They had tried to schedule the appointment at night, based on Rennick's idea of the killer's rhythms. But Cleary had simply refused, so they were arriving in the morning. Rennick wondered if that had been an intentional "screw you" move by Cleary.

Rennick saw Talon throw a handful of antacids into his mouth and start chewing them.

"Danny, you doing okay?" asked Rennick.

"You keep asking me that. To be honest, Professor, you're the one who looks like shit."

"You sure know how to cheer a guy up."

"Tell you what," said Talon. "If I'm ever not fine, I'll tell you. So you don't have to keep asking me. Deal?"

"Okay. Deal."

They pulled up to Cleary's house and Talon cut the engine. As they walked to the door, Rennick had the incongruous feeling that he was about to meet a girlfriend's parents for the first time. It made him ache for Julie. She wasn't returning his calls, and when he'd gone by her apartment, she hadn't been home. He massaged a throb that suddenly appeared at the back of his neck.

Cleary yelled for them to come in. He remained sitting on the couch with his back toward them, engrossed in a TV game show. Rennick looked around the living room and saw that it was sparse but orderly; a life of spartan discipline.

Ron Cleary sat perfectly still and didn't move in response to their entrance. When they walked around the couch to face him, Rennick was surprised at how much he resembled Lisa. Although he was much more angular, they had almost the same face, and the eyes were an identical sapphire blue. He was wearing a white T-shirt that said CHEVY TRUCKS on the front. The muscles in his arms and neck were flexed, as if he were doing an isometric exercise.

Only his eyes moved to look at the intruders, giving them a quick examination, then returning to the television. There was a loud *ding* and an announcer saying "You're absolutely right!" The audience broke into applause.

"Mr. Cleary?" asked Talon.

"Yeah."

"We spoke on the phone. I'm Detective Talon and this is Dr. Rennick."

"Yeah."

"Could we talk for a few minutes?"

"Yeah. Go ahead." He didn't take his eyes off the TV. The announcer said, "No, I'm sorry," and the audience "Awww'ed."

Talon turned off the set and the picture disappeared into a dot of light. Cleary continued to stare at the screen and Talon stepped in front of it.

"Where were you last Monday night?"

"Home."

"Was anyone with you?"

"Nope."

"What were you doing?"

"Watching television."

"What programs were on?"

"I don't remember."

"Do you bowl in a league?"

Cleary looked Talon up and down. "Yeah."

"Where?"

"Mar Vista Bowl."

"Isn't that kinda far for you?"

"Yeah."

"So why do you bowl so far from home?"

"I used to live around there. I like to bowl with guys from that neighborhood."

"You know anything about the recent killings of young women in West L.A.?"

"Just what I see on TV."

"Are you aware that the M.O. is similar to how your wife was murdered?"

The reaction was subtle, but Rennick caught it. Cleary's jaw clenched, and he blinked rapidly a couple of times. That question had scored a hit.

"Not really."

"You were a suspect in that killing."

"Yeah, well, they always suspect husbands. I was never charged with anything."

"I know. What happened that day, Mr. Cleary?"

Rennick saw another jaw clench, and Cleary's pupils dilated slightly. He knew there was more going on than just a husband remembering his wife's death.

"How can that be important all these years later?"

"If it's the same killer, it could be real important."

"You accusing me of something?"

"Should I be?"

"The cops back then didn't think it was me. Why should you?"

"So what happened that day?"

"Her garden club called and said she didn't show up. So I came home and found her dead. That's it."

"You don't know any more about it?"

Cleary blinked. "Nope."

"Mr. Cleary," said Rennick in a calm tone, "I'm Dr. Rennick." He explained his role in the case. "I'd like to ask you some questions that may seem bizarre. I'd appreciate your answering them with whatever comes into your mind." Rennick paused for a response. None came. "What kind of car do you drive?"

"Chevy."

"What color?"

"Blue."

The answers were coming without emotion, almost robotic. He's a cool one, thought Rennick. And he's getting harder to read as the interview goes on.

"Do you have ivory-colored stationery?"

"No."

"Do you have a steady girlfriend?"

"No."

"Do you grow vegetables?"

"Yeah."

Rennick hadn't expected a yes. Still, there was no emotion, no visceral response. He was coming to the unfortunate conclusion that Cleary wasn't going to have a visceral reaction to anything; he was acting like a prisoner of war trained to give name, rank, and serial number. Rennick guessed the guy could have taken a lot of torture.

"Where do you grow the vegetables?"

"In my yard."

"Do you have a knife?"

"What kind?"

"I mean anything besides a pocketknife or a kitchen knife."

"Yeah."

"What kind?"

"Coupla bayonets. Maybe a Bowie knife for hunting."

"That's it?"

"That's it."

Despite the subject matter, Cleary stayed icy calm. Rennick realized they needed a different approach to get any kind of emotional reaction.

"When did you last see your daughter?" asked Rennick.

"A week or so ago."

"What were the circumstances?"

Cleary shifted almost imperceptibly in his seat. "She came around here."

"Why?"

Cleary's face broke into an uneven smile. "It was you, wasn't it? You put her up to coming here. I knew it was some voodoo witch doctor like you that put her up to it."

"What did you and she discuss?"

"Was it you?"

Talon broke in. "We're here to ask the questions, Cleary, not you. Now tell Dr. Rennick what you discussed."

"It was personal."

"Did it concern her mother's murder?" asked Rennick.

Cleary's face sparked angrily, then he controlled it. "Now I know it was you. If you already know all the answers, why're you here wasting time?"

This guy is good, thought Rennick. Time to turn up the heat. He pulled Talon aside and suggested another approach.

"How do you feel about women?" snapped Talon.

"I'm not a queer, if that's what you mean."

"I hear you're pretty useless in bed. Limp Dick Syndrome. You have trouble getting it up, Cleary?"

"No." His facial muscles were tensing.

"Oh yeah? I think you only like women when they're help-less. A few of the bitches even called the cops on you, didn't they?"

Cleary clasped his hands tightly in his lap, causing the veins along his forearms to rise. Yet his expression remained con-trolled.

"Real men don't do that, Cleary," Talon prodded. "Just sissies and pussies. Real men can handle strong women. You don't like that kind, do you?"

Cleary stood up. When he answered, his vocal cords sounded like they had been tightened to the point of snapping. "I didn't agree to let you assholes come out here for some mind-fuck games. So either book me for something or get out of my house."

Cleary walked over to Talon, shoving his face within inches of the detective's as he stared up at him. After a few moments of standoff, Rennick said, "C'mon. We're outta here."

Talon and Rennick turned onto the 405 and headed toward Los Angeles.

"I'm not sure if we got to him," said Rennick. "The guy is an icicle. My instincts tell me he's hiding something. Particu-larly about his wife's murder."

"Mine too," said Talon.

"My instincts also tell me we're not going to get it out of him."

"Probably not. But maybe we rattled him into doing something stupid."

Talon reached into the glove compartment, shook two aspirin out of a bottle, and swallowed them dry. Rennick's mouth puckered sympathetically.

"How does Cleary fit your profile?" asked Talon.

"Reasonably well. He's clearly a loner, with an ice-cold mind-set. He seems to be intelligent enough to formulate a plan and carry it out flawlessly. He's still in excellent physical shape, and easily capable of climbing through windows like a commando. With his hand-to-hand training, he could take these women down and tie them up before they blinked. We also know there was an older man who showed up at the pyramid class."

"His shoe size looked about like the size-twelve footprint we got when Bobby Mullins interrupted the killer."

"On the other hand," said Rennick, "these murders are sexually motivated, even if there was a rape only the first time around. The display of the women spread-eagle is meant to degrade and humiliate them sexually. Except for child molesters, sex offenders usually stop by the time they're out of their thirties. So he's not a perfect fit."

They drove for a moment in silence before Rennick asked, "Where was Logan last Monday night?"

"Another *Home Alone* story."

"What was he doing when Lisa's mother was killed?"

"I couldn't find much. He was a student at San Francisco State and hadn't flipped out yet. Or at least hadn't got caught at anything."

"Did you check out the women in his life?"

"His mother was a redhead who kept her hair shorter than mine. His sister was a brunette. No one remembered any girl-friends."

"What about Cleary?"

"I didn't check the women around him. Wait a sec. You just gave me an idea. Take the wheel."

Rennick steered awkwardly from the passenger side while Talon fished Martha Cleary's file out of the back seat and flipped through it. After a few moments, he took back the wheel and shoved across a picture of Lisa's mother. Her body was lying on a stainless-steel autopsy table, staring blank-eyed into space. Above the mutilations of her throat, Rennick could see she had shoulder-length, blond hair.

CHAPTER FORTY-SEVEN

Talon stood next to Mary Waters, the lab tech, watching her handle the envelope Lisa had found outside Michelle Harris's apartment. Waters put the envelope under various lights and devices before finally taking a thin blade to slice it open. She seesawed out the note with large tweezers.

"Why, it's a love note," she said, pushing her glasses up the bridge of her nose.

Talon looked over her shoulder and read:

Fuck You

Bobbi buzzed Rennick on the intercom in his office. "There's a Rocco DiMartino on line one."

"Who?"

"He says he's a reporter with the *L.A. Times*."

"What does he want?"

"Hold on." The blinking line turned white and then started blinking again as Bobbi came back on the intercom.

"He's doing a story on the serial murders and knows you're working on the case. He wants a quote."

"Get rid of him."

A few seconds later, Bobbi was back on. "He asked for Lisa Cleary's phone number."

"Lisa? What does he know about her?"

"Michael, this is a humble suggestion from your assistant, but wouldn't a dialogue with Mr. DiMartino be more efficient if the two of you spoke?"

"Okay, okay." Rennick punched the blinking line to find the voice on the other end humming "The Happy Wanderer."

"This is Dr. Rennick."

"Hello, Doctor. As I told your assistant, I'm covering the serial murders and would like to ask you a few questions."

"I don't have any comment."

"No sweat. Do you have Lisa Cleary's phone number?"

"Why do you want her?"

"My sources tell me she's a psychic who's been working with you and the cops. I want to give her the chance to tell her side of the story."

"I'm sure she won't have anything to say either."

"Isn't that her decision?"

Rennick's blood pressure was rising. "Of course it is. But I don't think it's right for you to disturb her."

"Doctor, I'm running a story about the two of you and I'm giving you the chance to comment. If you want to, fine. If you don't, then it goes without your angle. I'm on deadline, so I don't have time for a debate."

Rennick's rage turned to alarm as he worried that a story like this might seriously upset Lisa. She had canceled her last appointment, and he hadn't heard from her since she'd visited the Harris crime scene.

"Mr. DiMartino . . ."

"Call me Rocky."

"Rocky. Can we have an off-the-record conversation?"

"Sure."

Rennick was aware that "off the record" meant nothing unless he knew the reporter really well. Yet he didn't have a choice. "This lady is in a fragile psychological state, and publishing a story about her could cause serious damage. I'd appreciate it if you don't mention her."

"Doctor, it's news. And she's important to the story."

Rennick knew a little about the journalism poker game, so he played his ace. "Tell you what. If you leave her out of the article, I'll give you an exclusive interview. And I'll ask the cops to let you break it when they arrest the perpetrator."

"Sorry, Doc. She's too important to the story. My editor's holding a page-one slot because of the psychic angle." His voice was matter-of-fact.

"You're playing with someone's life. How can you be so callous?" Rennick put the phone wire in his mouth and chewed.

"I take it that means you have no comment?"

"This is outrageous."

"If Ms. Cleary wants to tell her side, have her call me in the next half hour. Otherwise, it's my spin. Have a nice day." The line clicked into a dial tone, and Rennick slammed down the receiver.

He knew he had to call Lisa. He had to let her know that the story was coming, so she could brace herself, and so she could decide whether or not to talk to Rocky.

Shit.

CHAPTER FORTY-EIGHT

The story appeared on page one of *The Los Angeles Times,* bottom left: PSYCHIC AIDS POLICE WITH SERIAL KILLINGS, by Rocco DiMartino. The article first recounted the murders and quoted the police chief's statement that it appeared they were all committed by the same killer. Then came the standard interviews with neighbors of the victims and a declaration that West L.A. was in a panic.

The article next turned to Lisa Cleary, a psychic, who was helping the police. According to "knowledgeable sources," she was working with Detective Daniel Talon and Dr. Michael Rennick, a forensic psychiatrist who taught at UCLA Law School. Another source said that the police were reluctant to use a psychic, but that Dr. Rennick had convinced them to do so. So far, she had "used her crystal ball" to find "several important clues." The article also quoted a "high-level figure" in the mayor's office, who was appalled. The mayoral source said,

"Next I suppose the police will be calling Dionne Warwick and her Psychic Friends Network." The story ended with the following: "Neither Detective Talon, Dr. Rennick, nor Ms. Cleary had any comment for the record."

Rennick finished reading the article and threw the paper across his living room. It fluttered to rest over the coffee table and carpet.

Logan sat at his breakfast table reading the morning paper. He laid the paper flat on the table and touched only the corners with a paper towel to get it into position. Logan had a sense that things around him were getting more and more contagious, and he needed to take precautions. One never knew who might have handled a newspaper on its way to him.

The story was revolting. Psychics? Please. At least that obnoxious psychiatrist who'd poured water on the table was being held up to the ridicule he deserved. And that detective looked like a bit of the buffoon too, didn't he?

He finished reading and washed his hands with Hivacleans, a surgical scrub. The germs disappeared down the sink, yet he couldn't shake the fact that the police were sniffing after him. If they couldn't prove anything, they'd just harass him until he cracked. The oldest strategy in the book. He was an idiot not to have seen it in the first place. He had to keep his cool. Don't let them rattle you.

Using another paper towel, he threw the newspaper in the trash.

Shortly before his morning class, Rennick walked toward the Law School. He tried not to think about the *L.A. Times* article. Or about finally reaching Julie and being reminded that she needed to be alone and to please respect her wishes. Or about the effects that the newspaper article could have on Lisa, who would truly be humiliated in a conservative accounting world.

He was within one hundred feet of the Law School when a voice boomed loudly. "Michael!" He recognized it immediately as that of Professor Dodd, an intellectual snob who taught constitutional law but whose passion was the medieval canons. Rennick ignored the shouts and kept walking until a hand clapped him on the shoulder.

"Good morning, Michael."

"Morning, Irwin."

"Nice article in the *Times* this morning."

"Thanks. Glad you enjoyed it. I've got to get to class."

"Say, could you ask your psychic friend to pick me a lottery number?" With that, Dodd started guffawing with such force that he bent in half. Rennick seriously considered some form of bodily abuse, then decided it would only make Dodd a martyr.

Once inside, Rennick saw that there were very few people in the hallway, which suited him just fine. He went into the classroom to find the students uncharacteristically quiet. No coffee, no paper rustling; just silence. And none of them looked up at him. They all knew, he thought. Dammit. He glanced at Julie, who wasn't looking at him either.

After class, Rennick was delighted to see Julie standing outside. He had an almost overwhelming urge to take her in his arms.

She spoke before he could say anything. "I'm not here to talk about us. I'm here to tell you that I'm worried about you. In class today, you looked exhausted, you lost your train of thought twice, and your voice was hard to understand."

They walked outside the building, toward Dickson Plaza.

She looked ravishing, and his heart fluttered like a schoolboy's on a date.

"I'm so sorry about how I've treated you," said Rennick. "I—"

"I didn't come to talk about us. I'm trying to tell you as a friend that you're—"

"You're so much more than a friend."

"I was worried you'd turn this into a discussion of us."

"I haven't been able to stop thinking about you. I . . ."

"Just forget it." She turned and walked away before he could respond.

He shouted her name after her, yet she didn't turn around.

Across the way, a figure had been standing by a giant Moreton Bay fig tree, watching. The wind blew the dead leaves on the ground into small whirlwinds on the sidewalk, causing them to scrape the concrete as they scurried in an endless chase.

The great Dr. Rennick, Psychiatrist to the Police. Too bad they didn't put your picture in the article. So close to fame and glory. Still, the article is a nice road map to the players in the game. A geeky shrink. A clown of a cop. A weekend psychic.

From their body language, it looks like the doctor is having a lovers' spat. Aww. What a pity. Not a bad-looking girl. Not bad at all. She doesn't fit the usual criteria, but rules were made to be broken. And shrinks who help the cops should know there's sometimes a price. These assholes think they can just apply their brainpower from some ivory tower. But that's not the way it works. If you get into the streets, you're gonna get dirty.

When Rennick and Julie separated, the stalker followed Julie.

CHAPTER FORTY-NINE

Talon called Lisa's brother for the fourth time.

"Mrs. Lance Cleary?"

"Yes, Detective."

"Since I've called enough for you to recognize my voice, you know I'm going to keep at it until I talk to your husband."

"Well, he's not here."

"And he hasn't been home at all over the last week?"

"He's been real . . . no, he's still out of town."

"My patience is getting used up real quick. Does he want to be subpoenaed?"

"I'll ask him when I see him."

Julie walked into her apartment just as the answering machine picked up her phone.

A voice spoke to the tape. "Ms. Martin, this is Dr. Edmund Childs."

She reached for the phone, then let the machine continue handling it.

Childs's voice went on: "I will be back in New York in three days. I must have your answer by then. Thank you."

Captain Louie Ramson had a neck like a stack of manhole covers, and his leathered skin piled up in wrinkles around it. A thick, single brow ran across his forehead and made him look like he was perpetually scowling.

"Shut the door, Talon," said Ramson. His voice was grated raw from years of cigarette smoke.

Talon sat down. He hadn't been summoned to Ramson's office in a while, and Ramson's expression said this wasn't a social visit.

"Whaddaya got on the serial killer?" asked the captain.

"Not a lot. Five victims whose primary connection seems to be their looks and the fact that they lived in West L.A. First victim was Myra Powell, a barmaid. The second was Betty Sanchez, a manicurist. Turns out they were friends. Third was a secretary named Andrea Baylor who didn't know the first two. Fourth was Tanya Mullins, a single mother, who was also a stranger. Fifth is Michelle Harris, a graphic artist. This time, he cut off her head."

Ramson gave a quick nod. "Suspects?"

"I located an MDSO named Marvin Lofton. He got a lawyer and denied everything, but he's a serious possible. We're also watching Ron Cleary, ex-military guy, whose wife was killed with a similar M.O. about seventeen years ago. He worked in radios, which could tie into the electrical bit. I also want to interview Lance Cleary, Ron's son, who's been hiding. I'm about to camp on his lawn."

"Cleary? They related to the psychic in the newspaper article?"

"Yeah. Father and brother."

"That's a weird coincidence. If it is one."

"Can't argue that."

"What else?"

"Unfortunately, this asshole leaves the scenes like a fucking operating room. He also drops us love notes. We've gotten typed letters, knives, gloves, and some other shit. All of 'em clean. Without physical evidence, it's gonna be real tough to tie in a suspect."

"That's it?"

"That's it."

Ramson cracked his knuckles and leaned back. "I'll give it to you straight. Wharton's got a hard-on for you, and he's set it up so your job's on the line. This newspaper article about the psychic was more wadding for his gun."

"Tell me something I don't know."

"You don't know that you're running out of time. If he pulls you off this case, he adds it to your other problems."

The reference to Talon's slip with the cocaine stung sharply.

Ramson continued, "That means you get pastured to Traffic if I can save your ass. More likely, you're history."

"How long I got?"

"Week to ten days max."

"Ten days! You know that's ridiculous. What could I possibly do in ten days?"

"Solve the fucking case. If you don't, it's over."

"So I'm fucked." Talon's chest shuddered.

"Unless you deliver, that's about it. There's one piece of good news: Wharton's gone so far out to hang you that if you do come through, you'll get all the credit."

"That's the good news? It's right up there with 'Other than that, Mrs. Lincoln, how'd you enjoy the play?'"

"Sorry, Talon. I've tried to help behind the scenes. Truth is, you ain't movin' cases the way you used to. Maybe you need to see one of those shrinks that the city keeps in their zoo. It might get you off the hot seat."

"I don't go for that shit. I'd rather go down swinging."

Ramson shrugged. "I gotta respect that."

Talon came out of Ramson's office and felt as though he'd been sucker-punched. His lungs ached so much that he bent forward to breathe.

That soft voice, hidden in the back of his brain, whispered, "Danny, you need a little blast of cocaine. You know how it stokes your thinking." The thought had strolled by and bumped him over the past weeks, but now it was creeping through his entire body. He remembered how sharp the cocaine used to make him. As a teenager, he could ace a math test with just one toot in the morning. The memories in his cells screamed for fulfillment. His nose began to twitch and he felt himself shudder. The voice continued. "God knows you could use a boost right now. Just this once. You won't need it again."

"Fuck you," he snapped, startling a woman who was walking past him.

Rennick dragged into his office, still stinging from Julie's rebuke after class. She was right. He had blown it. His perspective always seemed so clear after a woman rejected him. He wanted her desperately, even knowing that he wouldn't be so certain if she were back.

"I take it you saw the *L.A. Times* article?" he asked Bobbi.

"Yep."

"Well?"

"It made you look like a New Age space cadet."

"You didn't have to sugarcoat it so much."

Rennick sat in his office, playing with a magnetic toy that Bobbi had given him a few Christmases ago. There were a bunch of metal men, and you could stack them up three or four high, until the magnetic field gave out and gravity pulled them down. This morning they kept falling before he could even get started.

"Call Lisa Cleary for me," Rennick yelled to Bobbi through the door.

When Lisa came on the line, he asked, "I take it you've seen the article?"

She was patched in through a cell phone, and the connection was riddled with static. "Oh yes. *The National Enquirer* already offered me ten thousand dollars for my story. I suppose they'll put me under a picture of some two-headed goat."

"Hold out for top billing."

"The partners in my firm weren't so impressed. One of them called me in to say that our clients won't like this kind of publicity. Fortunately, a major account loves one of my proposals, so the firm needs me right now."

"Lisa, why did you go to the crime scene after I told you not to?"

"Detective Talon told you?"

"Yes. Why did you go?"

"I felt like I had to. It was rough, but it's made me stronger. I haven't felt this good in months. Even the article didn't upset me."

"You were lucky. Next time you may not be. You pay for my advice, so listen to me."

"Yes."

"Are you taking the pills?"

"I'm doing okay."

"Are you taking your pills?"

"When I really feel I need to."

"You must take them. This isn't a game."

"I know."

Rennick hung up the phone and went back to stacking his magnetic acrobats. Then he started hurling them across the room with enough force to chip the paint.

After leaving Ramson's office, Talon went directly to his car. He headed north on the Hollywood Freeway with no destination in mind. The road snaked through the San Fernando Valley, then connected with the 405 and finally with the 5. Talon opened the window while traveling at seventy miles per hour, and the wind slammed against his face. He pushed the accelerator harder and started weaving between the slower cars.

How could anyone expect him to pull off a miracle in the next ten days? He wasn't an organ-grinder monkey that danced just because some bastard turned the crank. Of course Wharton didn't really expect him to pull something off. He pushed his car past eighty.

A half-hour or so later, he saw an off-ramp sign for Valencia and cut diagonally across three lanes to get there. As he slowed on the freeway exit, the wind whimpered into silence. Talon headed east and drove through the old streets on automatic pilot. He rolled slowly past his childhood home and saw that the neighborhood had taken a beating over the years. His boyhood house had been badly neglected. The front porch of the little one-story sagged to the left, and the roof was a patchwork of gray tar paper that curled at the edges.

After making three passes by the house, he went to a record store, then drove to the cemetery. Even though it was cold, the sun was bright and the air crisp. The quiet stillness was only interrupted by a few birds in the distant trees.

It took him a while to find the white marble headstone. Beneath the carving of an angel with her wings spread, it read:

KAREN ANNE TALON
1949–1966
ETERNAL LOVE

Seeing the name somehow made it more real, and he gasped back a sob. The bastards who ran this place had let a bunch of weeds grow over her grave, so he knelt down and began to pull them out. The smell of moist earth filled his nostrils as the dirt permeated his fingertips.

He wondered if anyone ever visited Karen, and then he realized there wasn't anyone besides himself. He ached with the burden not only of failing her, but also of not having visited their parents' graves in Palm Springs.

When he finished the weeding, he took off his jacket and lay down on his back. The winter had made the grass stiff, and it felt like a bed of nails poking through his shirt. He ran his hands up and down at his sides, as if making a snow angel.

After a few minutes, he turned so that his feet were by the headstone. Just like he used to lie on Karen's bed, with his feet near her head. He reached into his coat, pulled out the cassette he'd bought at the record store, and slid it into the cheap player he'd also purchased. Then he laid his thumb lightly on the Play button but didn't press it. It had been years since he'd listened to rock music of any kind, much less this album. He'd avoided this one since Karen died, and he hadn't thought he'd ever listen to it again.

Talon closed his eyes and vivid images of Karen appeared.

They were lying on her bed, with a black light illuminating the posters on her walls.

"You promised you'd come back," he said.

"You know I can't do that."

"And you blew marijuana smoke in my face. Do you have any idea what that did to me? Do you know how hard I've had to fight drugs ever since?"

"I had to fight myself. At least you won yours."

Talon felt warm tears escaping from the corners of his eyes.

"Dance with me, Danny," whispered his sister. "Take my hands. Let's dance again."

Almost unconsciously, his thumb pushed the Play button and the Jefferson Airplane began singing "White Rabbit." His mouth moved with words he hadn't known he remembered, and Danny Talon danced with Karen. His tiny hands were swallowed in hers as they circled counterclockwise, leaning away from each other and laughing.

She grew lighter in his hands, fading into translucence as the song wound down. When the music ended, the dead silence numbed his senses, and he was cried out of tears. He opened his eyes and saw that twilight was darkening the sky.

Danny was sorry he hadn't brought Karen's beads back to her. The beads she'd given him in their secret pact. They lay untouched in a taped shoebox, hidden in his closet. He vowed he would bring them on the next visit, which would be soon. Instead of the beads, he placed the cassette on her headstone.

Talon stood up and took a last look at the inscription, now softly lit by the fading light:

ETERNAL LOVE

And he felt at peace.

CHAPTER FIFTY

Talon drove toward Culver City, energized by his visit with Karen. If they wanted his ass gone, he decided, they'd have to drag it out.

Talon had gotten the runaround from Lance Cleary's wife for over a week, so he decided to sit in front of the sonofabitch's house for however long it took. Culver City was a suburb near West L.A. that had grown up around the MGM studios in its glory days. The area was now mostly blue collar, with identical homes and apartments dotting identical streets, like they'd been ordered from central casting.

Lance Cleary lived in a 1930s-era greenish fourplex, whose shattered window had cardboard taped behind it. A small wooden fence in front had been hit by something years ago, and lay in broken pieces like a pencil that had been snapped and discarded.

Talon was parked for almost two hours across from the fourplex before the sound of a motor scooter perked his ears. He sat up as the scooter pulled into the driveway. When the rider got off and tucked a white helmet under his arm, Talon instantly recognized the Cleary family resemblance. Contrary to his father, Lance walked with a stoop that made him look like he'd been pounded down by life.

"Mr. Cleary?"

Lance turned around and his eyes narrowed.

"Who are you?"

"Detective Talon, LAPD."

Lance turned to face him fully. A heavy woman in a pink quilted bathrobe waddled out of the front door and watched them while she ate a white-bread sandwich.

"You the guy who's been calling my wife?" asked Lance. The heavy woman sidled next to him, chewing with her mouth open.

"Yeah," said Talon. "And if you'd called back, we coulda gotten this over a lot quicker."

"Well, I've been busy."

"Me too. Where can we talk?"

"I don't have anything to say."

"Lemme be the judge of that."

"You gotta warrant?"

"No. You want me to get one?"

"I didn't do nothin'."

"Then let's talk."

"I don't have anything to say."

"Let me put it another way. We can talk here, or we can talk at the Hollywood station."

"You threatening me?"

"Not a threat. Shall we take a ride?"

"I don't got nothin' to say."

"Mrs. Cleary? Your husband'll be back in a few hours." Talon took hold of Lance's arm and jerked him forward. Lance stumbled on the sidewalk and scraped his hand. Talon pulled him upright and led him roughly away. Lance lowered his head as several neighbors popped out to watch.

"Where were you on the night of November sixth?" Talon pushed a calendar in front of him.

"Hell, nobody remembers that kinda shit. Where were *you* that night?" asked Lance.

"You're a real smart guy, huh? You know where you were or don't you?"

"I don't."

Talon read off the dates of the other murders, and Cleary said he would get him information on his whereabouts.

"Whaddaya know about your sister and your father's recent activities?" asked Talon.

"Nothin'."

"You seen them lately?"

"I haven't seen my sister for years."

"What about your father?"

Cleary shifted in his seat and looked away from Talon. "No."

"Your hand is scraped raw," said Lance's wife, Cheryl. "You need peroxide on it." She dabbed a cotton ball on the mouth of the brown-glass peroxide bottle.

"What can they do to me for lyin' to the police?"

"You did the right thing not getting involved." She dabbed the peroxide on his palm. The strong antiseptic smell assaulted him.

"My father shows up after all them years, and I start runnin' around takin' orders like some fuckin' slave. Jesus H. Christ."

Cheryl kept dabbing. He grabbed the cotton ball out of her hand and threw it across the room.

"Look how upset you're getting," she said. She retrieved the cotton ball and put it in the trash.

"I wasn't under oath or nothin'. They can't do nothin' to me if I wasn't under oath, can they?"

"You did the right thing," said Cheryl as she screwed the cap on the peroxide bottle.

CHAPTER FIFTY-ONE

Rennick dragged himself into his apartment, feeling like one of those cartoon characters that crawl through the desert searching for water. Although he'd been able to work through his exhaustion during the day, it was now catching up with him. His eyelids were heavy, his throat felt scratchy, and he knew he'd get sick if he didn't get some rest.

Why wouldn't Julie at least talk to him? He just wanted to tell her how sorry he was. Maybe she'd come to her senses and call. His hopes rose when he saw his answering machine blinking with three messages. He threw his mail on the table and hit the button.

The first message was from Bobbi. "Michael. The dean called right after you left this morning. You have a command performance in his throne room, tomorrow at ten a.m. sharp. Did I say sharp? His secretary certainly did. About four times. 'Night." The machine beeped. Two messages to go.

"Professor? Danny Talon. Young Mr. Cleary was about as forthcoming as his father, and quite a bit stupider. I dragged him down to the station and got exactly zippo. My gut says he's scared about something. Call me if you wanna discuss it."

Two down, one to go.

"Dr. Rennick! It's Lisa Cleary." He was surprised at the panicked tremble in her voice, since she'd sounded so together in the morning. "I must see you. Call me any time of the day or night when you get this. It's extremely urgent."

A loud knock on the door startled him. He hoped it was Julie, knowing full well that it wasn't. He opened the door to see Lisa, with eyes wide in panic. Her T-shirt was only half stuffed into her sweatpants, and she wasn't wearing a jacket despite the cold night.

"The killer's after me," she said, waving an envelope in her hand. "It's the newspaper article. The killer now knows who I am. He must think I'm a threat."

"Come in," he said. He could see that her skin was coarsely goosefleshed. She rushed through the door and shoved it shut behind her.

"Tell me what happened," he said slowly, in counterpoint to her panic.

He could see her eyes rapidly searching the room, as if scanning for an unseen monster that was about to pounce.

"Sit here on the couch," said Rennick.

She lowered herself clumsily.

"Now take a few deep breaths and tell me what happened."

"This," she said, holding up an ivory-colored envelope. "The envelope is identical to the ones we had found in the park and in the garbage can near the last victim's apartment."

Rennick saw that Lisa's name was typed on the front and

there was no address. He felt a wave of panic across his stomach. "Where did you get this?"

"It was inside my front door, on the floor. I found it when I came home from work. That means he knows where I live."

He stared at the envelope. "We need to call Talon."

"Last time the police lab took days. I have to know what it says right now. But I'm scared to open it. Please, will you do it for me?"

Rennick worried that the contents might upset her even more, and he really should call Talon. It wasn't kosher for him to handle evidence. On the other hand, she'd already touched the envelope. Couldn't he open it carefully? His curiosity cast the deciding vote.

"If you really want this, I'll put on some gloves and open the envelope. Then I'll read the note and decide whether to tell you what it says. If I think you shouldn't hear it, I don't want any argument."

"But it's my letter. I have a right to know."

"And I can't stop you from opening it. If you want me involved, that's the only way I'll do it."

Her eyes twitched nervously as she stared at him. Finally, she nodded.

Rennick went to the kitchen and put on a pair of yellow dishwashing gloves. He took out a kitchen knife, clumsily slipped it under the flap of the envelope, and slit open the top. Then he gently pulled out the letter. It was folded like a thank-you note, and inside was a typewritten message: "You'll be sorry if you get too close."

He walked back to the living room, aware that Lisa's eyes hadn't left him. She was still sitting on the couch, clutching a throw pillow against her stomach.

"What is it?" she asked.

He read it aloud. Lisa looked puzzled. "What does that mean?"

"In scientific terms, I would say: I haven't got the slightest idea."

That got a smile out of her, although it vanished almost immediately.

"I think it's good that the killer is sending these notes," said Rennick. "It's the sign of an overconfident ego, which usually leads to a downfall."

Lisa stood up and walked over to him. He gingerly put the letter down on the table. She grabbed his arm with a strong grip that betrayed the tension under her thin veneer of control.

"I feel there's going to be another killing in the next few days," she said. "My name's been in the paper, and this note means I'm being watched. I'm worried that . . . that . . . I'm the next victim."

She released her grip and stood fully in front of him. Spiderwebs of red veins covered her eyes, but the intensity of her stare didn't waver.

"I can't explain this logically," she continued. "But I'm sure the killer knows we're on the same wavelength. Like there's a connection between us and I'm a threat. I know he'll come for me. I'm so scared." She paused, moving her lips silently, as if debating how to phrase the next part. Then she took both of his hands and looked into his eyes. "Can I stay with you?"

Before he could react, she put her arms around his waist and pulled her body against him. She began to massage his back sensually.

He disengaged himself and took a step back.

"Lisa, you know you can't stay here. You aren't interested in me the way you think you are. You're very vulnerable right now, and the psychiatrist's relationship of authority . . ."

She turned away from him and sobbed. "I knew you wouldn't let me stay."

"This is not a rejection. It's essential that I maintain a professional—"

She kept her back to him. "Don't. You've said enough. I'm leaving."

"Lisa, do you want something to calm you?"

Without turning toward Rennick, she took a shuddering breath and straightened her posture. "I only want to be someplace else."

She grabbed the letter and slammed the door behind her. He stood there, disoriented from the exchange, hoping she could handle what he'd done. He understood intellectually that there was no choice, yet it stung him to hurt her.

Rennick started toward the kitchen and noticed a familiar-looking envelope mixed in with his mail on the dining table. It had no address or stamp. Just his typewritten name on an ivory envelope.

His hands were shaking as he put on the rubber gloves and opened it. It read:

You'll be sorry if you get too close.

CHAPTER FIFTY-TWO

Monday.

I watched her again tonight. She was cooking stir-fry and running around the kitchen, listening to rock music. Oblivious to the world. Just the way I like it.

How will you like it, Dr. Rennick, when you see what I do to your little girlfriend? Last time the hacksaw gave out after the head. This time, I bought more expensive blades. And several spares. No reason to stop with the head. No reason even to start there. It'll be much better when the hands and feet go first. How would it feel to know you'll never walk again? Or never caress the face of your lover? I'm sure that whatever I can imagine about her reaction will pale next to the real thing.

Rennick hadn't fallen asleep until after 5:00 A.M., which meant his alarm woke him three hours later. At least he didn't have an early class, although he did have to see the dean. As he pulled himself out of bed, the lack of sleep made him feel like he was moving through soft, sinking sand. He promised himself he'd come home for a nap in the afternoon, and the idea was enough of an incentive to keep him moving forward.

He soaked in the shower a full fifteen minutes, trying to wake up. Then he went to his office, where he found Bobbi acting bright and chirpy.

"You look like hell," she said.

"Thanks. You really know how to brighten my day."

"No problem. And in case you didn't get the message on your machine, the dean wants you at ten a.m. Sharp. They called again to remind me this morning. I guess they were worried that I'd finally get around to that lobotomy I've been promising myself."

He patted her on the shoulder. "Thanks, Bobbi. And in case I fall asleep, come in and throw some water on me."

"Sure. I'll use Diet Coke. It'll make you feel sticky all day, so you can relive the moment."

Rennick tried clearing the fog in his brain enough to prepare his afternoon seminar. He hoped doing something intellectual would distract him from being exhausted, and from thinking about Lisa and the murders. And Julie. So far, not so good.

Bobbi came in with a can of Diet Coke at 9:50.

"Aww. You're awake. Pity."

The dean's waiting room was larger than Rennick's office. It was paneled in rich mahogany, dotted with pictures of Dean Roland Stanfield next to presidents and Supreme Court justices. The dean's secretary, Miss Brodie, was a tight-lipped woman in her late sixties, with dark gray hair that was mostly captured in a bun. She sat straight-backed behind a desk that guarded the inner sanctum, and was talking into a telephone in hushed tones. It was rumored that she once smiled in 1967, but the story was unconfirmed.

Miss Brodie told Rennick to have a seat in a tone that invited no reply. The only reading material was an international law journal that discussed the pending constitution in New Guinea, and Rennick was too worried about dozing off to risk picking it up.

The intercom was also trained to buzz discreetly, so as not to spoil the atmosphere. He barely heard it, but Miss Brodie immediately picked up the phone.

"You may go in, Mr. Rennick."

He stood up, took a deep breath, and walked through the mahogany paneled door.

Dean Stanfield's office was similar to the anteroom, only much larger. One wall was covered with bookshelves, filled with claret-colored, leather-bound books. Most of them did not appear to have been published in this century. An oriental rug covered the deep brown oak floor, and the chairs were tufted, forest green leather. The dean's desk was a copy of Thomas Jefferson's and boasted a Tiffany lamp next to a bronze Lady Justice.

Stanfield was putting a volume back on the shelf as Rennick entered. The dean was a heavyset, gray-haired man, with a barrel chest that sloped below his belt line. He wore a charcoal-gray three-piece suit, with his Phi Beta Kappa key dangling at the end of a gold watch chain. His face had a perpetually somber expression beneath thick, white eyebrows.

"Please sit down," said Stanfield. His voice was deep and resonant. The use of "please" was irrelevant, as the dean spoke only in mandates.

Stanfield picked up a letter opener in the shape of a sword, about eight inches long. He put the point against his index finger and slowly twisted the handle, causing the point to burrow into his flesh.

He spoke addressing the sword. "I'll come straight to the point, Michael. You've missed two faculty meetings. You're late with your *Law Review* article, which leaves a gaping hole in the next edition. And you're looking . . . quite tired. Do we have a problem here?"

The use of "we" thoroughly annoyed Rennick, as it sounded like the dean believed he was the King of England.

"In our experience," Stanfield continued, "this kind of behavior is a distress signal. Meaning something is wrong in your life. We generally have good feedback about you, so this is a concern. Is something wrong in your life, Michael?"

Rennick thought, Oh, my girlfriend dumped me, my patient's on the verge of psychosis, we're hitting a dead end in the murder cases, I'm the laughingstock of the students and faculty for working with a psychic, and I haven't slept in a week. No, everything's peachy.

Rennick answered, "It's been a rough period, but it's almost over. In a few days, everything should be back to normal." As he answered, his voice changed from high to low like an Italian bus horn.

Stanfield placed the sword into a crystal holder on his desk. He then strode around the desk to Rennick, towering over the chair. The dean laid his hand on Rennick's shoulder, making him feel like a schoolchild in the principal's office.

Stanfield's slate-gray eyes, which had circles of milky white around the irises, riveted onto Rennick's. "Perhaps you'd like to take a leave of absence. Clear your head."

"I'm really okay, Dean. I'd tell you if I weren't. I promise this will be over in the next week or so." Or at least I hope the hell it is, he thought.

Stanfield held his gaze and his grip on Rennick's shoulder. "There is one more thing. This article in *The Los Angeles Times*. This psychic nonsense. I feel it makes the Law School, and by reflection all of us on the faculty, look foolish. I don't like to look foolish, Michael."

Rennick began to stutter slightly. "I'm terribly sorry, Dean. You know I can't control the papers. The public will be wrapping fish with it tomorrow." He managed a meek smile, which bounced off the granite facade of the dean's face without leaving a mark. "It will all be over soon."

The dean took his hand off Rennick's shoulder and returned to his desk. He picked up the sword again and twirled the point against his finger.

"I'll take your statement as an assurance that I won't hear of this again."

CHAPTER FIFTY-THREE

Lance Cleary fidgeted with his keys as he sat in the office of Pastor Shawn. His tie felt like a noose around his neck. First the meeting with his father, then being taken downtown by that cop, like some animal in a shipping crate. This shit had to stop.

He watched the rainbow of colors that sprayed across the pastor's desk from the sunlight coming through the stained-glass window. Lance hadn't spoken to a clergyman since he'd been in the army hospital almost dying from pneumonia. He remembered how much better the guy had made him feel, and right now he needed to talk to somebody who didn't have an ax to grind. He'd met this pastor once at a wedding, and the guy seemed friendly enough. If he turned out to be some holier-than-thou bluenose, Lance figured he could cut and run.

Things had been chugging along just fine until now. He'd found a way to do his job without anybody bugging him. The same way he'd gotten through the service without being shit on. Why'd his father have to show up? Lance hadn't thought about the night of his mother's death for years. Now he could hardly keep his mind off it. He knew what had happened. Or at least he thought he did. Maybe he only remembered what his father had said. He was only seventeen, for chrissakes.

Through the wall he could hear the choir practicing in the chapel. He flipped through a copy of the New Testament whose pages were worn and smelled like old paper. Finally, he looked through a two-page pamphlet titled *Putting Christ Back in Christmas.*

Paster Shawn came in, wearing a black-and-white collar and a small gold cross in his lapel. He was a gentle-looking man, with neatly trimmed salt-and-pepper hair, doe eyes, and a soft smile. Lance stood up, and the pastor motioned him to sit again.

"Are you one of our parishioners, Mr. . . ."

"Cleary. Lance Cleary. No, Reverend. I met you at Jules and Corky Phillips's wedding." Lance played with the coins in his pocket.

"Ah, yes. Lovely couple. What brings you here, son?"

"I got some things I'd like to, uh, discuss."

"Certainly. I have all the time you need." Pastor Shawn leaned back and clasped his hands across his stomach.

"Is everything I say here, like, secret?"

"What do you mean?"

Lance didn't look at the pastor as he spoke. "I mean, uh, can anybody make you tell what we talk about?"

"By 'anybody,' do you mean the law?"

"Well . . . yeah."

"The law can't pry into what we say. Everything is between us and God."

Lance sat quietly for a few moments before he spoke. "Well, Reverend, my family's real fu—I mean, we got some problems. I've been carryin' around these sorta secrets for an awful long time. And there's some recent stuff goin' on that I think, you know, might be, kinda connected. And I'm real tore up about what I should be doin'."

"God is always there to help us with our burdens, son. Tell me what's on your mind."

"Duke?" barked Logan into the phone.

"Hello, Mr. Logan."

"They're watching me."

"Who?"

"The cops, you idiot. Who else? Get a court order and stop them."

"Why do you think they're watching you?"

"I can sense it." Logan had always known when someone was watching. Maybe it came from his having watched other people for so many years. You developed an instinct when you were in the game.

"Have you seen anyone?"

"They're too smart for that. Quit arguing with me. Get a court order."

"First of all, unless you've seen them, we can't be sure they're actually doing it. Second, if they are watching you, I can't get an order because they have probable cause."

"You're not exactly giving me comfort."

"I'll call some friends of mine on the force and see what I can find out."

"Call me back in fifteen minutes."

"It'll take longer than that."

"Fifteen minutes," said Logan as he hung up.

                    *   *   *

Logan hadn't heard back from Duke for two hours. He called and found that the man had left for the day. If the bastard didn't call back tomorrow, he'd look for a new lawyer.

Later that night, Logan walked quickly along Broadway in downtown L.A., certain that the night's darkness was there to comfort him personally. He wore a faded pair of blue jeans, sneakers, and a ripped gray sweatshirt. He had left all of his jewelry at home, and replaced his ten-thousand-dollar Rolex with a thirty-dollar Seiko.

During the day, Logan went into the tall office buildings surrounding this area and sold software to the businesspeople who came in like ants every morning. When they left after dark, iron accordion gates grew across the storefronts, as if some spider were spinning a black web over the city. That was the signal for the true denizens to reclaim their land. Logan looked at the winos, vagrants, and hustlers sitting in the door-ways and cardboard boxes, and he wondered how many people could feel at home in both worlds the way he did.

He pondered what it would be like to do it again. The neon lights beckoned him, and the thought of choosing began to ex-cite him. As much as he could get excited anymore.

After a lot of window-shopping, he made his choice. Fantasy World. He went inside the booth and dropped in a five-dollar token. The screen rolled up to reveal the glass wall that sepa-rated him from the next booth. On the other side of the glass was a young blond woman in a hot pink bikini. She had stretch marks on her stomach, and a little too much makeup. The dark sockets around her eyes spoke of a lot of mileage. Still, she had big tits and was the best of the lot. He picked up the white telephone, and she picked up hers.

"I'm Tammy. What's your name?"

"Willy."

She giggled. "You got a big willy, Willy?"

There was a time when this would have given him a jean-ripping hard-on, thought Logan. Now he could barely feel his dick. The fucking drugs. Yet the thoughts still excited his brain. You can't take that away, you fuckers.

"Whaddaya like, Willy?"

"Touch yourself."

"Mmmm." Tammy cradled the phone against her neck and leaned back on the footstool. She put one hand inside her bikini top, and the other into her panties. As she massaged herself, she started to moan.

Logan's mouth was getting moist.

"Take off your top," he said.

Tammy opened the middle of her top in front and pulled it aside. Her tits sagged to her waistline. Logan liked the nipples. They were like dark, silver dollars.

"Pinch your tits."

"Ooooh. I like your style," giggled Tammy, as she complied. Her nipples grew erect.

"Take off your panties."

Tammy slid off the bikini bottom and spread her legs toward him. The bottoms of her feet were dirty.

"Do I get to see you?" she asked, continuing to touch herself. Logan knew a lot of guys came in here and whacked off while watching girls through the glass. He thought that was disgusting. Not that he could come this long before his shot.

"No."

Tammy moaned more and more toward orgasm. "It'd sure turn me on to see a big willy like Willy's," she purred.

Why was she pushing this? His eyes went to the filth on the

bottoms of her feet. The reality of the germs around him was sinking in, and what little horniness he'd had was almost gone.

"C'mon, Willy," said Tammy. "Show me what you got."

Logan yelled into the phone, and was surprised at himself even as he did it. "Look, you bitch. My privacy is none of your fucking business. Now you've fucked up everything, you filthy whore-slut."

Tammy sat up and covered herself. "Who you callin' a whore, you fuckin' degenerate?"

Logan smashed the phone into the glass, which turned out to be a plastic that wouldn't crack. It rattled the booth enough for Tammy to yell for the bouncer. Within seconds, Logan was out and back on the street.

Lisa's work had been piling up heavily over the last few weeks. She sat staring at her desk, unsure even where to begin. While her secretary had stacked everything neatly, the in-box was so full that she'd created two additional piles beside it. There was also a thick stack of three-by-five pink While You Were Out phone messages.

Lisa called her voice-mail extension, and was told that the mailbox was full. It was so disheartening that she hung up without listening to the messages.

She had to force herself to start something. She decided that arranging the piles into categories, which she could then prioritize, wouldn't be too difficult. She put one of the in-box stacks in front of her just as the phone rang.

"Lisa, it's Phil. C'mon down to my office." From the tone of his voice, she knew this wasn't good news.

She walked quickly to his office and he waved her in. "Close the door, please. Have a seat."

She sat with her knees tightly together.

"Latham Oil says they're still waiting for that VAT memo. Benson Packaging and Fredericks Hardware say you haven't returned their calls for days. I've tried to cover you, but I'm outta room."

She started to speak and he cut her off.

"This isn't like you, Lisa. You're obviously going through a rough period. I think you should take some time off and get things together."

"Phil, I can handle it. Is this about the newspaper article?"

"No. Fortunately the firm wasn't mentioned, so all I had to do was move you off the three accounts that complained. This is about how far behind you're getting. I know you're having some personal difficulties. I'm sure you'll get through them, and I think it'll go quicker if you have some downtime."

"I'm better off working. It keeps me from dwelling on myself." She was talking faster and leaning forward in the chair.

"I don't think that's best."

"I promise this won't affect my work. If I work a few nights and weekends—"

She stopped because he put up his hand like a traffic cop. "Lisa. This isn't a suggestion."

She didn't speak for a moment. "All right." Her voice cracked.

Lisa walked back to her desk, threw her purse over her shoulder, and left without looking back.

Outside, the crisp air hit her face with a refreshing splash. Even though there was a chill, the bright sunshine began to warm her disposition. She took a deep breath and started walking briskly.

A block later, she realized she had nowhere to go. Maybe the gym, and a push-to-the-max workout, would purge her anxieties. The gym was about two miles from her office, and she decided to walk.

Lisa began cursing Phil under her breath. You finally got your chance to shove me down, didn't you? You fat-ass defender of the glass ceiling. I'll bet you're laughing right now. Tonight you can have drinks with the men and talk about keeping the bitches in their place. They'll slap you on the back. "Way to go, Phil." "Score one for the good ol' boys."

The vision blasted through without warning, like an angry drunk barging into a room and looking for a fight. She saw a mutilated body, more vivid and gruesome than her other visions.

Lisa stopped so abruptly that a man ran into her. She was frozen in place as the pedestrian traffic flowed around her and the vivid scene continued to play before her eyes. The woman was being cut apart. Hands severed from the arms. Feet cut from the legs. Then the head sawed roughly from the neck. The head rolled across the floor toward Lisa, and she looked down at the victim's face.

After screaming so loudly that she silenced the area, Lisa began to run at full speed.

Rennick's freshly laundered shirt felt stiff and scratchy against his skin. The bright morning sun warmed his office, yet his hands were cold as he tapped a pencil on the desk. Every few minutes, he paced back and forth, jittery as a young boy asking a pretty girl to dance.

The sound of the door opening startled him, and he instinctively stood up. Julie walked in with a somber look on her face. She looked gorgeous, dressed only in faded blue jeans and a navy blue wool sweater.

He started the speech he had memorized this morning.

"Julie, I apologize for the way I've been. I know I blew it. I'm asking you for another chance. Please. I've been thinking about you constantly since you left. What can I do to get us back on track?"

Julie didn't say anything. He could see a softening in the corners of her eyes. Or maybe he just wanted to see it.

"I came here because I thought I should tell you this in person."

Rennick's stomach elevator dropped several floors. "I've never heard a happy ending to a story that starts with those words," he said.

"I decided to take the job in New York. I've already told Dr. Childs."

Rennick felt tears in his eyes, and his chest constricted as he stifled a sob. "What can I do to change your mind?"

"Nothing. It's done. I'm sorry our relationship didn't work out. I have to move on with my life, and you need to move on with yours."

"Can't we at least keep seeing each other before you leave? We've still got a few months."

"I don't really see the point."

He couldn't think of anything to say. He felt like a child whose teacher had just told the whole class that he failed a test.

"This will only get harder if we prolong it," she continued. "Good-bye, Michael." She kissed him on the cheek, then turned and closed the door gently behind her.

Rennick started after her, then stopped, realizing it was useless and he'd only humiliate himself further. He sat down and stared at the door, imagining her walking down the hall, going farther and farther away from him. The memory of their first meeting played in his mind: how fresh and energetic she'd looked in her loose-fitting dress with no bra. He thought of the late-night debates they'd had over laws and ethics. Their bicycle race that took out his knee. Their weekend in the snow, making love in the cabin.

Rennick continued staring at the door she'd just closed and reflected how his last memory of her would be that door. A door he'd have to see every single day.

Shit.

CHAPTER FIFTY-FOUR

After Julie left, Rennick sat alone in his office, stinging from her rejection. His elbows were on his knees, and his head was bowed into his hands.

A few minutes later, his intercom buzzed.

"It's Lisa Cleary," said Bobbi. "She's calling from a pay phone and says it's urgent. She's babbling about another victim, and she really sounds over the edge."

Rennick fought through his funk and punched the blinking button.

"Dr. Rennick. Thank God. I've seen the next murder. It was much more vivid than the others. I wasn't sure if I should call." Her voice was raw, as if she'd been screaming for hours. "I feel torn, like I felt about Sarah, the little girl with the horses. I think I should tell you, but . . ."

He took a deep breath. "You were right to call. Tell me what you saw."

"The next murder is very soon. Tonight or tomorrow. I can tell by the intensity of my vision. And I saw the . . . uh . . . face of the next victim. She was . . ."

"Yes?"

"The night I came to your apartment, I saw a picture of a woman on your wall."

"Julie?!" Rennick unconsciously shot up to a standing position. He dropped the phone and raced toward the door, smashing his almost-healed knee against the corner of the desk. It sent a sharp, piercing pain through his leg, which caused him to yell and collapse on the floor. Bobbi came running in with a horrified look on her face. He waved her off, pulled himself up, and limped out at the fastest speed he could endure. He yelled back at Bobbi, "Call Julie's machine and tell her I need to talk to her urgently."

Rennick hobbled outside the Law School Building to the courtyard and looked around. It was between classes, so large groups of students were milling about. He yelled, "Julie!" loud enough for most of the heads to turn toward him. Her head wasn't among them.

He went up to the Law School Library and moved between the tables, bent forward to see the faces buried in books. Then he went through Lu Valle Commons. Finally, he fanned his search away from the Law School, across campus.

After an hour, with his knee on the verge of collapse, he had to abandon the effort. It took him almost fifteen minutes to get to his car, and almost a full minute to curl himself into it. He turned the key. Nothing. Julie's lecture on the electrical system played in his head as he kept trying to start it. Finally, the engine kicked over.

*   *   *

Rennick drove to Julie's apartment, sat by the front door for a half hour, and then left her an urgent note to call him. He went home, lay on the couch with his knee elevated on top of a rolled-up sleeping bag, then called Julie. She was either ignoring him or still out, because he got her machine. Next he called Talon, who was also out. So he called Julie again, even though it had only been five minutes, and left another urgent message. He didn't want to leave the specific information on her machine, for fear it would panic her, so he called every fifteen minutes and hung up on the recording.

Julie finally answered just before noon.

"Julie, thank God. I have to talk to you."

"Michael, why are you doing this?"

"No, no. It's not about us. It's about you."

"Huh?"

"Please. Listen to me. Don't panic."

That of course panicked her. "What are you talking about?"

His words tripped over each other. "Lisa called me right after you left. She had a vision of the next victim. She says . . . it's . . . you."

"Me?" Julie's response was a combination of shock and nervous laughter.

Rennick tried to sound calmer than he felt. "She also thinks it's very soon. Maybe even tonight."

Silence. Rennick continued, "Look, there's a chance this is all nonsense. But her visions have been accurate enough that I think you should take some precautions."

"Like what?"

"Well . . ." Rennick hesitated. "I thought you should move in with me for a little while."

Julie's answer was sharp and swift. "Michael, don't start that. If we keep seeing each other, we'll only—"

"No, no, no. I'll sleep on the damn couch if that's what you think. I've been chasing you down because I'm worried about your safety."

"Well, you don't have to worry. I live in a security building with a large manager." She sounded impatient, patronizing. "Besides, your name was in the paper, not mine. I wouldn't think your place is such a safe haven."

"Fine. Do whatever you want," he said, slamming down the phone.

CHAPTER FIFTY-FIVE

Rennick painfully climbed the steps of the Hollywood Police Station because he was too embarrassed to use the handicapped lift. With great relief, he fell into the chair next to Talon's desk.

Rennick saw that Talon had organized his desk and was systematically going through several neat stacks of papers. Talon's color had returned and he looked energized.

"Danny, you look good," said Rennick, adjusting his knee position with his hands.

"I feel like I'm real close to a breakthrough. You get an instinct when the puzzle pieces are about to fall in place."

Rennick noticed that Talon didn't say anything about Rennick's looks. "Anything on the ivory notes left for me and Lisa?"

"Lisa never brought hers in. Yours was clean."

"She's pretty frazzled right now." Rennick explained about the vision of Julie being murdered, then said, "Remember, Lisa called me on the night that Michelle Harris was killed. She knew it was happening right then."

"Yeah. You told me."

"So, Danny, I came by because I want a favor."

"Shoot."

"Do you think you could get someone to watch Julie for the next couple of nights?"

Talon's chair creaked as he leaned back. "We've never bull-shitted each other. I can't do that based on what we got."

"But she could be in serious danger."

"We only have the prediction of a psychic, and as accurate as she's been, I can't justify this. You know how close I'm being watched. If I send a cop out because of a psychic, and if nothing happens, I'm toast."

Rennick's knee throbbed in pain. "How about this: Logan looks like a real suspect. And Lisa's father and brother are serious possibles. Couldn't you at least watch them?"

"That's easier to justify. But we can't be sure it's one of these guys. In fact, her brother's alibis checked out. He was in Florida during one of the murders and out with friends during another. So he's not even a serious suspect. Though I'll bet next month's paycheck he's hiding something."

"Then can't you watch the other two?"

"What makes you so sure something's going down tonight?"

"Lisa's premonitions. And I have the same gut instinct."

"So now you're turning psychic?"

Rennick's eyes stung. "Danny. It's Julie."

Talon rocked his chair back upright. "The hardest part of what I do is when it gets personal. You know I'd take a bullet for you, Professor. But put yourself in my shoes. I just can't."

Rennick bit the edge of his lip. He continued to stare at Talon, pleading with his eyes.

Talon finally said, "Get outta here for fifteen minutes and lemme see what I can do. On second thought, stay here and save your knee."

Talon left and came back a few minutes later.

"Okay. My ass is on the line, but I'll send out undercover guys to watch Ron Cleary and that Logan creep."

The news rolled over Rennick like a gentle wave in a tropical ocean. "You're a pal. I owe you." He started toward Talon.

"If you kiss me, I'll snap your neck like a chicken."

Talon sent Rennick home and continued going through the files on all five killings. The rush of being near a breakthrough buzzed through him.

He was halfway through Myra Powell's file. His eyes were beginning to water from the reading. The barely legible notes of Rojas, the first detective. The lab and coroner's reports. The evidence list. Her phone records.

That's when it hit him.

Powell and Betty Sanchez, the second victim, were friends. They went to the *Vibrations of the Pyramids* classes together. According to the guy who ran those seminars, they worked out together, shopped together, and so on. If that was true, why hadn't Rojas found their phone numbers on each other's records? Had he missed it?

Talon grabbed Sanchez's file and realized that her phone had been shut off a month before she met Powell. Talon remembered her brother saying she hadn't paid her bill. So much for that. No. Wait a sec. Rojas hadn't found Bart Heath's number in Powell's records. How could they have been dating if they never called each other? That didn't make sense, unless he always called her from pay phones and no one connected him to those random numbers. He was on the road a lot. Still . . .

A cellular! That was it. He remembered seeing a cellular phone in Powell's glove compartment when he went through her car at the impound. Rojas's phone company inquiry should have turned it up, yet there were no cellular records in the file. The cellular must be in someone else's name.

He called Powell's father in Nashville.

"Do you know if Myra had a cellular phone?"

"Why, yes. Matter of fact she did. I gave her one as a birthday gift."

"Whose name was it in?"

"Uh . . . it was in my business's name. I'm ashamed to admit it, but I charged the cost as a tax write-off. I hope you won't say anything to the IRS or—"

"Could you give me the phone number and the carrier?"

Talon got the information and called Western Air Phone. He told them to get Powell's records and fax them over immediately.

Because Ron Cleary had been in the Special Forces, Talon assigned Carl Adams to watch him. Adams was one of the LAPD's best undercover agents because he was invisible. That wasn't because he hid himself. It was because he was so nondescript that people didn't notice him: medium-built guy, in his early thirties, with hair that some called brown and others called dark red. Adams dressed in blue jeans and a work shirt, and always worked from his personal Camaro that had faded into an indistinct powder blue.

When Adams got to Sunland, he put on an orange vest, set up a few traffic cones, and pulled a surveyor's tripod and sextant out of his trunk. He could stand around all day in different street positions without anyone getting suspicious. He even brought candy to keep the kids happy. Anyone who knew anything about surveying would know it takes two people, one to work the sextant and the other to hold the measuring pole, or whatever it was called. Adams hoped no one in the neighborhood, especially Cleary, knew that.

It was a sunny day and, other than being bored, Adams spent the time pleasantly. By late afternoon he was planning his evening move to the car, where he could sit in the shadows. Before he got the chance, Cleary walked out carrying a bowling bag. He tossed it across to the passenger seat of his car, then climbed in. Adams quickly folded the tripod and headed for his Camaro. As Cleary pulled out of the driveway, Adams radioed Talon.

"Our Green Beret is on the move."

Arnie Bishop drew the job of shadowing Logan. He knew from the briefing that this guy was a layman, so he was unlikely to spot a tail. Still, Bishop wanted to keep it cool.

He had a perfect vantage point, parked in front of a fire hydrant. Bishop could see both the windows of Logan's condo and the garage exit. Nice place this Logan lived in. Seven-story condo complex on McClellan, just off Wilshire Boulevard in Brentwood. Probably a half-million minimum for each apartment.

Logan drove into the garage just before dark, and a few minutes later, the lights came on in his unit. Bishop could see his shadow moving behind the curtains.

He settled back in the car and popped open a warm can of Coke.

Adams watched Ron Cleary pull into the parking lot of the Mar Vista Bowl. The bowling alley was within a couple of miles of the apartments of the two victims, and it wasn't far from this Julie Martin's apartment that Talon had briefed him about.

Adams had a few candies left over, since the kids hadn't bothered him much in the street, so he popped a sour cherry into his mouth. As soon as Cleary took his bowling bag and walked in, Adams got out to see if there was another exit. A hundred yards up the street he saw another door, which was located so he couldn't see both exits at the same time. He went inside.

Mar Vista Bowl was jumping with leagues. All the lanes were full, and the crowd was raucous. Their laughter and cheering mixed with the crashing of pins and rock music on the jukebox.

Adams's eyes darted back and forth, looking for Cleary. According to Talon's report, he bowled with a team called Olympic Metals, in a yellow and red shirt. Adams didn't see a team with those shirts, either bowling or waiting around. Then he realized that Cleary hadn't been wearing a bowling shirt when he left. How had he missed that?

Bishop sipped his Coke slowly. Normally he could drink a six-pack within a short time. But on stake-out, having to piss is, well, inconvenient.

The lights went out in Logan's apartment, and Bishop sat up. He stared at the garage exit and waited.

Talon pulled the fax out of the machine before it finished the page, almost causing a paper jam. WESTERN AIR PHONE, it said across the top in letters that were stretched by the fax to look like bar codes.

He walked toward his desk, reading the calls placed to and from Myra Powell's cellular phone. He forced himself to go slowly so he wouldn't miss anything. About halfway down the page, his eye caught several calls to a number that looked familiar.

He knew that number. Whose was it? It was an 818 area code, meaning someone in the San Fernando Valley.

Talon called the phone company's "back door" for law enforcement.

"I need to know whose number this is. Pronto," he said to the operator.

"Certainly, Officer. Just a moment."

Talon drummed his fingernails on his teeth while he waited. That number looked so familiar. It's—

"Ronald Cleary," said the operator.

Sonofabitch! Talon got on the radio to Adams, the officer tailing Cleary. He didn't answer, which meant he was out of the car. Talon snarled out orders for a squad car to get to Cleary's house.

CHAPTER FIFTY-SIX

Julie sat at the breakfast table, revising her Ph.D. treatise. She was finally getting her mind off Michael and into a tricky theory of jury bias when she heard a noise. Her head snapped up. What was that? It sounded like scraping metal. She looked around her apartment, yet saw nothing. Whatever it was, it was quiet now. She forced her eyes back to the book, hoping her mind would follow. Yet she felt an uneasy sense of being watched. She told herself that was silly.

Adams walked quickly through the bowling alley and the coffee shop. He checked the men's room, then asked a woman coming out of the ladies' room if she had seen a man inside. He looked behind the ball racks and benches. The bastard had dematerialized.

When he ran back to the parking lot, he saw that Cleary's car was gone. Shit.

Adams reached into his car to radio Talon.

Julie's phone rang, breaking her concentration on the treatise.

"Julie Martin?" came a woman's voice over traffic noise. It sounded like the call was being made from a pay phone on the street.

"Who is this?"

"I'm Lisa Cleary. Do you know who I am?"

"Yes."

"I know you probably think I'm crazy, but you must listen to me. I've had a psychic image that you're going to be the next victim of this serial killer." Lisa's voice picked up speed and distress. "A little while ago I had another image of it. It was so vivid that—well, the details aren't important, but the point is, I'm sure it's tonight. I never see things like this unless they're really close. You've got to get out of your apartment. Now. Don't waste time. Go to Dr. Rennick's. Go to a friend's. But get out. Now!"

Julie's mind went into overload and couldn't process the information. She didn't speak.

Lisa started up again. "Look, be rational. If I'm wrong, all you lose is a few hours."

Abruptly, the words connected to Julie's sensibility. "Okay."

"Talon?" came the voice over the radio.

"Adams. Thank God. Get Cleary in here. Now!"

"Uh, that would be a little difficult. . . ."

Rennick had used Julie's skull-topped cane to get to his car. It had then been an excruciating operation to actually get behind the wheel. That was when he discovered that the damn thing wouldn't start. He tried seven more times before giving up and pouring himself out awkwardly, actually falling onto the ground before he could stand up. Time for Plan B. Except there was no Plan B.

How could he get to Julie's without his car? He didn't know anyone who could get over fast enough to help. Cab? Could be twenty minutes before they arrived. Rennick only had one way to do it in less than ten minutes. And he wasn't happy about it.

Julie snatched the Pooh bag of toiletries and threw it onto her bed. She took an extra pair of blue jeans and a sweatshirt, then grabbed her underwear and a jacket. She quickly shoved everything into her backpack, then pulled the pack over one shoulder and went to the living room, where she stuffed in her textbooks.

With the last papers halfway into the bag, she froze. What was that? She was sure she heard something. A cracking sound? Maybe it was her imagination.

She zipped up the backpack and reached for the keys to her car. She didn't even know where she was going to go.

That was when the lights went out.

CHAPTER FIFTY-SEVEN

Talon sped toward Lance Cleary's house with his blue lights and siren blaring. He knew the little prick had the last puzzle piece, and Talon wanted it.

When he arrived, he pounded the hollow-core door so hard that it bent under his blows. Lance's wife opened it a crack, and Talon shoved the door so hard that it slammed into her. Her mouth dropped open as she pulled her bathrobe around her neck.

"Where is he?" demanded Talon. She pointed limply toward the bedroom. Talon took that as an invitation in, and he stomped across the living room. Cleary was in the bathroom with a mouth full of toothpaste. Talon grabbed him by his pajama shoulders and shoved him against the wall. The toothpaste dribbled out of his mouth, making him look like a frothing animal.

"All right, you bastard. I want what you know about this

case and I want it *now!*" Talon was screaming, with his face about three inches from Cleary's.

"If I talk, I want some assurances."

"The only assurance you get is that you'll have my shoe up your ass if you don't cooperate." He again slammed Cleary against the wall. "The next time your mouth moves, it better be telling me everything that's in your brain. Nod if you understand."

Rennick limped back to his front porch and threw away the cane. Then he unlocked his bicycle and mounted it for the first time since he'd injured his knee. Tentatively, he used his good foot to push off the ground, causing the gears to click rhythmically as he coasted down the walkway from his porch. Fortunately, it was slightly downhill and he didn't have to pedal. Yet.

The first part of the trip was also a downhill run, and he wanted to pick up maximum speed to help him through the uphill part. Using a combination of the hill and as much pushing as he could stand, he was able to get moving at a fast clip. Then, as he was hitting his stride, a car changed lanes in front of him and he had to brake hard.

It wasn't long before he had to go uphill. He gave himself a mental pep talk, which made him feel like the Little Engine That Could, and stood up on the pedals. Rennick yelled with each stroke, which seemed to help. He rode the pain like a surfer on a nasty wave, still wondering if he could make it all the way.

Julie stood in the dark, disoriented. Her eyes were unaccustomed to the dark, and she could only see a slit of light beneath the door to the hallway. The slit told her that the door was a few feet in front of her and to her left. With each passing moment, her eyes grew more accustomed to the low light, and she could make out shapes now. The door was three steps forward, diagonally to the left. Not too far. She could see the outline of the doorknob. Grab, twist, and run like hell.

She took one step, as if walking in slow motion. The sound of her foot against the carpet seemed to crush loudly, and her breathing sounded like a strong wind blowing into sails. Only two more steps to go. Concentrate on the knob. She slowly took the next step.

Suddenly a figure leapt between her and the door. Julie shrieked loudly. She heard the rustling of a plastic raincoat and could see the outline of the figure contrasted against the faint light in the room.

Could she run? The front door was the only way out, unless she crashed through a window. Her eyes looked around for an escape route, and her mind raced for alternatives.

None came.

Rennick arrived outside Julie's building, out of breath and with his knee feeling like it was the size of a basketball. A throbbing basketball. He dropped his bike on the sidewalk and started toward the building. It had about ten steps leading to the front door, and each one was agony. He cursed the fact that the building was constructed before handicap codes.

When he reached the top, he repeatedly buzzed Julie. No answer. He finally found the manager's name on the framed directory and tried the same eight-buzz technique. This time he scored.

"Yeah?" came a slow reply.

"This is an emergency. Julie Martin in one-o-six is in great danger. I have to see her."

"Did you buzz her apartment?"

Gee, what a great idea. "Yes, I buzzed her. No one answers."

"I can't open her apartment up for you. It's against the law."

Rennick held his mouth less than an inch from the microphone and shouted. "You can in an emergency. I'm a lawyer, and I'll take the responsibility. You can walk in with me. This is very serious. Her life could be in danger."

"Okay, okay. I'll come down and getcha. Hold your horses, pardner."

Rennick let go of the buzzer and grabbed the front door. Maybe someone had left it open. He pulled roughly three or four times, yet it only rattled defiantly. Then he looked at his watch. Where the hell was the manager?

The figure in front of Julie exuded an eerie calm and control. She could hear slow, measured breathing, and then a soothing, gentle voice.

"Please come with me to your bedroom. If you'll lie down quietly on the bed, this can be over quickly and with very little difficulty."

A gloved hand, which Julie could now see was holding a knife, gestured toward the bedroom like a high school student opening his car door for a date.

Julie began screaming, and within less than a second the intruder's fist slammed into her solar plexus. She collapsed into a helpless rag doll and held her stomach in pain, unable to scream or even catch her breath. The figure wrenched back Julie's hair, exposing her throat to the ceiling, and then stretched a strip of duct tape across her mouth.

The killer next moved behind her, grabbed her across the throat with one forearm, and pushed the sharp tip of the knife into her back with the other hand. Julie was forced to her feet in order to avoid being strangled, as her windpipe was almost cut off from the pressure against it. She felt the knife prick into her back, followed by a warm trickle of blood seeping against her blouse.

The apartment manager lumbered toward the front door, while Rennick gestured for him to hurry up. He was an immense man, with chest hairs sprouting out of his shirt. He walked very slowly.

When the manager opened the door, Rennick yelled "Hurry!" and hobbled down the hall as fast as he could manage.

Rennick arrived outside Julie's door and began pounding on it, shouting her name. No answer. He looked under the door and saw that the lights were out. Maybe she was gone. He hoped so. He looked back to see the manager plodding toward him, still not showing much concern.

"Open it!" Rennick panted.

"Are you sure you'll take responsibility for this?"

Rennick considered kicking him in the balls, then decided that would only slow things down. "Yes. I'm sure. Hurry!"

The manager sighed and took out a large ring of keys.

"You don't have a passkey?"

"Older locks. The owner's too cheap to get a master-key system. Those locks cost twice as much. I've told him over and over—"

"Please. Which one is hers?"

"I grabbed the spares in my haste, because *someone*"—he looked directly at Rennick—"told me to hurry. So I can either go back and get the marked keys, or I can try these one at a time."

"Which is faster?"

"Six of one, half a dozen of the other."

"Just start trying, okay?"

"Okay."

The manager started trying the keys one at a time.

"Nope." He dropped that one with a jangle and went to the next key on the ring.

"Nope." He repeated the same procedure.

As Rennick paced back and forth in the hall, his rage was rising. On impulse, he went to the opposite wall and then ran to Julie's door, throwing his shoulder into it with the weight of his body. The startled manager dropped his keys.

"Dammit!" said the manager. "You mighta warned me. Now I lost my place."

A sharp pain stabbed into Rennick's shoulder, and he stepped back, rubbing it. Before the manager started trying the keys again, he said, "Looks a lot easier in the movies when guys crash through doors, huh?" He chuckled to himself as he started over.

"Nope," he said, discarding the first key.

Julie was on her back, spread-eagle, being tied to the metal bed frame with strips of her panty hose. She weakly tried to resist and was rewarded with another punch to the solar plexus that hurt even more than the first.

The killer now began cutting off her clothes. First the blouse, by slicing up the front. Then the arms. Julie heard the fabric tearing as her clothes were being dissected, and she could feel the chill in the room stinging her skin. Next came the skirt, also sliced up the front. Julie could feel the other side of the blade denting her skin. Next her bra, cutting each side and then the straps. Finally her panties, from the leg holes to the waist on each side.

She began to quiver and then shake uncontrollably. She tried to pull her arms and legs free, and the bindings gashed deeply into her wrists and ankles. With superhuman effort, she briefly managed to lift her body off the bed, arching her back and writhing up and down. She could feel the circulation cut off, and her feet and hands went numb as she collapsed.

Her final effort was a scream into the duct tape, which only produced a faint buzzing sound. Finally, exhausted, she lay back on the bed, shivering as perspiration beaded on her naked body.

The manager finally got the right key in the lock. Rennick heard the click and shoved him to the side as he burst into the apartment.

"Julie? Julie? Are you here?"

He could hear the manager behind him. "Now, you're not to touch anything, you understand?"

Rennick flipped on the lights and rapidly looked around the living room. "Julie?"

He went into the kitchen and then checked the bathroom. Finally, he turned toward the bedroom. The manager trailed behind him. Rennick sensed that something was wrong. Someone was there. He slowed down, fighting the urge to run away. "Julie?" he said quietly. No answer.

Finally, he walked into the bedroom and turned on the light. His knees buckled, and he collapsed. "Call the cops," he gasped to the manager.

CHAPTER FIFTY-EIGHT

Rennick's arrival caused Julie's head to snap toward him. Her expression transformed from terror to hope.

Standing beside the bed, like a surgeon about to perform an operation, was a figure in a plastic raincoat, wearing latex gloves and holding a shiny kitchen knife. Behind the bed, Rennick could see a broken window. The figure didn't interrupt the ritual, preparing to make an incision. Rennick found himself momentarily wondering if he were really there or simply having a vision. If this was real, surely the killer would have at least turned to look, if not run. Yet the movements continued like they were on automatic pilot.

Rennick knew what to do.

"Lisa!!" he yelled.

At first it sounded like a distant voice, like her dad calling while she was playing down the block. The next words would probably be "Time to come in for dinner. It's getting dark outside."

Only it wasn't her father. She probably needed to answer, but she really didn't want to. She was having so much fun with her friends.

The voice again. Calling "Lisa!" Rats. She did have to go. I'm sorry to leave before we finish the game. Do you guys mind cleaning up?

Then it felt as though a wall crashed down. On the other side was a room that she never knew was there. A woman was standing in the other room, just as surprised to see her. The energies of the two rooms were flowing together, creating a powerful swirl. Lisa needed to hold on to something to keep from being swept away. Daddy? Help me. I'm scared. I don't know what to do. Don't let Mom do this to me, Daddy. Help me. I love you. Daddy? Daddy? You'll be proud of me. Look. I'm standing up for myself.

Now more images. Her mother beating her with a knotted electrical cord. Lashes raising welts across Lisa's back. Daddy, I want to stand up to her. I'm not big enough yet. But I will be. I'll be just like you. You'll see. Daddy? Daddy?

Lisa looked down at her hands and saw that she was wearing latex gloves. There was a knife in her hand, and a false mustache stuck across her lip. She was wearing oversized tennis shoes that were stuffed with gym socks to keep her feet tight.

Rennick watched Lisa's expression go from an emotionless calm into an anguished, twisted grimace. Her posture slumped as she looked down at her hands and threw away the knife. She backed away from it, shaking her head in denial. Then she peeled off the mustache and collapsed into a sobbing heap.

Rennick collected his thoughts enough to grab the knife on

the floor. He then cut the bonds and pulled the duct tape off Julie's mouth with a ripping sound. Julie threw her arms around him and squeezed with such force that he could hardly breathe.

He heard the sound of a siren approaching, followed quickly by footsteps running down the hallway. Two uniformed officers came into the room.

Rennick began to speak, while Julie held on without loosening her grip.

"We've found the killer," he said, nodding toward Lisa.

"Her?!" exclaimed one of the officers.

"Her name is Lisa Cleary," said Rennick. Lisa looked up blankly at the sound of her name. "Call Talon."

One of the officers walked over to her. "Would you please get up, Ms. Cleary?" Lisa stood, without looking at him or the others. She offered no resistance as the officer handcuffed her and led her out.

Julie still clung to Rennick, crying softly into his chest.

CHAPTER FIFTY-NINE

Rennick walked past the line of people that overflowed the emergency and admissions lounges of Los Angeles County Hospital. He reflected how poor people pay with their time instead of money.

His injured leg caused him to lean from side to side as he hobbled down the sixth-floor corridor of the aging, concrete and steel building. At the end of the hall, he saw an unmarked door with a chicken-wire glass panel. Beyond it was the psychiatric wing, and at the far end of that was an armed guard in a green metal folding chair. The guard sat next to a locked door that even he couldn't open. A door that led to a holding section for the criminally insane, or the prison ward, as the staff called it.

Rennick sat on a metal bench that jabbed him in several places, waiting for Talon. On another floor, an officer was taking Julie's statement. He knew that the interview had to be independent of his own, to avoid any contamination of their stories, yet he felt like he was letting her down by not being there.

Talon stood in a light jacket despite the cold night air. The hum of generators feeding spotlights buzzed in his ears, and he was oblivious to the smell of burning diesel fuel that they were belching out. The mayor was approaching a podium that had been hastily placed on the hospital steps. Several reporters tried to edge in front of Talon, but he held his ground.

The mayor tapped the microphone and it shrieked in response. The crowd quieted.

"Thanks to the efforts of the LAPD," began the mayor, "I am pleased to announce that we have arrested a suspect in the murders of five Westside women."

Talon saw Wharton edging toward the mayor.

"Such an accomplishment is the effort of many people. However, I want to single out one man who worked tirelessly to bring about this result." The mayor glanced discreetly at a note card he had palmed. "Detective Daniel Talon."

Talon broke into an embarrassed smile. In the corner of his eye, he saw Wharton turn toward the back of the crowd.

"C'mon up here, Detective."

Talon was suddenly cold in the night air. He awkwardly shuffled forward as the crowd parted for him. The lights of the cameras blinded him, and several of the reporters clapped him on the back. When he arrived at the podium, he shoved his hands into his pants pockets and looked around for some idea of what he was supposed to do.

The mayor put his arm around Talon, and the flashbulbs exploded like Fourth of July fireworks.

"This is an example of the finest we've got. Excellent job, Detective." The mayor delivered the words looking at the cameras, not at Talon. Talon's mouth labored to hold a strained smile, and he hoped this was going to be over quickly.

A few moments later, Talon left the podium and was still seeing bright ovals from the floodlights that had been in his face. Ramson, the captain who had warned him about Wharton, grabbed his arm and pulled him to the side.

"Nice one, Talon," said Ramson with a wink. "I expect you'll get a commendation to hang on your den wall."

"I can't say I give a shit about the piece of paper. Unless you think it'll piss off Wharton."

"Good chance."

"Then have 'em frame it in gold leaf."

Rennick sat in the hospital corridor. His adrenaline had subsided, and a fog of exhaustion now clouded his consciousness. As he leaned forward and allowed his chest to rest heavily against his thighs, he felt like he was floating in Jell-O.

He heard the sound of elevator doors opening and looked up to see Talon walk out energetically. Rennick tried to stand and almost collapsed on his bad knee. Talon hooked Rennick's arm as he passed, supporting him as they walked toward the hospital's prison ward.

"You'll probably be interested in what I got out of Lisa's big brother," said Talon. "Seems their mom used to flip out now and then and beat the kiddies with an electrical cord. Sometimes she even tied them up. Guess what she used?"

"Nylon stockings. Danny, could you slow down?"

Talon had been pulling Rennick's arm forward as he walked ahead of him. He dropped back.

"Sorry. So when Lisa got bigger, she decided to get even. The next time Mom tried her routine, Lisa punched out her lights. Then she tied Mom up and slit her throat. Dad came home later, figured it might have been Lisa, then pretended it was a random murder. He told Lance what he suspected, then swore him to secrecy."

"That all fits," said Rennick. "Lance couldn't handle the situation, so he left home and never came back. And Ron separated from Lisa as a way of protecting her."

"Which would explain why Ron wouldn't tell us shit. By the way, he's still in that separation mode. I sent a squad car to his house, and they said the old man cut and ran. He swept the place clean."

"You going to chase him?"

"I dunno. Maybe. We got a real different response from our Mr. Logan. He showed up at police headquarters right after the mayor's speech, demanding a written apology."

"I'm sure the bureaucracy can crank one out in a year or two."

A loud, grating buzzer opened the door to the prison ward, and they walked through. Talon folded a stick of gum into his mouth and said, "Lance thought Lisa wasn't even aware that she killed her mother. Is that possible?"

"Yes. I think Lisa's a multiple personality. Classically, that starts when someone is beaten as a child. Prolonged physical abuse causes the normal personality to shut down, and a hard, tough personality, 'takes the pain.' Later in life, the tough personality becomes violent, and the 'normal' side isn't even aware of it. Her case was unusual because images of the murders were leaking from one personality to the other. And thank God for that. She saved Julie's life by warning us."

Rennick realized that this other personality was also the root of Lisa's dreams about a door being guarded by her mother and father. Symbolically, the door was a barrier that her conscious mind wasn't allowed to cross.

"Here's a present for you," said Talon. He pulled several pages out of his jacket and gave them to Rennick. "Seems our young lady kept a journal of her escapades. We found it inside her heating duct, hanging on a piece of twine. This is a Xerox. The original's in the lab."

Rennick looked through the journal as they walked. He grimaced at what he read.

A guard with a thick black toupee led them to the observation room next to Lisa's cell. It was lit only with a low light, so as not to illuminate the observer. Through the one-way mirror, Rennick saw a stark white room: the walls, the floor, the bed, and the single guest chair. All brightly lit with fluorescent lights that were recessed so they couldn't be used as a gallows. Lisa was sitting on top of the bed, wearing a white hospital gown over her bare feet. The sockets of her eyes were dark, giving her face the look of a death mask, and she was staring intently at a blank wall.

Rennick put on a set of headphones that looked like they had once belonged to Samuel Morse, then gestured for Danny to start the interrogation. He continued reading Lisa's journal while he waited for Talon to enter her room.

A few minutes later, Rennick heard Talon begin questioning. Lisa answered in a monotone, with little emotion in her voice. The audio was low and distorted, and Rennick concentrated hard to understand the words. Between her disjointed answers and the journal, he began piecing together a picture.

He inferred that she had an overwhelming need to be close to her father. A need that was intertwined with Lisa's childhood experience with horses. The journal recounted how Lisa and her father helped a mare give birth to a colt. In the process, Lisa placed her hands inside the mare and was covered with a thick mucus. Rennick now understood her repeated images of sinking into horses, as well as her lack of sexual experience. When she had such an intimate episode with her father—reaching inside a living body, covering herself with a sticky substance—Rennick believed that she associated the activity with sexual intercourse. Thus, subconsciously, Lisa thought she'd committed incest.

In addition, Lisa harbored a deep resentment that Ron Cleary wouldn't stand up to his wife and defend his children. When Lisa killed her mother, she became the protecting father she had always fantasized. These actions also displayed her strength and cunning, which were designed to inspire the love and respect of a military man. Lisa even wore a mustache during the killings, to mimic the one her father had when she was a child.

Using information in the journal, Rennick theorized how the murders began. Myra Powell, the first victim, was dating Lisa's father. Powell came into Lisa's gym with Ron, and Rennick reasoned that seeing her father with a woman who looked like her mother reignited the old psychoses. He believed that Lisa felt her mother had come back to hurt her, and therefore Lisa must stand up again. The other victims simply had the misfortune to look like her mother. Except for Julie, who was an attempt to strike at Rennick for getting too close.

The electrical cord was an obvious symbol of the cord Martha had used to beat her children. Lisa obliterated the victims' eyes and ears so that they couldn't spy on her like Martha had done. The journal told him that she used gray cords because her father had worked with radios and taught Lisa the resistor color code. Gray is number eight. For eight o'clock, the hour when her father left for bowling and her mother gave out the punishments. Lisa killed all the victims at eight, then changed the clocks to throw off the investigators.

When Talon finished his interview, Rennick took off the earphones and stared at Lisa through the smoky glass. She sat motionless on the bed, gazing without expression into another plane of consciousness. Rennick leaned back in his chair and closed his eyes. How had he missed this? He should have seen the clues in Lisa's therapy. How many women could have been saved if he'd made the connection?

Talon opened the door. "Professor?"

Rennick kept his eyes closed and didn't move.

"Professor? You okay?"

Talon shook his shoulder roughly.

Rennick slowly opened his eyes. Then, without talking, he hobbled past Talon into the hall.

The hospital cafeteria smelled of antiseptic and was deserted, save a few sleepy interns and nurses drinking coffee from white Styrofoam cups. The low hum of a floor polisher, guided around by an Indian man in a black turban, was the only sound.

Rennick made his way in with difficulty, holding the wall for support. He painfully lowered himself into a chair.

"You okay, Professor?" asked Talon.

"You once told me not to ask you that."

"Oooh. Sorry."

They sat in silence for a long while, until Rennick felt a hand on his shoulder. He turned to see Julie with a small blanket draped across her shoulders. Her eyes were red from crying, and her hair was stringy with perspiration. She looked stunning.

He struggled to stand up, now oblivious to the pain in his knee, and cupped her face in his hands.

Talon took the cue. "I gotta get back to the station. You need some help getting to the car?"

"No. I'm in excellent hands," answered Rennick, putting his arm around Julie's shoulder and leaning on her.

As Julie and Rennick walked down the hall, he said, "I don't know where to even begin apologizing. I'm embarrassed and humiliated."

"We've both got a lot of healing to do," she replied gently.

Rennick stammered the next words. "You were right about the things you said. I'll never have a long-term relationship unless I change my attitude. I've decided to go back into therapy."

She lightly kissed the hand that was draped on her shoulder. "I'm happy for you."

They walked in silence until they reached the front door of the hospital. "Isn't there anything we can do about . . . us? Are you really set on going to New York?"

She looked up at him and ran her fingers through her tangled hair. "I'm committed to New York for four years. After that, who knows. If we're meant to be, Michael, it will happen."

Two weeks later, Rennick woke up alone. He was aware of a sour taste in his mouth as he sat on the bed and rubbed his eyes.

Rennick yawned deeply and arched his back in a stretch. The bedroom seemed unusually quiet, as if no birds were out today. And the morning seemed darker—maybe because the winter daylight hours were growing shorter. All of the mornings had seemed darker lately.

He made himself a cup of coffee and noticed the mess that

had recently accumulated. Open books, unwashed dishes, piles of coats. All of them exactly where he'd dropped them.

After a few sips of coffee, he splashed cold water from the kitchen sink onto his face. Then he lay back on his bed and balanced the coffee cup on his stomach. It undulated as he breathed.

A few minutes later, the idea came to him in a flash of inspiration. He sat up quickly, oblivious to the hot coffee he sloshed on himself, and reached for the phone.

At five-thirty the next morning, Rennick bounced up the steps of Julie's apartment building. He buzzed the intercom several times before she answered through the speaker.

"Yes?" Her voice sounded groggy, with a touch of alarm.

"It's Michael. Let me in."

"What are you doing here? What time is it?"

"Let me in. All will be revealed."

Rennick walked quickly to her apartment, where she was already opening the door. He saw her standing in the doorway, her face creased from pillow edges and her hair matted and flailing.

"Get dressed," he chirped.

"Get dressed?"

"Yeah. We'll be late."

"For what?"

"I made us a reservation in Hemet."

That seemed to wake her up. "Hemet? Skydiving? You?"

"Yep. I even asked that obnoxious pilot to take us again. C'mon. Let's go jump out of an airplane."